GW00870404

Blonde on board

Zoë Phillips

Published by New Generation Publishing in 2018

Copyright © Zoë Phillips 2018

First Edition

The author asserts the moral right under the Copyright, Designs
and Patents Act 1988 to be identified as the author of this work.

All Rights reserved. No part of this publication may be
reproduced, stored in a retrieval system or transmitted, in any
form or by any means without the prior consent of the author,
nor be otherwise circulated in any form of binding or cover other
than that in which it is published and without a similar condition
being imposed on the subsequent purchaser.

www.newgeneration-publishing.com

 New Generation Publishing

Love, hate and something in between – in my quest for adventure and true love, part I

Small things end. Great things endure.
Basel Art Messe, 2002

My book!

Think of it as a key to connect you directly with another world, one that would mutually be better with you in it....

The story unfolds to reveal what lies behind a girl's mind, the complications, the thoughts, the hopes, aspirations and dreams, the heartache, underlying with a surfeit of messages for guys, what to do, how all your actions are interpreted and prepare girls for what choices may lie ahead. That nothing turns out the way you think it would, that you've got to always remember that things work out a certain way for a special reason – believe it....A passionate yet hilarious account of what goes through your mind in one year.

A story which tries to analyse why a London girl decided to pack it all in and head to Switzerland, taking advantage of a job offer with her company, whilst struggling to come to terms with the love she thought was of her life. How she battles with love – past, present and future, her life – what she wants, and why, the decisions ad choices she's faced with and within that year abroad, what she gets up to, with whom, and why she gets up to it! Facing realities, sometimes painful and deeply thought provoking and emotional, finally facing up to reality and deciding whether she should return to the ol smoke or not. It's a story of passion, betrayal, heartache and soul searching. It reinforces what opporunities we are faced with in the world and the excitement, but also creates a lesson to all of us that are put under similar situations, for similar reasons. It delves into the mind of a girl feeling very alone, and we start to uncover her hopes, aspirations, insecurities ad how they change with her over time.

It may be a true story about the adventures of 1 girl, 1 life, 1 year, 1 love, it may not, but it happens to us all.

Sometimes a painfully honest story of love, loss and hope and untangling the 'corset of life'.

Foreword

Within this book I have to admonish responsibility for any feelings hurt or otherwise, no intention was meant to cause offence or otherwise. However, the characters outlined within this book are completely fictional but true as can be to life.

Tip: When you get to the end of a rope, tie a knot in it!

OK, Dedications...

I would like to dedicate this book to ...

To JB, who, if you hadn't have dumped me before I came to Switzerland, I would never have had the time to write down all my feelings and findings.

To every single person I name within this book, without whom I would never have had a story to tell, even the terrible Andreas.

To my Mother, who I don't think knows that life can be so entertaining, exciting, upsetting, and yet fantastic all in one year but who also knows what it is to have truly loved and lost.

To my Father, without whom I guess I just would not be here and though I hate him for how he turned our young lives upside down, I guess if he had not done that, I would never had been able to put any meat on the bones of this book. I would certainly be a different person, so thanks Dad.

To my wonderful nephew and niece, Tim and Beth, with the hope that before they may ever have similar experiences, that they can learn something from me. I dedicate it also to my latest niece Rebecca, who came along way after this book was conceived.

I dedicate this to every one of my girlfriends who helped get me through those lonely nights and days, to Kate and Nadia, Liz and Jen, and Smooth Al – because he may as well be an honorary girl, he shared so much with me. To my special girlfriends from Basel and who I met in Switzerland, who helped me along the way: Rita, Ermen, Cara, Julie, Claire, all of you and all of you I have not mentioned here.

I also dedicate this to the men I loved and those men who loved me. I hope I didn't break your hearts and if I did, I apologise. I apologise because I was always, deep in my heart, holding out for my one true love, my hero and I'm sure you've felt like that at some stage in your life, or at least I hope you will because if you don't life just isn't worth it, believe me.

I dedicate this book to M who never knew and perhaps never will know just how much I loved him, or perhaps he did. Without him, I would certainly not have had any inspiration (and I write this with Shola Ama playing in the background...You are my only love). Mike says he'll start crying once he reads this, I'm not so sure but hey ho, M, I would still feel the same whatever, no matter what.

I also dedicate this book to my other loves. In one way I suppose I am lucky to have really felt incredibly deep feelings for 3 guys. All 3 have thrown my emotional stability completely off kilter. On the other hand I lost 2 of them for sure and well, the third just couldn't make his mind up.

So without further adieu, let's start at the very beginning. Let the journey begin...

Life is like a tin of sardines, there's always that little bit left in the corner that you can't get at.

But whatever you do, hope a little, move on a lot.

"If you have a dream, do it or start it today, for boldness takes courage, strength and greatness" but for God's sake, make your mind up!

Robert Swann, the explorer, May 2002

Finally, for Mum & Dad,
even though you parted ways, because you made me

Introduction – "Easy Rider"

March 3rd 2001

A cold and grey Saturday morning, it's about 04.30am and I wave goodbye to 14, Limburg Road, Battersea SW11 1HB. Who knows for how long? There goes my little flat in London, that tiny spec in the distance of my wing mirror as I turn the corner and make my journey onto the A3 towards the M25, bound for the channel tunnel.

Jane peers out from behind the closed curtains next door and waves to me. I can read her lips: "Good Luck". I smile, wave back and open the car door.

An early start. I began by dropping a rather abusive letter through the letterbox of the (definitely) ex boyfriend, JB, who was just oh too busy to wish me 'Goodbye' the previous night – well, I suppose I did put the telephone down on him too. Bastard. Well, he wasn't the one anyway.

It took little more than an hour to reach the tunnel, checked in by a rather pleasant monsieur and boarded at about 8am. Very straight forward, I was impressed. Just me, my car, 5 of my favourite cds, 5 of my favourite work outfits, loo roll, a load of books and mags, my squash racquet, all my gym gear and of course, saving room in my tiny impractical boot for my ski boots.

Moral in the story: finish packing the night before you leave and remember to have filled up the car with petrol (it's pricey in France). Don't forget to pack your kettle in the car, oh and hangers. And always finish off such messy business as ex boyfriends.

My car (who we shall name Midge – because that's how David and I always used to refer to it, no, him) and I passed over the "sheep dip" disinfectant due to the ongoing foot and mouth crisis rife in the UK and I was asked to dispose of any milk/meat/dairy products on board – that's when I realised I'd left Charlie's champers in my fridge and a whole bar of white chocolate toblerone – damm and double damm. It's also when I realised that I had a rather splendid piece of cheese from the cheese man on Northcote Road – I'll be dammed if they take that off me, it was expensive and it is gorgeous.

The "Le Shuttle" (to be continental) is a bit like driving into a tin can and out the other side, 35 minutes and £114.00 later. Tres excellent! Spent £4 on the most expensive bottle of water I know and then wow, hit the A15 en France (eventually) having taken a couple of wrong turnings out of the service station – typical woman driver. I arrived at my first payage, which was just £10 (well, French Franc equivalent, they're not into Creative Inc yet, another 10 months to go of their glorious independence) for the 1st leg, then about £2 for the next, then £22 for the next leg and now we're well on our little way and en route to Strasbourg.

We're moving through the champagne region near Alsace – all these wines around me and non in my little car. I keep thinking about the note I sent to M, hope he takes it the right way. Oh well, if not, he's not as witty as I thought he was. I keep thinking about our night out last Thursday, playing squash and then munching pizza at my favourite restaurant, Pizza Metro, down my road. I had a really great time, I can't wait to write to him to tell him what "Fuzz night" (AKA Basel Fasnacht) is like and whether I'd told my boss to "Fuzz off" as he had suggested when he wakes me at 3.30am. (I doubt it!) It's a shame M's not on email yet, still letters are nicer – I would prefer to see his handwriting anyway and at least it feels a bit more personal, like he's here with me too, oh how I wish he was here with me.

JB. Such a waster – wonder what he thinks of the rather rude note that I shoved through his letter box at 4.30am –

swine – what a pathetic prick. If he wants to, he can contact me. Think he's got a bad case of foot and mouth. Oops, I rang his doorbell too at so early an hour. I am such a bitch. Still, I think he deserves it.

I think of all the things I've left behind – the papers, the music. Will I know what's hot and what's not? These French radio stations are crap.

I stop for a bite to eat – bread and oops, some smuggled cheese from Hamish Johnson on Northcote Road – too nice for the waste bin, foot and mouth or no foot and mouth – I'll chuck the paper away now in France – at least I won't be responsible for spreading foot and mouth en Suisse.

My case is still holding on to the bike rack on my boot. At least there's no snow or rain, (yet), so at least my knickers will stay dry.

It was so beautiful driving through Kent this morning down the M20, there was snow all over the fields and hills. Rather fitting for a move to Switzerland don't you think?

OK, now I'm heading for Strasbourg.

I'm so glad I became part of the "Battersea set" by purchasing a pashmina yesterday (OK, only from the market but who cares and now that I'm no longer in Battersea, what the hell). Anyway, it looks beautiful here, and it's warm and light blue, my favourite colour.

It's suddenly become very snowy around the motorway and I'm starting to see mountains. All the cars have skiis on, Yipee!! I had thought I'd be reading a lot but I hope I won't have time.

My 'phone rings. It's a quick call from Hans-Peter, my new boss, eek, he's off to a client meeting ("But it's Saturday Hans?!") Am I expected to work that hard too I wondered? And panic suddenly set in. For a few more Francs (or Franks, should I say, ho ho!) No, I want to ski and have a life! I want to work in order to live and NOT the other way around, life's too short and I've decided I do not want "Zoe was an excellent worker" on my tombstone for sure.

I hope M pops over soon – I think he might.

Jane the neighbour at 12 Limburg, was really sweet as she waved to me just before I left this morning, it was so early.

Midge has caused quite a stir wherever he's taken me so far – I'm actually quite proud to have him here now. Sod Londoners who think I must be a rich git driving around in an MGF (which I wish I was, well, not a git, but rich at least, you know what I mean). I'm slowly getting used to the idea of driving him around Switzerland, especially in the summer with his roof down.

All the guys in the shuttle stared at him (sad bastards). As if they'd never seen one before? Oh well, he is special and I suppose they'd never seen one stuffed with so much junk and kit.

Toilets are another thing. Mmm, I find it's better to stop at Esso garages en route through France. The rest of the service stations provide just holes in the ground. Hey, has anyone done a good loo guide here? Now there's a business opportunity.

David Gray is playing on the radio at this Esso garage – Babylon – that's the CD I gave M for his birthday last year. It's still the way I feel about him.

I'm at Saverne now. Strange, I've not seen an English car for ages although, hey, one's just pulled up here at the station. Hello hello….I feel like I'm alone in the middle of the ocean and nobody speaks my language, so the English car seems familiar and the registration number seems so friendly, almost smiling at me. However the tattooed driver emerging from said blue Ford gives me a grunt before making a huge belch and walking away to pay for his fuel. Mmm, the not so friendly or necessarily attractive Brits abroad…

Here we are at Strasbourg. Bloody hell, suddenly there's a

load of German BMWs racing each other past my little car. Eek, suddenly I feel very vulnerable and...lost. Strasbourg always sounded so pretty but it actually looks pretty ugly to me especially when you're lost.

Damm, it's raining. My knickers. Urgh. Now, I've crossed another Duane (border) into Deutschland. Something inside me makes me feel like I would have preferred to have driven on the French side (call me old fashioned, maybe it has something to do with the fact that I haven't brought any Deutchmarks with me – roll on the Euro! – it's surprising how insecure that makes you feel). However Hans-Peter wants to meet me at the German border control to Basel. Urgh, it sounds like I'm about to join the Gestapo, or escaping vis a vis the Vontrappe family a la "sound of music".

I feel very nervous of driving through these German tunnels. Urgh. Everything's so 'German'. It's grey. It's bleak. It's raining and cold and miserable (even the people look miserable).

Ah ha, I see my first sign to "Basel". Yipee! Not far to go no doubt now. I'm feeling a bit jaded. It's 5.10pm now, so I've been on the road for over 12 hours.

I've come to the conclusion that driving in Deutschland is one of 2 speeds: dead slow or dead fast and nothing in between. Your average Welcome break driver would be left for dead by now.

Drivers here just come from nowhere, drive up your bottom. Everything ends in "fahrt" too. I need a dictionary and lessons rapido.

Wow, it's cold at Freiburg and everything is well covered in snow.

I had to go for a wee. Yuk.I don't think much of the German service stations I have to say. Vive la France!

Et Viola! Here I am at the border control, Basel. Now to find Hans-Peter, nearly 700miles later.

I receive text messages from Kate, Charlie and Emma.

Great, I really feel thought of, it's so nice of them to be thinking of me – they're out tonight. I can only imagine the laughs and music and life there and what I have got in front of me? An unfurnished flat with no TV, no stereo, for goodness knows how long, until Pickford's arrive.

Hans-Peter and his daughter, Daniella meet me at the German border. We went shopping for a few bits and pieces. You know, bread, milk, orange juice, toilet paper etc. Guess what the bill came to? About 34CHF (£18) for about 4 things?!! He joked and said that obviously this was not the usual cost – blimey, I certainly hope not! I should ask for a salary rise, now!

We drove into Basel (thank goodness I could follow him). I had absolutely no idea of where I was going in the dark. We popped into their house to collect a camp bed he thought of (thank goodness for Hans – although I think he thought I'd have something). His wife, Denise, asked me to stay for supper. I said that would be fantastic (the thought suddenly crossed my mind of sitting cross legged on my wooden floor with 1 travel adaptor, 1 side lamp, and now a camp bed, stuffing my face with the white chocolate toblerone I bought at the channel tunnel shop and the water from the service station. A healthy combination or what?

I smiled to myself, after the stories I've heard about the Swiss...as we hurled the campbed into Denise's little Fiat Punto along with the mattress, a duvet and a pillow. The campbed overhung the tailgate by about 6 inches. Daniella, Hans-Peter's daughter, told me that if the police saw us, we would receive a "big fat fine" even for this 2-minute drive around the corner to my apartment. Surely not, after all these were mitigating circumstances, well weren't they? Anyway, fortunately there were no PC plods skulking around any trees and now the bed is here. My first piece of proper furniture (OK so it's temporary but it's comfortable – I've just woken up!)

Sunday, 4th March.

I send a text message to Kate et al. So nice to think of them all back home. Dinner was lovely last night, then I returned to my rather minimalist apartment (wow, how trendy am I?! Philip Starke would eat his heart out here). I'm glad I brought Smooth Al's flowers with me – they at least make the place look a bit more friendly/cosy/warm/ and I remembered to bring a vase too (mm, some people would question my priorities when I moved abroad – other people may think of more practical things like toilet paper etc etc. OK, so I'm learning).

Sunday morning, I'd slept so well. A full 9 hours, wow, I opened my shutters and let in that sunshine – urgh, it's raining. Come on! It's so dull. Why? Cold, dull. Still, I cannot seem to get this underfloor heating to work.

I'm thinking about JB. Bastard. What a prick he is, coward. He had obviously turned off his mobile too. He just couldn't face talking to me. What a little shit. I wonder what he thinks of my letter. I don't really care (well, I do I suppose deep down). But I hate being used, ignored etc. Oh well, it's his loss. He could have had some fab city breaks here ... I wish I could share it with someone. I feel a bit like I'm in a convent for a year. Oh well, out to explore today. I can't believe it, I've promised Hans-Peter that I will pop into the office later. I have to meet him at 3pm – I hope I remember the way to their house.

I scribble a route.

Oh yes, I forgot to say that Basel was covered in snow when I arrived. It's quite pretty but very cold. It must be a bit strange for Midge too. But apparently, whilst it's minus 4 degrees tonight, it is going to be +14 degrees by Wednesday. Global warming?

But now, it's raining. Most of the snow has melted.

Now my adventures begin again.

I discovered a gym down the road this morning, ran by an orangutan called "Guido" – well perhaps it's just his big hairdo that makes him look like our furry friends. Once he showed me what every machine did for my 'beeeeceps' and 'treeeeceps', he offered me a free session (work out, of course) so I may pop back tomorrow to work up a sweat. I don't know whether I'd like to go there permanently though, it's very small. I also checked out a local pool – which is great for kids – and then stepped into Midge for a trip to the Migros supermarket at the railway station.

Isn't it amusing (or frustrating). Cashiers, wherever you find them, whatever the country, always seem to have to race to shove your groceries over the price check before you've had chance to load them into a plastic bag, I'm sure they're all trained to be on this mission. I'm sure they take some sort of sadistic pleasure from it.

However I managed to keep up with the Frau checking me out, Ha!, and left Migros with 2 massive bags filled with goodies, all fresh and ready to eat, as I still have no pans etc.(Quite a survival course this is turning out to be!).

I also find out that of course, everywhere is closed a) because it's Sunday b) because it's Fasnacht – yes, M's 'fuzz night' is about to begin this evening.

My alarm went off at 3am, and I had to meet Hans at a tram stop at 3.30am. I made a complete cock up of it. I caught the bus, but missed the tram stop I should have stepped off at, so I ended up walking back a stop, then spotted Hans in his passing car, waving at me frantically to get in. "We're late. Where have you been?" was all he said. "I have woken all your neighbours by ringing your doorbell" he continued. I apologised profusely (he is my new boss after all) and explained how I had not understood the German bus announcement and had therefore missed the tram stop by one stop. I felt terrible but never mind I thought, it's too early to get depressed about something like that.

We trudged on, found a parking space, dumped the car and ran into town picking up a lady called Anne en route, who had flown in from the US to be with Hans-Peter for a credentials pitch the following day in Rome. I bet she was pleased to be woken so early, jet lag and all! Not!

Anyway, it was all worth it.

Basel 'Fuzznight'

What an amazing experience. Anne, Hans-Peter and I arrived somewhere in the town centre. All the streetlights were extinguished and then, the clock tower struck 4am, lights came on, lanterns were lit and an enormous noise filled the streets. We followed floats, drummers and piccolo players to name a few, all around the streets of Basel. What a weird site it was. Quite bizarre. It was cold but fortunately, the rain had stopped. These people seemed to know how to party (or is it just that they're not allowed to normally?). The masks, costumes and music were unbelievable. (Eek, that's an expression Peter uses... 'Unbelieeeeeevable' ... think I'm picking up his accent, next I'll be saying... 'Terrrrrible'... and ... 'beauties' and wait for it ....'just a seckie' ... yes you heard me right. It's quite amusing, or it sounds amusing to an English speaker).

Hans-Peter and Anne left me in the street after half an hour. After I'd got over my initial panic at looking totally insane and meandering these novel streets at some ungodly hour in half light with weirdos dressed up and banging drums around me. My mother would have wondered what cult I had joined. So, I thought, OK, why not, so on I went, following these 'troupes' around for another couple of hours. I popped into a small bar for some cheese flan – sorry, I've forgotten the name of it, but it's traditional on this occasion – and a glass of gluwein to wash it down (it's a bit strange at 6am). Anyway, it was pretty good and the partying went on until I saw dawn break over the Mittlebrücke. At 7.30am, I thought I'd best return home to either sleep or, have breakfast. (Hans-Peter had asked me to be in the office at 9am even though it's a bank holiday here and even though I'd been awake since 3am. Am I a mug or what?!)

Hans-Peter left for Rome with Anne. He suggested I visit town again this afternoon, Tuesday afternoon and Wednesday afternoon (so good of him to give me the time off...I wonder what is planned though?) I got lost on the way back driving from the office and although I discovered a really cute restaurant, at the top of some hill, I will probably never find it again. Also I discovered a riding school. Yipee!

OK, this is my route to work, which I have to try to remember:

Hirtenbuendenweg – that's easy that's where I live
Im Kugelfang – think of fangs
Embeerden - strawberries
Holzsomething
Paradise Street – what I'm looking for!
Neubad rain/drain, something
Neu bad strasse
Roundabout
NB take the 3rd exit, not the 2nd, or I'll end up going to the office via the Flughafen again (airport).
Then think of Morgan something
Remember Rita something
Morganstrasse
And I should be able to recognise the way from there...
(Clock on wall, bus terminal, huge green glass building, M for Migros, supermarket on corner to Blotzheimerstrasse, only you cannot take a left turn so drive to Migros and turn around in the road).

Do you think I should fly back to the UK for JB's Birthday party? It would cause a bit of a stir wouldn't it. But you know if I saw him affectionately, patting some other girl, could I take it even if I don't love him at all? What if I turned up with a 7 foot Guido chimp on my arm?! So he'd probably laugh, then I'd point to his beeceps.

Where would I stay? I could kip up at Charlie's perhaps, see if she's up for it? Could I stay? Oh so much to think about. Perhaps I could swing a UK visit that Friday or Monday with work as I'm due to go over soon for a workshop thing.

I forgot to mention, I met a really sweet lady last night and her son in the cafe. Her mother married a German – an interesting story - he escaped from Berlin during the war. It was quite open of her to tell me everything since we'd only just met and shared a table with 2 Germans. She gave me her telephone number and address. She asked me to pop by some time for German lessons. Mmm, that could be useful, but I'd better check out what's happening at work first.

I've a party to go to on Friday night – we've a new CEO and CFO of Switzerland, Frederik and Otto respectively. Good, some excitement.

Why can't I stop going to the loo? Think I may have deli belly, foot and mouth etc. perhaps it's just the water? Or that damm tart that I ate? Still, my complexion will do well be getting rid of all the WCT (white choccie toblerone) that I devoured last night).

I do hope my social life picks up or I'll be destined for cardiovascular disease and arteries clotted with WCT as well as a WCT belly and thighs and zits etc etc. (I must look good if I do decide to go to JB's party).

Monday.

It's a Bank holiday and guess where I went? Yep, right, into the office. At least I managed to suss Microsoft Outlook email in German. Poor Bee – everyone's Personal Assistant - is still on crutches, I feel really guilty about asking her to do anything. I feel very tired as I've been up since 3am.

I went to the carnival again this afternoon. Don't think I

11

could ever fall for a Swiss guy, knowing how much pleasure they seem to deride from dressing up in womens' clothes and chucking confetti and sweets over everyone. They are ever so serious about their piping flutes and drums. Quite extraordinary. It's a bit like Notting Hill but with no violence. Nobody's pissed either, quite refreshing! (Hans-Peter threw a wobbly on seeing 1 policeman last night. I told him he should be in London, where to see just 1 policeman, would be strange – he did not get the joke).

Nice tea tonight though I say it myself. I just roasted some veg in some tin foil and put cheese on top – a better pizza than last night's and melon (v expensive for the poor quality).

I met some guy named Johann last night. Typical, from Sri Lanka and short – why could it not be tall dark handsome Brit abroad or Swiss guy (?!) (I was also approached by 1 Swiss guy but he was in a massive fasnacht outfit, mm, not my type! Definitely a turn-off). Oh well, Johann's someone who can introduce me to a few bars here at least, I just hope he doesn't get the wrong idea, I want nothing more than friendship. We've arranged to meet at 6pm on Wednesday outside Papa Joe's. Nothing ventured, nothing gained...

Tuesday morning.

I am still feeling a bit uneasy. My first impression... I'm definitely returning to London after 12 months (get me out of here!) No, give it a chance I keep saying to myself. I have to meet the landlord this morning.

The meeting with the landlord went well, although he didn't speak a word of English and I didn't speak a word of Deutsch. He didn't know anything about how anything worked either, just provided me with instruction booklets, which describe everything in German, French and Italian but not English. I've so much washing to do, I'm half tempted to just do it (without reading the instructions).

The 1st proper day at work went OK. Hans-Peter and I had a meeting this afternoon with Chameleon Pharma. It went well but 3 and half hours later at 6.45pm, we arrive back at the office. It was a long day. Rita from Mexico (one of my clients) has asked me if I'd like to join her and her friends this evening for drinks for Fasnacht, so I manage to meet up with them. (She's also offered me her spare stereo, which will be fab – instead of having to sit in silence amongst my...2 sleeping bags and vase of slowly dying flowers on the "living room" floor).

Tonight, wow, more men in drag on the streets. I can't believe the number of spectators – this must be the whole of Basel +++. I saw the 'Guggemusik' (bands who play tunes out of tune – mm, why I wonder?) they parade around the streets (even at 1.15am when we were on our way home playing the same old dreadful tuneless and irritating 'melodies'). I visit "Andreas Platz" which is very beautiful and hundreds of yet more tiny streets, which I've never seen before, and which I hope I will be able to find again for my guests.

I visit a little cafe bar for the traditional Fasnacht onion tart and hot chocolate, and then we all went into a "Clique" - an underground bar - which was interesting. There was lots of storytelling, in German, of course, performed by lots of people who had dressed up in some weird and wonderful costumes. I tell you what's interesting – they never ask for money, yet in London, that would be their sole objective. Here, they just seem to enjoy it?!

We visited the Münster platz with its array of illuminated lanterns. Quite amazing. Ooh, have booked a night away in a ski resort this weekend – yipee! – it makes it all worthwhile. So I'm off to 'Murren' this Saturday and Sunday – I am to catch the early train Saturday and return Sunday night.

Tonight, I met several people – Magda (here for 8 years, from Milan); Maria (here for 3 years, from Germany); Nicolas (15 years, from Brazil); etc etc. The rest I cannot remember their names but I feel sure we will meet again – they are in Rita's gang! There are lots of ex-pats, mainly from Germany. Oh and John Junior, some loud mouth from Nuttley, New Jerrrrrrsey. Urgh, why so loud? They are meeting tomorrow night, but I am meeting up with Johann. This is going to cost me a fortune – a piece of pie and a hot choccie cost about £6 and the taxi fare home (because the trams had finished) cost me £12 for about 4 miles, if that! Can't believe it.

Day 2 at work (Hans-Peter gave me unofficial half day today, mind you it is a bank holiday!) and guess what, I put the washing machine on, opened it when I returned home from work and now the kitchen floor is covered in water, like Lake Geneva. Great! I must try to translate the instructions.

I have managed to suss out a flatter route to work, along which I could cycle without feeling too much burn before I even work out. I think I'm slowly getting to know my way around a bit.

On talking to people, I can't believe how long they seem to stay here and I guess that's what scares me too. Do I, don't I want to stay here? I don't know. God please tell me to stop worrying and just let my life go on "C'est la vie" Kay sera sera, whatever will be will be, the future's not ours to see, key sera sera.....

Chapter 1

Wednesday.

Another day at work.

I wonder what's going on back home? Called Charlie at lunchtime, I just had to speak to someone with a) an English accent b) the same sense of humour as me!

9am – meeting No. 2 at Chameleon Pharma. Feeling very tired after such a late night. Still, apply myself properly (as JB put in his card). Oh yes, did I tell you, he sent me a card. Now who feels a complete prick?! Me, yes! Urgh! Wish I'd never sent my awful letter. Still, that's the way I felt at the time, I just wanted him to know how much he'd let me down. His card is so sweet though too. Urgh, here I go again...No news from M, well, I suppose I've only been away a week, but already I feel I've so much news etc etc, must keep stumm for a while – let all the fuss blow over. Still Fuzznight, so will pop out this afternoon (half day bank holiday – have you heard of such a thing, half a day?). Am meeting that Johann tonight, I mean, a guy who lives in Switzerland for 8 years and doesn't ski...no, not my type, certainement! Oh well, will let you know. I absolutely do not fancy him at all and must make him know that from the start. No problem! Got it, I'll tell him about my "boyfriend". JB, can I borrow you back for a bit?! Thanks, or M (yes, please) or whoever!

Thank goodness Rita's lent me her portable stereo. Fab, life in my flat. Bee helped me translate my washing machine instructions. Well, here goes, 2nd time..I'm hoping I'll have some clean undies for skiing this weekend.

OK, I met that Johann, made it clear, don't think I'll ever see him again and am quite glad. He's ok to find things out from. Went on a boat trip across the Rhine, behind the Munster, through "Klein Basle" = small Basle (saw big store, Manor, there's a roof top restaurant apparently, and saw H&M in Basle too, open until 9pm on Thursday –

apparently – great, at last, civilisation).

Back across the bridge and we wandered into an underground bar amongst the "Clique's" for a glass of white wine and then to a great place, wine only wine bar. – I had Edesse white (a local bog standard white wine) and Johann had Rioca (Spanish bog standard, no class). Then went to Wongs' – a sort of Chinese motorway self-service station in the middle of Basle city (oh, I apparently live in Basle land which is outside the city). It was OK, walked past La Bodega – apparently a great place for Italian (and pizza) and Fumare bar (tango on Thursday nights) and the university, where there is a tropical garden. Oh yes, apparently, you can climb to the top of the Munster for 2CHF as well – for a great view of Basle, I'll have to do it in the summer.

Decided enough was enough at 9pm. He had friends to meet anyway. Abdull and Sarah (who sounded a little crazy and pissed on the phone I have to say). Anyway, last night was a 2-o'clocker so could do with an early one. Back to apartment – jogged back from the tram stop (one stop too early) quite out of breath, gosh, I must suss out the gyms soon. I may take Guido up on his offer tomorrow night – I need to get rid of the toblerone in the fridge (and in my stomach).

U2 are in concert on Rita's portable stereo – cool!

Had an email from Justin and Lisa, JB and….Jeff. Tried to reply to the 2 former, not the latter. Also, messages from Kate and Nadia and sent an SMS to M to wish him a happy Fuzznight.

OK, so what did I discover today? Another way to get lost on the way to work (I think I know the corner to turn down now – restaurant Waage on RHS, then turn left, but you can't turn left, so go straight ahead then turn back and turn right opposite restaurant wagge. OK, restaurant wagge, restaurant wagge). Oh and IKEA!! Yahoo! Bought 2 pans, smashing. I won't have to eat bread tonight and I can cook something more spectacular, like, wait for it ...pasta.

Have more or less decided what I need to buy – I discovered a "start up" kit of wine glasses, plates, tumblers, cutlery etc. all for about £40. There are a few other things on the "wish list" too:

Wish List:

Sofa	either 299 CHF or futon 199CHF
Table	about 39CHF
Bed – v.simple	299 CHF
Mattress though as well	270CHF
Bedside table	39CHF
Drawers	179CHF
Hanging fold up wardrobe	199CHF

... by the time I can afford everything, 12 months will be up, and I'll be home! Ooh, and there's the dining table 59CHF – I found this garden type of table

Chairs	19 CHF x 4
Shelf unit	39CHF

Saw a box plant too, ab fab value, about 19CHF. On Northcote road they're about 50£ each for tiny things! This is fab value, I'll love to get one – had to hold myself back and told myself to get a grip, a box plant is not exactly a priority when I'm sat eating dinner on 2 sleeping bags.

Spoke to Kate tonight. It was great to speak to someone without an accent (think that may begin to bug me after a few months).

Got a bit embroiled in an office politics today – last thing I wanted – can't believe 3 days into work and I'm already a bit scared of stepping on too many toes. Wish M or JB would ring, or write – I guess I'm a man's girl.
Oh and I spoke to the washing machine people today (they have a fab little tool on our network at work called "twix

tel". You just type in the name of the place you want to find out about and the town and lo and behold, all the variations that fit the bill in the directory come up. I did this for the washing machine, found out a telephone number and hopefully I'll be able to get my washing out tomorrow!)

Phoned Pickford's today, my things haven't even left the UK yet – they are waiting for my documents from customs etc – urgh. Why didn't they call me to let me know? God, I think I should write a book about re-locating and things you need to take into consideration!

Which reminds me, I must sort out the following:

Mobile phone
Home telephone
Bank account   a) here
                  b) in UK
Mortgage direct debit from my new bank account
Gym – must must must – I miss it madly! I feel like a potato already yet it's not even been a week – all this bread and toblerone.

Gosh this pasta tastes sooooo good. Thank goodness I brought JB's olive oil in my hand luggage too, he was useful for some things I suppose. Feel really bad about that letter I wrote to him. But I missed him saying goodbye. I wanted to just say goodbye. I wanted to ask when I would see him again.

I know what's depressing – at least if there were 2 of you, you could both go halves on the furniture. On your own, you can't. That also assumes that whoever wants you, would like your choice in furniture etc and leave no opportunity for them to introduce their own touches, which would be awful. Perhaps that's what puts men off – everything's a fait accompli with me?? Sorted? Why would I want a man to go in and introduce some bog ugly leather 40's sofa with pink cushions etc (OK, if I loved him enough perhaps I'd put up with it, would I?). Thing is, I know I couldn't go out with

18

anyone like that (or could I?!) but I think I felt the former when I went to Jeff's house – everything was sorted. Done, dusted (and in a taste almost as bad as the former referred to design. Urgh, I'm just remembering his nauseous pink pink kitchen he referred to as "terracota". Mmm, think he must be colour blind – or, his interior designer must have been having a laugh! (When I hear the name Jeff all I can think of is that awful programme on TV that we used to (have to) watch as kids, "Rainbow" starring Bungo, George, Jeffrey and that silly blond tart who swayed her hair from side to side). Poor guy, I shouldn't be too harsh, at least he sent me an email, though I was a little worried when he said I should call him upon my next return for some "quality time" together. Cringe.

It feels like a squat here. What have I done?

I must put these shower curtain hooks on tonight. Another IKEA purchase, so I can hang my shower curtain.

So, yes, I discovered the motorway and IKEA – oops, I nearly crashed on the way home as I took to the LHS slip road instead of the RHS slip road. Fortunately, oncoming drivers flashed me just in time – yikes, a close shave!

New Vocab to date:
Gruezi = often used now, hey I sound local.
Bitte schon
Danke schon
Wiedersen
Ausfahrt
Eingang
IKEA (well, it's foreign)
Stüble
Guten morgan
Guten tag
All my old 1-term of German when 11 years old is flooding back
Guten nacht
Zimmer

Perhaps it would be cheaper to rent my furniture. They rent furniture here, honestly, what a strange business opportunity.

Tomorrow I have a party to go to at Creative Inc Zurich – that will be good – at least interesting anyway! I will drive as I intend to catch that very early train tomorrow, Saturday, to the ski slopes ☺.

Gute nacht!
A demain!

Friday 9th March 2001

What a bizarre day it was today. Got up leisurely late and made porridge (yahoo, my new pan). Can't believe I'm so excited about a pan. Managed to find the office without getting lost. At lunchtime I popped to UBS, Binningen, OK I'm officially Swiss now, with a Swiss bank account (banks are all the same, I felt like I was being given the 3rd Reich when opening my account. Led away into some little grey room with filing cabinets on the 1st floor of this little bank and was interviewed by a very severe and austere (but not bad) looking guy. No overdrafts, no visa, until you put 5,000 CHF into the account to cover it – ridiculous!) No wonder all these Swiss are so well off. Then ventured into town to sort out my mobile. After some language struggles a Scottish girl and boyfriend walked into the shop and spoke in fluent Swiss German. Eventually we managed to say goodbye to 0044 7788444834 and hello to 0041 79711 6786 (wow, I can remember it already).

Went back to car (via a display of fasnacht drums) and on the way picked up a ticket for 12 bus and tram rides (much cheaper than single tickets).

Back to car and guess what … a "big fat fine" was placed on my windscreen. OK, great, Thanks guys. I'd even displayed the 1 and half hour parking permit Bea had given me, so unsure what had happened. The fine was 140CHF, pretty steep. Bastards. When suddenly I turned around and

"Gandalf" was in a car opposite (did you read the hobbit, the fab wizard that turns up just when you need him). Whilst he did not give me a ring to make me invisible (read the hobbit!) he said "Give that to me, I will call them. You will not need to pay it". Well, I just held up my hands – what more can a girl say?! (Sometimes it's great to be Blonde, female and British).

Tonight, went to the party at Creative Inc Zurich and wow, another world...(after I'd negotiated the motorway). Had a wonderful night, champagne reception, quintet, meal, said farewell to Rene, the old CEO of Creative Inc and founder of Creative Inc Switzerland, and goodbye to his CFO, Gerry and hello to Otto (new CFO) and Frank Bodin (new CEO – only mid-30's, fairly good looking guy in a weird sort of Swiss-French way, if only he was more than 4 foot high and didn't wear such dirty old trainers with his Armani suit). He says he "vil pop over to zee basil one day". Drove back, very late, very tired and am catching this very early train tomorrow to ski!!!!!!

Well, here I am, sat on Basel train station platform. It's 06.34 and 10 seconds (sorry, I'm becoming a bit Swiss I think!). I missed the 1st train, the 06.17 but it does not matter, at least I've picked up my travel savings card, die 'Halbtax' for 12 months, which enables me to have half price travel across Switzerland now.

I left the house at 05.40am, just missed the No. 34 bus to the tram stop, so was no other bus until 05.59, then the tram at 06.08. No chance of making it, laden with my backpack. Arrived at station at 06.15, 2 mins to go, oh well, I thought, take it easy etc (just wished I'd eaten more breakfast though now). Ticket cost 62CHF (about £30) and the rail card 160CHF (about £80). If I come skiing twice more, I will have paid for it.

OK, lesson number one (get up 15 mins earlier) to catch the right bus and train.

No.2 pack breakfast the night before (oh and perhaps

have an earlier night)

No. 3 Book a seat on the train (obviously the non-smoking carriages are fewer than the "fumare" carriages .- bring back the UK with all non-smoking carriages!) then it's a case of trying to find a free seat – most being reserved.

So here I am, aboard the 07.04 and it's 06.53 and 1 second. Managed to find a seat that was not reserved and guess what, it's next to the window (and the buffet car – mind you, not a lot of choice on the buffet menu, save for jambon=lard and fromage=cheese obviously. Am glad I brought my fruit).

Must write to M soon.

Wonder what JB thought of the group email that I sent him? Sent an email before leaving for the party last night – attached – Swiss e-newsletter number 1!

Hope they didn't think it a bit off-putting. Had to rush before I sent it, so no chance to check for typos either – yikes! No doubt threw in some real horrors.

Purchased water at the station – wow, nothing changes, 3CGF (about £1.50 for a really small bottle).

I'm settling into my seat when Ok, here we go, cattle class is arriving. Am a little worried as there are lots of skiers on the opposite platform. Lots of boarders on this train (Cool!).

Forget to mention, last night was an eventful night, I met a couple of wild wild girls – Tanya and Indie – it was surreal. They were so confident and full of themselves. Indie is PR (obviously darling) born and bred Swiss (obviously darling) and very proud of it (darling).

Tanya at Creative Inc consumer agency in Zurich, school in London, University LSE, worked in Hong Kong, Sydney (where she lived with her boyfriend until he decided he didn't want to reference her extended visa permit – a bit of a handful I can imagine). A globe trotter (obviously darlings) and now lives in Switzerland since September (her mother is Swiss).

God this train's getting packed.

3 mins to go.

I think this is going to be a journey from hell.

The 06.17 is obviously the train to get. At least some skiers are aboard now, which reassures me and we're off, it's 07.04 precisely (obviously!) 2 mins into the journey and just typical, having traipsed the whole platform to find a non smoking carriage, I end up opposite the only 2 chain smokers on the train, typical! Try to open the window, it's locked. Small boy gets his Swiss army knife out. Twiddles with the screws and lo, it's open. So I decide to pop to the toilet.

OK, made it to Spitz. OK, so far so good. Fantastic lake on RHS as I arrived in Spitz. Now it's looking like the Switzerland I always imagined. Little wooden chalets nestling in the hills surrounded by white capped peaks of mountains. Another beautiful lake. I change trains. The next train is much nicer, less crowded, no smoking carriage (try again!) v v smooth and quiet. Unbelievable to think these things go on every day. Wow, that lake is huge.

And, here we are at Interlaken Ost (East, hey, my German's improving). Just rode past the most amazing blue blue blue river – so blue it's beautiful. Must be careful what I write now as many Americans here (oh no).

I must buy a phrase book, this is ridiculous.

And it's pouring down here in Interlaken – hope it's snowing at 1,634m (there's a map on this train to show you where you can go and the heights of the resorts. It also indicates the Jungfrau which is 3,454m, top of Europe – on a clear day, what a fab view). This is where the 007 revolving restaurant is, on the Shilthorn (at 2,971m), wow, perhaps I'll even be able to get up there too. Whatever, just take it steady. Wish someone was here to share it with me (yes, ok, namely M or JB).

There's also the Jungfrau here which is 4,158m! asl- above sea level.

So now, I'm going to admire the view and the weird little trains (noticed some stickers that are postcards – must buy one for Tim).

I can't believe I'm here on my own...arrived at hotel about 11am, changed, went into room, it's fab with beautiful view over the village and balcony (think the owner, Anne-Marie, has treated me specially). The air is clean and fresh – no cars allowed up here in Mürren.

I had a bit of trouble getting to understand the labelling of the runs – not so clear in Switzerland, but once you get the hang of it, it's ok.

Oh the church bell is chiming, must be 7pm already. It's a lovely little village. And, found a cheap grocery shop – although spilt most of my groceries over the road – a good way of getting 2 Italians to help me (although their girlfriends were not too pleased) and went to the top of 007's revolving restaurant at Schilthorn – fantastic views even though it was a bit snowy – we managed to have a few breaks in the cloud and it was beautiful (once I managed to get a bit of colour to my cheeks by tonight – though could be exhaustion having woken up at 5.15am! And, guess what, skiied down from the top!!! Yahoo!! Terrifying but the rest not quite so bad – very powdery though, lovely and a few bumps. Had a hot choccie and carrot cake in James Bond's place – mm, Mr Bond! Mmm, what should I do tonight? Eat in the restaurant or elsewhere? Would I look odd on my own? Probably better to stick to the hotel? But mm, food in hotels is always so average. May look around town for a pizza place.
    Lost a glove so had to buy another pair, then the hotel

found it tonight. Urgh, 95CHF later (about £40) could have been a lift pass for 2 days. Never mind, at least I have an emergency pair now.

What an extraordinary night I have had – as I sit here on my balcony with a glass of hot milk – with a smidgeon of rum in – medicinal I do assure you – reflecting on what's in store for me.

I'm scared, scared of liking this place too much, scared of not liking it. It's growing on me. The people are so nice and unpretentious. I just wish so much I could share it with someone I wanted to share it with, it seems such a waste (but no, I'm writing this, which will probably bore you to tears, but I guess I'll be sharing it all with you, with someone).

Ok, so what happened tonight…

After shower etc etc, went downstairs, where…thought I'd check out if there was a pizza place etc around. (Really felt like a gluwein and the hotel smells like gluwein when I arrived back from the slopes – obviously someone apres-skiing!) Anyway, made my way outside, determined to escape from a usual "hotel" and found an excellent bar in a small hotel down the road. Very cool, jazz, live singer (but chilled and cool) and candlelit bar. I felt OK and at home – v relaxed especially as the light was dim, so no-one would be able to spot me – urgh…girl on her own, sad. Ordered a gluwein and wrote some postcards (to mum, to M – hope he doesn't mind; to Paula and Mick). Had a good relaxing drink. Then, went in search of food. Passed a Chinese (no, really, in such a sweet traditional village?!) then came across another place. Thought I'd check it out and spotted "fondue" of all shapes and sizes on their menus outside. Excellent, love fondues. Went in. It was crowded but room for me to squeeze on the end of a table (one benefit of being alone). Had an excellent salad grün/vert, then cheese fondue savoyarde – normal – fab – garlic, kir, gruyere. Just finished when something extraordinary happened. There was a sudden commotion on the next table in the restaurant with cries of "mama mama" then a guy lifted a lady up from under the table. Oh shit, I thought, she's having an epileptic fit or something, or it's diabetes. Neither of the above. What can I do? She stopped breathing, her eyes were rolling in her head and she started to look really pale. The restaurant owner shouted "Docteur Docteur" but the son-in-law (I think) just grabbed her and said "No, stay calm" (I think anyway, because it was in German) and then I thought, she's choking why aren't they pushing her stomach? Instead the guy made his way around the table – where everyone else had left. I cleared a space – at least it would give her room and air. Eventually, after much frothing etc at the mouth, the guilty piece of "das brot" emerged. Thank goodness. Daughter (I guessed) was relieved. I offered all the support I could – water, napkins etc etc. She seemed ok after a while but wow, the whole restaurant was in stunned silence and shock. What a lady! I felt guilty to leave although really did not feel like finishing my wine but I felt that it would only make the old lady worried if I upt and left right away. I wrote my final postcard to Anna and Juha, finished my wine on the adjacent table, helped them get their table back together, read my book a little (the one Dr Maurice had sent me) and then asked for the bill. The waiter said that they would like to buy me a snapps or tea, but I said it was ok, just glad she was alright (in my pigeon German/Swiss/French). Later I left. They bode me goodnight and wished me a pleasant evening in excellent English so I did to them too and said "bon soiree" also which I know means have a good evening indicating to the old lady that she was to stay off the brot from now on! Quick walk around town then back to my hotel. Suddenly Mürren had grown on me so much.

And as I sit here on my balcony for a cost less than my 2 day ski hire, I thank Hans Peter from work for putting me in touch with Anne Marie and hope that if I do go elsewhere, I will receive a similar warm welcome – or perhaps I should come back here? But then if I'm only here for 12 months, I'd really like to find other places despite Anne Marie's kind hospitality. Gute nacht x

Good morning and wow, what a view at 07.09! Switch on the TV (oh what luxuries) love one of the channels – has a live camera which rotates around Manlichen (tells me it's 2,230m high, windstill, -6degrees.Cool!) with all this dinkly twinkly Swiss music.

Schilthorn, wind 9km/hr, 2,970m, -6degrees, www.schilthorn.ch (15km/h in the west). And Jungfrau "Top of Europe" Spinx 3,571m, -8degrees, wind 21km/h süd – feel it's a must to check out. Eiger run offnen, the typical swiss music could be irritating after a while but to a visitor like me, it's kind of funky, or, intriguing! Perhaps I should ask Kate and Jason to pop over to Grindelwald – runs around the Mannlichen look really fab and cool. Quite high too.

Ab fab breakfast – muesli, fresh fruits, bread (love the Swiss bread). Now off to the pistes!

   Had a wonderful day skiing. Up and down Winteregg a few times, then decided to go over the other side of Mürren and bumped into 2 German guys I'd bumped into yesterday – unbelieveable! Mind you, Mürren is a small resort so I guess it's more than likely you bump into someone someday. Peter and Joe, from Dusseldorf. They're quite good fun actually – went up the other side of the mountain together and had a few laughs and giggles. We nicknamed Joe the "mountain goat" as he went "cross country" having missed the piste. V funny. Went up the Schilthorn together and whilst Joe had to go down to meet their friend, Peter and I stopped for lunch in James Bond's rotating restaurant, I had a lovely vegetable canalloni, Peter had "James Bond Spaghetti" (yeah right!). I said to Peter I wanted to ski the Schilthorn one last time "But it's black" he said "I know," I said but I would like to do it one more time before I have to get my train. I think he thought he could not let a girlie beat him (he was going to get the gondola) so in the end, he joined me.

As it was, I was glad of the company. The going was pretty tough – fresh powder snow everywhere, if only you could see it – you could not see anything in the driving rain and snow. I could not even see the path we were going, so I had to keep waiting (for Peter) and for someone else to come along, bet Peter thought I was really stupid wanting to do it, but hey, we made it! It was a great feeling when we arrived at the station of BIRG gondola to then get a lift down to "land on the ground" as Peter put it, for the final trip back to Mürren. I took my skis back to the shop 48HF, not much for a full day of fun, said goodbye to Peter, wished each other well and I went back to the hotel to collect my things. Said my goodbye and thanks to Anne-Marie's team – she was on her lunch break unfortunately, otherwise I would have thanked her personally – I am sure she "upgraded" me – it was not a single room but a double and had the best balcony in the hotel (must remember 323 is the number of the room, if you ever want to go, or if you want to go with a Lurver!)

And so, I'm on my way home and guess what, some other bizarre incidence... I happened to notice a couple of guys who kept looking at me – obviously son and dad. Son was quite nice though blonde – don't usually like blonde guys. Anyway, we arrived at the Mürren hauptbahn changeover and got out. Stupid me, I dropped my purse and had not realised it! Fortunately, Mr Good looking was right behind me and picked it up and guess what, gave it to me when we left! Eek! 1st thought = alarm bells = language problems! No problem, alles klar – he spoke pretty good English (obviously!) . We caught the next train all together. Quite funny, a New Zealand girl and an Ozzie girl were sat opposite me and we were just talking and the guy and his father were just talking with me. We exchanged names. He said he was called "Pieter" – I laughed and remarked that every guy I"d met in Switzerland was called a version of 'Peter' – the girls started sniggering, it was all rather funny.

Anyway, I ended up sharing the train with Peter and his dad all the way to Interlaken (where his father lives and where Peter spends most of his weekends). He is an engineer, works for the government in Bern, lives in a 1 bed apartment in Bern but visits Interlaken to ski most weekends (except this weekend, as the weather had been so poor).

We exchanged cards (what am I doing?) but hey, why not. Weird thing happened as we descended from the Interlaken train – when guess what, another guy handed me his card and asked me to put it deep into my pocket! So... I did.....?!!!?? I noticed that he'd written something on it so thought I would read it later. Peter's father had obviously noticed (mm, typical) and so Peter wanted to know. I just said I think I met him on the cable car in Mürren and that he had helped me down the Schilthorn – urgh! What could I say?! I didn't even notice the guy, do not even know what he looks like? Urgh, he just disappeared very quickly. Ends up – urgh – he is a guy who lives in Michegan, this is what he wrote....

I would love to correspond with an English young woman – please write me! Bruce J. Butch, 1210 Blanchard Av, Flint, Michigan 48503 USA.

Who on earth was he? Obviously not American or English because of the English grammar. So bizarre? Wonder what other bizarre things will happen to me while I'm here?!
    Oh well, here's Swiss boy, Peter's card. We 3 went for a drink at the "thai restaurant" Interlaken (a contradiction in words). It was so embarrassing, Celine Dionne from "titanic" was piping on the overhead stereo. It was pouring down with rain outside (shame) but we had a laugh (the 3 of us: Dad, Swiss boy Peter and moi). He said he would like

me to go to Bern and he would show me around, or, would like to come to Basel for me to show him around. However he also said that he would like to go skiing with me next weekend. I said one of my friends was thinking of coming over (well, Kate and Jason are hopefully popping over) but that it would be good to meet up. Who knows, possibly we'll be able to. I mentioned I was thinking of going to Grindelwald (but that a guy at Mürren had said that Port du Soleil would be better because it was higher) so may prefer to go there. He also mentioned Gstaad "because it is full of beautiful people like you" he said – gosh, how sweet! (or, cheesy?)

Anyway, after helping me with my bags (his father had obviously said something to suggest that he did this), he kissed me the Swiss regulation 3 kisses on each cheek and I left for my platform (buying a "Daily Telegraph" en route). SBP's very sweet. Bet he's a fab skiier too – urgh – they just have that sort of "look" about them. Not great outfits, but great skiers.

My arms ache quite a lot (lots of T-bars in Mürren and a few button lifts too). But I'm so glad I went. Cost:

CHF 86 for hotel (inc. Hot milk and rum)
CHF 48 for ski hire for 2 days
CHF 95 for lift pass for 2 days (though could have got a cheaper one, because apparently Peter says that after 12.30pm they are cheaper, damm, because I only hit the slopes at about 12.30 anyway)
CHF 10 for Choc cake (sat) in James Bond's restaurant
CHF 10 for soup and roll in Winteregg rest for lunch
CHF 6 for gluwein in fab bar at the alti palace where I wrote M's postcard
CHF 31 for fondue in bizarre restaurant with poorly lady
Drink with Peter and his dad – free
Ooh, lunch, CHF 20 in James Bond's restaurant today (Peter insisted on paying the rest – probably would have cost 25CHF)

Train CHF 210 (but that included 160 CHF for the halbtax train pass, so I have half price travel now wherever in der Schweiz)
Oh yes, bought some groceries in Mürren Co-op, CHF 6
And the gloves CHF 95

Total cost approx 450CHF, eek, about £200 but then hey, why not, I feel I'm on holiday! So, about the cost of one measley Nicole Fahri top and guess how much fun I had this time.

Just remembered, this was embarrassing: my electric toothbrush went off in my bag when SBP said he would carry it for me ! I wonder if SBP thought it was some sort of pervy dildo (do they understand such things in Switzerland?!)
    No-one's ever given me an orgasm since M. I'm tired of doing it myself – may as well be on my own.

Telephoned Kate and Charlie and Lynn tonight. Desperate to speak to someone and tell them all about my adventures. Only got hold of Charlie. We had a great chat. Down to 58CHF on my "pay as I talk" phone – gosh – spent 22CHF already (about £10 on one phone call!!)

OK, so Monday, and received 2 emails and a phone call from SBP – whey hey! Phoned Kate to discuss. Jason couldn't believe my early success – 1 week in a brand new country and a new man already! Is this a record? Perhaps I should apply to the Guiness book of records. Apart from that, a bit pissed off that my things are going to take another 2 weeks approx. Pickford's estimate. My washing machine instructions in English have still not turned up so my washing stays locked in the machine – argh!! So annoying.

Tonight, went out for dinner with one of my clients – Axel. Fab restaurant/bar, pretty cool. Will definitely go there again. Especially as it's around the corner from my gym.

He chose Shiraz chardonny to drink and I chose Toscana wine. Came in little jugs – v cost effective for 2 glasses of wine each. Wine reflected him a bit – bit like a Yorkshire terrier, snappy, bit spicy, cheap? Whilst mine, I like to think was a little more refined, smooth (yeah right). I ate smoked salmon (lachs) and risotto of wald champignon (wild mushrooms, yum, my fav).

Also, checked out the squash club today – ok, not a nice club but it's ok and you can just pop in to play squash. On the less good side of town, border of France, Allschwill, and pretty run down. That's where that Johann works too – strangely I have never heard from him again, not surprising but quite glad really).

Had to cut SBP off the phone tonight as I arrived at Chameleon Pharma when he called, hope he doesn't think I did it on purpose.

Kate and I plotting to go to JB's party a week on Sat. Mmm, could be cool, if I turned up. May muster up the courage to phone him tomorrow – his card was really nice thought..mmm, we shall see. Is he worth it?

Here I am, embarking on another day, another journey, another relationship ?

I am worried about money, if I don't receive a reimbursement for my meal last night with Axel, I will not be able to afford to go skiing this weekend with SBP (gosh I hate the name Peter so much, reminds me of lazy Huddy from the London office, overweight , alcoholic, such a pity).

Wonder if SBP will speak to me today? (Gosh down to 30CHF already on my phone – must have cost about £10 to call Kate last night – will have to be careful).

Must pop SBP's mobile into my mobile, so I know when he's calling. He reminds me a little of Michele a) because he's foreign b) because he's a bit of a whizz on skiis (as his father was fiercely gesticulating on Sunday night) – probably been a bit of a ski instructor in his teens.

His father was obviously desperate to "pair him off" with someone. I remember his father asking (in German – SBP had to translate) whether I had a boyfriend and SBP said "Why not?" "You are soooo beautiful" (yeah right, I mean, I don't even know him, it was a bit much to be honest but ok, I'll take it). I said I did have one but that he did not like me coming to Switzerland. SBP said that perhaps he will come to Switzerland. I shrugged (hoping obviously that M would indeed one day come to Switzerland). He asked if I skied (bit obvious as I was in a train from Mürren with 2 things in my hand that looked like ski boots and ski pants on – doh or what?) (Both JB and M ski – I can imagine pretty well too). So I said yes (ridiculous that I'd not been on a ski holiday with either JB or M and such a fab and romantic hol too). I told SBP that I doubted he would come over as I had written a "terrible letter"... (wow, if I went to JB's party with SBP, what a hoot! Tee hee, play JB at his own game. See who's done better! No, that's terrible, besides, I can't afford to go home yet).

Sent Andy his birthday card yesterday –gosh he'll be 39 I think on 17th March! (how old?!) He's lucky at least he looks younger (in some ways – though he shouldn't drink so much).

Wonder how his love life with the "Child bride" is going? (22 – wow, it reminds me of my own father when he ran away from home at 40 to be with a 25 year old from Austria). Men. Typical!

(I have not heard a thing from dad – wonder if he will ever contact me? Perhaps I should just tell prospective friends and boyfriends that he died. Might as well – wish he could have helped guide me financially and with work decisions so much).

Oh yes, I had an email from that Tanya yesterday. It was amazing, she was going on about money. She's probably just like me and has spent it all on clothes etc in the past to live up to something she was trying to be (she kept mentioning how much more cost effective it is to buy "Joseph this Joseph that" here in Switzerland than in London, darling – I was a bit embarrassed as I had chosen to wear my one cream Joseph suit with black shirt, bought in the sale from Joseph London last year. I kept trying to hide the label, after all, she'll think I am rolling in it if she saw it).

The following day…

Wow, my face in the mirror this morning looks pretty brown – skiing tan. Except for the graze on my chin (when I landed over the crest of a hill into what can only be described as a "hole" in the slope on Saturday – urgh, typical. At least my bindings broke and my skis came off so I stood up laughing instead of crying, or at least stood up!)

Oh, while I remember, things to avoid in Der Schweiz:
  …processed chesse Gauda – it's terrible, tastes like dairylea.
  Also, cottage cheese (yuk yuk and double yuk – and looks like frog spawn – brings back memories of that terrible semolina at school. Nothing like M&S cottage cheese).

It's not raining this morning (for a change). Beautiful blue blue blue sky and I've tuned into "Radio Guten Morgan" (thank goodness for Rita's stereo). The station plays English music, so makes me feel more at home.

I should not be too deceived, although it's nice and warm in my apartment, it's bound to be pretty damm cold outside. (This underfloor heating is marvellous – even though it goes off at 10.30pm until 05.30am, because if "the law" as my landlord, Herr Rengli told me).
  Late night tonight – joined the Heuwagge (gym) in town. Ab fab. Feel less cheesy fatty now! Amazing they have disinfectant and wipes against every machine almost – and I thought I was anal in cleaning my flat so much (once a week).
  Ooh, I got my washing machine to spin too! Sabina at work helped me to translate the instruction booklet! Wow, my floor is covered in washing (should dry quickly because of the underfloor heating).
  I left a message on JB's home telephone number and also wrote to M tonight. Hope they get back to me.

SBP sent me a short email later today too.

Eek, bit late this morning. Alarm went off and I put it off and fell asleep again.

My washing's steamed up the apartment this morning.

Oh, Zurich party tonight.

Another late night, just driven back from Zurich – had a cheese and spud party (typical swiss food, mm, my stomach feels like there's a canon ball floating around in it). It was good cheese, ok, just as well I went to my new gym this lunchtime with Heinz from work.

Translations: "Sie machen ein gutes training" = you're doing ok!

Didn't manage to post M's letter today but will do so tomorrow.

SBP called at about 4pm.

Wants to meet up tomorrow, so I'll go to Bern.

Petrol is expensive here. Put CHF25 in – barely quarter full. Also, they don't take visa, just cash (no wonder these Swiss roll in it).

Another day, another dollar. I went to the Post Office to post M's letter (at 8am, it's great, everything opens at about 7.30am, except the gym, typical!). I also went to the bank at 8.10am, and then to the office. Went to the gym at lunchtime – even found my way without getting lost, worked pretty hard all day until about 8pm, when SBP called me on the mobile – before it cut out – ran out of Swiss francs on my pay as you talk).

Hans-Peter (the 'boss') thinks I'm working hard (I am) so that's good. We had new phones fitted today too, it's all starting to come together – quite exciting really, like setting up your own office and I feel totally in charge of how I want to handle my clients. Boss has complete trust in me too, it feels good, unlike how it felt in London so often – always feeling like someone was about to stab you in the back – except Steve – yeh, real turn up for the books. I never knew what to make of him (or what he made of me) until this job offer. He's been a real rock, really solid and offered me some fantastic advice. I like him, he's ok. (I think Andy, Trim, may have been right that the real "fly in my ointment" in London was Paddy). I don't know. I liked him enough socially but at work, my God, I never felt good enough for him (especially after he took me off the Chameleon consumer business, that was not fair, he just wanted all the glory).

Perhaps that was my fault, I tried too hard for him. I wanted to be more than a "Yes man" and he knew it perhaps. Perhaps that's why he decided to set me free. Or, perhaps it was because everything seemed to roll downhill after M and I broke up, it is hard to describe just how devastated I was and, (I suppose), still am.

Anyway, so work's going well so far – the clients have been away for a 2 day external meeting. At last, chance to breathe...

I finally fixed the washing machine I think too, so the apartment's coming together. I asked boss Hans-Peter about my relocation allowance and it's being sorted – just cannot wait too much longer until I get paid! (It is more expensive here – Swiss Edam's about equivalent of £2.50 compared to about £1 in the UK, bread about £1.50 – for any loaf as opposed to Carluccio's yummy special ciabatta at about 80p, I miss that so much). Cottage cheese (the absolutely disgusting one) is about £2.50 – extortionate – for rubbish! Come on, Tesco and Sainsbury, get your act together and take over the Migros empire. (Still, I cannot quite see Tesco running a gym or a restaurant network of this quality).

Friday night, still no news from JB – oh well, I meant to send his packet out today but Bea had a half day and I had to go to a meeting at 4pm at Chameleon – I knew it wouldn't be quick, so I missed the post office – damm, will have to go on Monday.

Urgh, my client, my God, they work like dogs. I mean, it's Friday night for goodness sake, and I left their office at 6.55pm. Well, I'm sorry, but I want to live a life. Tough! They can work until midnight if they want but I'm not with them on that one.

I went to the gym after work – so eventually arrived home at 10pm. Again a late dinner – should have had an early night too as I'm meeting SBP at 9.20am at Interlaken Ost tomorrow morning. Eek, will he be fanciable? Will he still like me? Will we recognise each other? Eek. He telephoned today again – I can't believe I've spoken to him every day this week. Funny thing is, I quite like it – the attention. (He asked if I ever wanted to stay in Bern that I could stay at his..."I have a nice flat" and "with 2 beds" – so that's ok...? Why doesn't he want me to sleep with him, is he gay?! No, no no no Zoe, perhaps just a normal bloke, taking it steady and making sure I'm not put off by a guy like JB who just wanted to get a girl's kit off, have his wicked way (as my mother would say) and then disappear into thin air, I mean, who did he think he was? James Bloody Bond? A mystery. Pratt, yes, Zoe, that's how you should think of him. Just remember the sex, it was shit (especially compared to M). (M M M– God, yes, I miss M). And, remember when JB slapped me on the bottom and called me "Bitch", bizarre, freaky, not romantic, in fact, terrifying. I think he was more into masochistic and kinky rape than making love and being with someone. Well, his loss, he'll never have a fulfilling life and I hope I never succumb to anyone like that again. I hope he gets off with that girl who was at Robin's party – God, she was awful and all over him like a rash so overtly so showy, so yucky with absolutely no dress sense whatsoever. No I'm not bitter, just honest to be frank.

Oh M M, M,. We got on so damm well, and everything was

going just so fab – let's do it again (had a dream last night and I hope it comes true – he was holding me so closely and I could feel the warmth and the scent of his body against mine, I felt so happy when I woke up, ever had one of those dreams?)

Arrived home and had 2 messages on my mobile (Oh goody) but no, it was mum "I miss you" (Ok,OK,OK, so that was nice) and one was boss Hans-Peter (still thinking of work – Hans-Peter, go home man, it's Friday night for goodness sake – forget it until Monday – no wonder he's been divorced before – I couldn't put up with it, no life with your husband. Thank goodness Denise his new wife work's so hard too. She's actually ok, and Daniela, their daughter is so sweet. I just think Denise and Hans-Peter's relationship is probably just how Andy and I were together. It's no life. Guys, watch out, wait until Denise's meets someone like M to absolutely blow her socks off. Perhaps she's not into that now – too settled and after all, Daniela's lovely).

I wonder if M received my package yet? I guess I only just sent it though, when was it, Wednesday or Thursday? No, he probably will get it on Monday or Tuesday next week. Can't wait.

Oh well, guten nacht and hello to SBP from Bern in Interlaken (can't believe I'm doing this!)

Ok, adventure number, whatever...

Dreams…

I couldn't sleep last night but must have slept a little. I can remember having some dream about boss Hans-Peter, me, and JB.. all haunting me.

So this morning, bright and breezy and nearly missed the 05.59 and zero seconds bus to Kroneneplatz to pick up the tram to the station. But had some cereal at least this week, so won't be feeling too weak and feeble when I hit the slopes. I'm also a little excited at meeting SBP. I guess it's that "unknown factor".

Result. I managed to suss the smoke free part of the train this morning (discovered that any carriage is in fact divided into 2 halves, a smoking and a non. Smoking section). However have now settled into a large 1-seat division. A lady walks in with a huge Irish wolfhound (they do make them big over here). Can't imagine that on a BR train! I notice that very few seats are reserved this week – not half term possibly too, but lots of people are now climbing about. It seems they wait until the last minute, then all shuffle on, Swiss trains are so predictable and then perhaps so are the people.

Someone's been at the alcohol last night – I can smell it pouring out of their pores – yuk – some things about train travel are just the same everywhere. (Boss Hans-Peter suggested I drove down – Bern, Thus, Interlaken, but it's just so easy by train). Also, discovered I'd been overcharged last week – this week I've been offered a "rack n' rail" ticket, which not only covers me for skiing for 2 days in the whole Jungfau region but also my train ticket. CHF 75 instead of last week's CHF66 for train and CHF 95 for ski pass – yikes a huge difference, now that's fab value and so important when I'm on a budget (the Gods must be with me for a change I think).

(Urgh, just caught a glimpse of my face in the window, I

look so "bog eyed" as mum would say – should have slept last night, but so excited. So worried, nervous etc etc etc).

Oh well, 07.04 and zero seconds and we're off – another spotless journey. Even the dog's asleep with his nose firmly on the floor of the carriage (lest he be court marshalled by the station master). Oh, bought the "weekly telegraph" from the station (my contact with normality) I've discovered the kiosk where it's 5.50CHF (about £2) instead of the usual 7CHF (£3.25). I also had to buy the extortionate water – where was my planning yesterday?!

Having changed at Spiez. I am now feeling nervous. More nervous than when I'm on my own. Bizarre! I had a bit of a fright – I wanted to buy Tim a sticker postcard, just made it in time as the next train pulled into Spiez, so dived out of kiosk and made it with just seconds to spare. Yikes, but I have the card. Yippee! CHF 9.50 spent (water big bottle).

OK SBP, so here I come...

Yikes, met SBP at station – train had arrived so climbed on board and saved 2 seats. SBP arrived about 5 mins before the train was due to depart, adorned in a one-piece (urgh, my heart sank), complete with ski boots already on and skis. Ok, so no stop over with me in Wengen, good, that gets over any embarrassing moments. Fine by me.

We had a great day. Dropped my things off at the hotel (which is a bit like something out of "Fawlty towers") – even from the guy that collected us from the station, who we nicknamed "José" because he was Spanish, very glum looking and didn't speak a word of English). A weird set up. Room's not very nice (especially compared to Anne Marie's last week at the Jungfrau – that was so special). This seems cheap and not particularly friendly but hey ho, it's a room for one night in more expensive Wengen, obviously more tourists here, so hotels are more expensive, ski hire is more expensive, but I did save on my life pass – Rail n' ski or whatever, which is fab although am a bit worried whether

41

it is a pass for tomorrow too. I don't think so although I asked for it. I will have to check tomorrow at Wengen station. Anyway, SBP and I skiied all day up the Kleine Scheidegg – the runs are good here, big and wide, compared to Murren and there are plenty of them too. We stopped for a drink about 1.30pm and didn't leave until 3.15pm. I was desperate to get back on the slopes but I don't think SBP was. It was snowing hard (but I am the "crazy English woman" as he's started to call me, who's determined to ski if that's what I'm here for).

Cringe…

SBP kissed me on a chair lift – well, 1st in a gondola, which was highly embarrassing because 2 people were sat opposite. He seems to really "care". It's a nice feeling and it's nice to feel like you're in someone's big strong arms again. He's a lot taller than me too, much more my kind of man (just like M was). Still haven't sussed his age though – damm, missed my chance, apparently he has a brother and sister 14 years older than him, queue me to ask his age "how old are they then" quite innocently, but I didn't – doh, plonker! His mother and father are retired (but obviously still shagged late into life) (ooh, that was embarrassing, his father waved us off at Interlaken Ost station too – he's a real sweetie actually, SBP calls him "The Chief" with a grimace in his voice). Anyway, getting back to the age thing, that makes him...I don't know. He knows how to treat a girl though (I think) and how to kiss (ok, a bit slimy) and he paid for the chocolate, that makes him...well brought up. I have to ask him tomorrow.

We skiied a little more after lunch and then arrived back at the hotel at 5.45pm, it was raining (please stop tomorrow). He asked if he could come to borrow the hairdryer (nice line, hey boys, original, give him that) so we adjourned to my room..mm, well, nothing actually happened, although it could have done (but God reward me for that at least) I resisted all temptation and the farthest we went was a fumble and a lie down. We each had a shower and then popped down the road for a pizza. I was so hungry and thirsty. I chose a fungi pizza and SBP had a salad (which we shared) and a lasagne (more like "cheese zuppe" he kept saying, such a shame as he said he didn't like cheese fondue either – oh no). After his ongoing complaints (after which I was becoming rather bored) we both had vanilla ice cream – he kept saying "ein boule, ein boule" which again was rather irritating – I was still famished. It was not that good a restaurant (also ran by SBP quote unquote "very lazy" Spaniards – again – as he kept saying - suddenly, I discovered that we had very little in common actually and was becoming very rapidly bored with all conversation, but in true girlie style, I persevered). Still, we had to eat.

SBP left his skis at the lock up in the station and caught the last train back to Lauterbrunnen (looked rather funny still in his ski boots at midnight!)

Anyway, we're meeting at 10.30am tomorrow at the station again. (I would have liked to go earlier, but don't think he wants to, don't think he likes skiing that much).

Woke up this morning, the sun is breaking through and I'm skiing on the alpes, in the far distance, probably Klosters etc, is Prince Charles and his mates, so here's for the Queen. It really looks spectacular out there. I really hope the sun moves and breaks through the 1 or 2 clouds that are roaming around the mountains here.

(Yesterday was good to ski but the conditions were terrible – it was so foggy. I was so glad I was with SBP who knew the slopes like the back of his hand and would probably be able to ski these slopes blindfold). Come on sun, it would be fantastic – I want to feel that sunshine on my face! No rain, no snow, no fog, no cloud. I want to see Jungfraujoch in all his glory (yesterday SBP pointed out where it would be but that was all it was, just a yellow/grey mirky fog. Amazing how the weather changes).

I can't believe I didn't drink anything last night –

Saturday night and not getting a wee bit tipsy. It's good, I don't mind, in fact since I've been here I've drunk very little – Andy would never have survived. It was his birthday yesterday, St Patrick's day. I sent him a card, geburtstag! = Happy Birthday!

And, it's JB's birthday party next Saturday. Well, JB, if you don't call me, I think I'd like to go skiing instead, so stuff you!

I wonder often if SBP gets frustrated at not being able to speak Swiss Deutsch with me. It would be so much easier I guess if I knew how to. Also, I'm sure I would get to know the real him – at the moment we're still making small talk...weather...parents...sisters...brothers...places we've visited...holidays...birthdays... nephews... nieces... blah blah. It's getting a bit boring though to be honest in monosyllabic answers. We've not even started on boyfriends/girlfriends (save for him asking me last week:"why do you not have a boyfriend, you are so nice" and "so you're not married"..!!!??!!!) I must ask him about his (I tried to pry it out of him yesterday at lunch by asking him who he went to Cuba with last November but he apparently went alone – boring?! (Urgh, translation necessary?) He must have had girlfriends before, he certainly knows where to fumble (but there again I guess all men do), but you would have thought he'd have seen a pair of boobs before (wish mine were bigger) and yet he kept gasping like a child with a new tommy the tank engine.

The sky is starting to get blue – hoorah!

* OK; last night, I didn't tell you everything...1st, we started with a kiss that developed to a ...snog. Then we snogged more. And then more. (He obviously likes snogging, or trying to, it was wet and slippery and not actually very nice).

He was still in his ski jacket, and pants – I refuse to admit to snogging ANYONE in a one piece. The window was open. I could feel my temperature rising and falling (his was obviously close to boiling point). He put his hands on my bottom (obviously a big step forward. There they were,

44

planted. Strange move) but then he began to squeeze. We snogged some more. It was, nice. (OK, not quite as nice as M's but when did M snog me last). We hugged. We carried on snogging. He was still fully attired, except of course for the ski boots. I had only removed my jacket and watch at this point, brazen hussy that I am. We snogged more and then more intertwined with more hugs (urgh, began to cool down a bit and wished he would either get on with it or go!). Gradually what remained of the light outside became dusk and then dark. I asked him to close the window as I could feel the temperature dropping significantly (or was it just my feelings towards him?). We were both quite turned on. Him with my bottom, now proceeding to one hand inside my pants, on my left bottom cheek and I felt a huge lump on his right leg (which unfortunately turned out to be his mobile phone – what a disappointment). We kissed more. He inevitably put his hand up my jumper and just held me (not the usual UK man approach or, rush). Eventually, he undid my bra and then 1 then 2 hands were on my breasts and he just kept lifting up my jumper, starring at them and then carressing them, and then gasping. A bit odd. (I was just being turned on by his mobile phone, almost to the point of reaching orgasm) He removed my jumper and (thankfully) his ski jacket part of his outfit and T-shirt beneath. Oh my god, I thought, this is going way too far, but it was not too fast – after all, it was now 8pm. We hugged and kissed and then he undid his trousers – typical, all men the same – and then mine. I was determined not to make love, least of all here (in this bizarre hotel) but we caressed each others' bodies. He sat me on the bed and I could not believe it, he ducked his head and there he was, straight into me, eating me up, caress, caress, caressing me. (I had not strayed farther than his chest, shoulders – nice and big – and waist). He made me reach orgasm (with a little help from my hands too) and was obviously so wild about it that he continued to try to get me to orgasm again and again (I can usually do this, but after a 5.30am start, I was just too tired). Eventually we both just hugged. I said his legs must hurt as he'd been kneeling all that time so we both lay next to each other on the bed. He took his underpants off (well, I did not want to). We both nearly fell asleep, then I could feel his hardness against me. It felt a turn on and he started to caress me again. I felt I had to caress him too. Bit of a shame.

(There again, I remember when I was making love to M and having groaned with Andy, because he'd liked it, M said I didn't need to do that, which was funny because I didn't really want to do that anyway). I wondered if I should have to put up with something like that and then think, if it was right and I wanted the relationship to last I could have said something about it, like M did with me I guess.

It must have been so difficult in olden days – girls just having married without any experience with other guys and so, no choice what they had, who they had, but compromise. (If I had a choice, guess who I would choose, yes, ok, pretty obvious isn't it).

I know sex is not everything, but to me it's jolly important and having experienced something that just worked so well with M, I don't want to accept anything less.

SBP muttered something (probably in Swiss deutsch) and then said "Excuse me" and I thought "Stuff you, JB".

We cuddled a little more and then had the shower. He still wanted to kiss and caress me (good sign) and then off we went for the pizza.

We returned the hairdryers downstairs (she must have thought it had taken a long time for our hair to dry?!)

Oh well, Swiss experience number one – not that I intend to clock them up and he's quite nice if that's anything to go by.

Well, I just said goodbye to SBP after our 2nd day on the slopes. Both looking a little more healthy now (even he could look more healthy?!)

Day 3

Had a good breakfast – fruit juice, fresh fruit, muesli, bread. Packed and went down to the village for about 9.30am – SBP's train was due in at 10.15am/10.20am. Had a look around. Bought 2 postcards and sent one to mum and one to Paula. Spotted some Easter things I would like to send Tim and Beth. SBP phoned. He was going to arrive in 5-10 minutes so I hung around the station to wait for him. Then his train came in and he came bounding towards me with a grin from ear to ear, gave me a big hug and kiss (so nice) – felt so guilty after writing all these things about him last night. So anyway, perhaps he does still like me after last night, I thought – perhaps because he hasn't quite had his wicked way with me yet? Damm, damm, damm, I still haven't asked him how old he is (but found out that his nephew and niece are 18 and 14 ?! Gulp!) that makes his brother and sister about mid-40's probably/early 50's I would think, so I guess he's around mid-30's – sometimes he seems a lot older. Sometimes I just cannot tell. Does it matter? No, not really I guess. (I know he's older than 29+++ he's been to so many places and he's quite worldy. He did a 4 and half year engineering course, he was then in the military service for about 2 years minimum therefore a minimum of 35 years old! And I think he's got quite a good job now as he seems to have a fair bit of responsibility). My god, all that brain work and I could have just asked him.

We're planning this week. He says he'll phone or text me tomorrow and would like an email from me (does he like bossing people around or something?) then he is coming to Basel on Thursday – hee hee. We're thinking of going to Engelburg next weekend to ski (Heinz at work suggested it to me).

Can't believe boss Hans-Peter has just called me, it's 6.45pm on Sunday night and he's talking about work, says he's really ill so will not be in the office tomorrow. He really should stop worrying so much. I can handle everything!

Sunday night is obviously the night the army boys are

returning from their weekends back home with mum and dad. There are so many of them returning to Bahnhof SBB to catch their trains home. Me off to catch my tram home, and then number 34 bus.

I've just received a text message from SBP to thank me for a great weekend and to sleep well. "Kisses". I sent a reply "xZx".

Chapter 2

Another day, another dollar, or, swiss franc. – boy it's expensive here. Another £5 equiv spent on bread and cheese, one tomato and a piece of fruit for lunch (when do I get paid next?)

Had email replies to my Swiss Cheeslette newsletter – Ben Ledge (over in Brazil at the mo), Andrew D, Anns, Rosy gal, Dan, James McClean. None from JB (ex-JB) and no letter yet from M – sod them.

Work was quite stressful today – trying to organise a meeting of about 10 country managers in London on 6th April (yippee! A chance to get back, catch up, etc etc) I hope Kate and Charlie are around for a drink down Northcote road etc. get my hair cut, highlighted. I did book an extra appointment this weekend but having not heard a jot from Lord JB, I guess I'm not invited – ooh, so sorry not to be part of the "in crowd" – I didn't enjoy his friends much anyway at Robin's party anyway, all seemed very shallow I have to say . Preferred his mates at Ellie's party – I wonder if they're going on Saturday, probably, wonder if they take that Elysia, pretty name, but I think she had her eyes set on JB at Ellie's party, and since JB was talking to her for most of the night, she probably fancies her chances anyway. Why am I so worried, envious, annoyed, jealous etc? Why? Because we never did get to see "Noises off" at the theatre and I would have liked to. Why? Because we had quite a good time when we went out and obviously turned each other on quite a bit. Why? Because I really did fancy him quite a bit, a bit like M (fancied M more though I have to say). Well, I suppose I fancied SBP too a bit when I saw him initially, a bit "blond" looking but very warm friendly smile, he's so innocent sometimes in a strange worldy way. Gosh you can't get anything by him though – his understanding of English is better than some English people I know! He telephoned me tonight as I left Interio – another furniture shop boss Hans-Peter suggested I looked at (would be great for setting up a pad with SBP but bit expensive for cheeslette who doesn't know whether I'll be here in 12 months' time).

Sometimes I like Swiss life, (the skiing), sometimes I hate it (the shops are closed, there's nowhere to go near my apartment, I miss my friends, my telephone, my TV, my video, and god it's so expensive here most of the time – just as well the rent's a bit cheaper).

I had a couple of bills fowarded to me from the UK today – that will be the next nightmare, trying to organise money transfers etc – urgh! Are my nightmares about to begin? Sometimes, I wish I was just back on the farm in Styal, milking cows, for my living and starting all over again.

I'm unsure about embarking upon a new relationship with SBP too, but SBP obviously isn't – he's obviously so keen, I can't quite believe it. It's like trying to restrain a puppy. I kind of like it though, for a change. A bit like B (but far more life to him) and sounds a little like Michele on the telephone (help, bizarre). I wonder how Michele is doing now too?

Dear God, make me stunning and beautiful and make M and JB wonder why they ever gave me up. Make them miss me so so so so much more than I miss them. I hope they're thinking of me as much as SBP obviously is.

(I sent JB's present today – cost about £10 to send. Hope it generates a response. Otherwise he's a massive loser with a capital "L" and he knows he's lost a really great girl – because I am, aren't I?!) Am I? I hope I am? (I mean I have a good job, a company that's paid for me to come over here, an apartment in London, a car, am sporty, love to ski, cycle, rollerblade, gym, walk, sing, dance, music, cinema, look ok I think, have good legs (or so M mentioned once), I smile a lot, am generally happy, am interested in people, always have something to say (ok, possibly too much sometimes), have a bit of fashion sense, love my men, like to cook and entertain, am a go-getter, fall in love, love beautiful things and kind people, look for the best in everyone and everything. However, even Andy doesn't hassle me anymore – why? Am I not good enough anymore?

I worked hard all day today and it's only Tuesday. Managed to learn a few more tools on my German computer. My face looked brown this morning but is peeling tonight.

Had an email from SBP – he's keen to go to Engelberg next weekend and it looks good (if I can afford it) having checked the website. (all my UK bills are starting to be forwarded to me now, yes, you can run but you cannot hide and somehow they just come back to haunt you). Boss Hans-Peter said Zurich will give me a loan at work but I said I have commitments back in the UK, so I need to know how much I'll get pcm before I will commit to (another) loan. Especially as they didn't tell me the annual salary is divided into 13 months, not 12, so that you have 2 salaries in December – great, no furniture then until December. They say that I have no further relocation expense left either despite having paid nearly £1,000 over what they gave me. Great! Work in Switzerland, feel like my house is about to be reposessed in London, so many bills to pay and I just want to ski at weekends! Urgh, feel like the world is closing in around me again and I thought I'd escaped all that and left it behind in London. How naive of me. Only one way to go...up! Get rid of my loans (only 12 months to go and I'll be 2 loans better off already, then only 1 more year to go to pay off my car, then I'll be laughing and can do what I want, or even save to get married etc with who I want – I wish).

No news from JB – it's his birthday tomorrow. He wouldn't call me today, it's too obvious. Perhaps I should call him tomorrow?

Had a message from Charlie tonight on my combox (= swiss mailbox).

Good point...where is my mobile? Oh, forgot to unpack my bag tonight, it's in there. Oh there's a message on it – great – my message has been delivered to Lynn. Hope she's ok (and keeping an eye on M for me at ceroc dancing!).

Wednesday morning, JB's birthday.

I wish it would stop raining. Even London's not this wet. We've had 1 really beautiful day and even that ended in rain! I can't tell anyone at home, they'll all be thinking that it's beautiful and sunny out here, clean, crisp and bright. Well, I suppose the first week was fairly beautiful but it did more or less result in rain by the end of the day.

We went out for lunch yesterday from work – hoorbloodyray! Heinz, Laurence, Sabina and I. We went to a great pizza lunchtime place in Allschwil. For about £10 equivalent per head, you get salad (plus the most fantastic salad dressing) pizza of choice (I had a La Maison, with Thunfisch) and a dessert all in! Good value. Eventually I'm getting the impression that it could be cheaper to eat out. We had a good time, discovered all our horoscopes. Sabina's a Capricorn (like Paula, yes, temperament is similar, but her heart's in the right place), Laurence's a Leo (yes, I guessed it, slightly loves himself), Heinz is a taurus (never would have guessed, mind you, I don't know any taureans – he seems too understanding for a taurus, we had a long chat tonight about life, love and whatever – says he has a scorpian rising sign, so does that explain it?!). They are all intrigued by SBP from Interlaken who works in Bern and feel he must have a lot of "fire" for me, if he wants to visit Basel and then also go skiing at the weekend too – if only they knew that he just won't stop kissing me – and that's a bit embarrassing sometimes, I mean he wants to do it everywhere, on the slopes, on the chair lift, in the gondolas etc etc. Thank goodness we've not been on a T-bar together, that's all I can say. If he tried to kiss me on that I think I'd just thump him – if I had a free hand that is – it takes me all my time to hang onto those things as it is. No, he's a real sweetie (as Sarah would put it). Oh, I had an email from Sarah yesterday, she's returning to freelancing – I don't blame her – wish I could afford to open the "Pinchos" shop (that B and I saw in Barcelona) and get away from people you just don't want to work for and with. To just be out of this rat race.

(I know I'm doing a good job but god, the politics, half the time is spent wasting time thinking about whether you should copy someone in on an email – your mind goes backwards and forwards about the implications..to him..to her...to urgh...You click on the name. Delete it, put it in again. Delete it. Then decide to save it as a draft for another day anyway! It's just as bad inter-agency as it is inter a company such as Chameleon. Talking of which, I should get in a bit earlier today as I've 2 such emails to discuss with Hans-Peter..laters...

Tonight is the first night I've been home in daylight – hoorah! I had to get home to see the "Chimmèe" who was to fix my fireplace – although he's just been and all he did was say "also" "Das gut" and something which I think meant he'll have to come back. Boy, it's difficult not speaking Swiss, I can only imagine what it must have been like for stone age man trying to communicate with each other.

Chapter 3

What a bizarre day I had today. Into work, ok, lots of praises from Hans-Peter (who's back from having his bad cold – Denise said he had a full 3 days growth of beard and looked like a grey version of Don Johnson. I suggested Sean Connery, being grey, but we both laughed, poor Hans-Peter, not quite! And Hampe (Hans-Peter) he says I've made quite an impact on Zurich – eek! I want to be good but that good? The higher you get, the more scary it becomes. I didn't hear from SBP today – I sent an email to him about the weekend, wonder if he even tried to email me though as I had to leave slightly early. Also, at lunchtime, went to the gym. When I arrived back at the office, parked the car and the damm door would not close. Urgh, typical. (It did that last Wednesday on the way back from Zurich). In the end I had to climb out via the passenger door so I called an MG garage in Munchenstein (sounds like a cross between the hobbit and Frankenstein). I took a trip down there and yes, typical, got there and the door works (typical). So, back to the office. OK, so it worked until I had to go home and then, OK, I stopped at a shop in Binningen and yep, it didn't work again. Aargh! The door would not open or close again. Had to climb in and out via the passenger door again. It will have to go back to the garage – I'll call them tomorrow – more expense, damm. All I want to do is to clear my cards and start again without any debt. And I would love to go skiing again this weekend, perhaps SBP was put off by my suggestion of the hotel – eek, just looked at the booking again and discovered it's ... kosher,..it's Jewish, Jewish food, I'm not sure what that is. Eek, I've booked it on the internet too.Oh shit, oh shit, why didn't I just wait until tomorrow night, perhaps I should just call him (anyway, I need to know when he will arrive from Bern).

I was going to go to a party tonight with Sabina, but it's her boyfriend's friend's office party so not really appropriate (oh, did I tell you, she's 35, so is Heinz – I thought Heinz was a lot older, well, say 38 and Sabina a lot younger, late 20's early 30's, but wow, she's a year older than me, yipee! Spoke to Kate tonight – had a giggle – I still haven't sussed out SBP's age).

Later this afternoon I called JB to say Happy Birthday. He asked me how I was doing and then asked if he could call me back as he had someone on the other line, so I said it wasn't a problem, gave him my number and then, 20 mins later had to leave the office anyway. Don't know if he called, it's torture not having voicemail, just a message set up by Bea or Laurence – hope Laurence answered the telephone – yeah, with his lovely voice and good English, make JB know that I'm working with really cool people here. Should I send a text? Why not. It's only once a year and it's an opportunity or a reason to call as opposed to just calling (wonder what he's thinking now then?). Wonder if he received my card etc? OK, so I just sent the following text message:

Hi. Left office shortly after I called – don't know if you called me back. Have a good birthday. Hope you got my card?!Z

And it's arrived with him, as I've just had the notification. Ha! At least I know it's arrived.

Oh yes, heard from Rod at Lundiss Pharmaceuticals today, I sent him a copy of my swiss cheeslette news – he replied with "Excellent. Keep us informed" and something along the lines of whether I missed the trains, weather, dog muck, Westlife!! (I replied that I had to look "Dog muck" up in the swiss dicto!) Made me laugh – can't wait to go home in a couple of weeks – it would be a laugh if SBP could come back too but hey, let's see, take it one step at a time!

There's a song on Rita's radio stereo playing. I think it will remind me of my time here, sounds pretty continental and reminds me of SBP (well, of him singing it to me, urgh, cringe, not sure I feel the same way about him though)...

"why I love you so, Baby I'll never let you go, tell me what's going on" "Oh baby just come to me.. the little things..blah blah.. I can see your face..." blah

Just spoken to SBP. He says he can't wait to see me tomorrow (eek!) (oh well, fuck you, JB no reply).

New words I've learned today: der Frau – woman's ..
Das gut – I assume, that's good
Bitte schon – that's ok
Foto – Photo, make a photo (for my permit, which will be here in 5 days)
Also, I have to tell you this: Danke und gute fahrt! – that's actually relates to roadworks and means thank you and have a good journey
Fur abwaehlen – to slow down (gym)
Sie machen ein gute training – you're still breathing
Halbweiss brot – half white?
Eingang – entry/ ausgang – exit
Einfahrt – entry also

Chapter 4

Sorry diary, missed you last night. Back v late. Went out with SBP. It was OK, we had quite a good laugh although I wish he'd stopped kissing me anywhere and everywhere – I mean, in the wine bar, Caveau, in the street outside a huge window to a Brötli bar and in the pizza restaurant we went to. I think he forgets everything else, what he's doing, and just concentrates on kissing me. No, it's actually v nice but I do wish he'd close his eyes – what is it with men who keep their eyes open – yuk, it's scary!

We've planned our weekend – staying at a little hotel he found in Engelburg, he had print outs of just about every hotel in Engelberg, so sweet, and all the train options we could take. Very impressive. So well organised (almost too much for a guy). Ahhh, he bought me a little chocolate with chick on it – v sweet!

Oh yes, discovered his age – remarkable – he's 34 too. 35 in June (9th June '66). Yes, same year (just as well it wasn't 6th June 66 then I'd be worried). Anyway, we had a good night and he caught one of the last trains back to Bern (thank goodness) at 23.30. I managed to catch one of the last trams back to Hirtenbuendtenweg – v turned on, from our last 15 min kiss on the station platform (I know what's going to happen this weekend, if we want it to). Eek, problem is, I don't know how long I can just go on playing around like this. Oh yes, having switched off my mobile last night, then switched it on at lunchtime today and received a message from Lynn, hoping I was OK and.... a message from JB "Hi, I did try to call. Hope all's well. J" mmm, so I should mail him today (Friday) to say I can't make his party – so that is his licence to "thrill" Mr Bond (as we used to joke). I hope he thinks of me. I'll see if he'd like to meet up when I'm back on the 4th. Hope he says yes in some ways (oh, no, when SBP's planning to go rollerblading together in the summer and to New York – eek, SBP, my money's running out, which is another thing, I hope I can afford this weekend).

Chapter 5

Friday, back from the office...
YESSSSSSSSSSSSSSSSSSSSSS!!!!
M wrote!!!!!
☺ ☺ ☺
Suddenly I'm so happy, so full of life and energy, refreshed, girl who can do anything, love you, love the world, love JB, love SBP, love boss Hans-Peter, love the old bag at Migros supermarket, love you everyone. Especially love you M!

Wow, cut that a bit fine, woke at 6.15am, this morning, finished writing M a letter – was so excited he had written, had to write back immediately!! Am now sat on a train for Luzerne. The ski season must definitely be on its way out as there are no skiers around Basel Bahnhof SBB today. Hope SBP caught his train – perhaps I'll send him an sms just in case, to meet him at 9.25am in Hergiswill – gosh, must get the time correct – what I've noticed here, the buses are so bang on time that everyone stays in their houses until they're due and then out they pop to the bus stop! Amazing! It's like clockwork orange.

Yesterday, had a good but long day at work. Boss Hans-Peter went home with a migraine for part of the day so it enabled me to just get on with work, with going to the gym, at lunchtime, with writing my swiss cheeslette newsletter for week 3. (Oh, I've just sent them to the Telegraph to see if they want to publish them in the weekly ex-pats section) Oh yes, had a reply to my swisslette news week 2 from Robin – my god, JB's mate – I sent him a reply to say it was great to hear from him, blah blah, about not attending JB's party tomorrow night, but do wish I could go, if only to see his face drop! (I sent him that email to say sorry I couldn't make it but of course, no reply. Grow up boys) (No, perhaps he's taken the day off to prepare).

Bought some water today from migros – lot cheaper than

at kiosk.

Ooh, last night, opened a bottle of bubbly in the office, only Laurent, Heinz and I left in the office, so we opened a bottle – they told me to take it home (quite glad really as I've not had any alcohol in the appartment for nearly 3 weeks – not found an offie that open later than 5.30pm, mind you, I've not really missed it, too much to do. Migros doesn't sell alcohol, it claims, in order to keep its "prices down" – I'd like to see it's "prices up" that's all I can say.

Oh well, off and about. Hope my money doesn't run out though – may have to ask SBP if I can pay for the next hotel if he pays for hotel Chrystal this time. It feels good not to have an overdraft though – in one country anyway! Just hope that my rent gets paid soon from Pascal, can't believe the jerks at KHF, the estate agents, had not set up my account and she's been in there for over a month – typical estate agents. Wow, am passing some beautiful chateaux on this route. Now, I'll send SBP an SMS (Sissach, ok, a pretty village).

Following a pretty run of the mill type of journey, we've turned a corner and wow, there are the mountains, which never fail to impress – it's then that I realise why I'm here. Staggering, quite beautiful. Lots of pine trees now too – not covered in snow – it's far too mild down here in the valleys. Awesome, that's what it is, awesome!

(Just had the most amazing toilet experience – it was a hole quite literally straight down to the track – bizarre, quite scary really and a little chilly on one's posterior, and not conducive to a wee).

Well, I'm now on the train at Luzerne having spent the weekend with SBP in Engelberg. Engelberg was ok although not many runs at all – skiing not so good. Saturday was a dreadful day weatherwise, well, it wasn't too bad but really windy and v v steep and the queues for the Titlis gondola took about 1 hour to get up.

I can never tell if SBP's in a bad mood or not. Are men all the same? Only Andy used to make a joke of it, Brad used to moan about it afterwards, JB used to go on and on and on about it ("I mean"). Wonder how his party went last night? Hope it was awful. Hope he didn't end up snogging anyone. Hope he had lots of questions about me, how I was doing etc etc., just to embarrass him and make him think about me . Hope he received my present – wonder what he thought?

The inevitable happened with SBP and I as we arrived at Hotel Chrystal with the Stimmel himmel (Star heaven sauna – mmmm). We both wanted it to happen, yet I didn't want it to happen in many ways. I don't know whether I just did it to spite JB though which is not right, I know, (in the same way as I tried with Michele in Passo Tonale on the ski trip to try to forget M when in fact all I did was break down in tears – and Michele thought it was because I was going home). SBP made me reach orgasm again twice before we went skiing (no wonder I kept falling over). He just would not give up. We could have stayed in the room all day and then never done any skiing. Sat night, I felt dreadful. I asked him to settle the hotel bill until I was paid – well I had to pay for my ski hire etc etc. Would have loved him to have said "listen, you do the next hotel" but he didn't (I gave him 70CHF for the room on the train on the way home – ski hire only cost me CHF45, with the 10% hotel discount).

Sat night, we went walking around Engelberg. And found a (dreadful) restaurant. The ones I would have liked were just too expensive for me – as I knew I had a serious budget to maintain (it's ridiculous, as M's booking a luxury apartment now that I'm not with him, in Croyd, instead of the ymca type place he was going to stay in and second rate bedsit, eating dreadful food etc etc, mind you, I'm skiing and I can only assume, as I never actually made it to Croyd with him anyway. Wish I had, it would have been a laugh).

I wonder sometimes how long the conversations with SBP will last. I think he knows that. We can only kiss for so long (my chin just won't take it anymore. It feels so sore from his stubble growing through., how come I never had that trouble with M).

SBP wants to go to Zermatt for Easter – I'd really like to go too (at least he comes up with new ideas, unlike Brad). I'd love to, but depends if I can afford it. (Now I realise why most swiss have no dress sense but are fantastic skiers). For Easter, I really fancy going off with Kate to Klosters or Zermatt for some girlie fun. (SBP just doesn't seem to realise that whilst kissing and cuddling is nice, sometimes I'd like a breather and time to absorb the spectacular scenary. There is nothing that a sagitarrian hates more than that feeling of being trapped. He tells me he wants to sms me tonight).

At least today, Sunday, the snow was ok and it was beautifully sunny. Thank you god. I had prayed to him! Don't think I could have coped with a grey day.

SBP keeps going on about taking a photo of me just with skiboots on, or my mountain boots – just imagine! Friday night, I showed everyone my photos on CD, can you imagine again if I had a CD done and a piccie of me was on it!! I think I should be more choosy I mean, what do I want from a guy. Do I want kids? What type of father would I like him to be?

I wish SBP would use antiperspirant too – last time I nearly collapsed, overcome by the body odour smell. Now, I suppose I've got used to it (oh that's awful isn't it, I'm not going to drop my standards).

As he put it, I need someone strong (gosh even he, a foreigner, noticed that!) So I wasn't wrong when I wrote to Brad. That was his problem, he had to be strong, stronger than me.

I must finish M's letter tonight – it will take a week to get there I guess.

Oh yes, fact file: this is interesting – scary but true... apparently, every boy in Switzerland has to do military service for 16 weeks after school or university or wherever, then they have to do 3 weeks a year until they are 30, then a week every year until they are 40, then they have to go to a "gun" club. They are then provided with their own guns which is scary, amazing that it's so peaceful around here, can you imagine giving a gun to every London boy and the nutters we have in town! Bizarre. I think the training must be good for them though, though a bit institutional?

Oh yes, another thing that was highly embarrassing, was going down to breakfast this morning, only to find out that the clocks had gone forward 1 hour. The waiter muttered something in Swiss German that I think meant "Where have you been, notification has been everywhere, are you thick or something?" I felt so embarrassed. Here's a Swiss guy that didn't even know that Swiss time had gone forward an hour (that's when I thought, mm, SBP, I don't think you're the one for me). He's so nice and right in so many ways but in other ways, so naive and not worldly, urgh, it's painful., even though he's travelled to New York, Brighton(?!), Bournemouth (hardly NY either), Bermuda, Mauritius, Barbados, Dominican Republic amongst 'the tops' on his list (nice to hear that good old Brighton compares with the likes of the big apple!)

Oh yes, were v v lucky today – as we literally jumped onto a chair lift together, SBP hitting my back, my glasses dropped off my nose. Fortunately, someone was going the other way across the lake and thank goodness SBP is fluent in Swiss German – he asked them to have a look out for them and once we were off at the other end of the chair lift, eventually a guy (boarder, quite tasty) dropped them off for me. Fantastic – thanks to SBP for asking the guys for help. (What a hero on the ski slopes. But wish he would stop snorting like a pig though, saying "oops la" more akin to a telly tubby, rubbing his hands together and wobbling his head like a weeble. (Also, wish he'd use antiperspirant). (Yuk). (Poor guy). (He let me listen to a tape of his guitar playing and his band, he's really quite good at that, with his friend on vocals and another on drums).

We discovered a bar whilst waiting for the train to go (at least he comes up with those sorts of ideas, it's not all dull and boring) even in a place neither of us know. We saw an English couple neither touching, talking, or even smiling to each other on the bus back to the station from the titlis lift, but they did have something between them, just a quiet, knowing confidence.

I'm a bit worried about my life in Switzerland. It is very quiet. SBP reckoned the bar was very Austrian (ie. v full of life, music, beer, etc etc). I just reckoned it was normal. (ie. Lots of people, about our age, relaxing, having fun, a couple of beers and a chat with mates. I haven't seen anywhere like that in any of the other swiss resorts I've been to). Now and again it's ok, but it depends who you're with – or … who you're thinking about...M.

That's another thing, SBP doesn't eat very much (except yogurt, rivella = like lucozade, and apfel krui – some sort of disgustingly deep fried apple balls, although the vanilla sauce = custard, was v nice). He hardly touched his pasta last night (Ok, it was nothing special but faced with nothing else to eat. Not like when M and I ate out, wow, we could put it away but really enjoy it too. Oh M, what are you up to tonight? Probably pissed or shagging etc)

I've just made the most fantastic pasta I've made here to date, probably because I used lots of fresh ingredients – ok so it probably cost me about £6 but hey, it's Sunday. I've *only* spent ...CHF 106 train/ski pass, CHF 45 ski hire, CHF 8 drinks last night, CHF 30 for dinner last night, CHF 10 for lunch yesterday, CHF 5 for drinks tonight, CHF 70 hotel – is it really worth seeing anyone except for the nookie?

Finished my letter to M today, and will post it tomorrow

morning – it's so great that he wrote. Guess what too, 1st phone call of the day (about 9.50am CH time, so 8.50am UK time, the clocks having of course gone forward an hour too) it was JB "Hi it's JB" in his usual deep husky nice voice (bastard) why do I still smile when I hear him. I have to say, he has the nicest voice of all my boyfriends to date.

We had quite a long chat on the 'phone, then boss Hans-Peter yelled over to me – damm, I had to go. I asked him how his party went, He said he had a lodger now. Said he had his house valued in Chester - £115K from when he bought it for £76K. He's done well. I asked him if he'd be around when I would be back over the next week but he said he was going to Chester and then to his mum's. He thanked me for the present, the video, and the chocolate and asked how everything was going. Asked if I went skiing yesterday. I sent him an email tonight before I left the office (about 8pm, again, grrr). Her wished me a good week, so I said, "Yeah, you too" and we said goodbye.

SBP sent me an email tonight but I didn't reply until about 8pm. He called me just as I arrived home, about 9pm, obviously wondered why I hadn't sent him any reply. (Get a life!) No, who am I to say, he's so sweet, almost cute and innocent. I just think exposing him to somewhere like London would spoil him (plus he may want to go to Soho all the time to investigate his fetishes?! I wouldn't mind if I wanted to do it with him but I don't). At least he wears nice boss T-shirts (like the one I bought JB for Xmas) and not the dreadful stripey thing that Michele wore (such a disappointment on such a hunky guy).

Everyone thinks JB is a complete waste of space. Going to Chester, seeing his mum, couldn't be bothered to catch up, blah blah... I know that's not the case, but you can't help thinking of things. What a prat though, the way he handled everything, it was completely the worst thing he could have done – what a complete and utter prick – just like his dick –

hope what goes around, comes around. I've never been treated like that before and I certainly don't want to be again. – I hope he gets someone else who treats him like shit because that's how he deserves to be treated. Hope he ends up with that really grotesque "Rachel" from Robin's party – god she really was grotesque – sorry god - with absolutely zero dress sense. Yes, perhaps he deserves her and they're a perfect match.

Sent SBP a quick text (to put him out of his misery). Asked him how Eric Clapton was – his hero - urgh ☹.

He replied (almost immediately, bit like his performance in the sac). "Hi Zoe. How doing you?(!!) What are you up to tonight. So I replied with "Masterbating" No, only joking, of course I sent a nicey response: "Enjoying my supper, singing along to my radio. Reading and writing to my friends" – ie, not thinking of you. I'm singing sad love songs because I'm not with M, and writing to him at the same time! He replied with "Hope Eric Clapton along" (?!)

Oh dear, had lots of dreams last night about M, about JB etc etc. Oh, sent M an sms today, to ask if he fancied meeting up at Zermatt over Easter with the boys? Have not heard anything yet. (Hope I didn't interupt any important meetings he was in). I am just so excited that he wrote. Oh and sent my reply back to him today.

Added to my expenses last night – I went to the cinema with Rita (client) and her friend Julie (She's from New Zealand and a little harsh looking, very serious). We met at Des Artes in town (near the Barfuserplatz), had some lovely risotto and a glass of wine (Australian Chardonnay – strange they're really into that here but at least it's the good stuff, none of the crap that you usually get at the Fine Line on Northcote Road etc that leaves you with a hangover etc. The risotto was fab – I asked for it in 5 minutes (as we were in a bit of a rush) and yes, it arrived in 5, a lovely asparagus risotto. V nice. Felt v hungry although I'd been to lunch with Hans-Peter at a Greek restaurant near work – Hermes – which was lovely too, had been to the gym after work so 'sehr hungrig'. We then went to the kino (yes, not to the cinema, which means porn movie as I quickly found out when telephoning the local "cinema" to find out what's on) to see "What women want" with Mel Gibson and Helen Hunt (who JB said looked like me - I thought she was pretty but she looked old, pointed face etc – urgh, so do I look that old and pointed too?) It was good but a bit predictable. Rita wants to see Billy Elliot on Sunday but I want to go skiing for the day.

Now, there's a beautiful sunrise in the East (so I have put all my love interest letters in the right part of my flat – the Southern-most bit of my bedroom, have to try as much Feng Shui as possible – I'll do anything to try to get M back!! (wonder if he's received my letter. Hope he's Ok about them – he's not responded to my text – perhaps like Lynn, he can't call abroad etc).

Well, it's Friday night and for the first Friday, I'm actually running around after a late night, trying to get my things ready for skiing in the morning (not that I don't want to go skiing tomorrow, it's great!)

Chapter 6

I missed writing in my diary last night, good excuse, I got home really late (I mean very late – about 2.30am) I went to meet SBP in Bern. I intended to leave work early/on time (for a change) but as always, best made plans blah went to pot! I eventually left at 6.46pm (urgh!) having had to take yet another call from the US – damm annoying this international business – they're always asleep when we're awake and vica versa. Am seriously wondering whether it's worth it – the idea of being a ski chalet type person is becoming more and more tempting!

So what were my thoughts as I drove to Bern (126km there and back – a bit far).

Well, for starters, the radio stations are crap down there. Then I thought of SBP and me. Urgh, what was going to happen? What should I do I thought to myself. Ok, so if he snorts in that stupid fashion, that's it. If I smell B.O., that's it. If he makes that silly laugh, that's it. If I spy his T-shirt tucked into his "jockey" shorts (yes, I noticed the brand) that's it – especially as he tucks it in so much, that it pops out beneath each leg of his underpants (urgh!). Ok, all practicalities aside, I know it won't come out while he's skiing, I mean, even if it did, where would it go, I mean, it can't exactly crawl out of one of the legs or even the waist band of his one-piece Descente little number and whizz off down the piste can it? So why does he bother to tuck it in so tightly even when skiing?! It's just that it reminds me so much of my mother dressing me when I was 5 years old and tucking my vest into my pants. Also, if he just continues to snog me in a very public place, that's it! And if he wobbles his head from side to side, that's it. If he orders a magnum of Rivella Red, or if he ponces around like he can't afford to buy anything except half a pizza with me, that's it!!

Poor guy, I haven't given him a chance really have I? How wrong could I be about someone?

I drove to Bern. Took the wrong turn – well, hey, how was I to know? And telephoned SBP at Rathaus parking lot, so I decided to call him (couldn't help sniggering as he said "Oh Yes, zee Rathaus parking lot. I vill meet you there. I vill be about 10 minutes" – more like 15).

So I parked the car and waited. Admired the view, beautiful city, beautiful buildings. Amazing river, so blue, even at 8pm dusk, (it's so light now that the clocks have gone forward).

I wondered what SBP would turn up in – which ski jacket and which T-shirt?

Oops, a second later, here comes this 6 foot 2 norse (well, ok, swiss) walking down the road in a rather cool looking black leather jacket (just like JB's but looks better on this guy) and oh, oops, it's SBP!!! Mmm, OK, so a little bit impressed. Underneath, a rather nice looking navy blue polo ralph lauren shirt (spotted the little red polo playing motif, now that's branding for you isn't it, well done ralphy). Urgh, this makes me sound like I identify people by labels – you could not be more wrong! Anyway, the shirt was open at the neck, just a shade, just right, to reveal his (little bit hairy) chest.

I appologised for being a little late (again!). he said I looked lovely – in my "work outfit" (Zara, tight brown trousers, top and jacket – the same thing I had worn the first night JB had seen me) and pink pashmina dead trendy (because I now know just how cold it can be in the evenings and my top was sleeveless).

Anyway, he took me through the old town (lots of lovely shops, cobbles, nooks and crannies) past the famous clock tower and to the most fab restaurant!!! ☺

It was called "Kornhaus Keller" and very amazing it was too – wow, I was so excited and I took a photo, sorry, very touristy I know – SBP called me a Japanese tourist – but it is quite beautiful. We sat at a lovely table and the waitress provided us with menus. Then SBP took my hand and said, "Vat vould you like. It's OK. It is my pleasure". (Urgh, I mean. Is it OK? OK? I took this to mean he would be paying, choose what you want). Anyway, fantastic, he looked fab, I felt fab. At last I was being treated like a lady! So, perhaps there was more to this guy than a pair of carvers? He did have a bit of civilisation in him after all (mind you, I couldn't help but keep wondering whether his father had:

a) told him to do something like this and

b) given him the money to do it with – after all, it was a pretty expensive restaurant even by Swiss standards – 24-39CHF for a main course – we both chose one at 29CHF.

Who cares, anyway, good on his dad if he had suggested it (I can't help but feel a bit like an experiment for him though).

We had a salad Caprese to start with – v nice, and then lachs, on a bed of squid ink pasta, with various vegetable ratatouille type of stuff . It was lovely. Salmon grilled perfectly. Classy place.

After the meal, we just snogged and kissed, kissed and snogged (I felt a bit embarrassed then). We kissed until we were then ushered out of the restaurant, quite literally. (no.one else was left there) and when the waitress came over, although I didn't understand a word she said, I got the jist of it ie. It's closing time, good night yoos fellas! We eventually left at about 1am, my eyes were really hurting. People were still in the bar upstairs and the music was good. Quite an atmostphere. SBP walked me back to the car park and saw me inside before leaving. Safe car parks, you have to have a ticket to get into the doors and even the carpark has a massive gate on the Ausfahrt, to ensure no-body can walk in that way, but cars can leave as they open automatically – quite astonishing and brilliant safety as a girl, come on Tony Blair, you should try this in Blighty.

Anyway, back in the car and I set off and guess what, my mobile goes off. A text message...it's from M!!!!!!

(heartbeat heartbeat).

"Can't make Easter. Finances forbid. Also, promised a home visit". ☹ but ok, because if SBP's so keen to go to Zermatt with me, it could have been awkward, mind you, it would have been worth seeing M's face if SBP started to snog me, no, urgh, I wouldn't want to put him through that. I would prefer to snog M so so much.

Anyway, I arrived back in Basel at about 2.20am, so sent SBP a text :-x (our code) then switched off.

Chapter 7

SBP sent me a text message this morning at about 7.40am, "Good morning Princess :x". But I went to the gym – I knew I wouldn't be able to go at lunchtime or after work – meetings at 1.30 and 2pm and knowing Chameleon's record, probably will finish work about 8pm again - how true I actually left at 7.45pm. I was very tired, and it's Friday night ☹.

Sent M a message later this afternoon "No prob. Never mind, there will always be another time. Coming to London next week, work, free flight. Any parties happening? Don't make me feel guilty about home visits!"

Perhaps he may take offence? Don't know. Hope he gets my letter and photos. Hope he likes them. Hope he's ok. Hope he's thinking of me as much as I'm thinking of him. Hope he'd like to catch up with me next week......hope hope hope... and then there's SBP – he's popping over to help me and Pickford's tomorrow – eek, I know I'll feel in a complete mess. It feels kind of scary, it's almost as if OK, the holiday's over, I'm in, I'm here, now all my things are here so I have to stay..I hope it all works out OK...

I heard from Rod today too – he's a good laugh, great client that I used to have in London.

Jeff also sent me an email – urgh! – he's over in Val D'isere next week so wanted to hook up. I told him I'd be in London! Heard from James McClean today too (my old treadmill buddy at the gym). He says nothing's changed in the gym – then I'm glad that I've come away for a bit.

Gave myself a facial and manicure/pedicure tonight. Sent mum's card – feel awful because it's her birthday on Sunday. Paula made me feel so guilty in her emails too. I've just had a letter from mum and a choc bar – yummy, one of my favourites, milky bar – yum, just what I need now I feel a little bit down and lonely – Moby making me feel like crying over JB; David Gray, making me feel like crying over M) blah blah blah.

Chapter 8

Saturday morning. 7am, I can't sleep anymore, partly due to the excitement/worry of having all my things delivered. A) how best to go about telling them they have 5 flights of stairs to climb B) when will they arrive – late morning? That could be anything between 10am and noon? C) What if they don't arrive? And D) Damm, it's such a beautiful day and I'm not skiing!

This morning, I try the new muesli I've bought, it's lovely – v sad now getting excited about a breakfast cereal – this must be desperation.

So I look around my apartment and here's a list of what I've survived on for the last 4 weeks:

1 single camp bed (and 2 pillows and a duvet from boss Hans-Peter) with my sleeping bag
An alarm clock,
One small side light;
4 night lights in 4 small candle holders from Anna;
2 vases – which were both full of the most amazing flowers from sSmooth Al plus those I'd bought form down Northcote road;
Dougal, my teddy bear from the day I 'stepped' into the world;
a kettle;
my mobile recharger;
one plug adaptor;
2 books – Perfect Storm and Dick Francis' Odds against;
one tube of neroli oil for relaxing;
my worry woman – don't ask but Paul from work gave it to me – you apparently tell her all your troubles before you go to bed and lo and behold, the following morning you wake up and they've all gone, disappeared – I'm not so sure, I keep trying, but at least M's sent a letter now! Well, anything's worth a try I figure.

What else…

3 piles of clothes (1 pair of jeans, 1 jumper, 1 jumper for work, 3 suits and a few blouses, 2 sets of ski wear, oh and there's a sort of 4th pile of my aerobics/gym gear, and then there's my small case full of knickers and bras in a haphazard manner)

oh and most importantly, my love letters (Michele, M, Brad, unsolved valentine cards etc, perhaps I'll assign JB's card to that pile too over the next few days).

Ok, so that's my bedroom fixtures and fittings. What's in the bathroom?

Andrex puppy Toilet paper (last roll now) from Sainsburys; shower curtains

towels – hand, medium, and large face cloth;

Aveda shampoo (which has just ran out), conditioner, shower gel, shaver and cream;

cleanser – about to run out, toner, moisturising lotion, eye gel, facial stuff, toothpaste, toothbrush, soap, vase and plant, plastic bag for bin, laundry bag, tissues, cotton buds, perfume, contact lens solution, etc.

What's in my lounge?

2 sleeping bags (as my sofa);

a vase – with what's left of the mimosa from fasnach – it looks a bit sad now;

Another magazine;

Papers;

Photos;

and Rita's getto blaster with 4 of my cds beside it.

And in the kitchen?

2 IKEA pans, sieve, 2 forks, cleaning brush and soap, 3 spoons, 2 teaspoons, 2 knives, a carving knife, small sharp knife, wooden spoon, bin bags, plastic bags, shopping bags

(they charge you for them here so you need to keep remembering them); what's left of a packet of special K; muesli, crunchy nut cornflakes, oats for porridge, 1 bowl, 1 small plate, 1 side plate, 1 large plate, 2 glasses, 2 mugs, camomile t-bags, instant coffee, sunflower seeds (?!) how did they get here? 1 tea towel plus things that are here already: dishwasher – not used yet! Fridge freezer, cooker, washing machine.

That's about it.
I think I can honestly say I've used every single thing that I brought over with me!

Things that are essential, most important/priorities = 1 kettel, plug adaptor, side lamp, tampax, bin bags, plastic bags, shopping bags, cleansers and toners etc, music, breakfast cereal and milk, UK toilet paper, towels, tissues, pans, ski gear, coat, gym kit, telephone /wish I'd had a landline fitted), alarm clock, toothpaste ad brush, shampoo etc, clean knickers, a mirror and some hangers.

Things I could have done with: a proper bed, fairy liquid, my little bin for the bathroom, wardrobe, cupboards etc for my clothes, sofa, TV, all my kitchen utensils oh and cleaning gear – yuk, I desperately need to clean up! And loadz of money so I could have bought everything I needed from IKEA week 1!

There's nothing like moving abroad though to make you realise just how much you spend on food and analyse the cost of every item of grocery you buy – call me a stingy person or what!. Oh well, must pop to the shop to buy some bread etc before Pickford's arrive! (SBP's due at 1pm at the station too, so I onyl have a few hours).

Things I've been gratfeul for: well, 1stly, M's letter!, then, boss Hans-Peter and Denise's camp bed, pillows and duvet. The main light in the kitchen and the bathroom, underfloor heating, daylight, sunshine! Bread, milk, cheese (urgh, ok, I have to admit it), pasta, swiss tap water (clean, pure, tastes good); Rita's stereo, my car (even though it only has 1 functioning door) and SBP I guess – a good friend when I'm feeling quite alone really. Oh and letters (keep them coming) and chocolate! Oh and text messages – just had one from SBP – wish it was from Kate/Charlie or even M etc.

Things I miss now...colour, vibrancy of London, my friends, smiling faces, Cullens grocery store on Battersea rise, my bed. Oh, just had another sms, yes, it's about my charging. Mmm, not sure a good message – spent so much on that call to the states Thursday night though, for work, hope Creatives Inc will reimburse me.

So Saturday, a busy day – Yipee!! Pickford's arrived at about 10.30am. Hoorah!

They were a little shocked to see the stairs – would probably have sent younger men to do the job. 'Paul and Rob', from Newcastle, moved my 23 boxes in (doesn't seem that much now a lot of the bathroom/kitchen/lounge stuff is unpacked. I'm sure they didn't think so at the time though. They were good fun and it was nice to speak to someone in English.

Before Pickfords arrived that morning, I discovered a little more about Binningen. After breakfast, I ventured down to the Migros double "M" supermarket in the village. It was really good, a nice atmostphere and free parking (especially as I had spent over £50 equivalent in CHF). I stocked up and bought fresh flowers. The 1st thing off the Pickfords van was my bike. I was so glad to see it, something familiar at last.

I popped him into the bike cellar. At 12.30, I searched for my bathroom bag (to find the shampoo), found it, showered and ran to the station to collect SBP who was arriving at 1pm to help me. (Help or hindrance...)

Eek I was going to be late for him AGAIN! Picked him up – he'd just left the station and was standing outside the station in the sunshine, he's worse than me in terms of seeking sunshine to soak up. There he was, about to call me I think, mobile in hand (oh, c'mon, I'm only 5 mins late I thought and he's already panicking), dressed in his jeans, navy blue PRL shirt again and black leather jacket (mm, a bit too hot for today I thought).

We arrived back to my flat and I took him upstairs. I think he was impressed. Well, it was nice hindrance. OK. And we had a fairly good day.

We unpacked a little, until he 'attacked' me. I made some lunch and we sat on the balcony with my 2 directors' chairs freshly unpacked, and used a massive cardboard box as a table, covered with a tea towel (also freshly unpacked) to make it look more acceptable.

I prepared fresh bread, butter, cheese, smoked salmon, tomato, cucumber, fruit juice, water. After lunch, heavy petting led to...mm, quite interesting (alas though I do hope nobody could see through my windows – which are everywhere). We left for IKEA at about 4pm (a bit later than anticipated but so what). Having tried almost every bed in the store, I ordered one. Not the most luxurious etc etc but managed to pick up a bed frame, supports and a mattress for 700CHF – about £300. Bit of unpacking (SBP was so good – and sorted my stereo out etc). He's a lot of common sense and then we caught the tram into Basel. We went to Des Artes for some risotto and ravioli and ein kugel (ball) of ice cream (that also irritates me about SBP, the way he orders a measly "eine kugel ice cream", I mean, come on, I'm hungry).

After, we went to Papa Joe's to see if Rita and Julie were there but we could not find them. Had a drink, missed the last tram, had to catch a taxi (urgh, 25CHF for a 5 min journey, absolute rip off). Arrived back home about 1am and in bed at 2am – suffice to say he found my candles and reindeer rug and likes the fireplace ...

Sunday, woke up at 7am, made breakfast, had shower. Beautiful day, sun was shining despite all the boxes around. SBP helped me unpack a bit more and then we left for skiing at about 8.30am.

On Sunday, we drove to Interlaken as we were going to go to Kleine Scheidegg for the day. What a beautiful day it was too. I met his mother (yikes) and she was so sweet, gave us coffee and some cake. We spoke in French – excellent practice for us. Given my knowledge of French, she then went on to ask me if I had a husband (un marie) in angleterre – eek, who does she think I am? (mind you, I guess she is only protecting her "vunderful" son, "a wonderful man" is that how I'd describe him? well, I guess he's a bit of a catch. No ties, never been married, skis well, rollerblades, has been everywhere, is really helpful and quite good looking-ish I guess – except when he pulls those really stupid faces etc etc).

We had an excellent day's skiing, I've really become quite brown as it was so sunny. I had made cheese rolls for lunch and we sat in a bar in the mountains eating them with some gluwein and ... yes you guessed it, rivella. (Ok, so it's not bad, I prefer the blue one though – like the ad campaign).

We went up the Eiger – black rock – and it literally was. Snow had more or less had melted but as SBP said, it was good training for me – especially as we didn't stop all the way down. Trying to catch the last lift up the wixi to ski down to Wengen alp for the train back to Wengen and then to Lauterbrunnen. We made it in the nic of time. Arrived at Wengen and I handed back my skiis. I bought SBP a little huski dog that he's named "Blacky" after the huskies that are kept at the top of Black Rock (the eiger).

We had a gluwein and caught the train back to Lauterbrunnen. We stayed in the car park fumbling in the car for about a further one and half hours like teenagers – just as well we were not discovered, and then we went back to his mum and dad's where they'd made us dinner (v.sweet although there was some meat). I left at about 9.30pm, fully fed and watered (with a little beaujolais too).

Back to Basel by 11.30pm. Quite tired. It was then a full week. So excited as I will be popping back to London on Wednesday for a big meeting on Friday at Heathrow.

Texted M and left message but heard nothing.

Urgh, my throat is v v v sore this morning – hope I'm not going down with anything – no kissing for a week will do me good.

Monday, work, US counterparts are starting to bug me big time, they want all the credit and none of the responsibility.

Oh yes, spoke to mum last night – it was her birthday. April Fool's Day.

Tonight, had to sort out finances. How I hope I can clear it up tomorrow. I want to order that bed from IKEA so desperately.

London

I stayed at Kate's on Wednesday night – it was fab to see her again and we met up with Charlie and went to the Fine Line on Northcote Road. Got very drunk. Back to Kate's, with 3 guys we had met, and danced around her living room floor – quite bizarre. One of them (I don't even remember his name) tried to stay the night with me, but I managed to fend him off. Thursday night, I stayed at Heathrow, then back to Kate's Friday night. We met up with some of her friends. It was an OK night, but interesting to see how different people appear now that I've been away – they seem so into themselves and no-one else, it's unbelievable. Everyone's so stressed. Thinking about appearance, getting pissed, getting married, having babies, buying rings from Tiffany's etc etc – do get a life I thought guys (and girls – they were terrible). I was immediately glad that I'd swapped life (albeit I didn't know how long for) for a more colourful one in Switzerland. (Or is it? I don't know, we'll have to see).

Saturday, I went to Canons, met up with my old squash mate, Ben Ledge and managed to beat him 3:2 (although I must admit, I was a little out of practice). Saturday afternoon, went to hairdresser's – good to see Massimo again. Steve's gone to Oz so Patrick did my highlights (and told me all about the ring he'd had made in Goa). He's gay, safe. He reminded me of Pat at work – v strange, he wouldn't even acknowledge me when I popped in to visit the office on Thursday, I still don't trust him.

Sunday was a little boring, and then caught the plane home at 6.45pm and returned back to buzzing Basel – yeah right!

No M.

Back in Basel

It's been a full-on week at work – again – though managed to do my expenses and write to everyone yesterday.

It's Easter weekend and everyone's happy. Lots of Chocolate bunnies around and the sun's up. I'm pretty tired now.

SBP popped over on Thursday to help me put my shelves up that I bought at IKEA). He stayed and I dropped him at at the Bahnhof SBB at 6am on Friday. He was really very helpful (even though he continually swore in swiss to himself most of the time which I found a little disturbing, I mean, much prefer it when men would say, "Blimey Zoe, for God's sake, what's this etc etc" have a laugh about it and end up throwing pillow cases over one another and then, make love. Somehow, I don't think SBP fits this bill....

I received an SMS at about 9.26pm UK time – don't know if it was from M – part of me wishes it was (I'm hoping it was not from one of the creeps we met on Friday night).

Aah, here we are in Bern, must close, I think this train's about to become absolutely packed. Every seat is reserved. I only managed to take these seats as obviously people didn't make it in Basel. At Spiez, I'll meet up with SBP.

Well, it's Tuesday night, seems like ages since I've written. It was an exciting weekend (to start with). On Friday, and Saturday, the sky was a brilliant blue. The sun shone, it was freezing cold (about minus 20 degreesat the top of the Kleine Matterhorn) but the snow was perfect. It was stunning and perfect...or so I thought....

We arrived at Zermatt at about 10.17am. Great, plenty of time to check into the hotel, organise my skiis, sort out a sandwich for lunch, perhaps a drink, and up for half a day's skiing. Sorted. Top of Kleine Matterhorn and after 2 and half hours sleep, hardly any breakfast, severe rush of adrenaline, as I ran for the bus/tram/train, I came over all weird – I felt really sick and dizzy and my eyes started to roll in my head. I had to stop. SBP was really good. He made sure I was ok, then we skied to the restaurant, sat down and after a couple of hours, a couple of heisse choccies, etc we went down the slope. I wanted to go back up the smaller slope but we'd missed the last chair – damm! I don't think SBP over exerts himself on the skis – think he's far more interested in getting a tan, god he's more vain than a woman sometimes! (and that's just the way he crosses his legs!!) Saturday was another beautiful day – woke up v v hungry (as he insisted on mucking around in the bedroom instead of going out. In total for dinner we had an apple each and some chocolate – great huh. He eats a lot of all the yucky things – chocolate, crisps, 'hals' whatevers – 'gorge claire' = throat cleaners I believe. Urgh, I find French so much easier and if I'm honest, I cannot stand the Swiss German accent that SBP has.

Ooh, last Wednesday night, went to the Basel theatre with Sabine and her boyfriend – don't ask me his name, cannot pronounce it! He's from Basel. We saw the Netherlands ballet company, it was absolutely fantastic. I really enjoyed it. Home on the tram, met a girl who was about to set up her own creche in Basel – she has a daughter named Rima – such a lovely name. She said I was full of courage. I replied that I thought she was.

Saturday night, we trudged around Zermatt for somewhere to eat and settled on a pizza place. Once more, the conversation focussed around my car, a photo pf me in a bikini in mountain boots, Robbie Williams and kissing – urgh, if he kisses me one more time, I swear I'lll scream!!!!!
    Saturday night we had a sauna too, which was good but he shrieked at the cost (oh, c'mon, be real, we're in a hotel,

I knew they'd charge, he's so naive). I wanted so much for him to say "let me take you for a nice pizza" or whatever, but hey ho, I should be grateful that he bought me a hot chocolate afterwards, just wish he'd relax a bit more and have a normal conversation with me. Urgh, is that how M felt I was with him, urgh, god I'm so sorry M you never saw the best of me.

Sunday, was a little cloudy but OK, it had been snowing all night, so looked really beautiful on this Easter day – Frohe ostern. (I sent a message to Marco – he was the mystery text messager, damm, damm and double damm, I thought, or had wished it had been M. Marco left a message on my combox too, to say it was him). I also sent a message to M – hope he's ok and had a good trip home. I hope he writes soon, even if it's to say "bugger off" – then I'd reply and say "no I wont. Come and tell me to my face". I still love him very much and still feel so sad that we're not together.

Jaks sent me an email today (Tuesday). She's split from Peter (at last!). He was never going to leave his wife. Jaks should make her own life, find a free man that she can settle down with. It brought all my feelings for M back up again as I understood what she was going through, when you feel that weird sick sensation deep deep deep down in the pit of your stomach – I still do and I still did when I wrote a reply to her. I felt a tear in my eye as I sent it and then told myself to pull myself together, I had a job to do (yawn).

So why do I miss M?

I miss his advice, his opinion, his everything, as well as his touch and his kiss. I miss his eyes and his smile. God, I sound obsessed. I can't believe it's been over a year and I still go completely crazy with joy if he texts me or wrote to me. No, WHEN he writes to me again, think positive, gosh, I mean, it's only been a couple of weeks in all reality, he will write soon, I know it...

Anyway, after that I couldn't concentrate on poor old SB who was still trying to snog me at every opportunity (now chin is now red raw). I spoke to mum and SBP said hello (perhaps I shouldn't have let him – he seemed a bit disrespectful anyway). He received a text message from "oh, an Anne" were his words as we stood atop the Kleine Matterhorn. He shrugged it off and said he didn't know anyone called Anne – now remember this because this is going to turn out to be hilarious!

Sunday evening, we went for a fondue (yumee!) although the conversation centred on how he didn't like to eat late and that's why he always went out for lunch and then had cornflakes and yoghurt in the evening (oh my god, lighten up, I thought, we're on holiday). Anyway, the fondue was fab (despite SBP making strange faces all the way through and playing with his fondue fork more than the bread). We met a few people in the restaurant, Thomas, Heidi, Claudia, and whoever (her German male creep weirdo boyfriend – about 50 and a dirty old man) Thomas and Heidi seem ok, but they drank bucketloads – bought us some snaps, herb schnapps and Prosecco at another bar. They wanted to meet up the following day at lunchtime. I think all they wanted to do was to have an orgy whilst watching us fucking or something – it just felt like one of those seedy storylines from one of those seedy German kinky vids – I remember the one M showed me, it was the last one I saw. I wonder why he brought it around, so soon into our relationship. Thing is, I was and still am turned on, just by thinking about him – don't need a video.

Monday, felt a little rough and by the time we left the hotel – god SBP takes even longer than me to get himself together – we only had half a day to ski and so we missed Thomas et al at fluealp (Thomas had actually left a voicemail message on my mobile but no number – as he had given it to SBP the previous night, of course, SBP would not give it to me to ring him back to thank him but to say no). pity, it would have been good to try somewhere else. But we must go to Cervinia on the Italian side – ab fab, and then back over when the mountain was then covered in mist and you couldn't see your hand in front of you (or your ski!). Anyway, it was time to get back.

We missed the train at 16.52 (SBP insisted on having a drink at about 4pm – which I had to pay for – and then he blamed it on me wanting to go to Italy – when I distinctly remember him saying that it would be boring to do the same slopes again, so why not go to the Italian side).

Things then went downhill, rapidly.

We caught the train at Zermatt after having had a quick shower at the hotel and changing, as we had time. (he was still asking in that pathetic voice if we could have a shower together etc etc – all I could think was: get real, SBP, we can't miss this next train, it's the last train, but the frustration was already there, he mentioned that earlier in the day he was ready at 5am!! For sex I mean – yes, well, what about me, it takes 2 to tango and I was just not ready for it. He can't just expect that I'll be there waiting for him to "do his duty" etc. That's what it felt like, a chore. Oh how dreadful.

We boarded the train to Brig, then at Brig caught the train (him to Spiez, me to Bern for Basel). He was in such a stonking mood – swore and shouted at me for wanting to help him load the bags onto the train – oh for goodness sake, lighten up I thought. I really wished I'd gone alone a) I would not have had to spend so much money b) I'd probably have enjoyed myself a lot more c) I wouldn't have to smell his body odour d) I wouldn't have seen his underpants – and the cheek of it, he actually suggested that I buy him some sexy ones – well, he can buy them himself. Urgh, I can't believe I bought him such a nice Easter egg from Carbonnel & Walker on Bond Street – he hadn't bought me anything and then produced this little chocolate egg thingy from the bakery in Zermatt, I think he felt guilty.

Anyway, we sat on the train at Brig waiting for it to depart and then...a girl walked down the aisle to find a seat.

"Oh"..."hello" said SBP with his irritating little wobble of the head. "Hello" replied the girl all gummy eyed and swinging her (too) long dark brown hair.

Fine, I thought, good, it's nice to see one of his friends. It was also a welcome break – he immediately stopped snogging and caressing me (which I hated because he'd just been so angry with me 5 mins previously). He was obviously embarrassed about something (but not half as much as I was when the ticket inspector came around to check our tickets and his silly idea of trying to get a 3-day ticket for 4-days took some explaining to the inspector as I knew it would, I was so embarrassed). Anyway, he finished bright red.

The girl and SBP started speaking in Swiss German, I had still not been introduced, so I held out my hand and said "Zoe, pleased to meet you". SBP then sheepishly introduced us. "urgh, this is Anne, she lives down my street" he remarked.....

Oh right, I thought, Anne, Anne, why does that name sound so familiar, where have I heard that name before .... Why, yes, on the SMS message he'd received.

Right, you little shit, I thought, I'll make you squirm in your pathetic swiss undies.
"Oh, so is this Anne, who sent you an sms?" I enquired, innocently. Anne gleefully nodded with full enthusiasm. "Perhaps you know who Anne is now" I commented.

"Oh, no no no" he said "at least , urgh, I don't know" and then he muttered something in Swiss German to her (quite handy when he knows that I speak virtually zero

German). She laughed. Body language says it all. It had been her message and there we all were, nodding, smiling, smiling, nodding, and then the train left and I got stuck into my English magazines.

Thank god.

The next few hours were spent making polite conversation with 'Anne' who stayed on the train opposite me, when all I really wanted to do was to read the mags I'd brought along with me, or be back at home, on my own, in a lovely hot bath.

Eventually the train reached my destination.

Anyway, I'd better go now, it's late. Catch up tomorrow.

(Oh, Marco sent me another text message yesterday and today – calls from the UK retrieval, it's costing me a fortune but it's great to know that someone's thinking of me back in the UK). Ooh, Charlie phoned too – she's organising her birthday party on 15th June.

It's a new day, a new dawn…

This morning, I turned on my mobile and received 2 text messages from SBP – I refused to reply. He also sent me an email. Eventually he called me – about 5.45pm – I was in a meeting, so had to call him back about 7.30pm. I was still at work. (I tried to sort out my credit card too, they are such bastards, stinging me on interest until I get under a certain amount – it's not fair, I'm not spending anything on it and yet the amount goes up every month. I wish I could miraculously inherit a couple of thousand pounds just to sort myself out once and for all. Serves me right. All those clothes etc that I bought when I was with Andy, just to look the best, the prettiest, in all those wonderful places that he took me to – all that investment for nothing, and I had to buy it out of my own pocket, while his new 22 year old girlfriend will never have credit card debt I doubt, because she'll always manage to scrounge money and outfits off her boyfriends no doubt – where did I go wrong?! Perhaps M thought he would have to buy me all the outfits under the sun. How wrong could he have been?

I received a text from Marco again tonight – god, why? He says he's over in Basel end of next week so would like to meet up if I was around – how convenient – knowing what I know of Marco, he's probably just after a shag while he sorts out his personal life and his current fiancée.

Anyway, yes, what did I discuss with SBP? Well, not a lot. He thanked me for the chocolate rabbits for "the parents" and said he would catch the train to arrive in Basel at 6.30pm on Friday. I think I need to make it clear to him where I think he stands. He said he liked "hearing from me" and "missing you" in that high pitched squeaky voice – I pictured the swiss y-fronts with the intricate "mountain goat" design on the front of them, and the bobbles from too many washes. Yuk. I was not missing them. I'm sorry. It's just not working for me. (I also pictured M's Calvins, yes,

yes, yes, ok, ok, ok...urgh. damm you M, write soon! x)

(Oh, I booked my air miles free flight to Athens – yipee!! Only work's so busy, I hope I'll still be able to go. Yes I will ☺ I need the break – the clients have been really really shitty today and asked me to take more of a back seat. They say they could tell that I hadn't worked on global business before – like how? Bastards! I could say that they don't appear to have ANY bloody experience working with agencies or, in marketing because they're so haphazard and disorganised, it's unbelievable! Oh well, fuck them. As long as I still get paid! The strange thing is and this sounds terrible, I can't help but wonder whether it was because I didn't let that particular client 'get off' with me.

Then, further to that, I was so busy at work today – I sent millions of documents to the lovely Axel (bastardo), so he'd have nothing more to complain about.

I cleaned my flat tonight – felt so good. Put the mirror up (managed to buy some screws from the hobby centre, (a DIY shop on the corner). Managed to fit in the gym after work – it's good, free parking in the blue lines after 7pm, not so rushed etc etc. but tomorrow will have to go at lunchtime because it's the company night out tomorrow evening. I tidied my boxes and letter writing things away and some UK bits and pieces.

Wish I would hear from M soon x

I feel there may be a letter winging its way to me, I just have to be patient – guess he felt in such a corner before, a bit like I feel with SBP – he sent me an SMS tonight about 11pm – left it long enough (I'll claim I switched my mobile off). I mailed him earlier today.

Tomorrow night's going to be a bit of a rush and then SBP's going to stay so probably won't get the chance to talk to you again until sat night. Ciao!

Sunday. I forgot to mention the bedroom number at the hotel in the Adonis. If you stay there, you have to stay in room 60. We joked about Robbie Williams staying in the room next door but I swear if he had been there he'd have been fighting for our room.

Anyway, it's Sunday night, my ears are ringing, I've just been out with boss Hans-Peter to the Atlantis bar. We went to see "Stan Webber's chicken shack". It was brilliant – v old rockers but it's amazing, although they were so old and grey, talent never fades! Drinks were fairly cheap – I bought a beer and a wine for 9CHF (about £3.50). Wow, compare that with the fine line with zero atmostphere (nul) etc etc.

Monday. I knew it was a mistake. Boss Hans-Peter told me that SBP was good for me (urgh) nice boy, honest (argh!!)

I took SBP to our company dinner on Friday night (couldn't let him down, but we talked on the tram. Actually he raised it. He asked me what Anne Marie (?who? familiar?!) had said to me on the train to Bern to me (paranoia or what?). I replied "oh this and that, just telling me what a nice guy you are, how long she'd known you etc etc". He then said "I'm sorreeee" "She used to send me a message every week on my work number" and so I said I was just surprised at how he had denied all knowledge of knowing who the SMS had been from. Anyway, he seemed to blow it over. He assumed he was staying – urgh, cheek of it. He stayed.

Saturday, we went to Zurich. Everything went through my head today. We really went because he had to off load his amplifier in a shop. Good job I had a car, the replacement was twice the size and heavy. We went into a department store. He was very sweet, bought me some eau dynamisante shower gel (Clarins stuff). It was so embarrassing in the menswear department though... initially we had a major clash of underwear tastes. I went straight for the Calvins or Hugo Boss boxers – yum, sexy. He went straight for the "hom" small clingy things – yuk, yuk and grosse yuk, unsexy, arhggh!

He could not believe the ones I chose, so I refused to buy him any, complete waste of money if he was not going to wear them. He selected a pair of socks (wow, how sexy, not) and at least accepted my (2nd) choice in these (charcoal grey, thickish, were my first choice, pale blue thickish my second). I could not believe it though, when the shop assistant handed him the bag containing the socks, he started to take them out, took off the hanging card thing, took out the receipt etc, the label, the plastic thing that always holds them together, even the washing instruction sticker was peeled off, and he started to shove them into the inside pocket of his nice leather jacket. I was hideously embarrassed. I mean, when you buy something, that's half the pleasure surely, unwrapping it when you get home. I felt as if I was with a shop lifter as he was stuffing them into his jacket, so I grabbed the bag, the labels etc, the socks and stuffed them all back into the bag and then headed out of the shop.

We headed to the Ladies section where I bought a little top. We had a wander around Zurich for some sports shoes for him (boy, it was a good thing I'd gone in a car. I felt a bit used and depended upon, even though he did not say it. I knew I need not have gone, but well, I wanted to see Zurich too).

We went for something to eat – I thought he was suggesting it but yes, we went Dutch again (how I wish he'd just say once "no, don't worry, let's go for a pizza, or, I'll take you for a nice pizza, after all, you took me to your work's dinner last night, paid for the trams to get there, gave Sabina and her boyfriend money for drinks afterwards, put him up in my apartment, went shopping to Migros for all that food – yoghurts, bread, croissants, fresh fruits, milk, tea, cereal, juice etc strawberries and ice cream for tonight and wine (red, because SBP prefers it, even though I don't). I know it shouldn't matter if I like him that much, if it's meant to be, but it does matter (it never mattered with M). I will then drive him to Zurich, then back, then to Bern to drop off his amplifier, before drving us to Interlaken where we will ski, where I will hire some skis, buy a lift pass (because he has his own skis and an annual lift pass because his parents live in the area and it's free, and I will pay for the parking in Lauterbrunnen, I'll buy the hot chocolates and sandwiches for lunch... The list goes on...urgh).

Fuck! What am I doing with him? Then my boss says he's "good for me". All he wants from me is my petrol tank, or that's how it sometimes feels! (I filled up twice this weekend), sorry but I may as well be on my own and not have to try to get turned on by some y-fronts with a picture of Eidelweiss or a mountain goat on them.

Yes, what am I getting out of this relationship? I give a hell of a lot. What do I get in return? Sex, a bout of cystitis, a sore chin, late nights, bags under my eyes, a hole in my wallet and a hot chocolate to share with someone. Great! Think I want something else.

Nov 3rd 2012
@@@@@@@@@@@@@@@@@@@@@@@@@@@@@@@@

So yes, today, went skiing (oh and yes, I bought the bread, cheese and tomatoes to make our lunch that we ate on the slope, which he exclöaimed – urgh, you're not hungry are you? As he stuffed his down him, and the rivella which again I purchased from the wonderful migros).

Urgh, we dropped off his amplifier thing at his flat in Bern. How dreadful. "Well" he said "I would rather go on nice holidays". Well, that's ok, I thought, I would rather have a nice time with my boyfriend, save for all the holidays you like, matey and you can have them on your own with your mountain goats. How I wished M was here, funny, I've completely forgottne about Brad and JB, latter especially.

Tomorrow's monday.

Hope Marco does come over this week, I need a bit of a sense of humour with someone.

SBP keeps going on about meeting up in Basel this week. Well, I'm just going to say "No" I'm busy. I can't afford to go out with him, I can't afford for him to depend upon me, I want to be treated now and again by a bloke and may as well go off sometimes on my own somewhere, meet interesting people, go to the gym etc, than go dutch somewhere I'd rather not be with someone i don't want to be with.

The snow was just superb today on Kleine Sheidegg – the sun came out once, unfortunately, the rest of the time it was a bit misty – snowing more and more at the top of the shiltorn, I can't believe they've shut everywhere – only 2 lifts remain open on the Sheidegg. When it's a white out, it's a bit like you are walking into a room and are waiting for someone to switch the lights on!

We stopped at his family's for dinner again – they're so sweet, his mum cooked lovely broccoli and asperges soup and sourkraut – potatoes and beans, which SBP kept making childish faces at. It was lovely. Had to rush back for the concert though. SBP's so ungrateful, he just expects dinner laid out in front of him, I can just imagine if you were married to him – wonder how quickly the heavy petting would die off. At least with British guys, you know where you stand from the start and then you can make your choice.

Fuck, M was so easy, write to me soon M!!

Wow, it's Monday and such a beautiful morning.

Work's pretty stressful and busy (isn't it always just before you go away? Funny that, isn't it)

Rang Kate tonight. Didn't ring SBP even though I said I'd send him a message – well, sent him one last night and he's not replied, so sod it (am channeling those mountain goat y-fronts).

Was great to speak to Kate, even though it cost me 23CHF (about £12!!) eek! I was served with a horrible letter from Goldfish Visa. Shit. Trying to apply for a visa or mastercard over here as I'll need it if I go to Chicago etc with work. Shit, this is looking so desperate. I can't believe I'm in this financial mess, I have to get out of it, then I can be with anyone I truly want to be with.

Even the bank will then be my best buddy. God, I'm so sorry for all the bad things I've done in the past if they are that bad, anyway, please forgive me, please help me to sort myself out.

Oh yes, that's another thing, boss Hans-Peter invited Laurence and I for lunch today, so we went to the huge Migros in Allschwill that's open until 8pm every night. Yippeee a shop that's open later than 5.30 bloody pm. We had lunch and though not too expensive, the thought did cross my mind that Hans-Peter would be paying since he'd invited us both to talk about business, but no, we had to pay our own. I mean, I think he is tight as "a fly's ass" is the phrase. My god, anyone else I've worked with would have paid for us – except Jules in London – but no, not Hans-Peter – bit like Axel the other week – how antisocial. Bit like last night at the concert – I thought he may have said, no, don't worry, thanks for getting me out etc etc but no "CHF 38 please" God, I feel like i've jumped out of the frying pan and into the fire sometimes when I look at what

I've got into being over here. Help.

Just spoken to SBP on the phone. Urgh. So sickly sweet it's unreal. At least his friend had a deep and husky voice. I've managed to put him off until the weekend.

Had an email from Paula today. She says mum's not well. Eek, I should be home. I felt really sad. I feel a bit helpless. Spoke to her on the telephone earlier today "Oh Zoe, I'm not well love" – sometimes I don't know whether to believe her or not, I know that sounds terrible but it's true, I guess, having known her for so many years, I've heard it lots of times.

Reassessed my finances tonight. I need to get straight asap. My year (at least) in Switzerland, will be a focus for me to do it.

Spoke to Marco and Andy on the phone tonight – wow, this is costing me a fortune, I must get a landline soon, although that will set me back the cost of the telephone and 500CHF to install it and I can't afford that yet, work will not pay for it, despite bringing me out here, I feel a bit duped to be honest.

But it was good to catch up – even though Andy still rubs it in about "them" going to France in June, doing the Carlton, the Eden Rock, the usual etc etc. All the places we used to frequent. At least he's offered me a token day at Ascot races on 19th June, as I'm over that weekend anyway.

So Andy's mailed me, and he's popping over on 24th August for the weekend. August bank holiday weekend, typical, bet everyone wants to pop over then but tough, whoever, whatever, I'll be glad to see them. (I must book my hair appointment tomorrow on 15th June 2001, with Steve or Patrick and Richard). (I feel a bit like Jemima Khan – running back to London to do all the vanity bits and pieces before returning).

I wish M would write again, well, I suppose it's only a month since I last received his letter but it seems so much longer ago – I'm dying to send him some bits and pieces I've been collecting, which I thought he may like –

something on mountain biking, and on email, and how it's not the most important thing in the world). Perhaps I should prepare what I would write if I did write. What about...

Hi M,

How are you? Sorry, it's another letter, you're probably sick of them already. Oh well, it keeps me occupied! How's life, how's work, how's London? Your tooth? Etc etc. If I repeat myself, sorry, I can't remember what I wrote last time – perhaps alzheimer's has set in early – can you get alzheimer's in your 30's? (just!)

Then what would I put?...

Something about my things having eventually arrived from Pickfords. Was great. Greeted by 2 newc'y boys (when I was expecting to practise sign language to 2 Swiss cheeses, so that was a relief) also so glad to hear the good old British sense of humour – urgh, that's what I'm missing, I'm terrified they'll drill it out of me here and I'll get to like this place and there again, I'm scared of hating it and not making many friends etc etc).

Anyway, I lived out of boxes for another few hours before I took to the local IKEA and purchased a few basics plus a bed (ahhhh, luxury...I feel like I have a body again 1st thing in the morning and my legs don't hang over the edge). It's a bit luxurious, I went for a king size, but well, it's an important piece of equipment isn't it?!!- apart from the balcony! ☺ by the way, that was supposed to make you smile, but it's still not quite warm enough to christen the latter! (Not that the swiss would appreciate it, I don't think) – you should see their lingerie departments, and as for the mens' underwear, urgh, pass – well, if y-fronts with little motifs of eidelweiss and mountain goats turn you on, well, this is the place to be, sorry boys! – ooh, I hope you don't possess any. No, I do think you may have more taste than that, but let me know if you'd fancy a souvenir.

Anyway, whatr am I talking about undergarments for when so much else is happening.

I also bought some of those simple shelf untis and a

wardrobe shelf unit with canvas cover (always wanted one) sounds dreadful but looks kind of cool (coz I'm just such a cool chick – yeah right) (but not so cool with my million and 1 items of clothing stuffed into them in some sort of disorganised organisation).

I'd tell him that I've bought a sofa for 199CHF (about £80) but it's great to have something to just veg out on. Also bought some simple table and chairs for the kitchen (actually garden furniture but I think it looks pretty good). It still looks a bit 'Philip Stark' but at least a bit organised and tidy now. Still no TV – another thing I miss – but at least I have my stereo and books and mags (stocked up on my last visit to the uk – sorry you must have been busy – never mind, so many people to see in such a short time – i managed a game of squash with one of my old squash mates and went out Friday and Saturday night, though I was absolutely broken. I worked really hard Thursday and Friday and quite late. Bumped into Jean from Ceroc at Clapham Junction when I arrived. It was really nice to see someone I knew. Then I stayed at my friend, Kate's, until Sunday lunchtime. It was great to catch up with her. We went out Wednesday night too when I'd arrived, drank a bit too much at that awful joint, 'The Fine Line', on Northcote Road – just had to find out that places like that never change, nor do the punters. We were chatting to a few people and we ended up all going for a pizza and then back to Kate's until about 3am. I felt like death on Thursday.

Work's been pretty harsh recently too, must have spoken too soon in my last letter. My client's have been really tough and unreasonable. Fortunately, my boss still likes me (I hope) and thinks the sun shines out of ..somewhere – thank god. Also thank god that I have a 12month contract so even if things went awol, they'd still have to pay me.

It was a pity you could not make Zermatt. Wow, what a fantastic place – I was overwhelmed by the scenary (and the 4,500m) as I wrote in my card – hope you received it. My first experience of altitude sickness (or v late night + little

99

sleep + v early morning + no breakfast + -20degrees + too few layers + brilliant sunshine = I felt v v ill. I just skied v v slowly to the nearest restaurant to sit down. Respect to some climbers I saw climbing the Kleine Matterhorn in the (huge) distance – my god, they must have been climbing sheer 90 degree ice at about 5K meters – I thought of you and Joel and your ice climbing, you have the ideal job for you here in Switzerland – as mountain rescuers.

Went inside a grotto at the top of the mountain and they were serving champagne because it was Easter. It was really lovely and warming. Skied over to cervinia – wow. I really didn't realise where all these places were until now.

I guess for you, if you want to/can/when you've enough money to pop over and ski, it's better to fly to Geneva or Zurich and catch a train from there (BA are doing special flights at the mo, £99 to Geneva, then the trains are about £109 return to eg. Saas Fee, and you can get a 2-day ski pass in with the train ticket – rack n' rail – for a lot less than buying 2 days at the resort – any extra days and you can just get a half day pass, or full day pass for about 40CHF – about £18) Anyway, just a thought if you wanted to meet up in a resort or whatever. Otherwise, fly here to basel, Cross Air or BA and you can stay here and then we could catch the train down to wherever or drive to a resort for a day (probably have to borrow my boss's car, a sensible car, for the day eg. If you and Joel popped over). Lots going on here, lots of jazz now apparently. (Also, in summer in Zermatt, you can ski in morning and mountain bike in the mittag – afternoon – sounds a perfect sort of day).

Went with my boss – for moral support – to a "gig" last Sunday night at a local bar – Atlantis – apparently v. famous (eric Clapton played there – whey hey?! – amongst others). Anyway, we saw some of his old heros – a guy called "Stan Webb and the Chicken Shack" – it was a pretty cool evening actually, the music was pretty fantastic. What a guitar player and singer – interesting to see that even though he was nearly 90, his talent had not aged.

So, when are you coming over?!!

I don't know what else I'd write – I hope he doesn't think I'm too pushy – it's just me. Oh damm it, this Friday, I'll just send something along these lines!

Wanted to write this letter tonight but back too late from work, so by the time I'd had a bath, relaxed, eaten some pasta etc etc, it's now 10.45pm – viertal vor elf, hey are you impressed? (Although I had a telephone call in Deutsch today – from the language school – oops, and had to ask her to stop and speak English).

My period started tonight, I was glad. Wow, that's a sign – the only time I wished I was pregnant was when I was with M, when we had split up. I didn't care if we never saw each other again, I just wanted his baby so much. Why? Gosh, I always thought Mrs T was weird and wimpy when she used to say that when she met Mr T, she just wanted his children. "Urgh, how can you say that, I thought?" (at the time). Now I know what she meant and how she felt. Poor lady. I'm glad I've spoken to Andy again, therefore. Mrs T and I did not exactly hit it off so well. Strange isn't it. I hope he'll write again soon. I hope he's thinking of me just a little tiny bit, just enough to put pen to paper and write a few lines. I don't care if it's on scrap or whatever.

I have to tell SBP it's a no-go.

He sent me this beautiful poem on my email today – probably told by his mum, dad, or mate, Richard to send it. It's probably a translation of one of Richard's songs anyway. Yes, I'm pretty sure SBP would not have written it. I just feel he's being told how to behave, what to say and do and occasionally, just occasionally, I see the real him which is either good and a bit funny, or really threatening (AKA Zermatt-Brig incident, or Lauterbrunnen-Wengen train incident this last Sunday). He always goes on about how expensive Switzerland is too and they say that people who go on about it too much will never be generous in love. I get the feeling that once he married, that would be it. I would become frustrated, as he'd probably just sit at the table waiting, like he does at his parents' home, like his father does, not help out like M – ok, M, you idiot, get your act together and goddamn get over here!

I'd have to relate to the incident of the kino and cinema to M – all about trying to book "billy elliot" and getting something more akin to "Willy elliot"
   And close "here endeth the nth letter – tell me if I'm being a pain – but then again, don't bother, because I'll be a nice pain, I hope!"
   Or perhaps "Given up waiting for your next letter so I thought I'd fill you in with some more stories from around the globe before I forget them. Hope you don't find it too boring..."

What do I say about my text messages when I went home – why didn't he reply? – perhaps I should ask but then, perhaps not, but then again, if I sent a message to a mate, I'd expect a reply at some stage. Then I start thinking..I hope he's ok, that his family's ok etc etc, perhaps he's away etc etc. Still wish he'd called me back but then again, if he'd said "Call me at "Bruce's" because I'm staying here for a couple of days, would I have called? Don't know. If I thought he was pestering me, no. if i liked him very much, possibly, if he was just a mate, yes, probably. But he obviously wasn't around anyway. Would there have been any point? Well yes, actually, it would have been nice to know how he's doing, or, just to hear his voice etc. I don't know. Perhaps I should just leave it as I suggested in the letter before. Tell me diary, what do you think? Tell me not to worry, that he'll write soon.

I had such a weird dream last night. Quite disturbing. Couldn't sleep afterwards. Dreamt boss Hans-Peter, Heinz and Sabina and I were left at work. We had the top floor office in a huge appartment block, a beautiful office (which ours is) and that we saw an aerolplane coming towards a building opposite and we saw it go crashing through it – the after shock meant that our building started crumbling. They were on one side of the office, I was on the other, we started going down. I saw the lift through the open door. It had people in it and was going down but then I thought I would rather die with my friends than stuck in a lift shaft with people I didn't know. We'll hang in on this together, I thought. All I could see was flames, red, yellow, dust, bricks beneath my feet. I woke up.

Hope it doesn't come true. I had a dream I had a massive zit on my forehead the other night and then, 2 days later, got one on my left cheek. Burst it this morning. Damm and Marco's over on Monday too – all he'll see is my spot.

Well, it's Friday night – had an interesting day, my cap fell out (tooth) so had to go to der zahnartz (dentist). Wrote all about it to M tonight – yes, have written him another letter – miss him so much, wish he missed me.

Urgh, SBP called me – he wants to go to the ballet with me tomorrow (that guy will try anything). Tomorrow's Saturday and I'm free!! To be me, do what I want, when I want, yipee!! ☺

I feel so stupid, my face is burning up. It's sunday night and I went skiing on kleine sheidegg again, thought the weather was not goig to be that brilliant but it was brilliant sunshine and as a result, my face is bright red!

Met up with SBP Saturday night – he came to Basel and I met him with his little rucksack, (from Egypt, apparently). I showed him my new handbag which I was very proud of – bought in in H&M on Saturday. Yes, I've found a nice department store. It looks very Italian, at least that's what I think. All he could say was "that's boring, from Basel, boring". How childish. Urgh, I wanted to scream. He asked me why I'd been so "frosty" this week so I just said sorry. I could not start to explain given that we had 20 mins to get to the other side of Basel in a packed tram, to meet with Sabina, from work and her friends. I looked at his shoes – those awful suede narrow things, really pointy, looking like he'd walked through a million puddles. At least his shirt and jacket were nice. As to the trousers – Ii didn't want to check them out too much in case he got the wrong idea and thought I was looking at his crotch – at which opportunity, he would be bound to pull me closely to him and start pecking me like a pigeon on the lips, just when I'd taken so much care over applying my lipliner and lipgloss.

I wore my zara pant and shirt set and joseph white fake leather jacket – probably a bit ambitious, but it had been a really lovely day in Basel. And then typically, once the performance had finished, it began to throw it down.

Met up with Sabina and Guy Claude and 2 of her friends from Germany (well, one who lives there, Astrid with the odd eyes) and the other now lives in Basel and is Sabina's boyfriend's ex-girlfriend – confused? Yes, so am I. The performance was really good – bit OTT contemporary, but it was interesting, and it was International Dance day after all. (I thought of the ceroc competition this time last year, then wondered if M was going to enter this year, no, I doubt it) I wonder how he is..stop it Zoe...wish he was thinking of me – god, why do I think of him ALL the damm time – it's terrible, even driving back from Kleine Scheidegg – even on the mountain when I hear other english voices, I sometimes feel like saying hi to them and showing off in front of them, because they may "know" M and report back to him to say that they saw this cool chick called Zoe and how fab she is – she's tough but beautiful – wish she was my girlfriend etc etc and then maybe he'd think twice about me and get back in touch. Every day I hope for this, why? I know it's so foolish and silly. I've never thought about ANY guy I've been out with as much as I've thought of him – over 12 months past now and I think my feelings for him are even stronger than ever.

I thought of M in when SBP cuddled me next to him on the train on the way down from Wengen to Lauterbrunnen. I felt like Kate Winslet from the movie 'Titanic', when she was "Rose" the old lady remembering her real love, the love she lost, and being with her family – obviously by another guy eventually, but I think I know that feeling (is it? Was it? How do we know? Do we ever know?) I wish so much he felt the same way about me too. I would love to show him Switzerland so much. I miss him so and SBP just cannot replace him.

I just find it amazing that I still struggle to even remember Neal, Jon, Andy (well, that's cool, he's coming over anyway), JB, Brad. And SBP...do I ever think of SBP? He's a kind man but...

Oh, yes, I had a card from Nicki (yoga mate from London), it was fantastic to hear from her and I can't wait to reply.

Marco's due to pop over tomorrow. I sent a message to his mobile, but I don't think it's gone through (I usually receive a "delivered" message).

Miracle of miracles, yesterday I had to fill up the car with petrol (again) on the way to iInterlaken. So guess what, for the first time, SBP offered to pay for it. Well, he said "I would have to get the train also from Zurich" (about damm time, I thought, good, fair's fair. I'm not a charity and nor is my car).

Think I have to compile a list.

Things I do like about SBP (and star rating):

****very caring (eg if I fall over)
** Tidy (although amazingly untidy flat)
** shows me where to ski (could do this alone though)
*teaches me a bit of German (though in an English Swiss German accent and when I get it wrong he laughs at me – I could take my own lessons)
*good at rollerblading, (although can picture him in gay type of shorts going around Interlaken)

Things   I   hate   about   him!
 (and star rating):

** music taste (eg.replacing Craig David with Billy Joel?!!)
***********Y-fronts
********* (* for infinity) body odour
**doesn't drive
***his weird temper (can't figure him out)
*******obsessed with kissing me (in a rather slathery way)
****dress sense
***obsessiveness about packing (eg plastic bags for each item in his overnight bag)
*accent (phrases like: the sister etc)
**doesn't seem to listen (eg no, I do not want sex with you, my mother is ILL)
*doesn't seem to have a clue about living in a civilised world (eg. Petrol/sock incident)
**skis off down the slope leaving me at the top, laughing in some sort of mad man way
*does not like horse riding/mountain biking

(Star Rating: *** equals really bad or good; * equals a little bad or good, but forgiveable)

Chapter 9

Another day, another dollar..

Tonight I feel really lonely, isolated, alone. I called kate, we had a laugh. Later Charlie called me. Everyone else seems to be getting their act together now just as mine seems to be falling apart (my credit card wouldn't even allow me to put £26.80 on it. Now that's desperate). That was for my ticket to Athens so there was a danger they would not clear it. (I'm scared about Chicago, when mentioning it to boss Hans-Peter, he just said "get a credit card", I can't talk to him about it. If we have to travel, we should have a kitty, some money, it's crazy!) I know he wants us to stand alone but sometimes, I just feel he's doing it as a personal vendetta against the Zurich office, not thinking of anyone else at the same time, we just have to put up with the consequences. I was at work until 9pm tonight – good job Marco cancelled. (yes, his meeting was changed but hopefully he'll be over tomorrow. Good, about time I am treated like a lady).

Thursday 1st May. Today was a bank holiday here in Basel. I wonder what everyone else did? I was going to go to the office, so thought I'd go to the gym first (as Marco was going to pop over today...yeah right) and then go to work. I parked the car, paid the meter (even though it's a bank holiday, it's not free here in Schweizland – no wonder there are so many rich people).

It was 7.50am – I thought they'd open at 8am as usual but one of the staff came to the door and muttered something in German followed by "neun uhr" which I recognised as 9am. Damm, they didn't open until 9 o'clock. So I wondered what I could do. I ventured back to the car and then thought I'd go down the road and check out the zoo. Anyway, great, it opened at 8am, so I decided to have a look around. It was superb. I saw gorillas, tamarind monkeys, giraffes, elephants, snow leapards, snowy owls, antelopes, ponies, goats, peacocks, flamingos, a goose that chased me down the path, snapping at the lace on my black trainers – she must have had a nest near to the path. Whatever, it was her territory and she obviously didn't want me on it! I was quite scared for a moment or two. What else, oh yes, an orangutan, penguins, otters, beavers, sea lions, lots of fish and things from the deep, jelly fish (medusa) worms in sand, mice, kangaroos, zebras, limas, even an aberdeen angus from Scotland (why not?)!

The restaurants look so nice, not like the yucky dreadful restaurants in the UK with their disgusting burger and chip type of fodder and discgusting sandwiches, here they serve tagliatelle that looks like tagliatelle, tortini, wine, water, ciabatta bread etc etc. Much more civilised. Eventually I was joined by a few other people, mainly older couples (it's so nice to see Swiss couples holding hands when they're old and still together. Holding hands, talking and laughing. They at least looked like natives, not just holiday makers, what a lovely way to start a day, I thought). I was glad other people turned up, then a few mums with kids, a few dads with kids and the zoo keepers were giving me strange looks – why would anyone go around a zoo at 8am in cycling shorts, but hey, this is switzerland and you can do anything, anywhere (as long as it's legal).

I was wearing my LEO Animal Health T-shirt over my gym outfit quite by chance too. Anyway, don't care, it was a nice way to start the day. I bought a little elephant keyring from the souvenir shop (I wanted to buy lots of little things for Tim and Beth and everyone, but I have to watch my pennies at the mo, Ii'm sure they would appreciate that more. I hope so, I'd buy them the moon if I could). (I hope I can buy my children things one day, I hope I have children and a caring and loving father).

Anyway, went to the gym afterwards, then into work. Boss Hans-Peter was already there. I worked until 7pm, made a couple of phone calls and then went to the Migros in the station to buy bread and essentials. Then to Boss Hans-Peter's to deliver a map that he'd forgottento pick up off the printer, then home to pack for Greece and make some dinner.

Email and text message from SBP, eek, he told me not to forget "SBP and Robbie" as they both love me very much – oh my god, not another one...I know I should be gratful but please God, tell me whether it's right or wrong, when all I think about is...M.

X night night X

Went to the gym first thing this morning – knew it would be a long day. Finished at 9.15pm, but at least I finished my report. I'd done my packing last night, so I didn't need to do that much there either. (I know I've packed too much, just hopeless at deciding what to pack, what not to pack, can never decide what to take with me, it's always the same… ooh, I've got this, and ooh, that reminds me about that – a bit like inviting mates to a wedding – inviting one reminds you of another etc and oh that reminds me that I'll need that bag and those shoes if I take that until in the end it looks like I'm staying for 3 weeks not 6 days!)

I'm looking forward to the break now, to catching up with people from home, to getting away from work and clients for a few days and from SBP (the sweetie! Eek, he 'phoned me twice today – think he's missing me already – why don't I miss him very much? With M, I couldn't wait to see him again. Still wouldn't mind. With Brad, it was OK, yes, if you're around, let's meet up. With Andy, it was always booked in advance, with JB, it was always a challenge, thinking it would be awful when we did meet up but ending up completely falling over each other, more lust (and I don't think I fancied him that much either). I bet he's with someone else now anyway – probably long forgotten me ... wonder if he still thinks of me when Moby plays, when he wears his leather jacket (the button of which I'd fixed), when he wears the Jo Malone aftershave, his black shirt, or his Boss underwear? No, probably not, probably he's thinking 'What boss underwear'. Huh, prick.

Treat guys nicely and they run away.

Perhaps I should be really really nice to SBP?

I replied to my email from Stonemaster69@hotmail.com. Still not sure whether that was Marco's unofficial email or that guy that tried to snog me at Kate's when I was over. (I think it was the latter but isn't that dreadful, I just can't remember, or why don't they sign off it would be more simple).

Anyway, to bed, must get some sleep, tomorrow's going

to be a 24 hour job, arriving at Athens at 4.30am! I may not take you with me, diary – if they find you, it would just be too embarrassing.

Well, this weekend's going to be either a complete disaster or fantastical success, absolutely nightmarish, and with a load of old cronnies. I'll let you know.

Today was one of the 1st warmest days in Basel for May 26 degrees, with a few more to go in May if boss Hans-Peter's weather report is anything to go by. It's so warm for this time of year, it's amazing, quite wonderful.

Chapter 10

Well, Hi. And so that was Greece and the cyclades!

Here I am, it's Wednesday night, I wanted to go to bed early because I feel so exhausted but it's already nearly 11pm. I think I'd better tell you about my Greek adventures tomorrow night...safe to say, Yannis = Peter in Greek (I met about 50 Yannis's – oh and one Theo, who's already mailed me. Eek!)

Cyclidian dreams

Well, it all started on Thursday morning. Typical, planned to leave the office at 10am, (wanted to go in because CEO Frank and CFO Otto were in, so wanted to make my impression). However, typical, Axel the rotweiller, argh, called at 9.59am (when I'd specifically told him I'd be leaving at 10am) and I eventually put the 'phone down at 10.20am. No respect at all.

Popped my head around the meeting room door at 10.30am to say a brief goodbye, was met by a scowl from boss Hans-Peter. I guess I picked a bad moment, but how to make an employee feel absolutely minus zero or what. (I must master "the look").

Anyway, eventually left the office at 11am, missed the Flughafen bus but arrived at the airport at 11.30 and the plane was delayed by 10 minutes. Flew into Heathrow and was hoping to meet up with Marco who I'd emailed and texted earlier to see if he was around. He was, great, at last! (Met funny guy on the plane, returning to New York – Danny, he'd been in a village in France just across the border from Basel for 3 months. We shared some stories, love, hate, where we wanted to be, with whom etc, he said even though skiing and boarding was close by, even that was not enought to keep him here, sometimes, I know what he means.

Anyway, I made my way from T2 to T4, dumped my bags, caught the tube into town. Marco called me – he was in Chelsea (where else I guess?!) so I hopped off at Knightsbridge, caught a bus to Sloane Square and met him at Oriel (wow, that's the 3rd person I've met at that place – sort of good vantage point/meeting place/lonely hearts club I think)

He bought a bottle of white, and lunch for us both – we each had salads, it was very civilised and how nice to be told not to be so silly when I offered to pay for half the lunch -– was actually glad as I only had £80 with me and had spent £22 in Harvcey Nicks on some bubble bath luxuries – ah bliss. We had a great chat, caught up and went for a couple of drinks before I had to leave at about 7pm and so did he. We both went our separate ways and I made my way to Heathrow T4 for my holidays! I almost felt like I'd already started them!

Anyway, at the airport I checked in my bag and the ground staff told me that I had a message and to look out for a 'Mark', in a bar in departures at about 9.30pm, when suddenly I had a tap on my shoulder. Expecting some hunk, I turned around to see a bearded scruffy old bloke. Hey ho, you can't have everything, (certainly not my type). Nice guy but after 5 mins, had summed him up as 39 and still living with his mum (I was actually spot on as I found out later in the holiday).

Anyway, bizarre, small world, this was Mark, who I had to meet for the holiday. We got on ok, he's a libran horoscope – just like M, though thankfully didn't look a bit like him – and we made it to the departure lounge. Scouted the duty free for cheapish champers to take with us, then in the departure lounge, we met his German friend who lived next door to him in Brighton and who was off to New Zealand possibly forever. Bizarre, yet again, small world. I tried out a bit of the German vocab I've been learning day after day in the gym – wo gehen sie? Etc etc.

We had a good flight (even though I was extremely miffed that the ground staff had actually upgraded me to biz class until Mark tapped me on the shoulder, so I forsook my special seat and glass of bubby to sit next to him – grrr, never again).

However the consolation was that we got the emergency exit seat with extra leg and rubbish room.

Mark befriended a stewardess who came from the same village in Hungary as an ex-girlfriend of his (had he no pride?!). The girl was obviously bemused, Mark thought it was fate. (Hearts floating…)

Managed to get in a few zzz's before grounding at Athens at 04.10! Urgh! Then, it was great, like being a student again, being free, being an explorer! We found the bus for Piraeus – the number E36 and took the 04:54 which arrived at Piraeus at 06.30 just enough time for us to find which ferry or hydrofoil left for paros.

We met some interesting people on the bus, an American guy who worked on Eos every year for 6 months; an English girl from Clapham – hoorah! Who lived on Paros for 6 months last year and was returning for another stint. Don't know where she was going but it was south of Clapham that's for sure. Also met an Ozzie girl who was just going to travel around the islands for 6 months. Also met a girl called Claire from Pfizer – from clinical research – her parents had moved to an island, so she just escapes there when work gets too much (bliss).

So, we caught the ferry to Paros at 08:00 and fell asleep on the sofas before it arrived at Paros at about 1pm, just in time for the boat. Met up with Steve (skipper), Phil (philanderer), Keith (mid-fortys, sex starved), Maz (puching 40 and sex starved), Elaine (head screwed on, divorcee), Annie (mixed up, angry, hots for married unobtainable like the Phil's of this world), Jeesica (lovvieeees), aren(depressed, rejected, but could be cool onec she gets her act togetrher again), and Ronnie (married, dirty old man with evil eyes and too much blubber). What a laugh. Saw the boat, a real beauty – 50 foot bavaria yacht named King Minos. After a few checks, this and that, we had to stay in Paros (we were supposed to leave for Mykonos however it turned out to be much better fun) and this is why...

Went to a beautiful restaurant and then to a bar where I met....Theo! and his friend, Andy, who plyed me with red vodka (urgh, never again). Anyway, turns out that old Theo is a pretty good windsurfer (champ of paros – so take that M!) ooh, what a hero. After dancing, dancing and dancing – the locals obviously impressed, the others left. Theo and I had a chat, he took me out of the club, we had a kiss on the beach and he kept telling me how he loved my dancing. He then went on to tell me how he'd been out with an American girl for a while but had not been out with anyone for 2 years. He told me that he liked me. Eeek (gosh these foreign guys are just so passionate, and boy do they move quickly and, never give up!) Eventually, (rough) he gave me a lift back to the marina where we kissed again and then he walked me back to the yacht. Nothing like a bit of flirting. Not a bad kisser either, not as good as M though (arghh, scream, M!!)

OK, so here are the kissing stakes:

At no. 1 spot: M (obviously, doh)

2a. Smooth al (interchamgable really with M but never actually went out with Al, just a quick snog once! And it doesn't count anyway, as I still fancy M like mad, so he just pips Al to the post)

2b. Neil (1st love or, 1st boyfriend, anyway, don't think I was ever in love with him, although did feel that tiny flicker in the pit of my stomach on a couple of occasions), he was a damm good kisser though, and so was Graham, I guess the first ever boy I kissed, who taught me to kiss one night in my bedroom about age 16. My mum went mad because we went up there alone, we didn't progress further than that though, it was more a lesson between two 16 year olds.

3. JB

4. Theo (though not sure, Theo could come before JB I guess)

5. SBP

6. Brad – a bit slobbery, lots of mouth and not a lot of content

7. Michele

8. Andy – useless, do you know, we only kissed once, the 1st night we actually stayed together – that was the first and only kiss I remember, why oh why gal did I put up with that for 6 years.

Anyway, Theo gave me his brochure – ooh, matron, you should see it – a bit revealing, a bit 70's, my mum would kill me if she knew I had it in my appartment. He looks absolutely fantastic on it though, I have to say – says he's been to Brighton, to Hawaii, to California, to Australia, etc etc – all to compete in some windsurfing championships. Wow, what a guy. Blown away.

He was really sweet too, very warm, not the jerky movements of SBP. (Can't believe that when I'd returned to work on Wednesday, he'd sent me an email already. I sent one back, but I still haven't heard from him).

Unfortunately, we left Paros on Saturday morning and went off to Mykonos. It was a pretty rough sail – force 7-8 and pretty cold all the way. We tried to dock at Mykonos but it was very very windy. After several attempts, we managed it after a while and caught cabs into the town centre, for a great meal out and found a great bar, where I met...yannis, the DJ, the Veranda bar. Phil was chatted up by a greek girl which he was obviously flattered about. She was called Infinity (think the name just did it for him and nothing else).

Could not believe Phil and Ronnie – couple of old codgers, they're a real laugh and out-stay all of us – dancing and drinking until 4am!

We were going to Daros the following day (Sunday) but the ferries were cancelled and it was too rough for us to land there so we just had a look around Mykonos town centre. I had a great time looking around with Mark. We did some souvenir shopping (I bought a beautiful hand made wrap, shoes and a bag) and we looked at some art, some exquisite shops (fantastic ideas for furnishings) and we went back to the boat.

Monday, we then set sail for Syros – a busy market town, very Italian influence, had a great dinner, with loads of starters, and then Tuesday went to Kythnos, sailing into a small harbour called Loutra. It was such a beautiful day there – we went to some thermal springs there too, fresh out of the mountain, it was incredible.

So we had a lovely meal in a restaurant – where the waiter lent me his jacket – a nice denim levi jacket. He had the most amazing eyes I've ever seen (even better than M's) and was called, guess what... Yaniis!

On the way back on Tuesday, we stopped at a bay off Kea, not very pretty but with a majestically beautiful sea and I managed to dive off the boat a couple of times with Phil and had a good swim.

Thursday we ordered cabs first thing for Wed morning to go to Athens airport. We had a great D.I.Y. dinner on board, using up all the odds and ends.

Wed took is back to where we'd come from – me to Basel via Heathrow, so felt exhausted.

It was an interesting break – talked a lot to Steve (who's invited me on a quick holiday to Roc, Cornwall, in June, it's the first week after I was planning to be over next so I managed to extend my holiday and go).

I spoke a lot to Phil – about boob jobs, kissing and boyfriends (the importance of eyes, nose, teeth, hair, height, fitness, legs, Switzerland etc). I spoke to Keith who was intent on plying everyone with "Freeserve" all the time – he'd just started his new job and was like a dog with 2 dicks (I think the saying goes, yes, Keith, I think we all got the jist after a few days, thank you).

There was Jessica who was (oh so very) in publicity/media/actors/ thespians/actor agent (and suited the part to a tee); Maz (a divorcee, pretending to be young, carefree etc etc, but I think very lonely and very hurt deep down); Elaine (divorced and setting up a new biz. Quite sweet and very Engligh – reminded me of Audrey Hepburn in African queen and always wore her straw hat); Karen (bit of an attention seeker, older but in control of herself, lost a lot of weight I think), and Annie (massive crush on Phil and I think very jealous of anyone else who had his undivided attention, which was anything practically on 2 legs I think!) No, he's ok really (telephoned me today, just to say it would be good to catch up soon).

Had another mail from Azad Zain – stonemaster. I am sure this is either Marco or that guy at Fine Linebut it's so annoying, I don't know which.

OK, so Kate's just confimred my suspicians, I think Azad Zain is the guy I met in the Fine Line that time with Kate and Charlie. Oh well, let's see if he's over the first week of June – would be fun – did not get the sleeping bag connection – was kind of hoping it was M in disguise. There's still hope.

Just spoken to SBP, sounds like he's been tramping around Bern all night to find a "special walk" for us around the old city. Urgh. The more I speak with him, the less I want to speak to him. He's become pretty obsessed – he had checked out my flight when I landed in Chicago, the weather there etc etc, my God, it's a wonder he's not interviewed the pilot.

Not heard from Theo since his email last Saturday – well, he's probably fallen for another blonde tourist by now. Anyway, his teeth were horrible and he looked a bit like Julio Iglesias, urgh! But quite sexy all the same, just something about him, wild and sexy man. Poor guy, I keep remembering his cries, they sounded pretty serious too. How can someone be so serious about me when he doesn't even know me yet? That's what worries me about SBP.

Off to chicago tomorrow. I'll take you with me, diary! Xz

Chapter 11

...amd voila! Here am I sitting on the 737 or whatever, sadly not in business class (would I travel anything less), en route to the windy city. Bit of a nightmare, flight from Basel to zurich was delayed but still took just 15 mins to touchdown in Zurich and then half an hour queing at the gate along with the shleppers. No chance of an upgrade, the plane was fully booked. Thanks Bea for your infinite wisdom in cutting costs for boss Hans-Peter's sake, I'll be stuck up here in the sky for the next 14 hours in cattle class and then be expected to stand in front of my clients (upright without throwing up). I wouldn't mind if I was doing it for me, but what really gets to me is knowing that the whole of Chameleon are lining up in 1st class and business and yet I'll be the one they point a finger at if anything goes wrong or if they're unhappy with anything.

Not only am I stuck in the middle of a nightmare, I'm squashed in a window seat above the wing – most nightmare of positions. At least I'm sat next to a mum and dad (Swiss) so will not have to make small talk with some awful yank all the way. I looooove the Swiss (at this moment in time).

See some wierd and wonderful sites on planes – it's just amazing what types of people you get on public transport. Black, white, yellow, Indian (lots of Indians, Turks, everyone going to Zurich from Basel – where do they get the money? Just as I've had yet another threatening letter from NatWest in the uk – God I hate that Ambrose O'bloody Sullivan, my personal bank manager, who just doens't want to know. I get the feeling he has a mssive chip on his shoulder and is very jealous of me being here to work abroad. I've never met him but I can just imagine him living in a Barrat house in Reading, married, but not happily. He has 2.2 kids of about 5 and 7 who go to the local comp and are not that bright and will probably end up to be "interesting" personal bank managers with droney voices too. He probably drives a Ford Mondeo in navy blue, with

5 doors and his wife probably drives a small red 1.1 Metro or Clio or something like that. They argue every night and they have sex once a year at Christmas. The thought just depresses me. I don't want to end up like that, trying to be happy – that's what makes me so worried about settling down with anyone. The only guy I really really felt excited about, constantly, and it was great fun was yes, you guessed it, "M" – that's what I'm going to start calling him so it won't hurt so much. Perhaps England is not for me after all. Everyone's so sad and miserable, just like the weather. So, God, if England's not for me, work's not for me, then why am I on this earth. Even mum keeps asking me "do you think you'll stay for 12 months?" I mean what does she expect me to do?! I have to work to pay off my credit cards. Once I've done that, I'll think about what I want to do, can do, where, with who etc – then my car will be paid off (only 2 years to go) and my loans (Woolwich and 1st National) then I can be with who I want to be with, do more of what I want without having to think about it all the damm time. Oh for that day.

Could I then tell "M" how I feel confidently, (wow, would I ask him to marry me?) Well, who knows? Sod it, life's too short to f*** around, but there agin, he must want to be with me too.

Just remembered that banana I put in my bag this morning, and it's squashed in that cupboard above our heads. Don't think my Swiss neighbours will be v pleased but I have to retrieve it, I do not relish the thought of a squashed banana lining the inside of my bag. (here it is, yes, just about to explode onto everything, so saved just in the nic of time).

The pilot's just announced that we have to unload the bags and reload them as someone's on board without a passport, unlucky! That's another worry, hope my bags arrive. I have to admit, the ground staff at Basel did not fill me with confidence as they advised me that my bag would be sent to "Orlando"?!! "Chicago" I repeated! Who knows where he's gone on his holidays then? Mind you, it would be a laugh to turn up at the Chameleon function tonight in my jeans and t-shirt – would just love to see the expression of Axel– hah! Wipe that silly German grin off his face!

Anyway, I'll write later. Do you think I'm mad writing this diary?

A rather irritating US woman sat behind me (typical) – she's not stopped talking since the passport queue. I hope she runs out of breath soon.

Just a thought, that's something that I do miss... variety. Just thought, in Switzerland, you fly Swiss air/Cross air/Swiss air or Cross air. In Britain, at least you can choose Swiss air, Cross air, Virgin, BA, AA, United, Air Lingus, British idland, even Easy Jet etc etc etc. It's a bit like their supermarkets really, either Migros or Migros or Migros!

And we're off..wow, it's quite surreal, seeing Zurich, the river, the lake and the mountains in the background, almost touching the clouds (what few clouds there are – it's a beautiful day, blue blue skies). The mountains are so crisp and clear with such sharp defined outlines, you feel like you just want to touch them so much. Even just prick your finger on the pointed peaks. The landscape is quite incredible. Amazing green fields and hills (quite flat in between the mountains) what a shame we didn't fly over the alps – it would have been a spectacular view.

Fields are arranged neatly, alongside each other blending harmoniously together with various hues, often separated by delicate lines. As if each had been given a free flight ticket to design and architect their own land. Where are the unsightly estates? Amazing the extent of the woodland (40% land = agriculture, 2 thirds = woodland, the rest = mountains and human habitation. No McDonalds culture, thank God).

Think I've just seen the Matterhorn – wow, fantastic.

Perhaps it's quite lucky that I'm in a window seat after all. An 8 hour 40 min flight – not bad – I thought it would be longer.

Just watching the in-flight TV. Apparently, there's a big festival in Zurich from 22nd June until 15th July (www.zurich-freispieche.ch). Think I need a rough guide.

Also on the info channel, Lucerne has a glacier garden palace (of mirrors) (the Alhambra). So many things to discover, how exciting.

Switzerland is an enormous meadow!
The alpine foothills and mountains represent dairy farming. One third of all agricultural production is via the cow. Fields of deepest green. Indiginous farms and chalets dotted everywhere. (Apparently tradition says that the devil flew over the area carrying a sackful of houses. As he did, he tore a hole on the rocky summit of the Säntis whereupon 1,000's of chalets tumbled out and were scattered over the landscape). (My mind wonders if he flew Swiss air).

Grindelwald even drew tourists in the 18th century. Vineyards are around Lake Geneva – the train journey from Zurich to Geneva is known as the "ticket vineyard".

Everything in Switzerland is shaped by mountains, valleys, rivers and fields. Farmers are the "landscape gardeners" of Switzerland.

Engadine has marvellous painted chalets, Emmental has farmhouses and Appenzella farms "gaden".

The Brits took skiing to Switzerland, to St Moritz and Davos in 1864/5 respectively.

Just watched a lovely film on the plane "Family man" with Nicolas Cage. It was so true to life (hope Axel saw the movie) and how I feel at the moment – also just read an article about women of 40 who've never been married or had kids. Gosh it makes me sound desperate but I don't want to be like them. Neither do I want to be married to a boring English guy (or Swiss guy) that's happy to settle for a 2-up/2-down Barrat house in reading. My guy's got to be special, with something about him – as Phil siad – a quiet boy, possibly, but there's got to be a hero hidden inside him to rescue me. Tall, handsome, sparkling eyes, generous smile, caring touch – is that so much to ask? And sense of humour/wit/life after work/a life of his own and friends of his own (that are not total pratts), with some things in common with me, who wants to be with someone, have fun and a family. I thimk of Brad and his claimed undying love for me. OK, so I do miss him a bit, just wish he'd been a bit more imaginative in bed as well as in other areas.

I miss M's style, his sense of humour, his eyes, his nose, his touch, his smile and most of all, his kiss. It's strange, I hardly remember the times we were together now but I still have this pain in my heart deep down and distant memory that however it was, it was fantastic at the time, I really fell badly. Perhaps it was because it was such a contrast to Andy. Andy, mm, yes, I feel I wasted so much of my life with him, so many of my "eggs" gone. When I could have been looking out for someone who wanted similar things out of life. He's already admitted that his new girlfriend will leave him when she wants kids. We're just good friends now, which is all I guess we ever were, just with sex (occasionally – which was totally NOT mindblowing – unlike how it was with M).

Apparently, we're over Montreal right now. Wow. It's 5.50pm (CH time) so I guess about Midday US/Canada time. I don't know, do I care? I guess I do or should do.

Well, here we are, starting our descent into the windy city. It's 12.10, that means we're 7 hours behind swiss time (urgh, I'm going to struggle later). Everything looks so flat and straight on the ground. Huge expanses of land. Fields, huge, long, highways stretching into infinity. Gosh when I think my Father's been to all these places, seen all these things, wish he could have shared them with me. It's incredible, lots of browm square fields. It looks like a grid map has been put down that they all fit into very neatly. It's so flat. There's nothing for miles. We're about to cut across Lake Michegan, and this is Lake Michegan. Surrounded by beautiful white sand around the fringes. The wheels are out. I know because I'm sat over them.urg, it's quite diconcerting over water. Have been flying for almost 11 hours now (including the Zurich flight). Never believe SBP again who said "oh it's not that long", it's always only "terrible" when he does it. I can see the outer edge of the lake. I can see thigs sticking out of the landscape on the far side – that must be Chicago! I think this lake's about the size of Switzerland alone. Hope I've brought the right suits etc to wear – I've lost touch a bit with the client side and feel a bit off my territory. Still, don't want particularly to impress anyone here (least of all Axel).

The houses are all like boxes, all identical with either brown or grey roofs but with exactly the same amount of land around each one and the same number of trees.

Well. Here I am, in yankee land. 1st impressions – not good. My bag's not made it. Possibly will arrive tonight? Has it indeed gone to Orlando. I'm so annoyed with the check in people.

Everyone seems to be eating things all the time, out of Big Mac bags. Shakes, burgers, coca cola, everything. The people are all fat, fat or fatter. Shared a cab with a "Herman" from Oxford, UK. Told him my luggage was lost. He mentioned that he lost his luggage once here and so he went to buy some more underpants but the only shop he could find sold ladies underwear – was he trying to tell me something?! Anyway, checked into the hotel. Had a wander around – trying to find the Chameleon market research sessions. Ended up at navy pier, but had to leave and come back here because I feel like I'm going to collapse (it's about 3 in the morning Swiss time now, even though it's 8pm here) goodnight!

Chapter 12

At least I slept really well – had about 20 hours sleep (or more, since it's 10.30am, 1.30pm in switz!!)

Don't like this place:

a) because I've lost my luggage
b) because my building is so tall, cement and glass, no character
c) because everybody is out for themselves yet so cheery (or is that just a facade?)
d) because I haven't got enough dollars and am worried even about paying the bill
e) because I have no-one to share it with and it's mother's day here in Chicago ("Roses for your mom") all I hear on the TV is "Iowa", "Wisconsin", that awful drawl. Get the feeling I'm not that happy here in "downtown" mind you, it would help if the people I were with made it more pleasant...

I have to say it was funny – on landing at the airport, you see signs for foot and mouth everywhere – if you have visited any farm or any agricultural premises, please advise our agricultural customs.

A British guy in front of me in the customs control queue was given the "nth" degree – do you live on a farm? No; Do you live near a farm? No. How far away is the nearest farm to where you live? I don't know . approximately? (Oh for goodness sake, give it up, he probably lives in a 2-up-2-down in the heart of Brixton – all Americans now believe that if you're British, you live on a farm) I wish I'd been interviewed – hee hee.

Urgh, the TV is dreadful here – a station just advertised a TV program on "Puberty" at 10am tomorrow morning. Oh wow, haven't housewives anything better to do here? I don't think so.

Interesting, last night I saw a few youngsters dressed up, all in meringue like ballgowns. Their kids (like their moms, dads and cars) are big and ugly. So are their ballgowns – did no-one tell them how hideous they look? Anyway, on the other hand it was lovely to see that the good old fashioned "prom" is not just hollywood fiction, but alive and kicking. And it was most chivalrous to see all the young men escorting their beauties to the boats along the pier (I just wonder how much illegal drugs and alcohol will be consumed once mommy and pappy kiss them goodbye?).

Well, today has been quite good. Woke up about 4am – typical, having fallen asleep at 7.45pm last night. Called Swiss Air but no reply (not like the BA UK 24 hour helpline). Fell asleep again. Woke up at 6am. Rang Swiss Air again. Still no reply. Telephoned reception for a toothbrush having forgotten mine. They sent one up. My alarm went off at 6.30am. Washed, showered etc etc. Had breakfast – awful – 1 bowl of Special K with hot water for $14.75 and they left "gratuity" blank (yeah right!). Walked to the Swiss hotel. Such a beautiful day and a little warmer than yesterday. Sky was blue (what little I could see from my room amongst the skyscrapers from my top floor – 200) There are too many buildings here blocking out the natural sunlight (that's what's wrong with this place).

Anyway, sat in the market research at the Swiss Hotel and met "Werner" from "Time Research". We had a great chat. At 1pm, had a call from "Geraldine" of "Time Research" to suggest that I made my way over to the survey centre instead (oh geez, I'm so sorry). So I went over there. Grabbed a salad from "Slice of Italy" (not at all) for Rita and I – gosh unbelievable, they could not make a sandwich, they said, unless they fried it first. (Yuk, no wonder people are so fat). Later Rita and I took the River Boat the Architecture tour, fantastic. It was her idea and so welcome. We were greeted by "Vern" and "Johhhhhaaaaana" who took us on a whistle stop tour all around the canal system of Chicago – did you know you can even reach the Mississippi and the gulf of Mexico from here!

Chicago was a swamp originally, named by the Indians who originally founded the place, then lots of architects built up all these amazing 120 floor tall buildings. Bit depressing I would have thought, to work here, everything's a bit tall and overwhelming (gosh is that how I would describe myself?). Not much character here either, but glass fronted buildings, amazing art deco design and amazing to believe that these things were being constructed from 1871! Lots of condominiums (urgh, dreadfully American – why can't they just use the term 'flats or appartments' like the rest of us) Flat sounds so...flat by comparison though I have to admit. Condo has something a little more exotic to it I guess.

Michegan Avenue is meant to be the shopping street to go for apparently – spotted Nordstrom (Ii remember that from the trip to John and Lolly's in LA, or was it from "Sex in the city").

Tonight, changed my room to a non-smoking and it's really much better, overlooks the river and part of the lake so fab view. Also, yee haa, some natural light! My bag arrived too – think he did in fact go for a quick holiday to Orlando via geneva – ooh, lucky him!

Out tonight with the Chameleon lot. Hope I have enough cash. Oh yes, good sayings here: "Champagne on the rocks" for the university that was on the old navy pier for a few years. "West Wacker Drive" just sounds so American – urgh. Gray line trolley car; Michegan Avenue; shopping and hacker observatory.

Am making up from my lack of TV over the last nearly 3 months by watching "The Oblongs"; "Seventh heaven"; "Dawson's Creek- the Graduation". Yes, I can see why many kids here may end up dull and dim.

Well, had quite a long day today – was up for a debrief meeting at 7am, which the market research company had fogotten about.! So ended up having breakfast (a decent one) with the client, then went into the research. Had sandwiches inside and then stayed in the research until about 4pm, then went off to visit the art museum on the old navy pier with Werner, the researcher. It was ok, really beautiful works of art. I saw the Lennon and Yoko Ono photo – the famous one, taken by Annie Lebowitz of them in bed, saw some warhole etc etc. Went to debrief at about 7pm and you won't believe what the client wants me to do tonight – call Switzerland at 1am Chicago time (9am CH time) and brief the Swiss to re-do 5 logos and pdf them to 2 of the clients computors, so that we can show them to the Doctors tomorrow at 8am, here in Chicago. Great. Thanks Guys.

Walked back to my minus 5 star hotel alone, whilst the client and market researchers stayed in the plush 5 star with a view around the corner. Although Geraldine had suggested meeting up with them all, I decided to stay in:

a) because my dollars are rapidly running out
b) Ali McBeal was on TV, then followed by Disney's "the incredible journey" (bit of a tear jerker)
   but mainly because..
c) I just could not face making poilte conversation for a further minute that night.

So, I ordered a pizza (which was probably one of the worst I've tasted in a long time) and ordered an alarm call for 1.15am.

Tuesday. Feels like Wednesday. Full morning of activity, adrenalin and extra grey hairs.

Shit. The hotel forgot to call me at 01.15. they called me at 04.00 to appologise and I then had to try to ring Switzerland. After much faffing around (there's no trust here – you cannot make an outside call unless you go through the operator and give them a credit card number – that works- or a calling card number). Life's a bitch without a credit card, I tell you. Now I wish I had not spent so much money when I was with Aandy. Anyway, at least I can laugh about it now. Anyway, in the end, feeling guilty, reception called Switzreland for me so it cost me nothing (Ok, so I had stomped downstairs in my PJs – shorts and tight T-shirt, and no fluffy slippers,that they all probably had in their 5* next door) I briefed the guys in Basel and they sent us pdfs – telephoned me back at 05.35 to say they had gone through. Then followed a full morning of research – and we still don't have the perfect logo. Groan. What do they want?

Anyway, back to the hotel to get changed and now have some fun. I went to meet Werner who'd finished his groups and we went for a walk down Michigan Avenue to visit a few shops – window shopping – and to have a bite to eat (Mozzarella and tomato sandwich with Caesar salad). We had a good chat – about why I'd gone to Switzerland etc etc and why he'd gone to England 10 years ago, our dreams, and ambitions, and all about 7-year cycles (and how apparently he believes I'm coming up to a pivotal 7 year cycle and that's possibly the reason why I'm feeling the way I do: confused, irritated, aggravated, worried, scared, etc etc, & ultimately, desperate to pay back my credit cards).

Anyway, another day here in weird Chicago. What a hot day – wow, so so hot and sticky. Greeted in elevators (that's lifts to you and me) by phrases like: "So it's $1.3 billion. Really, ohh" – is that all the americans think about – money money money. Passed by the "Steak and chops". The inhabitants here wind me up so much – can't wait to get back to miserable Brits or even Swiss. Had a wander around a few architectural landmarks – tried to go to the top of the Globe at the top of the beautiful building on West Wacker but unfortunately, there was a meeting going on (had to ask on the office on the 3rd floor – the security guard was fine with me going up there, 1st nicest Yank I've experienced on this trip so far). It was an architect's office, quite appropriate really I guess, they own the office in the globe.

Went to Nordstrom – tried to buy some Armani Extra shorts – material was beautiful – and a top, but my credit card would not go through. It's so annoying as Swiss Air told me they'd give me $100 worth of free clothes for inconvenience. I also tried a pair of jeans at gap at $52.00 (about £27 – a bargain) but still my credit card would not work – embarrassing or what!

Now, back to the hotel, waiting for Rita – she's just called, she'll be late. There's a meeting of some "Ram" society where all the women dress up like tarts on acid, even though they're about 500 years old, they look like trussed up turkeys about to be basted, god I hope my husband will tell me what a state I look if I end up looking like that. I can't believe the size of that old lady's heels, even by my standards – they're bright green too. Gosh they're not ashamed or embarrassed of anything are they? It's quite amusing really. Here's "Carter" looking positively out of sorts. Came down on his own in the lift, obviously been pushed out of the hen house in a flurry of feathers as the hen was preening herself. Carter's about 40, he has 2 little girls who are also dressed up – a little hideously – and are carrying dolls who have dresses on made of the same material as their dresses. They're obnoxious. Funny, with most children, I feel quite protective, I feel absolutely nothing for these kids. Here are some more, meet George and George junior (about 50) and my god, what's Mrs George Junior walked in wearing?! Ooh, there's another 'Vern' (by the way, I know all the names because they're all wearing name badges with big names written on them – I suppose just in case they'd forgotten their specs, the typeface is larger than 20 point and bold). Here's Arlein and Claude, Jeff amd Mave, Dirk and Charlie, Butch and Randy (gosh I thought all these names were just saved for the movies). I hope my Father did not like this place, I can see why perhaps he may have liked it at his age, the way of life/everything's quite cheap etc etc, but really it's all so pretentious, superficial, false, unreal, etc etc. OK, more later, here's Rita.

And so on my way back, here I am at Brussels airport – 2 hours between my connection (hope my bags made it this time). At least I'm in a little Saab 2000 (propellor plane- not seen those for years, but used quite frequently for "Swiss hopping"). Desperately need the toilet after all the water I drunk – managed to get a few zzz's on the American Airlines flight back, which was just as well as it was so awful. The girl next to me was sick twice too so I didn't feel too good when I disembarked. The film was family man again which I'd seen on the way out too – unfortunately no sign of "Chocolate or any other interesting movie, but it was just as well as I really needed some sleep. OK, so here's my last leg to Basel, back to the airport adorned with Swiss flags with the 1 token BA airplane on standby "alone amongst a crowd".

Oh yes, must make a note, on these hoppers you should book an "A" seat, so you're in the aisle in a little nook of your very own, there's so much more room.

Wow, we're caught in the middle of a fairly severe thunder storm so take off's been abandoned for a bit – I'm glad, there's thunder and lightening and driving hail outside bouncing off the tarmac. We're 1st in line, parallel to another Sabena flight, a BA and a DHL flight, all lined up waiting for the all clear from the heavens above. A small 6-man aircraft has just landed – that must have been bumpy.

Severe jet lag this morning – nearly sick and have bad diarrhoea. Did not eat, lost all my appetite which to those of you that know me means...it's serious! Do not know whether it was nerves yet excitement about the pitch we had to do today, which was with Serono down in Geneva. It seemed to go ok (the Americans who'd come over to do it with us seemed to think it went better but what a beautiful place – will defintitely return for a short weekend break or something).

SBP sent me flowers by post and some ginseng relaxing herbal bath salts. Damm, I must tell him sooner rather than later, I'd much rather be his friend than his lover (or as he calls me, his "sweetheart" yuk). I've decided. He keeps saying "Ooh, just a little kissey for SBP" on the telephone when he says "Goodbye". I just cringe at my end, knowing that he won't notice. (M has not written, still, Ok, I'm not going to mention his name from now on..perhaps next Monday I will allow myself 1 hour to think of him..that worked last time – and a letter turned up. I think he may write, just before I turn up at Ceroc). Damm, I want it to be a complete surprise. Would love to be able to just fling my arms around him and his around me as we grin from ear to ear on the dance floor – please God, that's what I want to happen. Right, that's it for now.

Urgh, SBP phoned me this afternoon at work. Think he's getting the message slowly but surely. He sent me an email to say that tomorrow he's playing guitar but could get to Bbasel by 7 or 8pm and we could "go out for a little something to eat" followed by rollerblading in interlaken on Sunday as the weather is going to be good. (I hate my life being organised by someone I don't particularly like) and that's what Andy used to do (ok, Andy was nice to begin with) and I don't know enough people or places yet to do my own thing.. Anyway, I wrote an email back saying that I couldn't do dinner as I couldn't afford it but may like to go swimming in the lake on Sunday and rollerblading. He called later to say "ok, I'll be in Basel about 8pm then" – talk about giving me a choice or what. Can't he get the message?! Can't he take me out for dinner perhaps for a change, instead of having to split the bill from the get go. Then I think I'm really using him as I think, well, maybe I'd like to go swimming, rollerblading, he can show me where, but I just don't want sex with you. Is that ok? I'm just not turned on by you, got it? Perhaps that's what M and JB thought about me? I'd love to know. That's awful, it's then you start to get paranoid thinking, how can they say that they don't want sex with me, goddess to the stars and all that –I'm so sad. M used to say he'd never done things like we did since he was 19 – was he lying – and B wanted me after we were supposed to have split up saying that he was not sure whether he was making the biggest mistake of his life in dumping me... Therefore I can't believe that I'm not a tiny bit sexy. SBP cannot get enough of me whenever he sees me and nor could Brad. Now I think of Brad just a little bit. Perhaps I was too quick. Perhaps I shouldn't have just dropped him. But he was 5 years younger than me (even though he acted about 5 years older than the oldest guy I've ever been out with) ... hey hang on, he could have contacted me to find out how I was getting on in Switzerland – I think deep down he was a bit jealous of the whole Swiss thing – I mean that's when things went hideously wrong (well, both that and not having the guts to tell me that he had to leave for Oz last November and knowing that he wouldn't know when he'd be back, just keeping me hanging on... Babe, I'll be back for your birthday..birthday came and went...babe I'll definitely be back for Christmas...Christmas came and went...Babe, any day now...any day came and went....).

M's response to Switzerland: "Wow, that's fantastic"; Brad's response "Well, thanks for asking me (in a very bad mood)" (before I'd even decided, this was on the day that Steve asked me into his office to discuss a telephone call he'd just had from boss Hans-Peter).

I feel a bit of a bitch though when Brad just could not say when he was going to be back and then moving on to JB, although when you see an opportunity, you should sieze it if you both feel the same..am I talking rubbish?

SBP sent me a weird SMS tonight. In german, don't know waht it was but think it was rude – yuk. Perve!

Yee haaa, I am now the proud owner of a visa and a mastercard from UBS!!!
Hallelujah. Sucess!!!! Now I can go on business trips more confidently. Hoorah!!

M must be getting ready for the Chelsea Flower Show right now – wish I could go, last year was beautiful and Paula really enjoyed it too – it's a shame Beth was too young to go with us. It starts this Tuesday until Friday. I hope he's thinking of me – wondering if I'll turn up.. and then waiting to write to tell me all about it. I hope his boss asks where the tall blonde is that was there last year. His boss seemed really quite a cool dude too, he's lucky working with fun people.

I hope M's ok, and his mum, dad, Sam and Russell and Humphrey the dog. I feel so close to him yet so far away. I felt almost adopted by his mum and dad, they were so nice, even Humph liked me as M said at the time. Bastard. You just don't realise how much I feel about you. Or do you? How do you feel? Am I just making it up, or were we really good together? Is it my imagination? All I know is that at the time I remember praying to God as I looked into your eyes, and at your nose and smile and I whispered to myself "Please God, please don't ever let this end" and for that reason I know something must have been good between us. I've never felt like that about a guy or felt like it ever since (and it wasn't just the sex, but yes, it did help!)

Sometimes I feel I shared too much with everyone (even Annie, who never rings or writes to me now, except to tell me what a wonderful weekend's riding she had in France with Edwin, Anders, and Jean. I wasn't invited. Jean never mentioned it when I bumped into him at clapham common although he did say he was going riding in France over Easter. Thanks mates. Perhaps she was a little put back when I replied with "funny, Jean never mentioned it" and "bet you're glad I introduced you guys then!" She's not replied since. I should kiss and make up, I like Annie.

I guess iI do feel a bit jealous of her – she has the perfect mum and dad, with the perfect brother, with a fab house in Bath for her to escape to, a perfect client job – one of the coolest places to work, Guiness, such a good chat up line with guys I'm sure – with fully expensed car. No debts. Little mortgage and a house in gGuildford. A share option of £20,000.00 about to mature etc etc. Why do I take it all? I feel like I've absolutely zero to offer anyone that comes into my life. Perhaps that's why M and then JB dumped me? I will just have to settle for an odd-ball like SBP who's obviously a mistake, 14 years younger than his brothers and sisters and obviously been treated as the baby of the family rather than the man – it would be like marrying Frank Spencer, no no no, I can't stand it. Otherwise, there's Marco, who's never heard from his father since his mother conceived him; Brad whose father ran off when his mother had breast cancer; Andy, who's father commited suicide.

Dear Lord,

All I want is a regular guy, with no strings and a whole bundle of fun (as well as a nice decent stable family). I guess that's another reason why M fitted the bill. He knows it and he wants to meet someone with the same "bill" of health. I think I'd sacrifice that though, if it felt right and if there was an enormous passion and just "something" between us....M, please wrote again!

Met my neighbour today, Saturday. Annie from Adelaide. She seems ok, a bit older than I imagined – divorced, 2 kids. Must earn a fortune – she buys them business class tickets twice a year to come over to visit her via London. Anyway, she taught me a few things – eek, rules I never knew existed. For example, if I continue not to pay for my rubbish (via little stickers you have to purchase at the Co-op), the police will open my bin bags and search for anything with my address on and come knocking on my door. Also, that apparently, you shouldn't hoover on Sundays, also, that in her last flat, the Basel law is that you can only do your washing every 2nd Monday between 7 and 9pm! Apparently, after 10pm, you're supposed only to have showers (to avoid the noise of bath water draining away) and that men, check this, should sit down on the toilet when you're going after 10pm, to reduce the noise (?!!) – can't wait to hear the news on lovemaking, or do they do it without any noise. (Did M know something I didn't when he said that no sex was allowed in Switzerland?) Aghhh! I said I wouldn't talk about him except on Mondays, damm. I sent him a text message today – it was such a beautiful day, I just wanted to share it with him. I wrote: "Hi there, hope you are OK. It's such a beautiful day 2day here in Basel! Tell me it's chucking it down in Blighty so I won't be so homesick! Z" but I've not heard any reply.

Talking of calls, SBPs not called. Strange, he said he'd be here by 7pm or 8pm and would phone during the day – now, should I call, shouldn't I? Should I bother? Yes, why not. I'm angry. Annie asked if I wanted to go out with her and her friend and I turned them down saying SBP was coming around. So much for that!

Well, he saved me the job. 8.15pm and he calls to say "Oh no, Zoe, I'm still here in Bern, I think I will now go to Interlaken". Oh right, thank you I thought. "I wish you'd called me earlier" I said "Because I met my neighbour today and she invited me out. Obviously I turned her down because you were coming over and now you're not – thank you" (well, not in that exact tone – I can never get angry, I must learn – perhaps tomorrow I just should, just as he did with me that time in Zermatt. Yes, it would be good practice. Because I don't need to be treated like that by a guy – I could have gone out and met someone else! Perhaps that's why he did it – probably, I'm starting to get that impression). I tried to ask him questions but he obviously did not understand. He told me to tell him when he was getting "too strong" but I didn't have the heart, but he wanted to send me flowers etc (urgh!).

I sent Theo from Paros a text message but I don²t think his mobile's switched on – it's still pending. Oh well, thought of him tonight (2 weeks ago last night, eek!) (If only SBP knew).

Had a dream last night (I'm usually right, call it female intuition). It was of SBP and I talking and he said it first: "Zoe I do not thik this relationship is working" and I agreed

136

"after all" I said "work's very busy, and I still have strong feelings for my ex-uk man and if we'd really wanted to see each other, I'd have been in Bern on Thursday or last night or he would have been here at 8.30pm last night. I felt it was moving too quickly anyway". Strange thing is, I woke at 5am this morning, heard the bells chiming outside in the clear air, and thought it was real and wondered what I could do today if I didn't meet him. I wanted to go swimming on the lake, to go rollerblading, but did not know where to start. (Although Annie told me of the "beach" place in Basel and the little strip of sand by the river – may be worth checking out soon).

Well, today, I "baptised myself" in the lake of Brienz – next to the lake of Thun and Interlaken. Yes, I made my way over to Interlaken and as I was about to leave my 1st motorway to get on the Bern motorway, SBP sent me an sms to say that he could be in Basel by 1pm if I didn't want to come over. Tough, I thought, (call me a cynic, but I guessed there was a thought of "zoe will be able to drop me off at the station in the morning and I can go to Bern – but tough, I don't think I ever want to sleep with him again, I can't stand his smell – that sounds awful but it makes me feel sick each time I smell it, it happened today, many times, as it was so hot – it was a beautiful day, we went rollerblading around the old airfield and then rollerblading to the top of Brienz see (lake) where we sat and sunbathed and I swam – SBP wouldn't, I'm not sure he can – huge negative star award – mind you it was dreadfully cold.

The water was so clear and almost turquoise blue though with a shimmer of pollen on the top, quite beautiful. Gentle lapping waves from the infrequent ferries that passed from one side to the other and the odd rowing boat.

It felt quite bizarre to lie with the grass beneath my feet and the mountains wrapped around me like a cocoon. We talked quite a bit whilst we were there – that was good, he knows now how I feel, he even said "I hope we will see you here again" as we said goodbye tonight. We went to his parents again, they'd prepared some supper for us and we sat outside – what luxury – what a backdrop for Sunday teatime!

Had some very strange dreams last night:
1. Watched, whilst sitting in Chicago with Max from sailing, an old Merc being washed away into the sea, then realised one of the bridges was opening. The lady who owned it stood there and watched it.
2. At mykonos, or was it Chicago, lots of huge boats arriving at port, in line, one behind the other
3. Some more, I'll try to remember later
4. Oh yes, in one, I lost one of my silver heart earings.

Wow, it feels like "living abroad" here (if that makes sense). The summer days are beautiful, blue blue skies, my favourite colour and the evenings, warm and balmy. I've become a star gazer and should buy a book I think, the sky's so cloudless and midnight blue and I've spotted the plough I think already. (That's always the easiest to spot). I cycled to work and to the gym after work and home. It was great. Sweating even at 7.30am in a T-shirt and cycling shorts with my backpack on – I feel like one of the kids with their regulation size backpacks on.

Oh yes, we won the Serene pharma pitch – yipee! Trips to Geneva!! ☺ They asked me to go to Chicago next Tuesday but Hans-Peter said it was too much (my God, he must be human after all – either that or he wants me for the Grundy pharma pitch on 30th! Yeah right, more likely! So we'll probably send Jeff from the US (I can almost hear his squeaky voice now, and shrill pitches and squeals of delight – aghhh!!)

Text from Marco tonight.

That only leaves M. He'll be at the Chelsea Flower Show tomorrow – wish I was there. I love May and June in London – there's so much going on.

Oh yes, boss Hans-Peter was going to warn Janick today

that if she didn't buck up – get her act together – we can't afford to keep her. Instead, she announced she was 2-3 months pregnant, had known when she had started the job but wanted to wait a few months before she said anything. So, great.

Now I feel I'm being left on the shelf. I have to find M (or a man!) before my seeds run out. Urgh, that's such an awful thought. I always remember Patrick's comment when Julian announced he was to get married in October and he asked whether he'd have any children to which Julian replied "No, I don't think so" to which Patrick said "oh why, is she an outspan or something?" I asked what he meant and he siaid "Why, seedless of course!" He could be very funny, I do miss that. I hope I'm not being classed as an Outspan orange.

Theo from Paros called me – I don't know where it's going – we only knew each other for 1 night but he's already emailed me twice and called me twice and wants to know when I'll be back in Paros! (He's just been to Italy to judge the world championships of kitesurfing – won by a 25 year old – I don't even know him or how old he is and he doesn't know how old I am, or does he, his friend is 27 and he said he thought he was a little young for me – great, do I look that old?!!Thanks!!Each day I look more closely in the mirror).

Snipbit: The sunset's are really quite dramatic – like pink and blue candy stripes across the sky – quite beautiful

Went out for lunch today with Janick – had pizza. The cheese on pizzas here tastes strange – the mozarella is more like ricotta and vica versa. Had text from Nikki – brilliant to hear from her, from someone! Marco also called tonight but I was in the gym – I called him back later and he said he'd call me back. Never did. I sent a jokey text to say "great, forgotten me already, off to bed etc!" Hope he takes it the right way!

Have to get some sort of work-life order or else it will be

all work and no play, making zoe a v v v v dull girlie!

Spoke to mum. Depressing. If it's not illness, it's a headache or something else. I'm sorry but I wish she'd met someone else or had some other interest in her life after Father left. I know she was devastated. We all were. We still are. I still think of him and cry often. But she should have not got over it, but had something else to do. I still madly, deeply miss M. I still deeply, secretly wish/want us to get back together again, in some serendipity kind of way. I always will, I think, but at least if I go to the gym, I work, I'm determined to pay back my credit cards within the next two years and then just maybe, something may happen and I'll fall madly, deeply etc again – wish and hope it's with big "M" but who knows. He as to be worth it.

Well, another breakthrough. I was paid today and I have been paid some tax back – it's 250CHF – I know that's only £100 but still, it makes it sound great. Now to sort out my bills etc. Also, was sent my PIN nos for the VISA UBS cards so now I can use them in cash withdrawal machines now even abroad which is good for work (and moi!)

Work, wow, it's getting longer and longer, now we're working with Toltzis in the US who begin their day at our 5pm! Great, not. Left the office at 8.45pm tonight, cycled to gym, was thrown out of gym about 10pm and then cycled home. Drove around to Janick's – who was officially given notice today. Just to tell her I'll give her a reference if she needed one and some moral support. She loaned me the maps for Colmar for tomorrow – I'm going to drive there. Bad news is, SBP wants to go there with me – OK – but then he wants to stay tomorrow night. He said you'll be going to work about 8am on the Friday, so I can get the train. I said Yes, but I'll probably cycle in on Friday (made him think). I've decided I don't want him to stay. He makes me mad and I feel so claustrophobic. I'm here for an adventure, life is an adventure, not for some dim wit who wants me for my car, my money (not that I have any). "But I simply don't understand" he said "you must earn a very good salary as you work so hard" yes, of course, but naive SBP, I have comitments, unlike you who just rents a broom cupboard and goes home to mummy and daddy every weekend for food, washing, ironing etc– the most expensive thing he has to buy are train tickets and for those he even has a halb tax card so gets them for half the price. Well, sod it, tomorrow will be the day of reckoning...

The following day:

Well, ok, feel pretty shitty at the moment, I know I've done the right thing though.

I collected SBP from Basel SBB this morning – I was a few minutes late but I know this sounds terrible, I could not be bothered. (Oh dear).

I could just picture him (unsmiling face), hear his squeaky voice, see his silly wiggle as he saw me approaching him (urgh). I am so sorry, no, I haven't used him but just takes time to discover another part of some people.

We spent the day in Colmar, just across the French border. It was really pretty – lots of beautiful buildings and canals. I didn't think SBP was really enjoying it though, he's not very interested sometimes in the world around him anyway … all will be revealed ...

I filled up the car with petrol, bought tickets for us to go on a train ride around the city – it was really good. Then bought 2 tickets for us to go on a boat trip. Should have seen SBP's face as I waited for him to pick up the bill for lunch – about £20 worth of French Francs – great value – but you should have seen his face – like a little lost puppy as I suggested he paid that (as I'd got the tickets etc etc etc, as above). "Urgh, Zoe, now let's see" he began, as he fumbled with the bill (also irritated me the length of time it took him to drink a glass of coca cola as he always called it) Arghhhh!!!

I noticed a couple walk in. A French couple, obviously in love (with each other) looked good together I thought; I don't want to look like SBP. He was obviously gaining a lot from me as in dress taste, manner, method of eating (previously stone age man type of eating!) – although only really seen him eat with his fingers when he's away from his parents (and when he eats there, he uses his knife and fork like shovels – just embarrassing!) (My 5 year old nephew has better eating habits than him) I want so much to be madly deeply in love, just as I was (am?) with M (ok, it's not Monday – I've forgotten about the Monday rule, or even about what day of the week it is!)

I feel like writing M's letter to him – SBP and I have nothing in common, we don't have the same ambitions etc etc (M, you idiot, you know how good we were together).

Anyway, I tried the swiss boy thing, "it just didn't work out". After 2 and half hour lunch (god it takes him so long to drink coca cola). We went for a boat trip. That was great – taken around by a rather tasty looking French guy – now their accent is pretty sexy. Half way through the trip, SBP started to move next to me, to put his arm around me, to sniff my neck again (yuk!), to kiss me – too much pda (public display of affection) – I'm sorry, he really had not got the message that I was just not reciprocating any of his moves.

We were determined to find a "Vin Caveau" to do some wine tasting, but one was closed and the other was a shop. Felt guilty but they let us try several different Alsace wines (reisling, cremant, etc etc). All v nice. SBP just snubbed his nose up, like a 5-year old boy (have you no voice, no point of view, iI wondered? I needed more mental stimulation in conversation than that!)

After that, SBP asked if I would like to go for a drink – so we went down to a bar by the river and had a drink – v cheap – wine and water, 50FFr!! Anyway, that's where I said it, where I made the ultimatum. The moment came up, quite by chance and so I just came out with it and said "I don't want you to stay tonight SBP. I don't think it feels right" (he'd previously said "urm, Zoe, tomorrow, will you take the car to work because if you do, it would be nice for you to take P to the station. I have a train at..." I didn't hear the rest of his sentence, didn't want to, I was just figuring out how I would say what I wanted to say. I kept saying I wanted space, time, etc etc, I felt like I'd been boxed in, frightened, clautrophobic etc etc. he grabbed my fingers and tried not to let go. I pulled away.

We left the table and I wanted to buy another stamp to send a postcard to Mum, Paula and Mick, Tim and Beth. I couldn't believe it, on being quite composed and as if nothing had happened in the restaurant, the minute we left it, he raised his voice and started to shout in that squeaky voice accent. I felt a bit frightened and a bit taken aback, I have to say. (He had told me that sometimes his father had shouted – is that a warning I thought?) I went to buy a stamp. I left the shop and we didn't really talk that much, he was just saying (or almost shouting) " I don't know what's changed. What's happened, what's changed? Zoooooee, what's happened? Was it Steve on your last trip?" As if!! He's just so narrow minded – "it has to be someone else" (urgh, was I like that when I was with M).

We were walking back to the car and suddenly it all came out again "In Zermatt" he said"I could not believe what happened with your credit card. Here is a woman (urgh, I've never been called that before, yuk, don't like it) with no money!" "It's all right for you" I retaliated "You have no mortgage, no credit cards, you have a really cheap – awful – flat in Bern, so you can go to Mauritius or wherever you want, a mum and a dad that you can go home to and get fed and watered and washed every week. I give you lifts to and from the station, buy all these tickets". Urgh, pretty ugly, it all came out. He replied "I would get rid of the flat in London if I were you".

I replied "I do not want to get rid of it. I love my flat in

London" and with that turned foot and nearly ran back to the car. He kept pace (about 10 foot behind) "You never really liked skiing did you Zoooeee" he said, with bitterness. "Of course I do" I replied (you jerk), 'just not with you' (was left unsaid). It is the most glorious sport, with the right people. He continued "I never wanted to go to Zermatt or Engelburg" he said (with a face pulled like a 5 year old puppy dog) "Well, if you didn't want to go, why did you, I would have been perfectly happy going alone. I didn't ask you to come with me". He replied "I only did those things because I luuuuurve you" (Urgh!)

We returned in silence to the car. I unlocked it. Of course he arrived behind. We climbed in. Interesting, the first thing he said was "Shall we take the roof off?" (what a subtle thing to say at such a time?!). Fortunately I didn't pull it back.

We drove the whole way back to Basel Bahnhof SBB in silence except for the radio playing "Suicide blonde" to which he tutted to as it came over the airwaves, and the sound of the persisitent rain as the thunder clouds broke above our heads.

I dropped SBP at the station – where he tutted again because it was 18.22 and the next train to interlaken was at 19.04 (tough I thought, this taxi can't help your silly Swiss train timetable and accurate train times). I left him there. He asked me to send him a message in the week. I said I'd think about what he said (to make him feel better). He just said: "Just remember Zooooeee, that if I'm your ski friend and you have so many friends in so many other countries, by the time you're 50, you will have just lots of friends. Keep attention, Zoooeee". What a horrible thing for him to shout out in the station.

I left him standing there with his little Egypt bag slung over his left shoulder.

That rather haunting melody by Moby is playing on the stereo (the CD I got with the Observer last year). It makes me think of JB and then... M. It just seems to sound how I feel about him – something buried that's still alive.

Chapter 13

Had a pretty busy day at work today and had to go to the PO afterwards so went with Heinz. It was such a beautiful evening I thought I can't possibly go back to my appartment and also need to find out where to take Steve next week, so dropped Heinz back at the office and went to explore – yipee!

I'd managed to go to the gym at lunchtime, well, a late lunchtime, so parked the car and wandered around. Found a few really nice restaurants there – wonder if that's the one Andy's thinking of when he reported a Michelin restaunrant in Basel (trust him to locate that one), would like to ask him but he'll probably just tell me that he's off to Monte Carlo, Nice, Antibes, Cannes, etc etc, just to make me feel really good (not). I settled upon a little bar facing the Rhein in Kleine Basel and had a glass of wine – ein glas rose wein, schweiz, which was quite nice. A brillinat musician played in the background, lots of atmostphere. I texted Kate and we sent each other about 3-4 text messages. She asked how I was. I said I felt good, not being suffocated by SBP. She told me that I didn't really fancy him so someone would come along. As boss Hans-Peter says, "There's a lid for every pot!" (think mine's just boiling over though).

So I wandered around for about 2 hours and then went back to the car. Oh, forgot to say, on the way across the bridge, I was accosted by this swiss guy who seemed to be telling me that he'd moved to Basel but didn't know anything about the town, and then asked where I was from. But I couldn't understand a word he was saying really so just said "Enschuldigung" (I'm sorry) "Ich sprache Englisch, ich bin Gros Britannien". With that I smiled, waved (as if to say thanks but no thanks). Think he got the message so he moved away.How odd. I was glad. I just wanted space, quiet, time not to spend a fortune but save my pennies and spend it with people iI enjoy spending it with.

I've put "beautiful south" on my stereo. Haven't heard it

for a while. Sounds cool and good. I keep remembering when M lay back on my sofa and told me I was really lovely and I said, "well, that makes 2 of us then". Wonder how he got on at Chelsea Flower show?

I sent a swisslette news letter out – didn't copy in JB this time – not worth it. Had lots of replies. Even Lord Huber came out of the woodwork. He said "I thought you were dead!" (Thanks!)

Ahh, yes, Theo called me again "Wen you come to Paros?" "I vant to see you again, it's lovely to hear your voice." My god, what did I do/say to him? All I can remember is running away from him as he tried to pull me onto the beach and kiss him.

Had an interesting day today. Cycled into town. Went to the market (it's becoming a habit) then to the gym. Saw the old Swedish boy in the gym, thank goodness we both recognised each other. I'm still reading my German book, but feel I am going backwards half the time.

This afternoon, sunbathed (topless and bottomless – ooh matron) on my balcony.

Thought about SBP and how good it felt to NOT have him stopping me doing what I want to do, plus no smell of B.O. to put up with, which really made me fell sick. This afternoon, rang boss Hans-Peter – he'd asked if I was free to pop around to use their pool if I wanted, so I thought you should never turn down an invitation – I went around there. His son (form his first marriage) was there – corrrrr!! (Blimey Hans-Peter, you never told me you had a hunk of a son – wow, he's gorgeous, where did he come from?!) he's called Oli and asked if I wanted to go to see Pearl Harbour with him at the kino! (eek, jaw drop!) anyway, played badminton with him and Daniela and splashed around in the pool. It was really nice and relaxing. Had a glass of wine and then went into town to have a wander again – went to a really nice bar opposite the Münster and met a German lady who told me about Freiburg and an art exhibition in Reimen. I'll go to both. It's amazing what you find out when you

147

start asking questions...

The streets are lined with outside bars and the cafes stretch onto the pavements in every street. There's music, laughter, noise. It's really a great atmostphere and everyone's in joie de vivre mode – there's generally a great feeling. I can't believe anyone who would find this place boring.

Town was alive tonight, it's all starting now – felt like a ski resort (a lively one) in the main cinema street – good fun. Everyone's coming out now, it's all coming to life. Wow, quite an incredible atmostphere. Now I know where to take Steve next week (and everyone else...M? Will you pop over? I hope so).

Spotted a hedgehog on the drive tonight – he's massive. Would not move so I placed a white handkerchief around him so that any car will at least see that then avoid him.

Ooh, Lynn sent me a text message. She was at a BBQ tonight in London. Said the weather was good (damm!!) I sent one to say I was enjoying exploring and it was so hot here (26 degrees at 8.30pm!)

I've woken up – it's 04.45am on Sunday. The birds are singing – so much song, I can't believe, the air's clear and it's a blue blue sky again, although the sun's not quite up yet. Must try to get some sleep again.

Well, Sunday morning. Left at 9am and it took me 1.5 hours to reach Weggis and how beautiful it is too. Sat in a cafe overlooking my bike and the lake. Just decided to have eine expresso. There's a ferry about to depart. I've sussed out a restaurant to go to with Paul eg. next sunday – it's really beautiful overhanging the lake. The nice thing about Switzerland is that you can go to the public toilets not in fear of catching anything – they're always spotlessly clean. Met dozens of like minded cyclists (M would love it).

I'm enjoying my freedom at last! Have seen a couple of hotels. Andy would be quite comfortable in and a few I could afford. I was just thinking of when people retire what a great place this is to be – as long as you have a car, a bike, enough money to buy your food and go out now and again, to go to stay in some places and enough for a ski pass all season. And off the ferry goes again, taking its punters for a tow around the lake and back to Luzern. I'm now in Vertilan I think. There's a small train up the Rigi mountain but there's also a cable car from Weggis so I think I'll take that. I heard some English ladies in the public loos, talking about how many tablets they've taken and how one of their husband's (I assume) had really bad heartburn. Blah blah, why do English people always have to be ill.

The longer I am here, the more and more I find myself avoiding the Brits abroad (and yet I miss my friends at home very much) – why is that? It's almost hypocrosy and I've almost taken on this "elusive" ex-pat type of persona – perhaps it's just I don't want to mix with tourists, more people that actually live and work here – true Swiss too. Shame it didn't work out with SBP but I really feel he has a lot of growing up to do.

Well, took a break just outside Gesau. Wow, I can't believe this place. It's fab, found some steps going down to a grassy area – guided by the music. Bit frightened because 4 guys were down there pumping iron whilst a girl was sunbathing. Still, there was plenty of room for all of us, so I lay my towel on 1 side of the grassy area, opened my bag and looked at the water, which after 1 hour cycle in the high 20 degrees looked pretty tempting. So after standing around for about 15 mins, finally plucked up the courage and dived in. I guess the difference between this water and ... the Aegean sea around the cyclades, is that once you're in the latter, it really does not seem so bad after all, compared to this water which, once you're in, just seems to get colder. (I suppose it is fed directly from the mountains!) I swam out to a "floating island" which was just far enough to merit exercise whilst not being far enough to give me a cardiac arrest in the seemingly sub zero temperature! What a fantastic way to spend the day though – I think of what I could be doing in the uk. Well, horse riding, if the weather was ok, (otherwise it's very unpleasant). It would be about 1-1.5 hours away though, getting out of London traffic, so probably equal time away from here to Basel. Then I'd probably have gone to yoga if I was back in time – depending upon traffic. Would have discussed with Annie all our men problems, felt even more depressed and driven back to Battersea. I would have called Nina, Charlie, or Kate, to discuss more on men problems, gone for a drink possibly at Base on Batt rise, fluttered eyelashes, thought about M, and how I could possibly get him back, only to go to bed, perparing my bag for the morning's trek to the gym, to work, to sneering looks from Patrick, and cutting remarks, to feeling like I had a spear in my back all the time.

OK, I don't have Annie, Charlie, Kate or Patrick here and lunch is not at pizza metro on my road, but my water and cheese sandwiches taste pretty good, I'm getting some fresh air, some sun, some exercise. There's the odd boat passing, the odd ferry, the boys playing table tennis, volleyball and games machines in the background and overall a fairly relaxed feel.

I think I feel good.

This air, and space is doing me good. I haven't spent anything except petrol to get here with, and my coffee, then just the cheese and bread, which I would have bought anyway. The families are all out and about, wow, what a great place to bring up kids.

I think about my bike at the top of the steps. I know it will be ok. I think about my car back in Weggis. I am certain it will be fine too, it's an official parking place. There's a few more people on the lake now – I'm not the only mad one – and 1 guy's just dived from the top diving board, wowee, that's brave. Think I'll wait until I have a bit more bottle. It's strange when you think of why you're scared of diving into a place that's obvioulsy meant for swimming and diving. It's safe, nothing will stop you on your fall, I guess it's just you know it will be freezing and you think you may have a cardiac I suppose. But you know that the feeling afterwards is so worth it.

I'm waiting for one of those guys pumping iron to come up to me and ask me for money for being here – I can't believe this is free. I don't really mind paying, it's worth it – music, loos, showers, grass, diving boards, etc etc!

I'm about to leave my little bay/beach here in Gersau. It's been good fun.

As Mark Twain's memorial puts it – this is one of the most delightful places he'd ever lived in, I can believe it.

Chapter 14

Had a few strange dreams last night. Went to a fashion show with Sarah Smart, we could not sit together. I thought of Sarah and how I did not want to end up like her, being single at 36 with no boyfriend (and not having had a boyfriend for about 5 years). The thought frightens me a bit..why? because I value guy's friendship and I like to have a male companion. I also find it so much easier to get on with guys most of the time. Anyway, in my dream, we talked about men, relationships etc. M cropped up, she told me she thought I was very immature in relationships. Perhaps I am. Perhaps that's what M thinks, perhaps he thinks that my letters are immature. Yet Nikki thought it was good. I also dreamt I received 2 letters, 1 from the bank, 1 a little thicker – and I think from M – I didn't open it for fear it wasn't from him but somehow I knew it was and it was going to be a good letter ... I woke up.

I want a relationshio which, even when you're 70, every time you look at each other, you still feel that little squeeze in the pit of your stomach that makes you go crazy with excitement to be with that special somebody.

A husband, that you just felt still so passionately about.

It's another beautiful day.

Another beautiful sunset tonight. Had dinner on my balcony/terrace. I thought it was the underfloor heating but it must be the sun – the flags are still warm – it's rather lovely walking outside because your feet feel warm. The moon looks like it's almost melting into a midnight blue sky. The reds, pinks, which had previosuly spread across the sky are now at last far from view – it is as if a painter had just dripped his brush in the pink paint and swept it around me in the sky, in an almost perfect line, quite incredible.

Cycled in and out of work – v warm. Went to the gym tonight. My hayfever is really bad though – I'm not immune to Swiss pollen unfortunately. It's not worth me wearing mascara because I just end up looking like a panda the whole day. Cute, I don't think so. (At least I'm not quite so big and furry though).

Discovered that they don't have pennies here. I totalled something at 120.63CHF. apparantly it's all rounded up to the nearest "0" or "5". Just amazing, it's taken me how many months but eventually i find out!

Boss Hans-Peter's being finiskety about my expenses – my God, he's a bean counter (and how much has it cost me to move here I askmyself?) At least he's generous in other ways (letting me use his pool, his map etc etc). I took Janick out for a pizza and he asked whether we did that sort of thing in London (Why? Where's he been?!!) I'm confused, it's important, I mean, surefly the 2 times I've been for lunch with him, he's put it on the company Amex card, so he's done it. Talk about double standards. Dear God, where was I when the gravy train stopped at Gatley station to whisk me to school in Alderley Edge?

I woke up last night and felt really frightened.
I've not felt like that for a long time.
I felt scared.

Every noise was someone coming into my appartment, every creak was someone climbing the terrace to get in. I was rigid with fear in my bed yet I know this is Switzerland, the land where you can just leave your bike overnight unlocked knowing it will still be there in the morning (in fact I feel a little embarrassed when I do lock my bike, I feel like everyone's watching me in surprise). I wonder why I dreamt like that?

Yesterday I eventually made a transfer from my UBS account to my NatWest account. Today, I must make the payments. I really wish I didn't have all these credit cards to pay back. I just need to persevere and pay them back little by little, gradually and keep my head whilst it would be so easy to lose it.

It's so warm, phewwee. Divine. Had email from Kate

today – she feels down because it is a year ago she split from her boyfriend. I think I know how she feels. Perhaps I'll just send her a quick message, I know it's 10.41 our time, but it's only 9.41pm in the UK. Wonder why Theo hasn't called – he said he wanted to speak to me in the evening – yeah right, probably found some other girlie to try to drag off down the beach claiming "it's been 2 years since I've had a girl, she was my last girlfriend, from America etc etc". Yeah well, it doesn't pull my strings my friend. I'll drop him a line then let's see whether he responds or not.

Cleaned and swept the flat tonight, ready for Steve. I'd better walk on tip-toe until Friday now! Ooh, there's my mobile, Kate's sent a reply. Must get it.

Oh yes, had a weird telephone call today, at work, someone rang my direct line and asked for me. I said it was me. He said "No" he wanted to speak with Zoe. I said "Yes, that's me". He asked where he had called, that I'd sent him an SMS this morning. I explained that I hadn't even switched my mobile on today. (The only person I've given my work number to via sms is Marco and he always says hi in his deep and husky voice – it's a dead give away, and is very sexy). This guy was obviously Swiss – sounded like it. He asked if I spoke German. I said I was sorry, but no, only a little (in German). I offered to pass him to my colleague but he did not want to. He put the telephone down...

That only leaves SBP...weird?! And I'd expect him to do something like that too. Obsessive!

Bumped into Heinz on leaving the office (he's off all week now doing his military service – every boy in CH has to do 3 weeks worth over the age of 30. They choose between looking after old ladies or shooting the asses off each other on a driving range). Heinz chose the former. More his style. After all, this is the guy that gets woken at 2.30am (yes, in the morning) to have a discussion with his guru in Hawaii or wherever. (The mind boggles, but there again, he used to work for a guru in India for 4 years, until that one died, and he seems fairly happy with himself. Perhaps there is something to be said for it, it's a bit like

"Echinacea Werner" who's due to meet up with me this Monday and Steve – think he's quite a spiritual bod – seems nice enough but a bit deep for me – strange though, I feel I can talk to these guys about almost anything, well almost anything.

Wow, another beautiful day, I so wish someone was here to share it with me. Oh well, as JB said, just have a fantastic time while it lasts.

Really felt like writing to M again tonight but decided against it. Wrote a letter to Theo instead. What am I doing writing to a Greek guy I've met once?! Sent a text to Marco and then he telephoned me. We talked for ages, had a good chat. He's a cool devil though, he's so nice yet he has a great girlfriend (apparently) so I guess he just wants to play the field before deciding – do all guys, I guess so and so he should be above board. I don't want to be a second choice though, no matter how cool or handsome he is. He says he'll call me tomorrow. Well, we'll see about that – bet he's just feeling guilty that he's not called for ages and I sent him a text.

Had a meeting with Axel and Rita today. We were discussing the frequency of topless cars that are appearing in bBasel now – it's becoming the norm, de rigour. I feel ok though because I am just one of zillions driving about with my top off (oh yeah baby). Anyway, eventually we discussed work (Axel is so materialistic) after discussing our ideal soft tops – I said a sleek black SL3 soft top (they are very beautiful, classy, sexy and, have 4 seats). Axel (of course) would have a Boxster – yes, well that just about sums it up, he has just got to be an Aries/Pisces or even Aquarian, Leo, I don't know – he's just so oh so full of himself! He'd make an awful father – don't think he'll ever be one – God help the girl he marries – bet he's really argumentative at home, you can just tell (strange though, he has his "estranged girlfriend or wife" who lives in Luxemburg yet all the guys think he's gay).

155

Had a dream last night that there was a tremendous thunderstorm. Woke and the sky was bluer than blue skies, went back to sleep. Woke up when my alarm went off and it was thundering and lightening and pouring down. Bizarre day. Worked hard until about 10pm. Marco called me (and sent me a text). It's nice to see that someone's thinking of me.

Steve's here tomorrow. Managed to give myself a facial but too late for pedicure and manicure – will have to wait until next Tuesday night.

x

Monday 4th June – had the most fantastic dream last night. Guess why? Groan!! Dreamt I went to meet M and he just ran to me and I to him and we wrapped our arms around each other and were grinning from ear to ear and laughing.

Then, I had another dream. I dreamt that Steve and I went to the Sir Charles Napier for lunch one day. A beautiful day. We were led to a table outside. Walking through the restaurant I noticed M sat at a table "pour deux" with a girl – I thought may be his sister. I just walked past and tried to ignore them. We had our meal and later, I walked through the restaurant and M was walking in the opposite direction. He gave me a huge grin and exclaimed "Zoe" and I exclaimed "M" and we gave each other a massive hug. We walked around for a while on our own, then his lunch "date" appeared next to him and made some snidey remark. I said I'd better leave them to it, but M said "no". His partner wlalked off to.. wherever and he explained he was "just seeing her" but had no real feelings for her (she was a client, a divorcee, wanted a bit on the side). I thought of M making love to her – I was really upset. He took me to one sideand kissed me. He asked me why I was with a guy like Steve, so I explained that he's just come to visit me and that we weren't going out etc etc although what was it to him? He started to kiss me passionately. I told him that I loved him

156

and had missed him and he said "I can't believe you love me after all I've done and put you through?" but I said "I still love you M".

Eventually, we each made our way back to our respective tables and partners. Later the "train" (?!) arrived to take us back down the mountain (?!). I left something on it, so went back up, and it started to go back up. I shouted for help and shouted "stop". Eventually the train stopped. I offloaded all our things (Steve's and mine) that we'd forgotten and then went in search of anything M may have left on it too. Then the train started to go back down the hill without me on board. It was the last train. "Please" I shouted, "Stop", "I thought you were continuing up the hill". The train ground to a halt and I was taken back down. Paul was at the bottom and I told him how I've bumped into "The ex" I really had not got over. He was excited for me and wanted to know who he was etc etc. He was really pleased for me.

I woke up.

I wish M would come over to Switzerland.

Chapter 15

Well, that was the weekend with Steve – my first visitor! It was great to have some company and it was a fun weekend, although a couple of things he said at the end made me question his motives for coming over and I have to ensure that he knows he means nothing more than being a good mate to me. The awkward thing is that I'm off to Cornwall with him and his friends in a few weeks' time. It's going to be either heaven or...hell.

The Steve weekend:

Friday night was a laugh (though I hope no-one from Creatives Inc Zurich thought Steve and I were an item! I collected Steve from the airport – he'd taken the green line bus from Victoria to Luton airport and the Easy Jet from Luton to Zurich – I must tell M! Seems very simple, and cheap. We went to the Biergarten at the back of the theatre where Deva was having his leaving do. We then went to find a bar/restaurant just outside of zurich – an absolutely fabulous place overlooking the lake where Steve paid for dinner. The food was wonderful and the view ...wow, delicious! Expensive but definitely worth it.

In Zurich we caught up with "OK Ya" Tanya and her mate Indie. We had a laugh. They are quite outrageous together – typical Chelsea/Fulham type of girls in the heart of Schweizland. Tanya keeps telling me I have to "find my vibe" to hang around with, my own "lizards to lounge with" – I think it's the hip trendy designer speak she's into, blah blah blah...

Saturday, caught the tram into Basel, to check out the marklet (buy some provisions) and show Steve the sights. The rain started then, relentlessly to fall. We stopped for a hot choc at the tea shop in the square that I'd found – we had to move tables, away from the smokey atmostphere as a French guy took a huge drag on his huger than huge cigar.

(Reminded me of M saying he fancied a cigar after dinner in the restaurant – 'the fish with no tie' at clapham junction – how I enjoyed that evening, he'll never know, and he said how much he wanted to pay for the meal too. I felt like a lady, and very much in love).

Anyway, Saturday morning, we spent walking around Basel in the pouring rain, visiting a few shops (even C&A – I can't believe he came all this way to go into C&blooming A to look for a jacket). He could have gone to Stockport.

We left for Bern quite late, about 2.30pm, so by the time we got petrol (Steve also bought me a plant for my terrace which was sweet (died a couple of weeks later) etc, we arrived in Bern about 4pm, just when the shops were closing. At least we saw the river (remarkable blue, such a beautiful colour), the shops, the clock tower and we had a drink at the Kornhauskeller where SBP had taken me – it was great, full of young people – at last!!! Fun!!! We left and arrived back in Basel to have dinner at Des Artes – we had a lovely meal and even shocked all the swisslettes in the bar by cerocing – eek! How embarrassing but it was fun for the lady who owns the place – she really congratulated us afterwards. She said we had such "charisma" on our faces (mind you, a blank sheet of paper may have more charisma to it than some of the Swiss faces you see I suppose, who tend to hold one of 3 expressions...miserable, quite miserable or very miserable).

Sunday was OK, but still the rain was relentless. We went to Luzern, primarily to go up the Rigi mountain to see the view, to cycle around the lake and to swim in the sea and have lunch on the terrace at the lovely restaurant in Weggis.

The Rigi was out of the question – I wasn't going to pay 35CHF each to go up a mountain, not to be able to see anything in the rain and mist, knee deep in snow too – I wasn't exactly dressed for it unfortunately. The bike hire shop had closed by the time we arrived there. Lunch was inside instead of outside (but the food was good). We drove all the way around the lake – found an amazing little junk shop outside of Hergiswil (lots of old people walking about and British – a bit disconcerting!) (My boss later told me that Luzern is the "drain" of switzerland and therefore the wettest area – thanks for letting me know).

Sunday night, I just made a simple salad and we stayed in and drank champagne which was cool, to celebrate my first guest! I was a little worried when, at the end of the eveing, Steve hugged me and said "We got on really well together, we did, didn't we? We do, don't we? We get on really well. I'd like to go on holiday with you you know" and all that – oh shit, I thought, don't say he's decided to try it on with me. I quickly followed through with "yep, cool, let me know when you're going but I'm thinking of doing this that and the other too" (I don't really want to hang around with him all the time – I think the few days in Cornwall will probably be enough. I'm just not into him, how do I say that?).

Monday, a little brighter but still not so hot as it had been. We went to Fribourg (disaster)- no, actually it was ok, just well, very German...

Bother it, I may write to M tomorrow – if I'm back home in time...

I prefer Switzerland to Germany iI think – much prettier. It's amazing that somewhere so close is so very different. Germany's just so... well, functional.

Nothing in its description allows "pretty", "attractive", "beautiful" except for a few buildings (called Martinsgasse, Martinstum, Martin this that and the other – arghhhh! He's all over me!! – I wish ;)

Monday night, had a few trials and tribulations going through the border – think it's because I went through Germany and returned through France. (We went to Colmar for a drink after Germany – it's so pretty). Anyway, we arrived home about 600miles later – good job petrol's a little cheaper here!

Monday, cooked Spargel (fresh asparagus) and mushroom risotto (spent a fortune on fancy mushrooms – at least he appreciated them).

Tuesday, dropped off Steve at Basel SBB so he could explore Zurich for the day before flying back.

I conceded, Tuesday night, I wrote a letter to M and to SBP (a letter to say how shocked I was at a horrid email he sent to me at work, and how I felt. It's just I hate people depending upon me and I never depend on anyone and I think he did depend on me a lot and that's why I found him irritating). I only want to do lots of things together when we're crazy about each other (like I am about M – arghhhh!) Here I go again.

I also conceded and sent Brad an email – to which he responded Thursday morning. Urgh! He's so nice – he said he was sorry it had not worked out between us and that he guessed it was just a case of really bad timing. Oh well, I'll reply at some point.

Spoke to mum briefly (more than that depresses and upsets me). She always has a great knack of making me feel incredibly guilty – do all parents do that? I hope I don't do that to my kids when I have them.

Even my theory about the cows and the birds goes out of the window. The cows have disappeared totally and the birds carry on singing even though the rain continues to fall (I thought they only started whenthe rain stopped).

What is it about weather? It's funny, when you say you work abroad, everyone assumes automatically that the weather will be better than in the UK. So far, it's been pretty warm for 2 weeks but apart from that, March was very cold but dry, April, a wash out and so far June looks no better – can't believe it's 8th June and it's pouring down out there –

makes me feel even more homesick! Called Kate briefly tonight but she was out and about and in a taxi. Had a text from Steve – he's ok, harmless (I hope) but I'm just not too sure about guys and their true motives.

Sent Brad a reply today, I've been so busy at work that I didn't send it until late. Bet he's having the time of his life. Sometimes I wish I could just start again, walk away and start again, 9 years ago, before I'd met Andy, before I'd gone out with him for 8 years and spent more money than I should have done on outfits and hairstyles I couldn't afford. Now that I can, I'm paying back all the debts I've acrued to date. Only when I'm out of this mess can I be more confident and confident enough to choose who I want, when I want etc etc.

I think of JB. Funny, I had a meeting with my new client, Roberto, from Serene Pharma – he reminds me of JB quite a lot (same hair colour, and smile – ridiculous I know but that's what I fell for – as well as his eyes – Roberto's are not as nice as JB's). (Stop it, Zoe, I do NOT date clients, no way) I wonder if Robin will be at Ceroc when I'm back? Will he report to JB? Will JB pop down there? (no way).

It doesn't help because I'm playing the cd that JB bought for me for Xmas – Craig David – and stuffing my face with "Farmer Flocs" (but it tastes so good on its own) – don't ask, but it's a tasty cereal. Anyway, I think I deserve it – my stomach muscles ache for the 1st time in ages which is brilliant – it must mean I'm getting back to proper training.

I think of Annie – shame, she's never called or anything – funny when it all comes down to it – where is she when you want her? It was all – ooh, fantastic exciting, yes, I'll come over to see you, yes, we can meet in Milan etc etc. Now I'm here, 1 email and that was it. (Perhaps I'm a little harsh, people have their own lives to live and it's not been that long). I do feel a bit "dropped" by her though. I hope that Andrew hasn't said anything – he was always suggesting that she'd said a few cutting things about me when he talked to me, which I didn't want to believe,

162

although I hope to goodness Annie's not told him half the things I've confided in her – perhaps that's why she's never contacted me since either. They all seem 2-faced. Only those who have actually done it and lived abroad are the ones that are in contact – they've seen it, done it, hit the wall and gone through it, chewed at the tough bits and swam in the good bits and survived, and must know how it feels sometimes.

Like tonight, when the CD's finished and you're all alone and it's raining outside and you're wondering what to do over the weekend if the weather's bad and you're thinking of all your family and friends and wondering if they're thinking of you. You think of the letters you've written and wonder how long it will take for them to arrive at their destinations and whether they'll be gratefully received or, not.

I think of mum and wonder how ill she really is. This sounds so awful, I know, but because she was depressed all the time I was at school – my only memories of those years when I was 13-18 years old were of going home on cold, dark, wintry nights, with nothing but the outside street lamp to illuminate the house when I used my key and walked in through the front door and I called up to mum, hesitantly, so as not to make too much noise, and there was a soft murmur from upstairs. I could not make toomuch noise. Ever.

I crept upstairs, frightened of making a sound, a single noise but took with me a cup of coffee which I knew would always make her sit up in bed and at least talk to me, but sometimes even to expect that was just too much.

I used to hear the ice cream man play his soulful tune as he drove down the avenue – my one opportunity to yelp in delight and think of the taste of that delicious vanilla stretchy ice cream wrapping itself around my tongue and the raspberry ripple topping and sometimes, if mum felt flush, we'd treat ourselves to a 99 each, which meant a chocolate flake being perched on top of the cone – yum! If I was cheeky enough, I could sometimes persuade mum to give me hers too.

I used to wish she'd get up, I used to wish she was healthy, I used to creep upstairs with a tray full of dinner and the puddings that I became quite expert at making – jam pudding, syrup pudding and custard, banana pie, all with lashings of custard. I would do anything to try to cheer her up, to try to make her proud of me, and to think of me rather than Father who'd upt and left us all to this dismal, depressive life.

He took so much away from us. He took my trust in men away, my belief in myself, my belief that I can be happy with anyone but mysefl, my belief of anyone that said they loved me and meant it.

Yes, Father, you have a lot to answer for. And yet, yes, you made me stronger and gave me the resilience to stand on my own two feet, the independence and determination to never want to give up, to never depend on anyone, whatever. And then I grew up. I realised that I am just as fallible as the next man down the street, the beggar at Bahnhof SBB, the druggies in Covent Garden. And yet, I still love you.

I sometimes read and want someone to help me out, to support me, to smile at me and with me, to joke with me, to hug me, kiss me, to take care of me and control me..I miss M so much because for the first time in my life I felt that he really had this massive input on me, on all those things. Why does he wonder whether I like him so much? I often wonder and then I know, he knows actually and that's why he couldn't be bothered because it's too easy. If only I could tell him, he wouldn't listen though, he's too wrapped up in his own life now I suppose I'm sure, to think of little miserable me stuck out here in der schweiz. Too many squash matches, cycling events etc etc. I bet he thinks I'm here, out every night squandering my money away, buying all the desinger labels, eating at the fanciest restaurants etc etc, when in all reality I'm not, I'm just sat here on my new

(1. Seat Ikea cheap) sofa, thinking of him, when I try so hard not to, and writing this diary. I wonder whether I will ever have the guts to publish it. Perhaps I should change his name to protect him. There again, there's more than one M in the world (as Freiburg demonstrated).

Marco sent me a text message last night: "Are you feeling frisky?" I replied that "Yes, as frisky as a Swiss mountain goat". You gotta be joking, I've never felt less frisky, I don't think "frisky" appears in their language, knowing the laws of the land and toilet habits for men as I do now. (You know, coming to think of it, I never did hear SBP go to the toilet). And he always made some squeaky noises and closed the door to go to the bathroom – as if I was going to stand there and watch anyway – really! Yuk! Mind you my "anti-man toilet seat" (as M called it) would have come in useful here I guess! Perhaps I should just pretend M died somewhere along the lines, and then I just have the wonderful relationship memories, like Demi More and Patrick Swazee in Ghost. Mmm, whatever. Whatever it was between the two of us, it's not dead – it's been buried alive – and I find it weird that I still feel this sort of pang in my chest, I suppose where my "heart" must be, every time I think of him or his photograph (I've not looked at it for ages). Why?

Why god? When I spoke secretly to you when I was looking at his face that morning, looking right in his eyes, and I asked you to "never never let it end" then, was it then God that you told M to finish with me? Why why why? I've learnt a lot since, I've met some great and interesting people. I've 'been out with' (not necessarily seriously) 3 different guys, 4 if you include Michele, 5 if you include Theo, but I still have this pain, it's like a massive "thirst" in the pit of my stomach.

I sent him a letter yesterday morning. It wasn't that interesting, well, I didn't think so anyway, toned down compared to my last letter, but with a hint of wit and sarcasm in there (I've not quite lost it yet). I hope so much that he likes my letters and that he'll reply one day. I didn't mention I'd be over in the UK next week – I just want to surprise him. I'm not sure whether to turn up at his shop in Notting Hill. I'd love to (as I'm around the corner at the dentist's) but then I think perhaps I should leave it until Ceroc on Monday night and then run across the floor and snog him. (Well I'm only human) Well, maybe ok just give him a massive hug anyway..well, that's my dream. Oh well, God, if I go to his shop, if he's there that's the right thing, and if he's not, then it's the right thing to just surprise him at Ceroc. Please God, just do what the right thing is to do for me, please.

It's strange, perhaps I'd look like an idiot, traipsing through Notting hill with all my bags, but part of me just thinks, well, it doesn't matter if I can see M – strange, I've never really given much thought at all as to how dumb it must appear, yes, it seems quite ridiculous. Does it? Would he think I am stupid? After all, he knows my dentist is just around the corner (well about a 10 min cab ride away) so I have a sort of excuse for being in the neighbourhood. Gosh, I feel a bit like Andie McDowell in Notting Hill. I just wish it would end up like that too.

I had another weird dream last night too. I dreamt I was at M's mum and dad's and we were talking about Switzerland and they were planning to come over for a weekend. The memory of them was so vivid..thier house was in Gatley though, one of the larger bungalow houses opposite Gatley Hill. One that we nearly bought as a family all those years ago. I jusr wonder if we had moved there, whether it would have made a difference to mum and dad's marriage? Would daddy have stayed?

Well, the new plant that Steve bought me is getting another thorough watering this morning – the heavens are open and it's chucking it down. I want to cycle to the market and go to the gym too – I will, but I'll be very wet! Oh well, it's only the same as cycling to Covent Garden in the rain I guess. The birds are singing still, so my theory's definitely out of the window.

Chapter 16

One of the houses opposite have lit their fire! (It's 9th June) Yes, it's SBP's birthday today. I sent him a gift and a card (a bottle of L'eau d'Issey body shampoo), since he uses the aftershave. Deodorant would have been more appropriate, but I thought that was a little too close to home.
Perhaps he wouldn't know how to use it anyway either.

Oh I'm a bitch. Perhaps I should have done though and then he would have understood one of the key reasons I decided I couldn't go out with him anymore – should you tell people that? It's very personal. He wouldn't get it though until next week – he's bound to be at his parents (again) for the weekend – get a life SBP, they probably can't wait to try to get him "married off" so that he will let them have their space.
What happened to him, even his nephew (Berndt – I guess the swiss equivalent of Bernard) at 14 years old, seemed more grown up and had a girlfriend, Charlotte, whose parents ran a hotel in Interlaken.

Anyway, so much for hoping to look brown, healthy and tanned when I return to the UK next week – at the rate of this rainfall, I'll be whiter than I was even back home. I wonder if Jeremy's BBQ is still on tonight?

Now check this for a voice message:

"Hi gorgeous thing. Zoe darling, it's me, Tanya. I just lost you sweetheart, you must be in an area of low coverage. Ok, listen doll, tonight, let's do this, why don't I meet you somewhere up town that's easy to find. There's a hotel called the Beau du lac and it's just down the road from Parada Platz. OK, Ya. BBBEEAAU DUUU LAAAAC. That's B.E.A.U. then du, then lac. OK, now if that's too difficult then let's meet at, urgh, hello, Parada Platz or the ummm, the Savoy hotel, that's right by Parada platz, but it's actually easier for you in the car honestly, for you to meet me at the Beau du lac, it's so much easier doll. See how you feel sweetheart, call me on my mobile, but I figure we should meet at about 7.30ish, 7.45ish. we should be at Jeremy's at um, 8, whatever suits you. Call me on the mobile 079 466 2119. Byeeeeee".

Fab.

That was Tanya!

So, that evening, I drove to Zurich last night, managed to forget my map, so I managed to get well and truly lost.

Anyway, good ol' Tanya, came running towards me on Urania Strasse, so we actually and remarkably bumped into each other. We went to Jeremy's and had some fantastic food (although felt I had to eat the meat things as I'd forgotten to say I was vegetarian) So, had a burger, (mind you it was home made and jeremy's wife, Silvie, is from Singapore and is a great cook). A Swiss couple were there, not sure of their names (they had that sort of impact), the husband owns an ad agency in Zurich and was telling us about his daredevil driving and acrobatic flying (much to his wife's dismay). His wife, a very slight woman, was a radiologist but not very talkative. She made a great rhubarb tart though which I'll have to make for my next guests.

(I should have drawn a diagram at this point: the ruhbarb bits, custard middle bit, rhubarb tart was all symetrical and perfect as everything else here in Switzerland).

Also met a "Xavier", originally from Brussels, but working in "Silicon" something in Zurich. That fitted as he rolled up into Jeremy's driveway in his sporty little metallic blue porsche 911, with a grin the size of a watermelon (wow, what an ugly set of teeth he had!) Actually he looks a bit like a horse I thought.

Poor guy, no hard feelings, at least he was a bit of a laugh (unlike the Swiss who seem to keep their faces as straight as pins, even when they make a joke!) we also met Silvie and Jeremy's son, who was very sweet (although I didn't think so when he wlaked into the bathroom when I was on the loo). He was at an American school in Zurich and told us how he just didn't like the other students. Poor guy. I told him it wouldn't last forever so to try to make the most of it. (Who am I to tell the poor laddie?) Anyway, he seemed to buy it. We also met Frederick and Dominic from Singapore, although Freddie is a student of design in London. Dominic is a consultant in Singapore. They were quite fun – I now know what I miss here, smiling faces (they smiled all the time, it was a joy) and were so happy and enthusiastic, it was a pleasure.

We left at about 1am (urgh!) so back in bed at about 2.30am! Up at 9am this morning, as must go to my riding lesson with Herr Griger in Binningen (this should be interesting).

Had an awful dream last night, dreamt that someone noticed that I'd put on a lot of weight on my stomach when I went back to London. Argh!!! Feel a bit down as a result of this dream ☹.

OK, after my riding lesson, me, my car, my bike and I went in search of the sun but I think the rain's followed us here – arrived at Neuchatel and it's still pouring, after a few breaks in the cloud along the way. The relentless rain.

Had a great lesson with Herr whatever this morning – he was really good. Strict but good. Ends up his mother in law is from Edinburgh, so he lived there for 18 years and knows Newcastle (?). It was quite good, with the odd little "wee" dropped into the conversation, in a Swiss-German accent. His wife works at Chameleon although I couldn't make out which department (I think it's too rude to keep saying "Wie bitte?" or "Pardon" so I just nod and say "Ya ya"). Anyway, he taught me how to saddle up, put on the bridle – gosh, I hope I remember by next Wednesday night, my next lesson. I've forgotten so much from Radnage As he seems very strict, even when old Sydney (the stallion I rode) dumped in the corner of the "tacking up area", he was there, quick as a rat up a drainpipe, with a brush and a shovel. He told me where his barrow and brush were kept and advised me that he expected his pupils to look after their horses. He looked at my feet. I blushed with embarrassment, I hadn't managed to clean them since my last ride with Annie in either Guildford or way back when, on that very wet day in Windsor Great Park in February, so my boots and chaps were absolutley filthy; and I didn't have time this morning – all my best plans went to pot as I overslept. I told a white lie, to say I'd been walking in them in the mud yesterday and that I hadn't managed to clean them. He accepted with a tut. (I felt really bad and asked if he'd prefer me to wash them first, admitting my cardinal sin and looking at Sydney, immaculately washed and groomed standing alert in front of me, and seeming also to be tutting looking at my grubby boots). I was worried and sudden visions of headlines within the "Basler Zeitung" hit me: "British Girl infects Basel stable with Foot and Mouth. Sydney really ill" and being sent to the gestapo to be shot.

For a moment, I thought Herr G would ask me politely to take myself and my grubvby little boots back to the UK and threaten poor Switzerland (with it's picture box houses and fields) with the dreaded F&M words. (I am an ec-terrorist I thought).

Anyway, we began the lesson, he with his Clipboard, and lunge tethered to Syd's bridle. He told me first to walk around the arena and to "introduce" myself to Syders, to tell him a "wee" story about myself. I managed to introduce myself "Hi Sydney matey, I'm Zoe and I'm from London" before the Herr told me that "halte" meant stop, "On pas" walk, and "Allez" for "go" (gosh I thought, even the horses are multilingual, now doesn't that put us brits to absolute shame. And our ponies). It was only later that I thought, hmm, that was actually a fairly brave thing to do, to go to a riding school in a foreign country, when I didn't even know how much English they would speak – the horses let alone the instructors. Am I stupid or what. Still, it was an experience and I really did enjoy it, he taught me how to trot properly while sitting with one hand , to stand, to canter, to bend my back, to stick out my bum, to adjust my feet in the stirrups, the measure the stirrups with my arms, and that the outside leg should be just behind the middle part of the saddle on cantering with the inside one working the horse and pushing him on.

Herr G calls me Mrs Phillips, despite me telling him funf hundert times that it's "Miss". He says it's better for him with a "wee" grin. (?! He's about 70 years old and 4 foot high, who does he think he is?!)

Silvia made a good point last night, even though the natives think they pay a large amount for their appartments (with lake and mountain veiw) she siad it's so important when you live somewhere to find somewhere with a view that sums up everything to you about that country and if you find somewhere like that, then you will always remember a place how you want to remember it. So true.

What else, well how to hold the horses head by pushing on his neck whilst holding the rein high with the other hand, it felt quite stable. How I should press on the horses neck to climb on, not the saddle, how to support my own weight by moving my right leg over the neck, sitting sideways, turning around and swinging my right leg over his bottom to sit back on again. (I failed with the left leg and my arms gave way, I just had to fall off) and all this within half an hour's lesson!
He taught me the proper way to move the horse – rein in left hand, push the neck to the right and move the horse. Never go behind him, to keep my left arm in the rein as I sorted out the saddle etc. (Gosh, I hope I remember where everything goes on Wed night).
He showed me how I should always clean Syd's stall of "apples" (i.e. small round lumps of shit) before taking him in – so he would not get his feet dirty, or me, mine. I picked his hooves – again, I did that wrong so Herr G showed me how to do it.

Anyway, here we are in Neuchatel. I think I'll get on my bike and have a quick cycle around. I must ring Sabina too, to check on tonight's plans. Steve's just called. I feel a bit guilty, he's offered me a room next weekend. I would rather stay at Kate's but Kate's not come back to me and I felt like she wanted to get rid of me last Friday night. I'm sure that's not the case. People have their own lives, just like me.

My brain feels like exploding sometimes, there's so many things I want to write down and put in you, diary, before I forget. Tonight, had a really lovely evening – just managed to get back in time to go to the theatre with Sabina and her boyfriend (gosh, I can never remember his name). We went to see a fab ballet production in Birsfelden, just north of Basel city. It was amazing, and I feel so stimulated and motivated to dance when I see them. Then we had a drink afterwards in the Ritzy bar at the theatre then they took me for a pizza. It was cool. Great evening actually to what started as a really boring potential weekend. We chatted – I discovered I have been cycling around illegally after all – it wasn't a joke when Laurence told me that I needed a licence to drive my push bike! I really do need a licence for my bike! Sabina's just been caught without one and fined 120CHF!! That's more than a motorway speeding ticket in the UK!! Apparently, I must buy one from Migros (of course, where else?!) for about 5CHF – that's another £2 urgh!

I found a botanical garden in Neuchatel today. Started to cycle into town and saw a sign to it, so just followed it – didn't realise it was at the top of some mountainous hill. Still, it was a good workout and an easy cycle down. It stopped raining too whilst I was there, so that was good.

Why couldn't the weekend be as nice as it is this morning? Monday, another week, but a short week – holiday from Thursday night.

Oh no, I had a letter from Steve tonight delivered to my letterbox. Urgh, I think I was right. He mentions in it that we got along so well and seemed to have lots in common, blah blah and one day might end up falling madly deeply and passionately in love with each other (urgh, yuk, I'm sorry but please. Please God, get M to call me for goodness sake). I mean, Steve's a nice enough guy but he's just not my type whatsoever. I don't even the slightest bit fancy his little finger. He's about as exciting as a cream cracker. I thought he was a friend. He's just a typical guy, fancying his chances. Well, I'm sorry, but what gives them the authority to even think it? The very thought of him disgusts me, I look at my photos of M, of Michele, the thoughts of Theo. No, I'm sorry Steve, I'm going to head South this summer on my own if M doesn't come up trumps, for some serious fun with some Latino lovers.

I feel awful now because I've just accepted his offer too, to stay at his flat next Friday, Monday and Tuesday. Oh God, please help me.

A full day today at work, but managed to escape by about 6.30pm, to get down to the gym. A few people recognised me now and say "Gruezi" (Hi) which is nice. It's really a different feeling in the gym here, they seriously train. It's not just pumping out like most people do in the UK. Here they seriously go for it – all shapes and sizes and all ages, most of all the oldies, I can't believe it, it's like a scene from "Cocoon" when they're all alive and smiling after 150 years and in tip-top shape. I feel my waist staring to shift which is good, I thought I was starting to lose it.

Tried to call Paula tonight but my phone cut out. 0.00 CHF left. So I will have to buy yet another credit tomorrow – damm, it's like water going down the drain. Of course she didn't call back. Too expensive you see, that's the problem with my family, cost comes before thought. I'm desperate to talk to someone here Mum, too, but will you call…no. Never. (well, twice since I've been here for the last few moth, over the last week, because she's been ill so needed some (more) sympathy).

I started packing for my trip home. Of course, first I need to think of what I could wear at Ceroc (to impress M –

pleeeease, Saffron, do your stuff tonight and tell M he simply HAS to be there next week, he simply must). I want to pop in on him so much in Notting Hill in his shop but I've a feeling I may feel and look dreadful (what with going to the dentists and before going to the hairdresser's). Oh well, if he's not meant to see me, he won't be there.

Gosh it's a good job I started packing tonight. I am trying to find the outfit I want to wear to Ascot but it's not there. Now I feel helpless. I'm trying to rack my brains as to where on earth it could be. Could I have left it at the dry cleaners? Surely not. I'm usually really careful about things like that, especially my fav outfits. It's funny though that I can't find that, a blue and white stripey jumper and some white linen trousers. Oh well, I'll have another look in the morning – maybe I missed it. (Why should a piece of material wind me up so much? How sad am I?!)

I called Marco tonight, he was in Bilbao in Spain, on business. Really felt like the big brush off although he said he would meet up for lunch next Wednesday. Mmm. One moment, as hot as rocks, the next, cold as a cucumber. Can't make him out. Oh well.

Theo left 2 messages on my mobile. He's received my letter and was obviously delighted. "Hello sweetheart. I receive your beautiful letter and now watch your photograph all the time. I would like to speak with you. Theo, Greece". A few mmms and stutters- obviously the English translation. He seemed quite sweet and keen – Tanya asked me how I manage to get so many boyfriends – perhaps I should be more choosy, like her…

Well, I didn't sleep last night because I still kept wondering where my suit is. In addition to that, there's my blue and white stripey T-shirt coming to think about it, my olive jumper and trouser set, so that just leaves the other bits and pieces. I telephoned Pickford's. They confirmed that they had sent and delivered 38 out of 38 boxes (it's a problem though, because as they pack things, they just put them straight into the van, box by box and you are so busy fetching cups of tea for them, making sure they're OK, that you cannot possibly count them as well. You just trust them..Oh, what am I saying? I'm sure they'll turn up. I have a fall back plan if the worst comes to the worst – either that or, I'll go shopping in Jigsaw.

Moral in the story: Try to count the number of boxes packed by removal vans.

OK, so Marco phoned me tonight – apologised that he didn't call me back last night (sweet – why is he so concerned?) I said "Hi". He responded "Hello, cool!" I said "Hello oh moutain goat" OK so he's still talking to me. He says he'll call tomorrow, before I leave and is looking forward to lunch on 20th, "when you can fit me in".

(I managed to scrounge another notebook from Bea at the office, so the saga continues).

Wrote a letter to M tonight (Wed 6th June – the night before voting day in the UK and I've gone and forgotten to organise my postal vote. Emily pankhurst will turn in her grave):

Dear M

Something tells me there may just be a letter hiding within your jacket pocket, just waiting for that right moment to be popped right into that London postbax on Queenstown Road, to wing it's way to Schweiz land. Mmm, I could be wrong – in which case, I enclose some useful info on how to write to me! (am I pushing my luck a bit far here? Sorry, I'm only kidding). I'd love to hear from you though, and hear all about your escapades etc etc – Chelsea flower show, footie, whatever, squash matches – only the ones you win! Your brain, your teeth etc etc. anything! I can't understand much of what s delivered through the letterbox so all letters are gratefully received. I hope yxou don't mind my letters either, hope they're not too boring etc etc.

What have I been up to…went to Bern a couple of times – really quite a beautiful town. Have you ever been there? This weekend my first visitor is arriving, 1 of my friends, I can't wait, 1st time to play hostess with the mostest (well of some things anyway). We may go swimming in the river if it's warm enough, the river is so blue, almost turquoise. It's amazing, it's beautiful.

I've been simming in one of the lakes near Interlaken – the Brienz – which is fed directly from the mountains, so it's pretty cold! (It's where I understand the dreadful accident happened a couple of years ago with the Australian canyoners). Last weekend, stuck for what to do, so drove down to Luzern = very pretty. Took my bike too and cycled for a leisurely 25km before deciding it was too hot, so found a great little place by the lakeside with people, music, and a place to dive in, an island to swim to etc etc. I must admit, I stood at the side of the lake for about 10 mins contemplating whether to take the plunge or not, contemplating why no-one else was in the water before I thought I must look foolish so I either had to go or not. I decided to go for it and in true British stiff upper lip manner took the plunge (I don't think the swiss could believe their eyes – one came running to the edge shouting "baywatch baywatch" with one of those rubber thingys tucked under his arm – really! I must admit though, when I surfaced I felt this little squeal come out of my mouth – that and a bit of laughter as I laughed to myself – either that or you'd cry with the pain of the temperature! It was pretty cold, but exhilarating. I swam to the "island". Funny, it felt really cold when I climbed on board it – my whole body really felt reduced in temperature (whereas you sort of get used to the sea temperatures in Greece/the Med/etc. It's strange here it just seems to get colder under the surface, with a little warmer layer at the top). Bizarre, still, it's nice and clean and must be ok because it's straight from the mountain (which still have snow on their peaks as it was later pointed out to me!). I discovered a wonderful little restaurant which overhangs the lake – really beautiful, so I've booked a table for this Sunday.

OK; so I sent my letter to M tonight.

Moral in the story: If you feel like writing, write and be yourself.

Oh yes, had my 2nd riding lesson tonight with the Herr at the stables. Fab again, I feel I'm really learning a lot – a.lot more than I would have done in Oxforshire, although perhaps it's just a different sort of teaching. Marcus drilled so much into us at Radnage and most has stuck. At least I can thank him for feeling so confident on a horse now, compared to 18months ago. It's strange to talk German and then French commands to them though, "Halte" for stop, "On pas" for walk and "Allez" for let's get moving dobbin! I rode "Spider" tonight. We were trotting around the school for at least 1.5 hours. Herr does a lot of shouting (in German, fortunately, so it does go in one ear and out the other for me). I met a girl and her boyfriend – they seemed really nice and askede if I wanted to go for a drink with them in a couple of weeks, once they're back from holidays – they're off to Lanzarote tomorrow.
    It was a lovely evening.

    I feel I'm getting to know this place more and more and making the most of it. I'm becoming more settled, more confident and more contented with what I've got, and London's calling – only 2 days away and I'll be there. Wonder what it will feel like – it feels like I've been gone for ages and ages and ages and...
    Wow, Thursday, a beautiful day, yet again, blue blue skies – wish I could sunbathe all day to impress everyone at home at how healthy I look ;) (despite not sleeping too well for the past few nights, feeling sad, stressed, working more hours than God intended I'm sure etc etc).
    It's going to be an early start tomorrow, so I'd better put my head down. After 2 nights of not sleeping very much too

I should feel more tired than I do. Sent Brad an sms to see if he wants to catch up tomorrow, so he's suggested I call him once I know what I'm up to. No news from Marco, and I have to switch off the mobile.

Chapter 17

Inspiration is the main cause of success.
A Compaq ad at basel flughafen, June 2001

Well, an early start indeed after not much sleep again. Think I've inherited Mum's "nervous system" Damm. (I think Mum stresses me too. Also I have such a packed agenda). However I managed to fall into a deep deep sleep eventually and to dream of horses, beaches, laughter, friends, skiing, sailing, swimming, flying. So, here we go, the safety presentation for the 1.25 hour journey home.

Well, here we are, touchdown in Heathrow and at once I notice the variety of tail fins and HSBC ads everywhere. Bizarre! So this is my home yet I don't know how I feel, where's all the excitement from last night? Still there but I don't know whether I feel happy or sad, or just … alone.

Sat pm, exciting. I arrived at Steve and Sarah's flat a little later than expected on Friday morning even though the route was remarkably smooth. Left Heathrow on the Piccadily line, changed to the Victoria line at green park, then headed south on the northern line to my destination at Clapham south. Let myself in, following Steve's instructions (key for back gate under bricks, behind back gate, code for alarm under large pile of bricks behind front gate). (We've just had a train announcement here on thew train as we're leaving Euston, in that dreadful rural Mancunian accent – greeted by that dink dink dink tune to introduce him – why oh why do they have that silly music sound? And the strange thing is, it's international – they even have that little introductory music in Switzerland too). (I had booked a seat on this train, but looking across at Coach D, seat 49B, I'd rather not be sat across for the 2 old blokes who incessantly chat in their broad accents, reading "rail" magazine – and was that an "anorak" mag too.

Stuffing their faces with cherries – oh they're so round and plump and sexual darrrling" they purr to each other – actually filled me with horror when half the train is empty anyway, so I'm sat here, where it's just me and the window, my books and magazines and I'm going home to Mum like the prodigal daughter. I just found it annoying.

Anyway, yes, where was I?.. Mm, Steve's flat. Then I made a quick call to him to say that "I was in" and in my best "Sean Connery accent: "The code is broken, where's the safe, we have 30 seconds" Actually, I felt a little like Catherine Zeta Jones in 'Entrapment' (as I said in my email following his instructions, perhaps it would have been more appropriate for me to wear a black sock over my head). The guys oppositeare quiet now, really into their "rail" mags – probably playing footsie under the table.

Anyway, after dumping off my luggage at Steve's, finding my umbrella (because Britain wouldn't be British without it chucking it down as it was when I arrived), I ran back to Clapham south tube station, to catch the tube to Bayswater, to my Dentist. I was 1 hour late for my appointment, but she was fab, still could see me, gave my an xray and cleaned and polished my teeth. Afterwards I went to Space NK to stock up on potions and lotions and then I thought"oh fuck it", I'm going to catch a cab and see if M was around at his shop – you know you want to Zoe and would regret it if you didn't even try. (Please God, I muttered, if it'smeant to be then let him be there, if it's not, it's not and he won't be there). In my heart of hearts I yearned for the fact that he'd be there sat drawing behind his desk.

I asked the taxi to drop me off a couple of blocks down the Ladbroke Road, so as not to make it look like I'd made any special effort to catch a cab, etc etc. Besides, the rain had stopped, I'd applied some lipstick and mascara at the dentists – in their toilet, and popped in my contact lenses too. I didn't feel the best – actually, felt quite knackered after such little sleep and an early start and an early morning, but I wanted to see him so much, to just give him such a massive hug……

My ears are popping, big tunnel, almost as big as the Swiss tunnels but the scenary, and houses on the other side are not quite so pretty as in der schweiz.

……."going somewhere nice?" enquired the cabi as I was getting out. "only to see the man of my dreams" was my reply. "ah, you don't want him to see you get out of the cab do you?" he added. He'd sussed me, we both laughed, heartedly – mind you I had asked for Lancaster Road and then stopped him en route to say "just here will do nicely thanks". "I want to surprise him" I said "He doesn't know I'm here". "Oh you're just off work then?" the cabio further enquired. "No, just back from Switzerland" I replied. We both smiled, I paid him (taxis are so cheap here compared to Switzerland) and he wished me well and hoped he'd be there for me.

I walked slowly and pensively up Ladbroke Road, catching a glimpse of myself in the odd window just to check my hair was ok, lipstick had not smudged etc etc. I crossed over the road. "OK, here we go, Lancaster Road" I breathed to myself.

My heart was pounding with excitement or was it nerves (I never felt I would feel like this).

My head was spinning with thoughs. I just wanted to rush up to him so much. But then, …what if he was dashing off somewhere. What if a friend was meeting him for lunch. He always used to take Friday afternoons off, what if he'd left and I'd be left heartbroken on their front step. What if he had to be somewhere and hadn't got much time (I know after all what I'm like). But I just felt so happy to be there and yet so sick with worry.

Why do I still feel like this?

After so long, nearly 2 years?

I felt so nervous, so excited.

So, so, all at once…

I turned the corner into Lancaster Road and recognised his shop right away, his street, eek, this was it. Would he be there? What would he think when he saw me? "Oh great?"

"Oh shit?" "what the hell is she doing here?" "I wish she'd get the message""I hate her"…etc etc, the demons were running wild in my mind. I don't know then what inside me made me but I just smiled to myself, switched off those demons, whispered "hey ho, here we go with Zo", took a massive deep breath and walked into the shop.

An assistant was standing behind the desk. She smiled at me. Last time I was here that assistant was Juliet his sister, (that's another story so funny, so bizzare) but not this time. I didn't recognise her. I asked sheepishly if M was in at all and she just smiled and said "Yeas, sure, just head down to the conservatory, you'll see him on the left".

Shit shit and shit. Iit felt more difficult than getting into Steve's flat and messing up the alarm system. My head was spinning. I wondered what I looked like, there was no going back now, after all he could just pop out himself and see me standing there."Keep calm, keep calm, stay calm" I whispered to myself. I thought of everything that my squash coach and Lee, my shiatsu masseur had taught me, "Breathe breathe" their voices echoed, don't panic, breathe deeply.

I spotted his boss, Tony "Shh" I indeicated with my finger over my lips and then smiled at him, I pointed to the conservatory to where I could hear M's voice on the telephone. I could not see him yet, he could not see me. Tony smiled at me and said "ok, ok" I heard M put the receiver down, so, bravely, I took a step forward all the while thinking "What am I doing here? this is the man I love with all my heart, does he know it? Does he realise? Does he care? This is the man I want to marry". My heart felt suddenly warm, and suddenly I felt, fuck it, this is the right thing to do".

I strode into the conservatory, where he was sitting behind his computer. He looked up. I looked at him and I grinned from ear to ear. He looked down at something he was writing. He looked up, he looked down again, he looked up and with a gobsmacked expression exclaimed "Zoe" and then "what are you doing here?!how good to see you!" I really didn't know what to say, I just said "hi" and "how are you" and "just thought I would pop in" and "it's great to see you" and and he stood up, walked around his desk and opened his arms.

Naturally, I stepped into them and we kissed each other on each cheek – God he's so calm I thought. At this point I felt like screaming, like choking, like crying, laughing, coming all at once in some sudden euphoria! My mind was all over the place. I still loved him with all my heart, I looked at his eyes, I still loved them. I looked at his smile, I still loved it, it strill made my knees buckle and my insides yelp like a puppy dog with excitement. I wished and yearned so much that he felt the same about me, about my eyes, my smile, (with my newly sparkling teeth).

"I, errr, just flew in this morning, just had a dental appointment, thought I'd surprise you" I said, "well you certainly did that "he replied "but look, look" he said, and waved the piece of paper he'd been looking at on his desk. "it's a letter for you" he exclaimed "so there you go, you may as well have it". "No" I retorted "send it anyway, you lazy so and so, buy a stamp. I'm bored of just getting German newspapers in the letterbox" (my mind was thinking, besides, that will be another day I can feel his thoughts, as if he were talking to me right now, I can spread him out to last longer. I don't just want it to be this afternoon's chance encounter). I wanted to shout "I love you I love you I love you" from somewhere but fortunately, sense prevaled and this was not the time or the place to say such words.(I'm certain I would have been locked away).

We laughed, we chatted some more, about life and love and things in der schwiez and things back here at home. Gosh, I was just so nervous and excited, I felt I couldn't speak properly, I was just freezing, and sweating simultaneously on the chair in front of him, I made silly sudden movements, but I just couldn't help it, I'd worked myself up for this so much sub-consciously, I thought I was prepared so much but it never works out that way. He was just so....arghh! cool that's part of what I loved about him, his ability to make me feel so calm, to be so cool, calm and collected. Yes, that's why I love him so much.

We stepped outside into the brilliant sunshine (although I'd taken my favourite cardi with me, I didn't wear it as it was too warm, but I just had on my small lilac jigsaw top – not the most sexiest of tops, but then that's the way I wanted it to be, after all, I thought, if you love someone, they've got to see you glamorous as well as warts and all one day!) I didn't think I looked too bad though (however he commented on my Swiss "mountain boots" which I then told him I'd bought in Meribel, France, but which are a bit Swiss looking I guessed, but comfortable.

Oh, yes, he spotted my "Birdsong" book, by Sebastoan Falkes. He said he'd just finished it and exclaimed at how good it was, especially the "passion" bits. I agreed, "Yes" I said, it was a fantastic book, very moving.

We walked down the road to a little eating place he knew of on Portabello road, a little Italian, which was buzzing and sold pastas, and salads, hot and cold, and seemed just a really perfect place to just have a bite. He showed me the score and I said I'd have a salad. He said he couldn't possibly have that as he opted for the fried meat, 2 types of pasta and together with a portion of vegetables. I explained that I was going to my friend's birthday party tonight and we were going to have pizza, so I didn't want too much. The waitress offered me some Italian dressing, but I declined. He had coke, I had water and he apologised "I'm so sorry" he exclaimed "I've only got a fiva as I didn't anticipate going out for lunch". "Don't worry "I replied"I'll buy, after all, I've dragged you out and surprised you." He laughed and said he'd grab a table then, so he found a little table against the wall.

(I've decided to tuck into my "granary torpedo" here on the train, rgh, the bread here is so awful compared to swiss bread).

Anyway, we talked and chatted, chatted and talked. I asked how his work was going and whether it was better

184

now. (They hadn't been to Chelsea Flower Show this year as it would have cost £30K for the stand alone – extortion). He asked how everything was going, and excalaimed at how exciting it must be. I told him as much as I could, hoping that I wasn't repeating myself too much from my letters.

There seemed so much to say but I didn't know how to say it, what to say, when to say it. I felt like I'd forgotten lots. There was so much I wanted to tell him, to share with him. He asked my advice about marketing and advertising his company, I was really amazed and flattered that he'd asked me. I told him I ought to write a book for people who are thinking of moving abroad. He said I should do. It sounded like a good idea (as I told him of my trials and tribulations of moving).

I told him all I was up to for the week. I told him I was going to Cornwall from Wednesday until Sunday. He asked where, so I said, Rock – I was so glad of Steve and of Friends and of being able to say that I was doing something interesting. He said he'd been there, so I asked him what it was like.

Oh yes, someone's driven into his car too and the car was almost a write off. He told me he was off to a Greek island, a surfing centre, in August, with Joel and Paul, Paul's brother and his girlfriend (good, not his own girlfriend, I thought to myself silently).

I related our experiences in Paros, said that we girls had met the guy that ran the surf centre there (sorry, Theo, it's most disrespectful of the way we actually did meet) and that he said he'd teach us. "Yeah right, I bet he did" was M's reply. "Yes, yes" I said, "and I also mentioned that if he had been 5 foot taller and 20 years youngere I may be interested". We both laughed heartedly. He asked about the friends I'd made. He asked about Swiss guys. I nearly landed myself in it, but just mentioned that I'd made buddies with some Swiss guys in Interlaken but that they were getting a bit "fresh" and I didn't really fancy them, so ran off. I told him that they seemed to have this "valley mentality", still living with their parents at 37 years old (which was not strictly far from the truth hey SBP. I know you lived with your parents Friday until Monday every weekend). I mentioned that I'd had dinner at their house a couple of times and hung around with the 2 brothers (ish), but we did have dinner with SBP's nephew once – and we skied with his mate a couple of times and he does have a brother so again, sorry God for stretching the truth here, but it wasn't far from the truth. I said I couldn't understand a word his parents said half the time, so he laughed and said "Their parents were probably arguing over which one would marry you."

(The inspector's just come down the train. There's hope yet – he said I should check my next credit card bill when it arrives as I should have only paid 50% for the ticket. He was a really friendly chap. How good of him. A shame not everyone in Britain is the same!)

M and I talked about my sailing weekend which was great I said, but one of the guys had written to me to say that we thought we had a lot in common and therefore perhaps fall madly and passionately in love with each other. He laughed and said "urgh" and so did I! We had a great giggle. (It was Steve's letter, sorry Steve, I know it was after you'd been to see me too, here in Basel). I told M that I sent an email to Steve to say that I'd rather just be great mates. He exclaimed "what, you sent that to him?!" "yes of course" I said, "I don't even like the guy" (I should have used my cream cracker comparison).

M's doing his triathalon in Windsor this weekend – it's his 3rd year he's doing it – he wants to beat Paul this time, so he's been training hard for it.

We laughed, joked, exclaimed, talked, discussed, tapped and touched each other on the arm. I enjoyed it a lot, I hope he did too. He asked how my Mum was. I explained that she'd not been too well but I was hoping it was not serious, hoping it was not "pining" or "munchausen's syndrome" type of self inflicted misery type of illness. I asked him how his Mum and dDad were (I could picture his Mum, Carol-Ann, she was so cool, great, I really really liked her; and his

Dad, Jonathan, aka John Major – the same specs and conservative look, yet in his own way totally endearing. I always remember the watermelon incident when I went to meet them in Hampshire – his Mum brought out some ginger to sprinkle on the watermelon she'd served and his Dad (perhaps rather too) generously sprinkled it over the melon. He then ate and began to cough uncontrollably – as the ginger dust had obviously caught his breath. "Oh Jon, for God's sake" his mum had exclaimed. I smiled, everyone was pretending they hadn't noticed. I was so glad she said it, because that sort of gave us all permission to laugh, and we all laughed so much and at once, the atmostphere was relaxed and great fun.

His Mum is now working in a gallery in Southampton – he suggested she put up a few paintings of his (wow, I'd forgotten he painted) and his father is going to fully retire at the end of August – he'd been working a 3-day week. I asked about Julie, Russ and little Sam. He said they were fine, that they were popping over in July and were in Greece on holiday at the moment. He said he'd love to see them and see more of Sam (such a great name) (ah, poor little mite was crushed a little in the womb, his arms and legs are so long – yeah, wonder where he gets that from?! – so he's wearing a cast on his foot for a few months, to try to straighten out his foot). He showed me a photo of him, and the one that's a screen saver on his computer. He's so so cute, blonde – like M's mum – and with the gorgeous M nose – M said "yes, he's got the family nose", I agreed and said, "Yes, it's your nose alright!" I exclaimed at how lovely, cute etc etc he was, because he was, because most babies are. He had lovely eyes too and really long fingers "He's going to be an artist like his uncle" I remarked pointing out his long fingers.

(God, what are the train spotting guys eating now? They've a bowl of split peas in front of them. It's a proper little glass bowl they've obviously brought with them specially. Bizarre, and they're very close to one another, it's a bit public).

I told M I missed Tim and Beth but that I was hoping to see them this weekend, but that because it is Father's day, they'd organised something for Mick "oh, thanks" he said, and scribbled down "Father's day". "I must get a card" he said and smiled at me.

We chatted some more and laughed and laughed. He made me a cup of tea, I bought a few things from the shop, oh and they gave me this little dog (because they're selling the retail arm of the company to some interior design woman, so they're getting rid of a lot of stock). This little brush dog was pretty ugly but he was all lost and forlorn. I think I will call him Brutus, because he's such an ugly brute, and I've already thought of sending M a photo of him together with Swiss St Bernard "Robbie" on my balcony perhaps with sunglasses on, on a beach towel. Yes, that would be funny. (Sometimes, I wish my brain would just die, it thinks of so many ideas all the time and of M).

I looked at my watch, yikes, 2.15pm, I had a hair appointment at 3pm. "oh dear, I'd better let you get on. I'm off to the hairdresser's. What do you think, should I get it all shaved off?" (Inuendo innuendo). We laughed (gosh, I rememberd his exclamation at my "naked puss" when we first made love) I was a bit slow there, I should have made a funny comment.

He said Joel was down in cornwall at the moment, raising money and doing the coastal cycle ride, so he said he'd call him and see if he was around there when I was down there. I said that would be great, I wished he would be there, I was feeling a tad anxious about the few days dwon there spent with people I hardly knew and with a guy who'd fallen for me just before I had left Switzerland to join him for his Cornish holiday.

I said I'd probably be at Ceroc on Monday night to see everyone there. He said he'd been to the competition, just to enjoy it, not to compete. I said that was the part of the day that I really enjoyed last year.

When I'd gathered my bits and pieces together, he came around the desk again and we hiugged and kissed, kissed and hugged (on the cheeks of course). He said "It was really great to see you Zoe, thanks for coming in and thanks for lunch and the chocolate and…"

I don't know what else he said, my mind was spinning. I'd touched heaven again. I'd felt his back as I flung my arms around his waist to kiss him goodbye. My lips felt his cheeks. My eyes had seen his smile. My ears had heard his voice, heard him say "Zoe". My eyes had seen his laugh, had heard his laugh. My cheeks had felt the warm brush of his cheeks against them and his lips. My heart had felt his heart. I so wanted the earth to just fall beneath me so that I could die happy, at that moment and wouldn't need to live through another day without him. Bizarre.

I floated down the road to Ladbroke Grove tube station. My parting words "Come and see me in der schwiez" echoed in my mind – he said he'd like to, if he could afford it.

Later that day, I went to the hairdresser's. They did a good job, as always, although their prices had increased marekedly, I'll have to find another hairdresser.

Last night, I went to Charlie's birthday party at the pizza restaurant and then met with Brad for a drink at 10.30pm in the Fine Line, Northcote Road. Brad told me that he still thought of me a lot (despite moving to a wonderful apartment in Fulham, ordering a brand new silver Audi TT convertible, going to Moscow, Latvia, Madrid, Barcelona, Copenhagen, Amsterdam etc etc). It was a bit of an anticlimax after lunchtime. I wonder if M has as good a time with every girl he meets/goes out with etc, probably. After all, what makes me so special? I have to ask myself and, then, I start to feel sad.

Saturday morning, Ben Ledge – not the ex-JB – oh, I forgot to mention, so funny, as I had a drink with Bad who should walk into the fine line but JB. OMG, the ex came over to say hello to me, he said he'd seen me walk past and recognised me, so wanted to pop in and say hi, I said hi as civilised a manner as possible and introduced him to Brad –

urgh, little did Brad know that this was the guy, follishly, I'd decided to give it a go with when Brad had returned to oz, with all those empty promises. Little did exJB know that this was the guy I'd decided to call it a day with în order to date him, what a fool I had been, or had I?!

Another learning curve, another life experience. Anyway, Ben Ledge came to collect me in his convertible Black audi TT, (seem all the rage with "up and supposedly coming boys about Battersea I guess, pretty materialistic, but if you're a girl you cannot seen to be with someone in anything less!

Anyway, we played squash at my old gym in Battersea which was great. It was good to see him and we had a good game – I won, yippee! (3:1) I have to keep up my record, but it was good to see him and catch up with no strings attached (or so I thought). Turned out there were more strings attcached than those just in our racquets. He's a nice guy actually, with lovely big eyes (accentuated by the fact that he's lost his hair, so shaves his head in the latest fashion) and has quite a bit about him, even more than say Brad sometimes. (Sometimes, Brad thinks he's just so cool and great although there's something about him that's so unsure and nervous. I cannot believe that he was such a total rebel he says he was when he was younger, he's just a bit too wet and wimpy. I prefer guys that are more sure of themselves and don't get used like a dishcloth. Perhaps that's a little too cruel, as he was always a real gentleman and treated me really well, never let me pay – except for the hotel in Barcelona.

(Urgh, one of the train spotter guys has just been on his mobile between Milton Keynes and Stafford.: "Oh, hi Gaaaaary, honey, how are you, it's Aaaaash. I'm here with Riiiiiiichard. How are you honeeeey?" Yuk! Richard's just sitting there staring out of the window, he's finished his split peas. Ash is raving about some shelves on the phone to Gary. "We must sort out another A&D date" Ash says on the line, as he puts his arm around Rich. "Is this a gateway weekend?" "Have a nice fart about honey""Ok honey, I'll

190

see you soon, oh yes, of course, we'll see you next week honey, for pride" (of course, it's gay pride week next weekend in Clapham Common, of course). Other totally obscure language followed: "When's the next 'voyager' weekend? Ok honey, blah blah....". Now he's talking about German food (?!) Shit, I'm so glad I am NOT sat opposite them, if they'd spotted that I'm from Switzerland, they'd probably want to practice on me!

Oh well, now the train's left Stafford. I've bought all these newspapers, mags and books and I've not read anything because I've had so much to tell you. (I've left Brutus at Steve's flat).

Moving on, the train from Manchester Piccadily to Gatley. It's terrible. I'm so glad I don't live here anymore. Yes, this train is totally depressing. No wonder they look so old, so young. I am sandwiched in a seat between a guy with greasy hair in front of me. He's effusing some sort of alcoholic smell from his pores mixed with sweat. It's not pleasant. It makes me feel sick, really ill. Behind me is a woman talking incessantly about "Bob" and how "Bob" had admitted 2 weeks after Irene, 2 weeks after "Bob" was admitted, he was. He was, you know, our Bob. Argh!!! Think I'm going mad! Fortunately, Gatley was the next stop, I could escape this torture.

I walked back home, the way I'd always walked all those years ago, from school. Trudging down the road, come rain, snow, sunshine, wind and more rain. Homebound. Nothing had changed, although some things had, not for the better. The signposts had changed now and looked cheap and tacky – high up so that vandals could not destroy or deface them at street level. Sad but a true sign of our times, in England at least. At least there appeared to be no litter around, although still dog mess scattered along the pavements. The Tatton cinema, once home to such premier screenings as the latest Bond, scene of many a first date and many a first fumble, was now all boarded up. It's closed. There's an Armenian (?) deli – mm, continental, in Gatley? In the village, I'm not so sure how the local residents, like my mother, will accept it. I'd give it a year, if that, what a shame (I bought some dip etc and it was lovely. Naturally, mum did not want to try it, after all, it was foreign – oh, of course, I'd forgotten she doesn't like to deviate from meat and two veg. I try).

Mum opened the door. After everthing Paula had said, I was exepcting much worse than I saw. She looked much the same to me, however it was written in her eyes that she was more morose, more down, and she started weeping and clinging to me, crying "Oh Zoe, Oh Zoe". I felt helpless. I'm probably seeing her as frequently as I did when I was in London and yet just a bit of water and a few more miles in between and psychologically, I'm too far away from her. It makes such a big difference. I try to cheer her up by showing pictures of Greece, of Switzerland, of skiing, by telling gher that I had had a great time last night at the pizza restaurant, that I had seen M and that he'd asked after her. I even showed her a couple of photos of SBP which should have been hilarious, but all she could say was: "Oh Zoe, you must realise that life cannot always be so exciting, you have your family to consider". (Oh yes, doom and gloom, come on Mum, rub it in, make me feel guilty for living a life, like you always have done, make me feel that I've abandoned you in just the same way "as yer Father did" as she constantly says, why not). As if my life has been all excitement over the last few months?!!! That's a laugh! If only she knew and understood the pain, the agony, I've been through mentally too. I gave her my all when I was at home, even when I was at University, I responded to every beck and call, to every shopping list, I ran back to the shops like a lap dog when I'd forgotten something miniscule. I did everything I could to the best of my abilities and now, now, what do I get back in return? Tales of woe, of how awful she feels, how many tablets she's taken. Yes, I know, I listen, I sympathise, and help as much as I can as I see fit, but there comes a point when you think, you really have to help yourself mum, just a little tiny bit, please, because this is driving me away from you).

Apparently, Paula started her off last time she was here, telling her she's not going to see her for a very long time and slamming the door behind her as she left. (Please Paula, don't say that, I know it's harsh. Please don't disappear and leave me to it, like you did when you went down to Kent to live with Richard all those years ago, when I was still at school, please don't disappear for years again).

I bought a video to help cheer us both up (because strangely(!) by now I was feeling pretty low too). "Hideous Kinky" starring Kate Winslet., which had some beautiful Moroccan scenery in it, and was actually quite a moving story, albeit a slow one, but I was interrupted all the way through it by Mum telling me about her tablets. I bought provisions from the deli and the supermarket to make pasta which mum said "oh, don't give me that, I'll just have a ham sandwich. I'll be sick if I eat any of that foreign stuff" (give me a break here mum, I'm trying, with a video and by making dinner. Neither did she want a glass of wine from the bottle I'd bought – I could have saved £5. At least she liked the strawberries that I'd bought but snubbed her nose up at the nectarines as she said they weren't ripe enough, although they were really soft and juicy (I had one).

Anything I do, I don't feel is worthy or good enough. Everything has to be greeted with a moan. God, I hope I'll never end up as bitter and miserable as this I think to myself…

At 9.23pm, I said I wanted to go to bed, I was so exhausted what with all the lugging of bags around the world, travel, trains, listening to the face of depression etc etc, but mum started on me: "Oh can't you stay up just a little longer?"and then whining, pretending to cry then turning her face to indicate that she no longer was talking to me in some sort of childish manner. Great, I felt really tired. last night was a lateish night though not too late and I haven't slept well over the past few nights. Mum commented "You were with your friends last night and you'll see them again this week, can't you just stay up some more? I'll be worse in the morning. "I suddenly felt very annoyed, very trapped, so I said, "Mum, I'm sorry, I'm tired. It's 10.43 swiss time, I've been travelling etc etc" Have I not a right to feel tired and go to bed I ask myself?

I woke at 04.55am, I've just woken from a fantastic dream. M and I. He put his arm around me, so I put my arm around him and I could feel the electricity, pow! We made love, we both climaxed, it was as good as it ever had been, even better. Such a weird dream. I dreamt of a condom filled. I wanted to make love to M when I saw him yesterday, so badly. I wanted to feel the warmth of his hands along the contours of my body. I wanted to feel his lips against my skin, everywhere.

Sunday was an "OK day". Got up late, was great to have a good sleep. Went for a paper, dropped back the video and made Mum and I some breakfast. I decided to pop into town to see what was going on and to experience the Sunday shopping again for the 1st time in over 3 months! That's what's wrong here I thought, the people have no inclination to do anything other than "shop" on a Sunday, there's nothing else to do. It was depressing. I bought a few bits and bobs for Mum from Boots (more tablets for her migraines and antacid pills) and then I found a Hobbs shop and bought myself a couple of things which I knew I shouldn't have done on my Hobbs card (but what else should I do? Stay in and listen to mum being depressed about life and the world, stay in the dark lounge, with the curtains half drawn, to Mum in her nightdress still at 5pm in the afternoon. I returned to make dinner once again.

Mum and I chatted all night (I gave up the idea of getting a video as I thought, no I knew, that Mum would only talk over it anyway). We had an OK evening and watched a programme on Princess Di (Hewitt's story this time). (I remembered the card I'd written to M after we'd broken up – to say hoiw I felt like Princess Di after she'd split from Hewitt to say how much she loved him, she adored him…I still do). Went to bed. Had a few more weird dreams – I dreamt I was making love to Marco – Oh shit! – I have to meet him on Wednesday. Then I dreamt I was a survivor in a really horrible plane crash – we'd landed but then had to take off again for some reason but there was not enough fuel. We landed on a motorway and went through a tunnel, the wings tearing off as we went through its gaping entrance. I woke up with a start after it at 06.55am. I didn't tell Mum, she'd only worry.

This morning, Monday, Andy called to arrange our meeting up tomorrow. Great 9am, he'll collect me.

I wish I could tell Mum to just "get on and do it", like we all have to do, even though we all suffer and cry sometimes. She's not the only one to hurt, but she thinks she is.

I popped to the Post Office, the chemists and the newsagent (I can't believe the number of packs of headache tablets I have to buy Mum – I wish she'd ask the doctor for something stronger if these don't work, she takes them like they're smarties, but she will not be told. The minute I try to offer encouragement, to suggest ways to help herself, of making herself better, and happier, it's only greeted with disdain and the words "impossibility" that in the end I give up. There's only so much you can do or say before you know that someone has to help themselves a little bit too. Perhaps that's why Dad left, why she has very few friends – no-body's phoned or visited for months, or so she says. If only, I wish, she'd make a little tiny tiny effort then people would want to be interested. Everything is such an effort with her for her. Everything is so expensive – I can't use the telephone. I can't have more than one banana a day. I have to split a tomato in half between the two of us and yet she orders a mass of milk, when she knows I don't drink it. The freezer is packed with loaves of white sliced bread like we're to expect a food ration at any moment. The fridge is filled with meats, sliced bread and freshly sliced hams, although I'm vegetarian. And she says it's all for me. I feel so sad, I'd dearly like to help her, to give her £1,000 to play with, to take her out, to make her move, to take her on holiday but I feel that even if I did that, it would not be good enough, it would not make her happy. Even with £1,000, she'd worry that she'd be spending it. It seems that no-one is worse off than her. I wish she's see that we all have pain and suffer a lot of the time. My God Mum, life's too damm short.

The following day, I feel so guilty about leaving, with my bags, with my new outfit and a heavier credit card, and with a smile. Why? Am I supposed to live in misery, to feel down all the time? No, surely not, I don't want to, is that so selfish? God gave me a body, he gave us all bodies, he gave us a laugh, a smile, a voice, life. Surely, he did not just want us to be miserable all the time?

I think I'll write a pocket guide to moving abroad – why not, it may earn me some money, but more than that it could be a really good and funny guide to work abroad. Who knows? I'll have a laptop soon, so will be able to write a little in the evenings too.

I've just finished my book, Sebastian Falkes "Birdsong". Perhaps the worst book to read on a train as I'm in floods of tears and desperately trying to conceal them under my specs. (Typical girl). It's just that the story rang so true, mirrored my life in so many ways (the passion about M etc etc). It seemed ironic that I chose that book to read on the way to the dentist's that morning and that M noticed it and that he'd read it, and also exclaimed about its passion etc. Oh M, you fuckwit, it's you, you fool!

So here I am on the train leg between Stoke on Trent and Watford junction. The buffet car smells horrible, as do the toilets and a few of the other passengers on this carriage. Again, I've not taken my reserved seat as I would have been sharing it with God knows who, but I found a little 2-seater where I am quite comfortably … alone.

196

Chapter 18

Last night, Monday, was awful.

I rushed around once I'd got back to London, picked up a hat, went to the Doctors for some more eardrops and returned to Steve's. I was called by work twice and then by a client. My God, can't they sort out things themselves? Then I went to Ceroc, or should I say Pizza, plus half an hour of dancing (I was really upset I couldn't make it earlier – I knew M would be there as we walked past his car on the way to Jongleurs – wow, there was a huge dent in the back, just as he'd said).

I felt the evening was really crap. I'm so glad I saw M last Friday. We managed to sneak a quick conversation together and 2 dances, but I had the feeling neither if us were relaxed, his mind wasn't on it, my mind was totally on his heart, plus he was being persued by a Tart, about 4 foot tall. He left without saying goodbye (well, he disappeared anyway. Mind you I was dancing all the time). When we danced, I purposely swung my hips into his and we danced quite closely together. It was a laugh, nothing spectacular, but then it never was, after all, I never fell for him solely because of his dancing, I just fell for him anyway. Our parting words were: Me "I'll look out for your letter then" with a wink and smile, and his reply: "Yes, sure, we'll have to sort something out". Where have I heard that before?

Tuesday, I was collected by Andy at 9am, and we went to Ascot for a lovely day and off to Nobu for dinner. It was lovely but my confidence was at an all time low due to hearing of his recent holiday exploits, him and his 22 year old GF, how she's sorting him out at home, how this, how that, how they've been here there and everywhere. How he's bought her a number of new outfits. Great. Thanks mate. When you don't realise just how lonely I feel out there in Schweizland.

Marco's not retunred my calls. Oh well, just another "fuck n run" man. I'm, off to Italy soon to find my own.

What a bizarre turn of events my life is on?

Today is Thursday, I've woken beneath a frame of voile and linen in the "artist's room" of the most magnificent house in Britford, just outside Salisbury, Wiltshire.

Oh but let me tell you about yesterday.

Wednesday, I dropped my hat back into the hat shop, then went to the Nurse to get my ear syringed – my goodness, it felt like I was sticking my head into Niagra falls – I've never experienced it before. Hopefully it will clear this sensation of me feeling like I'm in a swimming pool every time I move my head. Then I met up with Nikki for coffee at Starbucks on Northcote road, which was fab. It was great to catch up on all the girlie gossip. She's off to Vancouver with her Canadian boyfriend in a couple of weeks and is moving too, so it was nice that she could take some time out to meet me.

Then Marco called. We met outside Bibendum on the Fulham Road and we went to a lovely little Italian around the corner (in his new BMW3 whatever), people wagon type of car, it was amazing, like a much better version of the Range Rover Discovery). He bought me lunch and we chatted etc. He told me he's about to buy a house with his girlfriend but that he saw it as an investment, that he'd covered all angles, that he wasn't worried about her as she had lots of male admirers in the city where she worked (what is it about men, or about partnerships like that) I mean what is he saying, is he planning to stay in that relationship?

His business has been quite stressful recently apparently, I'm glad I could lend an ear. He seemed to be preoccupied (not least by every girl in a skirt who passed the restaurant) but he's off to Spain on holiday, so all's not too bad and he will relax then. I gave him some Swiss Chocolate which he kissed me for (on the cheek) and told me I was so sweet and thoughtful. He dropped me off and I grabbed a cab back to Steve's to help him load the car and the boat and we set off on our leg to Cornwall (not that I really felt like a 3- hour conversation with Steve, who's sometimes like an old mother hen).

(It's strange, apparently, Marco has already checked out "Co-habiting rights" for what he could get away with if he and his girlfriend split up – my god, it sounds like a really stable relationship, not, as he ogled everything that walked past the restaurant in a skirt…)

So, back to Thursday under my linen sheets in the artistic room. Here we are, Wiltshire. It's a beautiful morning. I feel I could stay here and have a holiday, it's so beautiful. At the moment I'm surrounded by fab easels of the most magnificent portraits (one of a very handsome hunk indeed). Charlie and Francois' obviously lurrrve good things. They have lots of art and I feel priviledged that they invited me. (In the corner stands a table by David Lane, on the walls hang paintings by John Miller – he's got to be my favourite artist now, he has such beautiful landscapes and sunsets).

Now I'm being woken by the sound of "Come on baby light my fire" emitted from a stereo downstairs, so perhaps I should get up after all. I'm listening to the rooks, crows, cockerels etc, it's lovely, and staring out onto Salisbury plain with the cathedral spire piercing the trees on the horizon. I think of M and wonder whether he'll call me to let me know if Joel's around our neck of the woods. Wish he would – it sounds like everyone else that is going to be down there is old enough to be my mother or father.

That's it, I feel like I'm in a scene from "Sirens" the movie, and some artistic hunk is going to walk into my room in any second and give me a good seeing to. Dreaming again – talking of dreams, I dreamt of Robin last night – very strange – I dreamt he owned a flat a bit like this house. I wonder if he met up with JB last night as he said he would, and if he mentioned that he'd seen me at Ceroc, hope he threw in that I looked stunning etc etc – yeah right!

It was strange with Marco, he said he'd never told Howard that we met up, because he didn't feel it was appropriate – likewise I hadn't told Kate that I'd met up with him, as I felt I would have broken his secrecy rule. Why? Not sure I like feeling like I'm a bit of an affair type of person, I couldn't be bothered with all that! I haven't even slept with him either.

Back to Wiltshire.

Last night, I met Harry, the son, 23 who wants to work in advertising:
"Why?"
 "Because I know it's the right job for me."
Urgh, my heart sunk, why oh why, when I think of the pain and aggravation I've been through over the past few years, the hyped up egos, the stabbing in the back, the larger than life bullshit personalities. The tears, the stress, the late nights for absolutely no reason other than the uber boss wants to change the presentation for the sake of it.
The accounts, the constant struggle to reach profitability, the clients, the demands, the impossible deadlines, the crap, the clients who are nice, the clients who are shitty, and who treat you like a piece of shit, even though you're probably better qualified than they are, the weekend work, the hours in Switzerland and the course of my career. So, remind me, why?

We had a lengthy conversation though and I hope I've dispelled a few of the myths and re-tinted his rose-coloured specs of the "sexy world of advertising" to give him a more realistic impression – the good, the bad and the ugly. I think if I'd had my own agency, I'd hire him as a receptionist or PA to me – he seems willing and able, but to check out his desire to work, to put in some effort, to find where his passion and anger lies. (Marco told me that I should start my own agency – yeah right, with what?! But I do like his belief in me).

This is a beautiful house, there are no other words for it.

OK, so Thursday at about 10.30am, we "set sail" for Cornwall. It was great (or could have been, with people my own age and my friends). We arrived at Exeter Sainsbury's at about 2pm and stocked up grabbing some bread and bits for lunch. We ate it in the car park and went on our way again. We arrived at the cottages in Roc at about 5pm, picked up the keys from the estate agents, John Bray (who must have a hell of a monopoly on sales and lettings in the area as their signs were up everywhere) and we proceeded to unpack everything. (It nearly drove me mad, unpacking toilet rolls, kitchen roll, crisps, water and milk to each and every house and being told off for getting the numbers wrong, as super-oragnised by super-organised Steve, but especially as a) they'd brought their own and b) some was off before they arrived on Friday evening. (God, he's so organised, he's verging on Mr Boring). Everything must be just "so-so", just so, and you can tell that he likes me (yuk) because even things that I started to do to annoy him, he just replied calmly, "Yes, that's correct" etc, in true BBC fashion (where he used to work, shuffling CDs). Well, Steve, I'm not a CD-disc.

Sunday, it's great here on the train, there are younger people. I'm starting to feel a bit more like myself again – fun and bubbly and young – why can't I be? You don't need to be miserable all the time.

By the time we'd unpacked, everyone else had arrived…Tanya (a fabulous chef) and her husband Dave with their 2 boys, Gearge and Freddy (the latter who has such beautiful, massive eyes and long eyelashes and a fabulous smile – he reminded me so much of JB, I even wondered what JB's kids would look like – ridiculous).

Mike (the gynaecologist) and his 2 boys, Alex and William – later to be joined by his oh so successful wife, Janie (the silk) and their eldest son, another Sam.

Malcolm (the barrister) and his wife, heavily pregnant Janine (due in October) and their children, Zoe (little Zoe!), Ellkie and JB.

Hubie (barrister number 2) and his wife, Wobbly (poor woman, I would refuse to be given such a nick.name) but she actually turned out to be a bit of a whiz on the waterskiis, and then there were their children, Katherine, Lucy, Joshua and Sam (baby Sam).

So, if that was not enough, on Friday, David (head of a branding agency and embarrassing to say so but yes, you could tell), and his heavily pregnant wife, Charlotte (due in 3 weeks!) and their painful kids, Oliver, Hugo, and Oscar. Actually, David and Charlotte were pretty cool, but their kids were a real handful and you could see where they got their mischieveness from, (their father David was unstoppable).

It's true what they say about married guys too, they are the worst, the most flirtatious etc. They all got so so drunk and it was quite pitiful to see their creepy behaviour towards me. (As was Steve, as I insisted on paying my way for something – urgh, he's so old, smells of BO, and has the most atrocious skin. Then you realise that despite his heart of gold, why he's never "cut it" with anyone. I'm sure he is very generous, but he's so typically set in his ways for a 48-year old – I can't believe that he even thinks that I would consider going out with him. I would feel physically repulsed). I think he's spoilt our friendship by writing that letter, or by the things he said in the letter anyway.

Thursday night, Tanya made a wonderful meal, followed by a Sainsbury's chocolate pudding from Mike, and strawberries. We drank so much red wine, white wine and whatever that we all had hell of a hangovers by the time we went to bed, never mind the following morning.

(We're just passing through "Saltash" on this train. It seems a really pretty place, it's such a lovely day again).

Chapter 19

I feel like I'm trying to find out where and with who I fit in, please God, help me out a little here.

Friday morning, Mike, Steve and I took out the boat and went around the 2 islands off the coast out of the estuary. I felt a bit seasick, although I dare not say so. The weather was beautiful, and we returned back to shore at about 3.30pm, so hungry and we were pleased to be greeted by Tanya and some real Cornish pasties (she was so thoughtful – she'd brought a vegetarian one for me too). I just wanted to get away from Steve after that though, to do my own thing, but he clung around me like the beach limpets, even when I said I fancied checking out Padstow, of course, he wanted to go too.

Over in Padstow, we walked all around the town. I bought some ice creams, Cornish of course (I thought twice about ordering vanilla as Steve had ordered that, and I just have this feeling that whatever I do, if he does the same thing, he thinks it's fate. But tough, I wanted vanilla, it's my favourite). We walked past Rick Stein's restaurant, although Steve was pre-occupied with how much it cost and not of the food itself.

Now, I've been joined by "motormouth Mike", just as a hunk has walked by and sat opposite, what a shame. (He had gorgeous eyes, hair, smile, reminds me of Michele). Mike's complaining about the train strike, his father apparently used to work for GWR (Great Western Railway, otherwise Mike refers to as God's Wonderful Railway, and waits for the laughter). He's talking about the "APT" system that Richard Branson's trains have – "Met him, you know, nice bloke" etc etc. oh Mike, shut it.

I've got to write this down quickly before my "train companion" returns. His name's Mike, he offered me a selection of his tasty morsels should I feel hungry – these consisted of 2 cigars, 4 pieces of Wrigley's Spearmint chewing gum, a packet of fruit pastels and some opal fruits.

He is quite bizarre, I wish I'd never told him my name, I feel a bit scared now as he asked me "Urgh, Zoe, you got on the train before me, which way is the buffet car" he then mumbled something about steam trains which he's into apparently (why do I always seem to get them sitting opposite me on trains?)

Thank goodness, I'm off that train now and on this coach, following a full 5 hours of listening to Mike's incessant conversation. Something strange – his father was a driver on GWR when he spoke to me yet when he befriended another young female lone traveller, his father was a policeman. "SAS you know" etc etc. (Yeah right). (At least Mr Fitbit, corr he was really lovely, gave me a huge smile when I left – reminded me of M).

"Shopping, leisure, housing, culture and…" here we are in Reading, urgh, that was the sign on one of the buses that's just gone past. Now the driver's done the headcount and we're off.

Goodbye "chick n chip" England.

Ah, Monday, don't you just love em? But at least there's a brilliant blue sky outside, the sun is shining, the radio's playing, I just wish so much I could share it with someone, (like M).

Monday night, I've written a huge lengthy tome to M but will not post it until I have the photos of Brutus and Robbie on my terrace.

Well, tonight, Wednesday, I collected my photos from the shop (an absolute extortion – I will never take them there again, it's so much cheaper sending them away). (The shop assistant said – just in the same way SBP used to say: "That's Swiss" urgh, if anyone else says that to me, I'll punch their eyes out!!) Anyway, I wanted to collect them to send M the silly shots of Brutus which I did. I read and re-read the leter I'd written, just in case (I get so enthusiastic and excited when I write to him, there's so much I want to say, to share with him, I hope he bloody well writes back this time

Still no sign of that letter he said he was writing – sometimes I don't understand men. However it has just been a week, come on Zoe, calm down, it will arrive, ease up a bit). I've sent him a lot of suggestions and zany ideas for Lloyds & Christie's, his work, I hope he takes it the right way, who knows. (Please God, let it catch him on a good day, when his heart is open, when there's a doorway for me, when he wants to desperately reply. Please God, if there's one thing I ask of you tonight).

I went riding tonight, and I felt really crap. I was put on a selfish brute called Moritz who had a mind and determination of his own despite his size – he must be the smallest horse I've seen. I felt really rubbish. I couldn't control him and was thrown off, great. I felt a real chump as Herr continued to reel off his rules in German – it bugs me sometimes. I asked myself why I bother, perhaps it was a silly idea to pursue a riding school who speak only Deutsch. I don't know, anyway, I'll persevere, not a lot makes Zoe give up. It rained so heavily outside, it was white. The thunder and lightening flooded the stables and when we let the horse back in, we were sloshing around in the stables. Unfortunately, I'd left my patio window open in the living room and came back to a "swimming pool" across my floor. It was a really terrible storm, yet interesting. Amazing!

Last night was fab – I was invited to a last minute BBQ in the forest at Birsfelden. It was fantastic – so warm. I just took courgettes, peppers, cheese, bread etc and joined Rita and her mates at a little hut in the middle of the forest. It was really brilliant. Lots of people in different little clearings, who'd cycled there with a picnic basket. What a life, I just wish so desperately that I could share it with someone. The pain of it is that I just know M would love it to bits. I miss him so. Will he ever know? Sometimes I wish I'd die and that's the only way I can reveal how I really feel to him. When someone shows him this book and he can read it, will it ever be a book, well I'm hoping so now that you're reading it.

Talking of men, I feel particularly low tonight. Look at them all, useless.

M who I'd die for.

Theo who rang me nearly every other day when I returned from Greece. I even sent the little shit a letter and he phoned me again to say that "all the time, 'e "watches ze photograph of you, Zoe". Yeah right. Suddenly the phone calls stopped and he never returned my calls etc etc.

Marco: "I'll call you from Spain" "I know my girlfriend will be able to meet another guy, she has so many admirers in the city" blah blah, I mean, Marco what what what are you saying to me? I don't have plenty of admirers in the city, so I'm a safe bet? You're about to buy a house together? I don't want to split anyone up if you're not sure. It's Wednesday and have you called, No, Do I care? Mmm, well, a little bit, after all, it's nice to feel wanted.

Michele: the Italian ski stud. Whatever happened to him? Texts everyday, letters, phone calls, photos (from his mother's family album), more letters, more texts, then....nothing? Absolutely nothing. I sent him an email to see if he wanted to meet up if I went to Locarno in a couple of weeks' time. Has he replied? No. What did you think?

All I get is Steve sending me creepy letters and saying how he enjoyed my company so much, how we seemed to have so much in common and making suggestions for passionate evenings together?!!. Then I see a photo of him from when he was over here. Yuk. !!!!!!!! (are there enough exclamation marks there?)

JB: Where's JB now, pathetic little pratt. I don't think it's me that cannot be friends. I think he's too scared of what he would do to me. I sent him a text tonight to wish him well at Ypres if he still goes to do his rally race there. I wonder if I will hear from him. Probably not.

Why is it that one minute, every single man on the planet seems to want to know me and the next, where have they all gone? I must sound like I'm desperate to meet someone. I'm not, but I don't want to be like Sarah – I don't think she's had a boyfriend for over 4 years, she's 37 and unlikely to meet anyone there in the countryside with her cats and her horses. Or is she, perhaps she's got it right. I like mens' company (sometimes!)

I felt really awful this morning. Went to the Post Office. Even the woman behind the counter was miserable, in fact I don't think I've ever ever seen anyone with such a miserable total personality. I went out and nearly screamed, "for goodness sake, you people, SMILE!!!!"

What happened to all these so called "Ski mates" too I met in Meribel? All so up their own arses, so they don't bother to keep in touch. At least Kate sent me an email which cheared me up. We spoke briefly on the phone. I must get a landline here, it's amazing how isolated you feel without a 'phone. I feel so alone and would love to talk to people.

Has Charlie 'phoned or anything to thank me for the presents I gave her, for flying back to the UK and taking holiday to be there at her party? Nope.

What's happened to Nina? Well, now that there's no man in her life (and no job I don't think), she probably feels she's got nothing to tell anyone, so no news there in 6 months despite my mails.

Annie, well, I think I've given up on her too – all she wants is a shopping partner in Milan, which I can't really afford, especially right now. What happened there though? We used to speak/text/email all the time. Suddenly now that Andrew gets his claws on my friends, no more news (funny, I thought he'd say more than a brief "hi" when I saw him at Ceroc the other week, but no, not a word).

I don't think I'm going to send my swisslette news anymore. People are so fickle. Well, fuck you all (except those that write now and again, I like you). Now I'll cry. Please God, I feel like a curse has been placede on me, please lift it away, I feel like I'm in a self-inflicted prison.

Chapter 20

What a fabulous night it was tonight. (Gosh, now I must sound like a schizophrenic after being so own yesterday). Anyway, I met up with Amir, (at Rochester pharma, lived in New York for 12 years), Dave (at Chameleon, a vet from Oz, and had just driven back from Milan, which took him about 3.5 hours – hey great, this really is the centre of Europe) and Nick (a lorry driver from the UK who's been living here for a number of years). I also met Chris (Swiss, nothing more to say really), Andrea (half swiss, half Italian and reminds me of Nadia – mad but huge fun), Marla (swiss, ex-Rochester,now at SwissAir and you can tell why with her typical stewardess look) and the rest of the gang at a fayre in the Kaserne. It was fantastic. Food from around the world – Thai, Chinese, Indian, yum, a real feast and made such a change from the usual bread and cheese). Clothes and goods from around the world too, lots of bars, music, a concert, it was all free and lots of laughter, excitement, really great fun.

Funny how you meet people. Amir is a friend of the brother of the lady who used to serve me in Pharmacia in Covent Garden – confused? You should be! Strange what a small world this is though. I had told Meena (the pharmacist in Pharmacia) that I was moving to Basel and gave her one of my new cards (boss Hans-Peter was so efficient, he'd had my cards made for me about a month before I even arrived here) and she said she'd pass on the details to her brother's friend. Lo and behold, here we are, 3 months later and this guy, "Amir" emails me and says he's now working for Rochester in Basel and if we want to meet up, he was going into town with a few mates, signed "a random guy, Amir"! (Now Amir turns out to be a great buddy all my time in Basel truly the organisaer of the Social whirl).

Half of me wanted to stay inside. Half of me wanted to go and explore on my own – another beautiful evening, but then Amir rang and I said "Whoops, I'm running a bit late", but so was he, so that was cool. I jumped on the bus – found out the bus outside my door goes all the way to Claraplatz (across the other side of Basel) in about 15 mins! Anyway, so I caught up with my new buddies there.

Wow, what a place. Music, dancing, food from the Far East, the Middle East, India, Africa, Prints, art and clothes, truly multicultural. It was fab, it felt like the whole of Basel were out. I ate Egyptian food, and samosas. I caught the last bus home, feeling a little tipsy after a few Sangrias and whatever cocktails! I must go back tomorrow. (I bought some pants too).

OK, and guess what, JB sent me a text message back: "Thanx for your support. Just scrutineering car before the start at 9.30pm. Hope all's well. JXX" (that was upper case kisses) (?!?!) I sent a message back later tonight to say "Let us know how you get on. Hope you beat the man in the mini"(always his biggest rival)"and don't crash!Zx"(NB lower case kiss, just in case). Oh well, we'll see if he replies – bastard! (No, at least he doesn't just ignore me like M - pratt!)

I noticed tonight, walking past all the watch shops that all watches and clocks in every shop were showing the same time, all spot on 15 minutes past 8. So typically Swiss. Arghhh.

Saturday, what a beautiful morning. I don't deserve to feel as good as I do at 7.15am, due to the late night last night plus sangrias. It's amazing that at weekends I can't lie in, there seems too much to do, to see, to enjoy – not like work, which you have to do, to see, to not enjoy. Therefore, you always want to stay in bed during the week.

Apparently here, schools take a day off by law, when it the temperature is 28 degrees at 8am and Heinz at work says that that happens quite a lot in the summer (I think the same should apply to work) The schools apparently broke up for summer yesterday.

Well, I cycled to the Market on Marktplatz, to buy bread, cheese, cherries (great value), tomatoes, pfirsch (peaches), spargel (asparagus), etc etc, via the atlantis bar, where they pla the jazz – I thought the number was 0900 555 222 5 as was on their window, but I got it wrong (later I asked Hans-Peter at work to call them – he wants to go to see a saxophonist on Monday night there and I can't call 0900 numbers from my mobile for some reason, so I asked him to buy 2 tickets anyway for us both. Anyway, it turns out that the number should have been 0900 55 222 5 and I'd made him dial a porn number!!! Oops!) (what a difference 1 little digit makes! Matron)

After a good work out at the gym, I washed, showered and had some lunch, sunbathed and read last week's paper for a bit then thought – what should I do? I telephoned Theo, to say hi but it was his answerphone. (Hee hee, he called me back later tonight – ok, all is forgiven theo – when I was getting a bus into town to say hi. I said I may pop over to Paros at the end of August/beginning of September which he seemed to be really pleased about. I told him I'd seen some photos of the rest of the island and that it looked beautiful etc. Then I wondered whether his hands were really as leathery as I remember them for some reason! Why? No, surely I'm thinking of Steve or someone else? I don't think Theo's hands were that bad, but I can't remember, well, there's only one way to find out, go back to Paros and touch them!

Anyway, Saturday afternoon so I decided to go to Bern for the rest of the day, to find out if it is true that people swim in the river there and yippee, I found it! And yes, I swam in the river! Yipee. I was laughing all the way as I bobbed up and down in the fast current of the water, lapping through the valley and it was beautiful, 18 degrees in the water. I swam in the freibad (an open-air swimming pool, which was free and fantastic in this fantastic hot hot weather). It was a great atmostphere. Everyone was swimming, jumping in the river, jumping out again, running down the side of the river and swimming again and I joined in.

Later, I caught up with Dave and Amir at the Kaserne

again, to buy a skirt and trousers and experience the food, a flavour of the Middle East again. In a way, I wanted to be on my own, I find out so much more, but in another way, I was so glad of the company. We went to "Café Des Artes" later and talked with "Steve" the pianist, who's from New york, but now lives in Basel although it was his last night in Des Artes, as he was off to play at the "Splendid" hotel in Zurich from Monday – I will have to check it out, it's supposed to be THE place. I asked him to play "Fly me to the moon" which is my song to M I guess. The moon? He'd probably fly me to Portsmouth docks, but I'd love it all the same.

I texted Kate and she texted back.

I texted M – I couldn't resist – sorry, he's still the 1st person I think of whe I'm really excited and have done something new and exciting. I hope it doesn't irritate him, but I just want to share it with him so much. Out of all the guys I've been out with, it's his face I see laughing as we'd both be bobbing about in the water, trying to scramble back ashore. I can hear us both laugh and joke together, I feel his hand gently touch me on my waist, his eyes look into mine, with their knowing smile and his hips against me as he tugs me closer and his lips caressing my lips, our tongues eclipsed in the most perfect embrace. And then I realise he's not here with me and I'm sad again.

Is this what you call love? (I would have hoped it had diminished after 18 months but sometimes I feel my feelings are just the same, sometimes less strong, sometimes stronger, but I still think of him day in, day out, I still wish we could laugh together all the time, I miss his constant text messages too).

Well, I visited a beautiful place today – very peaceful, quiet and a great place for a potential party.

I met Sabina and her boyfriend, Guy (his Indian name is Wobinden or something, even though he's far from Indian, he's Swiss, he lived for 4 years in India with a guru – it seems a lot of swiss do that. What are they trying to find?)

At 10am, then we drove to Pfaffikon, near Zurich, to "beard's" house on the lake. It was just like something from Scandinavia – a beautiful wooden chalet with a verandah and a path leading all the way down to a platoon from which you could dive off, or row away from etc etc. The lake was a mild 20 degrees (2 degrees warmer than the aare) and it was beautiful and so calm. Even with a spf of 16 in sunblock, I could still feel myself burning. We were joined by Beard and his sons, Marlo and another little boy (they were real terrors, and wild children, in fact absolute pains, the worst swiss children I've ever met). Their father was dreadful too, well, he just seemed so incredibly sad and depressed, just sat around allowing these kids to make a complete and utter mess, smashing plates, pinching food and throwing it all over the grass etc etc and he just didn't do a thing about it, just smoked about 20 fags during the day and never batted an eyelid or lifted a finger (even when Sabina and I prepared some food for dinner and cleared the table). What a dreadful mess it was. Both of the men seemed quite content to live in such squalor – no wonder their wives had left them, why should we be forced to force them to get their act together?

You know yometimes you read great novels and there's that boring bit in the middle, well, I feel this is it. Now, what other exciting things can happen to me while I'm here.

3 months later Beard was found dead in his bathroom. He'd electrocuted himself with the BBQ in the bath of his house in Basel. Sabina was distraught. I myself felt quite affected too, having spoken to this very man, stepped on his land, consoled him on the loss of his wife and how strong love is and that everything would work out for the best.

Monday, another beautiful day but am annoyed to hear that it's beautiful in the uk at the moment too, that is, until it started to rain at wimbledon later today – tee hee, as usual! Makes me less home sick.

I think of what Amit said. Yes, he's right. It was only London where he said he did not feel like a Pakistani, a black etc etc (even though h e's Indian anyway!), because there are so many Indians in London and I have to admit, it's easy to become a snob over here in Switzerland and not encounter any of the dangerous ones. Although in Battersea, you didn't really encounter any of them, it was all white, middle-upper class fmilies, that's the only place I could live in London – the rest is depressing 2 up, 2 down places, rubbish dumps along the paths of time, staying in a squat like Paul's all the time – I felt guilty at not paying more towards the Cornish trip or for my stay at his flat but there again, I think about what I entertained him with here…clean dry flat, lots of hot water, fresh towels, a spotlessly clean bathroom (which he always messed up with dirty footprints – don't men seem to notice what marks they leave behind or have I become that set in my ways and expectations?!) petrol and car trips everywhere, lots of food, champagne, etc etc. I really enjoyed having someone here so yes, I felt I'd earned my stay in London I suppose.

It's also quite true what Amit said, that when you feel homesick for London, you just need to think about what you'd do at weekends. At least here there's lots of things to do etc. What would I do in London at weekends? (At least I can ski here every weekend if I want to/can afford to in the winter and swim in lakes every weekend in the summer and mountain bike etc).

I think about what Kate wrote in her email today – initially she said it sounded like a great weekend I'd had, so I replied that it was, if only I could share it with people, to which she replied: "Let's forget it. Think about it, we've got great jobs, prospects, we're pretty etc let's not waste time thinking about men" and she's right, isn't she Brutus (I'm talking to the dog now, excuse me! I must be mad, he's not even soft and furry).Never mind, he has a cute and appealing face, a lop sided head, beady looking eyes and long floppy ears – just what I should look for in a guy I guess – as I asked in M's last letter. I asked him what he thinks?!! (I can't believe now that I worte that to him!). He now knows he was a pratt to dump me (or does he, perhaps he was right, I am the pratt?) but I have so much to give, am so generous (want to be), giving, loving, and happy (most of the time). He should be with someone like that not some 1 night tart bimbo, who's probably just lie there in the sac as he gave her one, wondering what would happen to her mascara! (I do think it was a bit weird, it always has been with him, even the girl to whom I suspect he's having his next dig n dump trick on, had a dress on, just like the one I'd chosen to wear that night when I went to Ceroc – quite ironic!We looked quite similar except I had blonde hair, her's was black, she smoked her head off, I didn't. Come on, M, she didn't look the type of girl to sail with you, to play squash with, etc etc. I remember our dance together and remember thinking as he swung me towards him, "Right, you bastard, I'm going to turn you on, like it or not" and I swept right into his crotch and stayed looking 'gangster bitch' serious, which I don't know whether was good or bad (I think I prefer smiling). We ended the 2 dances, smiling together and our heads bashed together by accident. I offered him another dance in order to bump the other side, to make it even. (Did he realise just how much I still think of him? Probably not). Oh well, it's another Monday night and he'll be there, dancing his socks off and trying to pull anything in a skirt I suppose, probably I am the furthest thing from his mind.

And what about me? I went to collect 2 sun loungers from Hans-Peter and Denise's and ended up having a glass of wine with them and some salad which was rather nice. They are good people, but work too bloody hard, but they are good to me – thank god!

Oh yes, I called Theo again tonight, to see how he was – to check he wouldn't be away or anything if I visited in September. He said he wouldn't be, in his usual charming way "Zoeee I vill alvays be ere for you darrrrlinnngee!"I thought of the girls in his office probably rolling their eyes in their heads! Oh well, who cares, I like the attention! He was busy though, that was obvious (his world championships start next week) so he asked me to call him again and we left it at that.

I called mum and received the usual half hour discussion about headaches, tablets, doctors, nurses, prescriptions, money, chemists, doctors, headaches, nerves, anxiety attacks, great people, horrible people, the way she's been treated by so-and-so, how it's too hot for her, how it's too cold for her, how she doesn't feel well. (Oh, and by the way mum,. I felt like saying, I'm really great and feel fine, OK, just in case you wanted to know! I wish!)Forget it, Zoe, her only interest is how ill she feels and how many tablets she's taking. Why oh why can't I have a normal mother, how so much I am never ever going to be like that with my children, if I'm lucky enough to have them, if I'm lucky enough to get the right man, to get my guy and have some beautiful little people.

Marco…no news.

JB…no news.

M…still no letter number 2.

Well, if I've an ounce of cellulite left on my bottom after today, I think I'll jump off… Munster Brucke! (a bridge). I went to the gym, despite it being another 31degrees, had a good work out, then tonight, met up with Lorena, Magdalena, Catherine (who's soon to leave for London – I met her husband, Dierck at Fasnach, when she played in one of the strange bands, he was very drunk but a funny man). We also met up with Peter and Niklaus and we cycled to the Black forest to go to find the cherries! And, yum, we found them!Millions of them, laden on the trees and we stuffed our faces until our lips were more crimson that the ripest fruits and so were our teeth. It was fantastic view – as we cycled right to the top of the hills and saw the view of the sun setting and the moon rising over the forest beneath us. It was quite surreal and studendous, together wiuth the flavour of the sweet delicacies melting in our mouths (our stomachs will probably live to tell the tale tomorrow).

We stopped at a little hostelry in germany and had a

(huge!) salad (thunfish!) 8and I had some of Magdalena's because I was still so hungry) and then we set off again. We'd cycled since 7.15pm (well, 7pm for me, as I left Binningen) and I arrived home tonight at 12.45!! Eek! With no lights. It was a great night, but I feel very tired.

Wednesday, another beautiful day. I went to the gym at lunchtime, then tonight went horseriding – back on Spider tonight, it felt good, especially when I'd been on such a little horse, then afterwards, I went to meet up with Philip Atkinson (the guy that popped into the office from roche the other day) and Susie (his girlfriend who's great, I want to be like her) and their mates at St Jacob's park outdoor kino – it's fab, it's an outdoor cinema screen, a massive screen with plastic chairs on the grass beneath it which you just arrange where you want to sit. We took rugs, there was plenty of grass to sit on too and a swimming gpool just in case you fancied a dip! Bizarre, well, yes, as all the shopkeepers say: "That's swiss"!

Philip, Susie and their mates seemed a great bunch actually, I really enjoyed the evening. The film was fab too, Taxi Taxi, a Luc Bessant film – with guns, cars, a hint of passion, but great, even though it was in French with German subtitles – non of us could understand a word that was said, but it's amazing how you can follow a plot in any language – the plot is a global language! – and even find yourself laughing at the appropriate parts (perhaps I understood 1-2 words, but I wasn't sure whether to try to follow the French or the German).

The air smelt of something interesting! Am I the last to know that Marujana is legal in Basel?!

Tim henman managed to beat Roger Federer from Switzerland at Wimbledon. Well done Tim, the Brit!! It's a shams in a way, I felt my allegencies torn because Federer is from near Basel, Munchenstein. I wonder if anyone back home thought of me? Eg. M, JB, B (yes probably, no, probably not) Oh well, I had a great night tonight.

Another late night but hey, you only live once!

I booked a flight to Paula and Mick's for this weekend –

I wish they'd contribute to it, since they more or less said I'd be disassociated from them if I didn't go back. But I know it's as difficult for them as it is for me (well, I think so).

Thursday night and I'm sat on my balcony. The tiles under my toes are still warm and the sun is setting – again providing a beautiful sweep of several shades of pink, lilac, blue. The tree that paul bought my (present for putting him up here) is shrivelling, which sort of resembles our friendship. Why can't blokes just be friends, they all have one objective, and that's to get their hands down your pants and then that's it, it's over, you find out how awful they really are, they are onto their next pair of pants to accommodate their hands.

It sounds like the good old swiss traditions still live on. Last night, after the kino am pool, one of the girls mentioned that she'd missed her "wash night" (I can't believe it, it's a bit like being at boarding school – or how I always imagined it would be, not that I ever was there, it would have been fun but lonely I think).

I had another message from JB: "U can see the results on www.Ypresrally.com" End. Fine. I naturally clicked onto the website this afternoon. He and his co-driver came 46th out of 60. He did well for an amateur. It was good to see that, but hey great, are you getting friendly again to come over because you haven't had a S.H.A.G. in 3 months?!

This chair is great. Hans-Peter from work gave it to me. The sunloungers are a bit old but they do the job and it was terribly good of him to think of giving them to me – they've bought 2 new chairs from Interio.

Tonight, I went to the Appollo gym (oops, I've just turned down my Moby CD, I don't think these Swisslettes will appreciate it now that it's past the 10pm watershed for noise, shhhh). Anyway, at Appollo, I saw Guido at his 'Muskulatur' class, and it wsa fun – especially deciphering the moves when they're all dictated in Deutsch (at least I can count to 10 and back). Actually, it's good to get used to the Swiss accent. Guido's hell bent on teaching me Deutsch too, he says it's better than speaking English when you're in Schweizland. (he may have a point). Guido, he's an odd-looking chap. He's all muscles a massive smile, massive specs and massive hair. He looks a bit simple but underneath you can tell that he's just a gentle giant and also intelligent (I think it's the specs that put you off him – get contact lensed up guido!) Also, the haor doesn't help much I don't think, but there again, I can see that Guido just would not be Guido if he had a haircut.

Marco called. He said he'd be over next week in Switzerland, I told him that I'd believe that when I see it.

It's funny watching the other members of the gym. There's an obviously efeminite guy who Guido obviously takes caution with – he doesn't smile at him, yet he beams at everyone else that walks through the door.

Tonight, I sent a message to Marco. He called me back and we had a good if not, inuendoish chat. It's OK, I won't fall for him. I always have to make the first contact so that he calls back and that's cool. Ok, I know where I stand. He doesn't want me for anything other than a good friend and that's cool. Perhaps I can have a guy as a friend after all.

The town was in mourning all day today, after Federer's defeat to the "Roastbeef" Tim, at Wimbledon yesterday. It was such a close match though. I can't wait until they're over here later in the year for the Swiss Open. There's so much to do here.

I wonder if M has my letter yet and box of goodies. I dreamt of him again last night. He said, "Now you don't think that just because you sent all this, I'm going to get back with you?" I said "No", smiled my usual smile and he gave me a massive hug and we laughed and kissed and made up. I then said "No, but you can get back to me because of other reasons!"

You're not going to believe this view I have as I lie here now on my bed. The moon's just hovering outside, bouncing along the tops of the roofs of the houses opposite. Its edges are perfectly clear and it is a waning, yellow colour, clear, clean, crisp, beautiful, patient – if a moon can look patient.

The phone's ringing to spoil this tranquil moment. I know it's going to be Mum because it's nearly midnight. Yes, I've answered it and it is Mum. (I would give almost anything to hear her call me and be happy one day) "I feel ill love"""Oh I'm bad" "I feel dreadful love". She doensn't think she'll make it to Tim and Beth's christening on Sunday. Oh, come on mum, pull youself together, I thought. "Oh no, I haven't washed my hair" to which my reply was" Well that's up to you really, it's not that important" but my reply did not go down at all well. Voices shouting, 'phone slammed down, and of course I called her back. Boy, I wish she'd just feel well for once, just once. That's it, isn't it in life, you must do different things, change, move, appreciate and see things from a completely different perspective sometimes, keep your mind alive, in control, active, happy, looking at views like this moon in front of me now. Smelling new smells like that of the honeysuckle that is growing in the porchway here at Hirtenbuendtenweg number 6. They all help me take my mind off M, of London, my friends, of JB etc etc. I still think of them a awful lot (yes, ok, you know who I think of the most) but I just have to hold that for now, to hold the memories, keep them there in a special place in my heart for when I need them again. I can't do anything about it. I've laid my cards on the table for him, I've been cautious with him ever since we split up – not wanting to get too close to get hurt again by him, but yes, not straying too far away that I lose him altogether because I just don't think I could bear that. But deep down, I still care for him very much – in my stomach, in my heart, still, even now I feel a tear slipping down my cheek, but Mum, look around you, look at how the world changes, how the world is big and beautiful and interesting. How there are mountains to climb, branches laden and heavy with blood red cherries, paths to cycle along, lakes and rivers to swim in, friends to laugh with, smile and joke with, and lovers to enwrap yourself in, hearts to touch each other with tenderness, hands to hold, eyes to meet, kisses to greet.

Kate and I emailed and spoke briefly today. She says she's no more time for time wasters who are not true friends. I replied to her email and said "yes, especially moving abroad, it soon sorts out the wheat from the chaff" and it's so right, sadly, there are a lot of plonkers in London (and I'm sure, the world).

Chapter 21

Ok, so here I am at Heathrow on a typically grey and cloudy day at 09.15am. And let me tell you the story so far.

The plane was delayed for 1 hour and 10 minutes.

Paula advised me of a 9am bus from Heathrow, terminal 1 which goes to Watford Junction. The plane arrives at 08.48am. It lands at Terminal 2 instead of 1. I make a dash to terminal 1. I see a "bus help phone" opposite me. What a great idea, I thought (and at the back of my mind: but will it really work after all we are here in London"). It worked, it rang. I spoke to a guy on the other end. "No Love, terminal 2 you want, bus stop 4, it's a little red virgin bus" "But I've just come from there" I replied "Are you absolutely sure, I was told I should be here in terminal 1" "No love, terminal 2". So, I put the receiver down, after thanking him and raced all the way back to terminal 2 from where I'd just come. (At least I did not take the 'trolley route' this time which takes you on a tour about the length of the great wall of china – not that I've ever been there either. I arrived at T2. I went to bus stop 4, where some Americans were waiting for a bus to Gatwick. Gatwick?!A red virgin bus appeared only on the other side of the bus station. Typical. I dashed over there only to see it deposit half a dozen virgin stewards and stewardesses and their luggage. Fortunately, I saw a technician and so I asked her.

"Bus 724 you need. Stop 1" she told me, so I went to stop 1. "It's a green bus" she added as I left her.

OK, so how much information did I receive, how many different colours of buses, of terminals, argh. Yep, I'm back in the UK, I thought to myself.

OK, the green bus, the 724 is on its way to Watford Junction. I just missed the train, so it gave me the chance to get some papers, some water and an opportunity to call Paula and go to the pharmacy for work research (urgh, why do I do it, when I won't even be thanked for it on Monday – you should have seen the awful letter that the guy in the

US sent to me yesterday, when it's me that's doing HIM a favour), I ask you? I didn't have the chance to see if I recognised anyone, or if anyone recognised me.

Last night I dashed off to Zurich for the "Nur Fest" – a kind of summer Fasnach. Apparently, Zurich parties from Friday morning until Monday morning non-stop. Tanya had called me "Darlingees" earlier in the day and suggested I went with them. "Sweetie, it's the only place to be gorgeous doll". Even though I only left work at about 7.30pm – Axel called me at 7pm, can you believe it? Friday night as well. I decided to go, even if it was just to "tick that box" (been there, seen it, done it) as it apparently happens every 3 years – the canton put a stop to it happening more often because of the 'noise pollution' and 'people pollution' – apparently over a million descend on the city – and the litter pollution is extraordinary. I can understand why – it does not really fit into the Swiss regime that I have discovered.

It felt like a massive massive fairground, with all the dirt, trouble etc that places like that usually attract (and a few drunk louts). There were some tremendous fireworks though at the end of the evening, sparking off in synchrony with hits from Titanic to Pavarotti. It was really quite spectacular over the lake. I then left on one of the 24-hour trams that had been laid on for the evening – it was packed, even at midnight. I'd left the car at the EURO car park on Gutstrasse. Easy. Then took tram number 9 which goes straight into town for 3.60CHF – quite good value! At least I've found a way around the expensive car parks in the city (as long as no-one objects).

Wow, I'm thirsty.

Some thing I hate about England:

1. A husband and wife screaming at each other in public. Him blaming her for going in the wrong direction (I mean, ok, so he could have made the decision, but the language is insane).

2. A bloke swearing "Fucking late again" when we waited at heathrow and who continued to mutter swear

words under his breath. I mean we just can't do anything about it I felt like saying to him, but who am I to say anything? It's in-built in our miserable lives.

3. The semll of this trendy perfume that I sprayed on me – it's vile and disgusting.

4. Shopping precincts. They're so depressing, with their attempt to be all things to all people, attempting to be all continental with branches of 'Bon Marche' (well done on the accent boys, when you can't usually get the English language correct) dotted here and there selling the sort of tat you certainly would not find in the best French markets.

5. The miserable look on peoples' faces (their mouths seem to turn down naturally at either side in the direction of the floor). The sun's not shining, but could it ever shine on places like Uxbridge? Watford? Watford Junction? Etc etc?

6. Older people here all look so exhausted, worn down, over weight, miserable, or complain about everything in such terrible accents. OK, so I don't know too much about terrible swiss accents yet but at least the old fogies smile, seem to have something interesting to say to each other that creates laughter, smiles, and jokes and they're super fit. In fact they're bloody fit. Those pensioners that regularly turn up at my gym at opening time, are so toned and fit and flexible, they would even make M look a complete slacker.

My mind constantly goes back to thinking of my bank manager in his 2-up 2-down model home in Reding; my mind thinks of Suzanne from Creatives Inc, London, in her red brick semi on the corner of a busy road in Kingston. How did she feel to come back here? Does she ever think she should have stayed in Switzerland? Why? Why not? All she has now is a loveless marriage to a tight-fisted Scot who doesn't seem to make her happy, yet she runs around doing everything she can for him and for their little girl, a demanding child. What is there here for poor little Heather? A life of drungs, violence, theft, sex, abuse, whatever, bastards who will use her as she grows into a beautiful young woman, suitors she will choose, suitors she will

223

unchoose, amd then the cycle will begin all over again, in a semi-detatched 2 up 2 down in on eof the estates surrounding Richmond. Not very pretty. Not very creative. My mind feels almost subjected to the crime and pollution that surrounds the roads here as we travel along. And, I'm sad. It saddens me to think that this is what's happening to London, to England.

Well, things looked a little brighter when I was joined on my seat by a little old lady. 89, who'd just moved into a 1-bedroom flat but who really enjoyed it. Her husband had died 14 years ago (he'd been in the war apparently, on the beaches in Normandy – she knew about the book: 'Captain Corelli's Mandolin', the book I was reading, on my lap). She'd fallen and broken her hip last December and then went to spend a month in hospital. She then got a clot in her lung following the operation and had been written off but came out of the operation still smiling. In fact she was just such a lovely woman and still in love with her husband "I still miss him" and I could tell and I could feel it and I felt like saying, I know how you feel because I believe I do too.

She asked where I was from and when I said Switzerland, I asked if she'd ever been there. She'd never been abroad, her husband had not wanted to - he said he wanted to see England.

I thought, Yes, it doesn't matter where on the earth you are as long as you're in love and together and you can be wherever – after my initial thought of "how dare he prevent this lovely lady from seeing the rest of the world, or, of letting the world see her smile" – I could tell that she had been really pretty in her day, her eyes were still sparkling. They would have been married for 70 years and I said I hoped I would find a man like her husband. She said one of her grandchildren was 30 and she was in the 'same boat' as me.

We arrived at Watford Junction and I had to get off. I felt happy. Once more, my faith had been put back into England, into the people and into the world.

I then had a swift train trip up to Rugby where Paula

collected me, and I spent a wonderful weekend with them. It was Mick's 40th birthday on the Saturday (I can't believe it). Then Saturday night, Paula took me around to one of their neighbour's houses, Hazel., who put me up. Why are you doing this to me God? Another lady who's been happily married for goodness knows how long and in love. Lost her husband last year to skin cancer and she still misses him (and still wore black). She has a beautiful daughter, son-in-law and an absolutely gorgeous grandson, Ethan, with massive brown eyes, sallow skin and dark hair.

Chapter 22

Sunday was a great day! I became a "Godmum" to my favourite boy and girl – Tim and Beth – they're so sweet (and so beautiful) I sometimes wonder what my babies would look like.

If I had them with M, wow, they'd be gorgeous 6-foot-tall boys or, lithe beautiful girls with beautiful eyes, nose and hopefully curly blonde or dark hair.

What would M be like as a father? I could imagine him with babies, but with older children, gosh, I don't know. Mind you, what would I be like? He'd teach them how to sail, ski, swim, run, jump, rollerblade, surf, windsurf etc etc, ride a bike. Wow, it would be such fun. We'd teach them to be so adventurous, perhaps with that little streak in me too.

What would children with Brad be like? Gosh, thinking back, his brother was gorgeous and about 7-foot-tall, dark, dark eyes, but Brad will be bald soon I think – his hair is so thin. He had no rhythm for dancing but would teach them how to cycle and how to be good at business. At least he's travelled the world and is a man of means, so I think they'd be sound of mind and secure.

And with JB? Beautiful eyes and teeth, mouth and smile. Not so tall though and could be inclined to be podgy (I bet he gets podgy one day). JB would teach them everything there is to know about cars (even if they would be girls).

With Michele? Gorgoeus dark Italian looks – dark eyes, skin, curly dark brown hair – or blonde – with that Italian style and flair (but possibly that Italian temperament too). They would be fabulous skiers, because their father could teach them, but then he'd possibly run off with a beautiful young Italian girl or guy one day (who knows these days?!)

With Theo in Greece? Bet he would be a good father (I suddenly wonder if he already is?!) His children would love the sunshine and the surf, he would teach them to surf really well. With dark eyes, and tanned skin, and beautiful dark wavy hair, but they would be short. They would be wild. Would we split up? Would I be saying "Your father in Greece" and me be in London or Switzerland? Would he fall for another girl in a nightclub in Paros, the way he claims he 'fell' for me? Could you trust a Greek guy – as my boss says?

And what about SBP. Well, I think he thinks he's still a baby in nappies anyway, so I don't think he'd know what to do with a child, not even which end would be their mouth and bottom. No, I don't think he'd have kids somehow.

And, why would we split? Because of….

And, on a scale of 1-10, where 10=fantastic, this is how M fared:

Sex   more than a million

Making an effort   7 (but he didn't need to much)

Being interesting and spontaneous   8

Being too demanding   10 (he never was)

Being too temperamental   9 (not really)

Different interests   8 (OK, so he was a bit more
                        sporty than me – is that possible?!)

Not fancying each other anymore   10 (I don't think I
                        could ever 'unfancy'
                        him even with no hair)

No time for each other   10 (I would always make
                        time for him above anything)

No kids/too many kids/ugly kids/demanding kids
                        We'd just have to work at it, his
                        mind's so stable I don't think it
                        could be possible

Not being in love anymore   and here I am 4 years later
                                   and still thinking of him
                                   every day

Falling in love with someone else
                         and how do you prevent that? I
                         would certainly not set out to
                         do that to anyone, I would just
                         trust that he felt the same way

not being caring/considerate/generous (in heart)
                                   7 (he's only a man!)

Thoughtful   7 (well, he can't be completely perfect
                                                 can he?)

Common sense/practical   10 (definitely one of his
                                              strengths)

Personality   10+++ (Come on, I fell for him hook line
                and sinker because of his attitude to life)

I wonder if M would tick all these boxes for me? How
should I know? The only thing I do know is that I woke up
in the middle of the night last night, crying, really missing
him and wishing that his long arms and hands were wrapped
around me as they once were.

And yes, if we'd been together for so many years and then
he died, I think I'd feel incredible sadness, I'd miss him
every day he was not around.

(Oh God, please don't let him be offended by my letter, I
am only trying).
    I bet Marco would be a good father. He would provide
everything and ensure you led a 5-star luxury life – until he
got sick of it? Would he? I don't know. He'd always had a

roaming eye – just think of all those girls that walked past that restaurant he took me to – just think of that dance that he had with me, was he with me or was he dancing with the other 2 girls around us? But I don't think his girlfriend wants babies and so he'll probably never have them unless he makes a girl accidently pregnant and then just pays her maintenance – yes, that's probably what will happen (as happened to his own father minus the financial support).

Anyway, how should I know what kind of father guys would be, or how they should be, my very own father wasn't much of an example.

What about Andy? Couch? Well, he knows he "never wants kids" and will probably be forced into admitting that an illegitimate child is his one day by his current bit in the side. I reckon she'll stop taking precautions without telling him and it will all be a bit of a shock and they'll never get married but will probably split but still see each other for occasional sex. He'll live in the South of France in an appartment overlooking the fine restaurants, beaches and bikinis. She would live in his flat in London – rent free of course.

The child would go to a Tooting school and become a druggie, like his mum, and alcoholic, before his 16th birthday. He would not be much good at sport or anything and will probably start to put on weight. He may be good at business though – taught by his father – and could set up in the East end in a market. He may well go for fishing trips with his dad, along river banks which would be energetic enough, and share a beer or ten. His mother would despair but have lots of affairs and probably die a broken woman.

What was wrong with M? Was I so bad? I'd love to know.

Tuesday night, Wednesday night. Home late and will tell you about it later. But arghhh, just as I'd started to givce up. YIPPEEEEE YIPEEEEE! A letter arrives from M!!!! I'm so excited, sick with excitement, I don't know where to open it, when to open it, to savour the moment, to bathe first in my favourite bath gel, to eat first, to eat afterwards, to brush my hair and unpack my bags first, not to, to go to the toilet, not to go until after?

It felt like the sun had come out after it had been raining all day long and I feel like a dog who's running around in circles chasing his own tail in excitement.

Bother it, eeeek, I've opened it and am sqwaking with delight, squealing, I'm reeling in delight and pleasure and a smile beams across my face, surely my neighbours are wondering what bright light has just come on at Hirtenbuendtenweg 6 which they can't extinguish. Why does he still do this to me, why do I still feel this way? I still feel exactly the same as all those years ago when our eyes fleetingly met across the dancefloor at Jongleurs off Lavendar Hill.

I sent an SMS immediately to Kate. Her reply "Sit down and breathe".

I sent an SMS to Nikki. I know she's in Canada at the moment, but I just wanted to let her know. It's still pending, I'm not sure she'll receive it. I want to tell everyone, but I reckon they'd think I've gone bonkers, lost the plot etc etc. (I probably have) I thank the Universe.

So, besides M's letter (oh, and an email – yes, he sent me his new email address, so I sent a 'testing testing' message this morning which YESSSS!! He replied to. Squeeze, hug, bliss, laughter, laughing out loud, sing, dance, be an idiot, I don't care (ok, so I am excessively happy). I'll print out his replies and save each and every one of them. I'm never going to delete them. I could never delete him from my memory.

So, what else? Tuesday night, I went to Kino am pool again but this time with Rita. We watched "What lies beneath" with Michele Pfeiffer and Harrison Ford. It was really good, very scary. (I swear I crushed this bottle of water about a million times in my hands, especially during the last half hour). What a movie. Anyway, home late again but it was worth it, I like Rita too, uncomplicated and easy to get along with.

Wedensday night, I stayed in Geneva after a meeting at Serene. I met all the International Product Managers there. Including a "Manfred" that reminded me so much of SBP. I am now so glad that I broke it off – so sorry SBP but you really were not for me.

I went out for a drink with Roberto, my client, and then for something to eat with him after the meeting. Scary. It all came out, about how his girlfriend was in the middle of a divorce from her current husband (she'd only been married for 3 months) but that her husband was now starting to make an effort, seeing that he was losing her and so she had lots to sort out (it sounded like he was being strung along). She is from Italy, works in Lausanne and had agreed to go halves on an amazing apartment in Geneva overlooking the lake. (He insisted that I accompanied him to his apartment whilst he dropped something off and whilst there, showed me his etchings – a painting he had done, a bit weird but imaginative – and his new road bike – a triathalon bike, only weighing 9 kilos – I think it was super light, with a very thin frame, very snazzy, but purple – very girly). He also showed me his fish. Yes, all right, I know what you're thinking, I have just got to write this in my next letter to M, it's so amusing.

It was actually a little creepy as he played "David Gray" on his amazing new stereo – I had mentiuoned that I am going to see him at the Montreux Jazz festival and felt obliged to ask him along (seeing as he is a client) and he had bought the CD to find out more about his music.

Anyway, we then left and had something to eat at "perle du lac" in Geneva, it was a lovely little restaurant overlooking the lake but quite expensive, considering what we ate. I insisted on paying (to state my place as the advertising business account handler). We walked back to my car and he let me out of the Serene car park. Also, creepy was the fact that he said that he'd loved to have joined me in Ticino this weekend – but I wanted to explore on my own – but that he ought to wait until he knows what's going on with his girlfriend – urgh, eeek, yuk.

Come on guys, who do you think you are? Excuse me, but did I mention I fancied you, that I wanted more than just a drink with you?

It was awful, I couldn't even blame alcohol as he has this enzyme problem which makes him unable to drink alcohol. At that poinht I was worried, but I hastily said goodbye, with the usual swiss 3 kisses on the cheeks and left post haste back to Basel.

Shaisa (as they say here) (=S. H. no 1. T). I have to go to Mantreux with him next Monday to see David Gray. Yuk and double yuk.

I managed to clean the flat tonight, Thursday, so I can go to Ticino with a clear head, knowing that it is clean. I think everyone will want to go for a drink tomorrow night, but I could do with giving myself a facial, face mask, pedicure, manicure etc. I can't let myself go to rack and ruin (I wished I was going to Henley Ball with M this weekend as he'd mentioned in his letter).

I went to Guido's "Muskulatur" aerobics class again tonight. Guido's class is a killer, but I swear my backside will look better than a firm tight peach by the time he's finished with it. So, it will be worth it. Met a guy called "Davido" Italian, obviously, "David in English" he pointed out (as if I was completely blonde) He's originally from Italy, but has lived in Basel since he was 11, so practically Swiss. It's great to meet some Italians, I much prefer them to the Swiss. (I wonder if Valentino missed me in the Appollo gym over lunchtime over the last 2 days – wonder if he'll be there tomorrow, a beautiful smile, probably not into girls and anyway, I should forget it, he's probably 10 years younger than me anyway. Nice body though, big brown eyes, lovely huge smile, longish brown hair – v sexy! Although he thought of M still turns me on – oh please leave my mind!)

Oh yes, the pitch for work we had today was postponed until tomorrow morning. Torture – another sleepless night.

I don't know whether my excitement, feeling of being sick etc are down to the pitch or to M's letter and email. I feel hungry yet sick, tired, yet awake, everything all at once. I feel like dancing, I feel like hugging someone. I told Sabine at work, even she's excited for me. What does he do to me?

There's a song on the radio, it goes something like this:

"I know I've felt like this before,
but now I'm feeling it even more.
It all comes from you.
I know I've felt like this before,
But now I'm feeling it even more.
It's all a dream to me, dream to me, dream to me...
All my life is changing all of the time,.
All my dreams are never quite as they seem,....

It's my song, it reminds me of M.

I sent an SMS to Michele to tell him I was going to be in Locarno tomorrow and if he was at home, it would be lovely to meet up. As it was not so far away etc etc. he replied almost immediately - ?!! – he was off to see his friends for the last time from the army (He must have left) in Palazzo and so could not go, but would send me his new email address. I sent him another SMS to wish him a good time, and yes, to send me his new email address. He replied again "Of course, I'll do" (love his accent) "and hope we can meet again. Michele" I wonder if we will. He's probably married with 50 kids by now anyway. Hey ho, I want to hold out for M anyway.

The next song followed on the radio, which also reminds me of M:

"What took you so long..."

and this song reminds me of my time in Switzerland, it's foreign etc!:

"la enta cen..
La ma vido….
D'amorice, beide,
De falla much better,…"
"Ciao mon est fatta…mon,
Oooh ooh ooh"

Quite catchy, Italian song, would be good to dance to.

Chapter 23

The weekend from hell.

Fuck. I feel quite alone and helpless and I feel like curling up in a tight ball and crying my eyes out.

I desperately want to ask for help but no-one speaks English.

I wantz to call JB – he'd know what to do with an MG, but it's only 07.50am in the UK, he'd kill me.

What's happened? Well, I left Basel at about 6am, for Lugarno – I was very excited, the thought of spending a weekend at the Italian border, with lots of beautiful food, lakes, sunshine, etc etc. However, the traffic on approaching the Gottard tunnel was unbelievable and as a result, my engine over cooked. I think the fan's gone.

Fortunately, 2 Italian truck drivers (who had been trying their luck to chat me up, honk their horns etc, as we'd been in the traffic jam, to whom I had given the 'V' sign to several times with nose in the air as I whistled past in my MGF, hair floating in the breeze…one of the trucks had a Ferrari in the back of his truck –what I'd have done to swap for it at that moment.

Because…

Midge just blew his top – literally.

The guys, ie. Italian truck drivers I had formerly been very rude to (and thank god they were there) came flying to help…flipped open the bonnet, flicked the lid off the coolant – as steam emitted in profuse clouds above us and a whole load of green stuff frothed out.

The car began to resemble something from the stomach in that Alien film – it bubbled everywhere, all over the Autobahn (oh no, I'll be fined, I thought) It threw itself everywhere, making a complete mess of the road.

The men were so brave and I was distraught and alone..

Anyway, between us, (lots of Italian, hand signals, smiles, gesticulations, hand books, and fuse boxes) we managed to stop Midge from blowing his hatchet.

One of the Italians was travelling to Milan, the car (Ferrari) was travelling to Naples. I never knew their names, then we were joined by another – a Daniello – on his way to Sicily. Thank god for them. They were fantastic. They must have been angels following me. Thank you. I managed with some trepidation, to pull into a parking space with the 3 guys in tow (One had taken my bike for me and I was sandwiched between these 2 massive juggernauts as we pulled into the last service area before the G tunnel).

They changed my fuse for me, made sure the fan worked, but were worried because the heater was not going down in temperature.

After 1.5 hours of Italian language being thrown at me from all angles, they left me to my own devices and now I sit and wait for the Swiss emergency services to arrive. I hope they come soon. As the minutes pass, I become more and more worried and afraid.

I tried Keens services but no-one's there yet – it's now 08.12 in the UK (09.12 here). I wish I'd tzravelled last night, when there would have been no traffic and no potential to overheat.

Daniello suggested I should go home, but such disappointment after having come all this way and the beautiful mountains, and blue sky ahead of me, I'd set my heart and my mind on seeing Lugano. Perhaps I should try to find an MG garage there.

Even my bike's fallen over now at the side of the road.

I feel very scared.

So, I sent an SMS to JB after all. I'd love his help right now, but he's probably getting it off with some tart he'd picked up last night.

I feel like crying my eyes out.

Daniello asked me how old I was. A funny question to ask in a serviceway parking lot to someone who's brokem down. I said 34 (the 1st time I've admitted my age here). He said he was very surprised, that I didn't look that old – that old?!!! Now I feel old.

The traffic looks terrible ahead.

Daniello asked why I was travelljg alone, had I no boyfriend. "No" I answered, I told him I'd left him in the UK. "Do you miss him" he asked me. "Yes, very much" I said (I meant M of course who I wanted to say, yes, with my whole heart). I also did not want him to think I'd fall for him just because he'd helped me.

I'm very frightened, I have about 100km to go before I reach Lugano (about 60-70 miles), or, about 200km to return to Basel. What do I do?

Perhaps I should call the SOS man again, I've been waiting for 1.5 hours now. It's not very Swiss. I felt so very far from anything, from anyone. "Alone in a crowd" even though there's a huge traffic jam ahead of me – at least it's moving a little now (touch wood).

Phew. I just had a message from JB saying "call me".

Cringe. I bet he's really pissed off with me.

Shit, I'll call. Now he's sent me another SMS saying, "number: 01550 777728".

I've called. He was nice actually and gave me some good advice – "turn the heater up full" he instructed. "Check the water, and beware of slow traffic, get to a garage and let them check it out. It could be the thermostat, the water pump, it sounded like the fuses are OK if I'd changed them – sometimes fans don't work after the engine stops" etc etc etc.

He was so nice. I cried. He told me to email or text him to let him know how I got on and to enjoy the weekend. (Of course, I sent him both and a postcard and and an email…Dearest JB, I take back all those nasty comments I wrote to you in that nasty letter, I'm sorry).

The SOS man arrived. I sounded so knowledgeable (armed with JB's advice). He checked the thermostat. OK: He checked the radiator, OK. He told me that the pump worked OK because the fan worked when the engine was on, but that the problem was the stationery traffic (of course my being completely fluent in ItaloSwiss by this point and sign language). He filled the coolant bootle up and advised me to take the slow road over the mountains "Let's go upstairs" were his excat words to which I replied "Pardon?" Anyway, so here we go, Midge and I set off once more into the distance.

Chapter 24

Well, that was the most expensive bit of coolant that I've ever purchased, but it was a cheap price to pay for reassurance and a helping hand. The mechanic charged me 150CHF – he said it was a bargain, "raffat" – compared to the 250CHF he should have charged me (apparently). I just believed him, wouldn't you? He made out a receipt for 200CHF, for the insurance company – yeah right! – and I thought Swiss were not corrupt?!

He wished me well and went on his way.

I sent the text message to JB to thank him and to let him know that the SOS man made it. I've not had a reply and assume he's a bit pissed off with me.

Now I'm here in Lugano. Mm, I need somewhere to stay tonight, so let's find a hotel.

I parked in a car park and made my way, by bike, down to the tourist office. By bike is the best way to get around and enable you to get out of potentially sticky men situations with little fuss and a smile, plus it's quicker than walking.

The tourist office was of course closed for lunch, so I thought I may as well find some food for me too. My nerves were still shaking after this morning's fiasco. I found a lido by the lake, ordered a salad and some water and set about reading and re-reading where I should go and explore, whilst I gazed out over the lake and having driven through some horrific weather, 'upstairs', found that it began to brighten up, but I spoke too soon.

I had a chat with the hostess who reliably informed me that there was a music festival on in the town tonight, that I'd have to check out and told me that swimming in the lake was forbidden except in specified areas, like their lido of course. It looked really nice and tempting but I had my contact lenses in, no towel and a hotel to try to book into, so I didn't swim.

I eventually found a room in Gandria, just outside

Lugano, and it turned out to be a bit of a find – a little like an Italian version of the place that I went to with Andy in the hills overlooking St Jean Cap Ferrat in France, but this time in Switzerland. There were winding little streets, narrow paths, all twisting down to the quayside. There were coves, cobbles, chocolate box houses. Red tiled roofs, that sometimes formed the pavement, rumbling down to the lake.

Now the heavens opened, so I sat in my little room and made some notes about where I wanted to see here.

- Paco Civico – East of the Casino
- St Mary of the Angles Church, Piazza Luini
- St Lawrence Cathedral, San Lorenzo
- Mont Bré – a drive on bus number 1, to Cassarate and then to the furnicular
- Melide – via the boat
- Gandria – via a boat then cycle back taking in
- Villa Heleum and Villa Favorita
- The customs museum, opposite Gandria
- Mt Generoso – a boat drive to Capolago
- Oh look, near the hotel there's a "Ferienwohnung zu vermieten-with 2 double rooms, 1 bedsettee, a bathroom and a shower, a kitchen and ubwaschmaschine. Hedy Wunderli, Niederbipp 032 633 2555.

Well I don't know how I got here but here I am anyway. I've landed myself in this pretty little fishing port and it seems that this is the only (affordable) place free in Lugano, due to the music festival. All rooms are fully booked, even the hostel seems to only have one or two beds free and no bedding. So here I am in "Fischer's See" hotel for 59CHF per night. There's a sink in my room but no toilet, no bathroom. My bike's outside, locked to my car – about half a mile away where the car park is and getting very wet at this moment in time as I'm sure this is a tropical torrential rainstorm happening.

Gandri, as I've mentioned is very sweet. Lots of winding little paths and cute houses seeming to dip their roofs into the blue blue water beneath (even in the tremendous thunder and lightening storm overhead, you can tell that the water is still very clear blue).

It seems weird that it's still Switzerland here – so far I've only been met by Italians and everybody in Lugano seems to speak Italian as their mother tongue. Still, I have a base for not much more than £20 which is cool. Now I think I may as well head back to town to check out the shops etc (but I wish I'd bought that waterproof that I saw the other week in Globus – but everyone was saying how beautiful and warm this place is. Warm it is, but it's like a monsoon out there).

The weather abated so I went for a long walk, down through the village, taking in a beautiful hillside garden where figs and apricots grew in abundance, tapping you on the head as you passed under their branches. I went down to the Villa Helleneum, which was unfortunately closed but all the same, it was a beautiful building. The gardens were also lovely, and I could imagine it in its former times as a wonderful regal house with huge gates and those steps leading down to the lake where the ladies would dip their toes ever so gently into the lapping waves.

It's a shame it's so overcast but it really warms up when the clouds part.

So, tonight I went to the Jazz festival in town. I walked around and took in the shops, to get my bearings, settling on "campione" for a pizza and an octopus salad (insalata polipi) and a glass of wine – a 2dl glass (2 glasses). The bill came to 29CHF, so not bad, about 13£.

I'm lonely. It would be wonderful, such a romantic place to come with someone you love, and I feel like a sore thumb sticking out really. (Even the waiter here asked why I am travelling alone." Such a laarverly ladee like urrrself"). It was time to go.

Still, I have my copy of Helen Fielding's "Edge of

Reason" with me which is cheering me up – in so many ways, I feel like my life is an episode from Bridget Jones' diary sometimes.

I can't believe it. I've just switched on my mobile phone, it's Sunday morning and Hans-Peter from work has left me a message about work!! I mean, as if I can do anything about it, he knew I was coming here to get away from work and have a weekend away. Well, I guess he would have asked me how Ticino is, so that would be nice.

The town is alive, it's packed with people. I don't think I've seen so many people in one town in Switzerland in one place since…I've been here.

They're surrounding this huge stage whilst a band (I'm not too hot on) bangs out some weird music. Very Swiss, very strange. I am chatted up by a deaf man. Is that all I can attract now? He makes signals to indicate my body shape (so he's obviously not blind as well) and a smacking noise with his lips and I thank him, (even though he cannot, apparently hear me), nodded in politeness and moved on.

I go to visit a postcard shop and he follows me. I buy 3 postcards and stamps. He insists on buying me 3 more with stamps too. I decline his offer. He insists. He gives me the paper bag with them inside. I thank him "merci, grazie, danke" oh, whatever, you can't hear me anyway, whatever language he understands from my lips. He then indicates to follow me, but I wave my hand and say "I have to meet a friend". I think he eventually understood my English as he smiled, shook my hand, made the body signal again, rolled his eyes and we both walked off in opposite directions. I felt guilty, but I cannot just be with someone just because I feel sorry for them, can I?

I must send a postcard to JB, to thank him. It was great to hear his voice (I do think he had one of the most sexy voices of all the blokes I've been out with). He knew so much about cars (I just knew he would) and he was really reassuring. I cried afterwards, I cried my heart out.

The clouds were coming over, I'd had to give in and

speak to him, I'd become a bit upset on the telephone. I wanted to be with someone, desperately, I wanted to cry. Now he probably thinks I'm a pathetic whining female.

Tonight, after I decided to head back to the hotel, there was an almighty crash across the lake, the show had truly started. The heavens opened and there was one almighty and tremendous thunder and lightening display over Lake Lugano. It was incredible. At first, I thought it was neon lights flashing across the lake in aid of the concert illuminating the sky, and I just stood there watching, mouth open wide with amazement. Then the flashes became much more frequent and formed distinct forks in the sky piercing the water, and the thunder started to rumble. The rain then came down like a monsoon again and I found myself running through the piazza Cirrcio (a beautiful park, not knowing really which direction to take). Everyone was running for shelter, my feet were slipping out of my sandals with every step.

Eventually I made it back to the car and drove back to the safe comfort of my hotel bed. I felt tired, exhausted, frustrated by the events of the day and by the weather. I slept until 8am the following morning, really soundly.

At least it looked brighter the following day. Just as I leave for Locarno. OK, I may have to take in a boat trip and a tour up the Mont Bré, who knows.

I had a weird dream last night. I was told I had fallopian cancer – don't let this be true, unless it's my turn to go.

I remember something Lord Lee said at Creative Inc in London one day, as I scuttled through the horoscopes. "Zoe, you make your own luck" he said to me and, yes, it's very true.

I've got it. All my clothes are half focused around being a lady in Cannes and not for packing something in a bag like for this weekend and walking, cycling whatever. The thing is that's what I want to do, wlak, cycle etc. I need to review

243

my clothing now that my life's changed and I'm unlikely ever to return to the Carlton in Cannes, without prostituting myself to some hitched guy – even Andy's found someone new now.

I need good walking boots and socks.

I need good walking shoes (I wish I'd bought those I saw in Globus last week in their sports department). They were perfect – I'll have to go back there this Thursday night for late night shopping. Oh no, that Frank from the supermarket wants to take me for a drink on Thursday night – because it's his afternoon off. Oh, come on Zoe, what can he offer me? Apart from his Dick? Zero. I don't think I want his affections, even though he has lovely eyes and smile. I think I will make sure he knows I am not interested in him on Monday when I pop in there for some bread. Sorry 'Frank'.

Sunday, I had a lovely day. Until now! (I'm sat in the car and it's torrentially raining again. I don't see a let up but there must be soon.

This is when I find several leaks in the roof of the MG. Great car hey? I've just refilled him with a litre of coolant and some extra water. I must buy some more at the next garage I get to).

I cycled into Lugano this morning after an early breakfast and checking out of the room No. 11. CHF 59 not bad. The standard of the 'shared bathroom' was very good too. I caught the 10am boat to Melide to check out the Swiss Miniature village – gosh I'm glad I'm not walking around there now, there was little cover, except for the shop and the self-service restaurant where I bought a coffee and a water. I got off at Melide a little worried because I'd left my bike in Lugano and the boat back was 1.37pm. I had 3 hours to spend here. However, I went to the Swiss Miniature village which was delightful – would be great for kids too. They had examples of symbolic buildings from across Switzerland, including Zurich airport (with all the Swiss Air planes), to the Münster in Basel, the clock tower in Bern, the Jungfrau mountains, grindelwald, the Sheel docks in

Basel (?!), an example of a farm here, a farm there, (complete with cows and cow noises), a factory in Emmental, and schlosses by the bucketload (lots of quite beautiful castles, they seemed very medieval). There was traditional music playing in some of the exhibits displaying traditional dancing in piazzas. There was traditional swiss alp music for the Bernese Oberland. It really was quite something.

I telephoned the hostel outside of Locarno for a bed for tonight. I hope I make it, the rain's atrocious and I need to tie my bike on the bike rack yet.

It was quite warm, the sun was out and so I decided to check out the town, I finished the swiss miniature in about 1 and half hours so I had time to kill. The town was pretty – lots of meandering around the back streets. Then I came across a lido, so decided to go for a dip (carrying my towel and swimsuit around now all the time, just in case), It cost 5CHF, so I swam, dived in 3 times, and swam. I had a great shower afterwards (one thing you can say about Switzerland is that the facilities are excellent). The swim was beautiful, Outside the temperature was 23degrees and the water temperature a breezy 21 degrees, quite acceptable. I'm surrounded by mountains as I paddle backwards. Beautiful.

I caught the 1.37pm boat back to Lugano – I nearly missed it because of some waiter (obviously Italian) trying to catch my eye as I left – they're like chickens, 2 of them were there, looking at me all coy as I left saying "Why you go so soon mademoiselle" etc etc in their smooth Italian voices (they just know they sound good).

I got talking to an English couple – they've been here for 2 weeks (zZermatt last weekend, Lugano this week). They were from Chester, retired. I asked them about San Salvadore which I had decided to check out (I am also glad I am not up there right now). They left the boat at "paradiso" and I stayed on to pick up my bike at Lugano. I cycled to

Paradiso and caught the furnicular up to San Salvadore. I went into the church on the top – it was beautiful, like a refuge. I said a prayer for M and climbed to the top of the church where the view was just spectacular (before the clouds rolled over to join me - This storm is still not abating). I hope it won't be like this tomorrow for Montreux. It's really dreadful now. (Dear God, are you punishing me for dumping SBP. I'm sorry, I did not love him though and I don't want his children).

Wow, I think the lightening is over my head now. It's dazzling and my radio's not working suddenly. I think this should be enough rain for the whole year not just today. I wonder how Valentino and his friends are doing in Zermatt? I wonder what the weather's like there? Right, it seems to have died down a bit, so I must get out, tie on the bike. Here goes.

That was messy but at least it's on now. Now off to Locarno.

Oh yes, if you want to go to the museum on San Salvadore, it closes at 1.15 every day (wed – Sun). Typical. I missed it.

I could do with a huge fire, a large glass of wine or heisse choccie, an arm around me and a beautiful smile in front of me (oh and a pair of lips to kiss).

The car's demister is now working again. All I can see of the lake is the first few metres and then a seething grey mass of cloud, water and cloud. I can't tell. I can just make out the outline of San Salvadore on the horizon opposite me. It's very faint but it's there, like a uge giant watching over us all.

Well, I've given up, along with a number of other drivers on the road on the way to Locarno. It's now thundering and lightening and throwing down hail stones, the size of peanuts. Each time one hits the roof or the window, it sounds like it's smashed through. I'm looking around for shattered glass/a roof tear. This has got to be the worst conditions I have driven in over here, I can't see a thing in front of me. The roads are flooded so it feels like you're going through a log flume at Blackpool pleasure beach. My eyes feel a bit paralysed because of the lightening – it's a bit like having a brilliant flashlight put in front of your nose every 2 seconds. It looks like a bleak November day out there. I could be anywhere, but I know that when the rain clouds clear, it will at least be beautiful and stunnig scenery. The sky is black and it's only 6.40pm, it should be sunny and bright, it's July. This is supposed to be the tropical part of Switzerland. It does feel tropical – tropical storms. Fabulous.

Sunday night, I took the car into Ascona for a walk around. I discovered a fab little restaurant 'San Antonio' where I had the most delicious rocket and parmesan salad and tagliatini with crevettes – it tasted wonderful. Afterwards I heard a pianist, so I asked the waitress where it came from. The bar next door. It was great, really cool. I stayed there for a glass of red merlot (traditional ticino merlot) and then made my way back, reluctantly to Barraca backpackers. I had a good night, although the church clock tower was just in front of the bedroom. I heard it strike 11pm, then 11.30pm, but nothing else until 7am, when I woke up. I must have slept solidly. There was only one other girl in the room for 6. She was German – a bit quiet, kept herself to herself. Anyway, perhaps that's for the best. I felt I was a bit of a cheat as I drove up in a car but she also had a car and a family were also staying and they had a people wagon. You need a car really, because it's quite far to Ascona, Locarno, the valley etc, but in a way, I'd have liked to have been a free spirit "ohne auto". Another time.

Monday morning, I took the bike and ventured to a

beautiful Roman Bridge over a waterfall and river. It wsa amazing. I almost slipped on a few rocks – they were still damp from the downpour. Then I cycled to another magnificent waterfall. I took lots of photos. I even had a paddle in the water beneath one of them and felt quite refreshed. The owner of the hostel told me everyone swims under the waterfall in the summer – it's meant to be summer now, but it's so cold and the water was freezing.

This morning I popped to the Co-op to buy some provisions for breakfast. A light came on in the car for the steering, indicating no power steering. It could have been tricky on these roads but fortunately, it went out. How I hate the unpredictability of cars sometimes.

And so, I find myself in a charming little restaurant here in Bosco Gurin, at the source of the River Maggiore. I'm tucking into a salade caprese (Mozarella and tomato) and it's good, though expensive (CHF14, compared to my delicious tagliotini last night plus wine for 20CHF).

Unfortunately, I'm sat opposite a group of 4 Americans who've just walked in (and taken over). They're from Tennesee and know the owner (well, came into this restaurant last year). The owner's in hospital at the moment. (Not that I listen in, they just talk so loudly). One's called Wayne. They're talking about Sherry and Jeff. It's a bit embarrassing, one of the guys talks "Did you notice that girl walking towards them wearing nothing but a long shirt" (it's me and they don't realise!) "She was very pretty though"the guy said as his wife advised him that I had shorts on underneath. "Geez this geez that" etc etc. I wonder what these guys here in the restaurant think of it all? Never mind, Nancy and her crew, it's turning out to be a lovely day (typical, just as I'm leaving) but just as well as the drive back down this windy road would have been extremely tricky in the rain (especially with no power steering – I give up on this car). So now, off to Montreux. I hope this car holds together.

Chapter 25

Montreux - Fantastic.

What a cool atmostphere – much better than the Zurich festival or Lugano festival.

I arrived a bit late and changed in the service station en route (as I passed by all these famous places like Zermatt, Saas Fee, Valais, Verbiers, Grand St Bernard etc etc). I saw 'Re' as I crossed the Italian bvorder, in which stood a magnificent cathedral, where the pilgrims had gone apparently after seeing blood appear on a statue of the virgin mary in 1930).

I was exposed to fantastic valley views along the way down Valley Centro to Domodosola. I saw the apricot wagons at the side of the road all the way through the valley as the farmers had harvested their first crop.

I saw the 2 castles on opposite sides of the valley in Martigny. It was fantastic. The power steering light had stayed on since leaving Bosco Gurin, which meant I had no power steering but I'm glad I'm on a straight road now. It's easier than those hair pin bends.

Anyway, I arrived a little late at Montreux, but Roberto and I met up – him looking like he'd walked off the set of eg. Casablanca, or something, me, in jeans top and cardi with mountain boots. There he was with slick hair, slightly tanned face, cosmetic smile, black shirt and chino trousers with strange European shoes – I'm sure they're very trendy in Holland, but I'm not so sure they'd go down a storm on Northcote road. He had a sparkling white jacket on too, quite the James Bond style, it matched his teeth. But I wished he'd smile occasionally.

Anyway, we progressed with the evening (although it was hard work). All I could think of saying was "Hallo Robert, how are the fish?" to which he responded, giving me the fine details of genre, species, colour, mating patterns at this time of year, and how he was going to Rotterdam to

250

find a specific rare species (I groaned secretly, I knew I shouldn't have asked him).

Apart from that he gave me the low down of the state of affairs of his relationship (again).

My goodness, I thought, decide what you're doing with each other. I mean, at least I invited M around and then (shit) followed him back to his apartment to tell him how I felt. (Ok, ok, so I wanted to say it, it had been burning up inside my for almost a year and I would not have done anything differently under the circumstances). I felt clearer though after that and amazingly that's only when he started to (sort of) talk to me again and seemingly to take an interest in my life (my ski trip and work in Switzerland, enquiring as to why I'd not been to ceroc for a few weeks – which was in fact due to sex life, being dumped again. Howver, I told him it was due to work).

It had felt like a bomb had been defused inside me. At least, I thought I'll be remembered. I'm no wishy washy smooth-talking fish expert, but I damm well know when I'm in love and I jolly well know how fantastic that was when I had it, and I never want to give up on that.

(I sent an email to M today. It's ok, I mean, I know he won't reply for a few days, but at least he knows, hopefully, in the right way, that I'm thinking of him. I hope he's thinking of me, just a liuttle bit would be just fine).

No new email from Michele. Italian, typical.

No email from Brad who lived in Italy for a while. It obviously rubbed off. Typical. He'll never know how comforting the sound of his voice was though.

I received an email from Brad. Yep. Nothing very exciting. It's strange how some guys make me feel excited (well, one in particular) and I think even the most boring news from them is exciting. Brad's unfortunately not one of them, nor I have to say Marco (yes, another Italian and yes, typically truly typical "I'll call, I'll call" yeah right). At least Brad is a true gentlest gentleman and he will call or whatever when he can.

So tonight Tuesday, a (relatively) early night for me I think.

Back to Migros tonight too, no more Appollo, but that's OK, Valentino will not be there for much longer either. So no flirting there and anyway, he'll be leaving soon too. I wonder if he'll ever call me or send me an email (half Italian = probably not). Gorgeous body, looks, smile, etc and probably knows it. Probably has about 50 girlfriends and anyway, he's probably 500 years younger than me. Humph, why was I born in the year I was born? why do I have a mother and father like mine? At least Paula seems to have turned out OK in the end, perhaps it's me that's odd?

Gosh, I had the most erotic dream last night, with M.
Well, I didn't dare send him an email today – it may have looked too obvious. Does he have dreams too. Like me?

The power steering's gone again on my car. I may ask Hans-Peter if Oliver his son can have a look at it, after all he's doing his "car course" and wants to be a mechanic.

I went riding tonight and had a drink with my 2 new friends now, I don't even know their names but they're nice. The girl's French and her boyfriend is half German, but raised in Italy.
I am desperately missing friends and company and a boyfriend.
Smooth Al sent me an email tonight – it sounds like his weekend's been dreadful too – poor guy, sounds as bad as me on the love struck front. I replied. Hope I cheered him up, just a bit.

OK. So, I feel like I've been dumped again (or dumped on).

I received an email from M. Usually, I would have been so excited about it, well I was before opening it, my heart was in my mouth, I was very excited, but somehow deep down I felt sick with anticipation yet excited, scared to open it, to ensure it was the right moment, that I could dissolve into the atmostphere and soak up the contents at ease without anyone around me disturbing me.

It started, very casual, very relaxed, then he threw in that he'd gone horse riding with a girl he'd been seeing for a while called Claire.

Thanks for that, I thought.

He said she'd given him 2 lessons and he was really pissed off so he got on his mountain bike and cycled off. He said his work had picked up with a couple of major orders. I felt like writing back immediately, to say "well, stick to mountain biking" or something along those lines, but I just felt for the Kleenex and went to the ladies.

Boss, Hans-Peter, came to my desk.

I just wanted to read and reread and re-read again but he wanted me to talk to him about clients.

Suddenly I felt sick, like a rag doll, helpless, stupid. Again.

Roberto from Serene sent me an email, I had to call him and sort it out but I really didn't want to. I had to email the USA and sort it out but really I didn't want to, I just wanted to get on my bike and crash it.

Bastard bastard bastard bastard bastard bastard I hate him I hate him I hate him. I love him so much. I emailed Kate, desperately wanted to call her but she was in a meeting, she suggested calling her later.

What does he care? I feel like thumping his chest with my fists, probably beating the air as his strong arms would hold my hands away from him so I couldn't reach him.

I wondered if "Claire" was the one that he used to talk about – his ex-girlfriend who he said had not been out with anyone in 12 months after they'd split up. At least I had admitted to *trying* to go out with people.

I must call Kate.

Later. I just sent Kate an SMS, my 'phone rang. I'd just returned from Muskulatur with Guido at the Appollo fitness centre. I thought, do I want to answer that? I felt like crying. It was Theo – what a star – at least it was nice to feel wanted (he said he missed me but that he had my photo next to him). I don't know sometimes what I'm doing with my life. Sod men, sod boyfriends, sod getting married and having a family, I hate them all, I'm going to die a sad old spinster, listening to them all telling me about their new female acquisitions.

I am calling Kate, perhaps she'll know what to do. I checked my horoscopes. Crap. Can't get through to Kate. Heinz told me to send him an SMS, but he's out tonight on his date, it's the last place he'd like to have a text message sent, I think I may have to go for the chocolate in my fridge, but I feel sick enough already.
I don't know who to trust anymore.
I don't know who to turn to anymore.
I don't know who to write to anymore.
I miss him still so much, the bastard.

Why not send this letter I've written, asshole, so that the Postman will push it so far up his ass that it squeaks.
I hope Claire's so boring that he's totally unhappy, bored and has zero sex life.
Now it's 10pm and I should be in bed.
Friday night.
I sent an email reply to M this afternoon – I waited until about 2pm, then having tweaked it for about 45 minutes, I decided I really did have to get on with work. This is what I wrote:
1. Stick to moutain biking
2. Glad about work. So I presume soon, finances won't

254

forbid you from popping over? Then I can show you some decent stables where the horses don't mind the smell of mountains bikes, and you can buy me lunch.

Meooooow, perhaps it was too snappy?

I then worte that I was off to Crans Montana tomorrow and Sunday, to a "multi-athalon" and told him that I was a reserve in a team for the swim in the lake and running parts and that I was a bit nervous.

I didn't sign it. I didn't say hi. I was not friendly but very straight. Perhaps I shouldn't have sent it? Bother it. He's got to see how I feel. Perhaps I should have just done nothing, stayed quiet, made him wonder what I was up to, but then perhaps he'd just forget me and perhaps by writing what he did, he wanted to see my reaction. Well, my reaction was "pisssed off" and I hope he read that in what I sent him. I wish I'd been even more brief.

I wonder if it's this weekend that his sister is over? Would she knock some sense into him? Who knows?

How dare he end it "Hope all's well". I keep going over what he sent me. What's it to him? I am so hurt by him so flippantly throwing in about his new girlfriend, he's on the same level as Andy. I really hope he realised how much he'd hurt me when he sent it. If he didn't I hope he does now. He will once he gets my letter. Should I send it, perhaps at the end of next week.

Meanwhile I spent the whole week dodging dodgy Frank from the supermarket. He's the assistant that asked me out. I mean, it now dawns on me, what more has he to offer me other than his oranges and lemons. I ask you, come on Zoe, don't lower your standards. Can you imagine our date? Him speaking half Deutsch, half French, me speaking half English, and half whatever came out of my mouth. And what would we talk about? Carrots? Fortunately, I avoided him all week. Thursday night was supposed to be our night out, his half day so that "'e could go 'ome and douche, before our little drink". I spent Friday skulking around the tins, dodging the bananas and making a run for the cashier, only to find him sat at the till. Oh shit! I said I was in a rush.

Eventually, I managed to get hold of Kate. "Silly arse" she emailed me. "Whatever made you think..." I felt really bad. Great. Thanks Mate, I thought. I never said that to her when her ex-boyfriend won't go out with her anymore. I am all for trying to get them back together again, encouraging her, telling her not to give up if that's how she felt.

What did I do wrong?

I start to compare myself to my girlfriends:

Kate, she's really nice, but smokes like a chimney and drinks like a fish every night, she must take care.

Charlie. She's OK but my God, so undependable, shallow – not that I think she realises it. So so very la di daaa.

Tanya here In Zurich, completely over the top, la di daaa, but fun, and very pretty, a bit OTT darlingeeeees,sweeties etc. but that's her style and it's great on her.

Nina, nice girl but a bit chubby and so paranoid about losing each guy she sees as soon as she goes out with them. She's like an animal though sometimes with them, and talks about them as if they're not there, when they're stood right next to her.

Lucy, who always seems as if she's half asleep (as does her boyfriend.

So many girls, they all seem to make so much effort to speak, to do, to get guys, and I'm not saying that I never needed to, but I'm not an arrogant or OTT person. I hope I'm not bad in bed. I think I'm ok, fairly level headed (apart from my fixations on a certain M person) I have no real hang ups (apart from the fact that I don't have a Double D and a huge bank balance - yet). But apart from that I'm ok I have a good job (not that that's what I crave for my whole life). I'm a fairly relaxed sort of person. I can love and be loved. I'm a bit jealous, but only if not reassured and supported emotionally. I'm very generous (perhaps too much) but if and when I want to be.

I love M so damm much.

I'm going to sell my car. Seems reasonable. Too many things going wrong with it and I'm just frightened each time I drive it how much the next trip will cost me. It's expensive. It must put guys like M off. I could do with saving the money. The tram system is good over here, I could always hire a car if M did actually come over, or perhaps get a cheap one once I've sorted out my finances.

I sent an SMS to Lynn. She's probably not interested.

As the weeks pass, I wonder if everyone's forgotten me?

Chapter 26

Well, what a beautiful and stunning place Crans Montana is. Here I am, I arrived with Ermen, Lorena and Magda in Magda's little Mitsuibishi Colt (she paid 10K CHF for it, with only 28K on the clock. It's a bargain, I think it's more sensible for me to sell my car and I'm planning the return trip already). I will call MG on Monday.

So tonight, am having an early night, because tomorrow, hopefully, I will be competing in the "Course a pieds" (5km of up and downhill running) in the team "Chevaliers rond de la table". I hope I can run. I've been SMS'g a guy called Marc all evening to sort out a time and place to meet.

I watched the "mini terrific" event today. It was so sweet, I ran around the course with the competitiors and Magda's little niece. Very cute.

Well, it's a beautiful morning and the sun is shining. The white peaks of the mountains are piercing the blue clear sky and it gives me hope, I feel on top of the world, so high.

I'm desperate to take as photo but I keep thinking to myself that the view won't run away.

What a fabulous Sunday. Unfortunately I could not compete – the Chevaliers found a mountain runner, but it was a great oipportunity for me to suss the course and check out the competition (and get a sun tan, have a swim in the lake - twice, go to the top of the mountain and walk around).

It is absolutely beautiful, so hot. It is covered in snow at the top and skiing looked fantastic (I had taken my boots, but only competitors were allowed to ski and I would have needed my own skis anyway).

So I saw Ermen start off on her rollerblades, fast as lightening. I saw her hand over to Peter on the mountain bike who made it to the half way station, I'm certain his T-shirt was saturated in beer from the previous evening, not sweat. John took over, in his international flag boxers (you have to hand it to him), and he made a startling run to the top of the mountain – half the track being covered in snow (just to make it more "interesting"), who handed to Catherine, who did the 1 minute downhill ski, who handed to Lorena, who made a sterling job of the Langlauf (Ermen and I ran the last part of her leg) and who handed back to John to run back down the mountain, or rolled part of his way on his bottom I think from the colour of his shorts), who handed back to Peter who cycled back down to Oliver who picked up the sweatband to run (this would have been my part) all 4.5km around the lake, to hand obver to Phil, who did the swim (I also offered to do this, but as they all wore wet suits, I would have looked pretty silly in my bikini – I think I may have been a bit chilly, or, embarrassed). Phil then handed over to Dierk, who was the homecoming champ on the road biking. Wow, phew, I feel worn out describing it, what a fun day though.

We finished off the day by jumping into the lake (Peter with his bike, to clean it, or, get rid of it, he said it was the last time he was going to go cycling).

So I jumped in too and everyone was laughing and happy. The lake was cool, but refreshingly so, because it was so warm outside and we were a bit sunburnt. (to say the least as I emerged from the bathroom last night). It was colder than the hotel pool, which was positively tropical by comparison.

We went for a bite to eat at a pizzeria (more friendly than last night and as good). The quality of the food is much better the closer you get to Italy). Then we drove back after another quick swim in the lake, in Magda's car. (I have definitely decided to sell my car, I would be able to do so many more things). Even the boss bought his golf cabriolet for only 9KCHF. I'm going to buy a little run around here too, perhaps a golf or polo).

Back in the apartment, I think of M and his email. He would have loved it today – he would have been in his element.

Monday night. I try not to think of M. The bastard. I

mean did he think he wouldn't hurt me to send such a flippant email? I can't believe it. I wish so much I could forget him. I feel such pain and anger and emptiness.

I hope M writes an email again to ask what I'm up to and why I hadn't filled him in. I hope he does take a photo of Sam as he promised to send to me. I've probably blown it now though in writing that letter to him.

I didn't see Frank in the supermarket today, thank goodness, a whole week and I've managed to dodge any risky conversation.

I played squash with Ozzie Dale the vet tonight after work. It was good to have a game. We went for a quick drink afterwards and discussed cars, Lugarno, etc. He's not a bad squash player and it was good to play with someone, I was glad of the company.

I was not so busy at work today, so I spent a bit of time writing my next Swisslette news. I really felt that my whole enthusiasm for writing to M has been blown apart.

Tuesday, I sent my Swisslette news to everyone under the sun (including M – well, stuff him, let him know what a good time I'm having here). I was glad that I thanked JB, personally, in it. I even had a text and a telephone call from ol' Marco (probably to defend the bit about Italian men).

Tonight, I went to the Kino am Munsterplatz. It was brilliant. I queued for tickets for "Chocolate" when I was asked by a Swiss guy in German whether I wanted tickets for tonight. (I understood "billets" because it's the same in French, so when I heard that, I said "Ya, naturlich. Haben sie zwei bitte, for Magda and I). I then asked him how much and he gave them to me for free. We had the best seats in the house too, I was so lucky, we had free Cornetto ice creams too and watched a lovely film starring Juliet Binoche and Johnny Depp – the latter who was very gorgeous of course, even with his Irish twang. The story reminded me of my meeting with that Valentino I met at the Appollo gym – I wonder if he'll ever get my note and whether he'll contact me again. Probably not!

Juliet Binoche's character, Vianne (and her daughter's

name, Anouk, short for Annoushka, I think that's a great name for a girl) reminded me of Magda, with a quiet confidence, nothing glamorous or extrovert, but beautifulo in her own way.

We met up with Lorena before the film started. It was good to see them both again.

Wednesday night.

I've just returned from riding (where I was congratulated by the Herr) on how my riding's coming along nicely. My goodness, what's happened to him, why all the complements all of a sudden? He must be in such a good mood, probably because he's going on holiday on Monday for 2 weeks, to Edinburgh, to see his son apparently. Anyway, I returned here to the appartrment and thought I'd quickly rinse my boots and chaps before going to bed. I'd stayed for a couple of drinks with Tobias (the German guy) and his girlfriend, Stefanie (French, loves cheese) and we met the wife of his boss.

Anyway, I returned home at 10.30pm. In the washroom, I was greeted by this figure looming in the darkness, from the underground passageway, who pointed to her watch and muttered something in Swiss German. Oops, I didn't realise they were so strict in these apartments and suddenly I realised that I am only allowed to wash on Monday nights between 7 and 9pm. Oh damm. How do I get out of this one? It's bizarre that these Swiss seem meticulous about cleanliness and yet they won't allow me to quickly dust off my dirty riding boots, surely, they wouldn't expect them to stay mucky until tomorrow? Anyway, so I had the wrath of Binningen thrust upon me and I'm probably cursed now for the next 7 years.

Thursday, another spectacular morning. I will cycle in and tonight, Muskulatur with Guido.

I keep writing about the mornings and how beautiful they are for when I'm deciding to return to the UK. Or not.

I had a bit of a late night – I went to see Charlie's Angels tonight at Munsterplatz. Catherine and Dierk were there and dangerous Dave (not) from New Zealand (he's a bit of an odd ball). Dale and Amir showed up – I bought the tickets so they bought me dinner. Also Dave and Suz were there. It was a good laugh, a bit of a no-brainer but it was funny.

It was very hot today, and tonight

Friday, yes, another day of blue blue skies. All my windows and doors are open.

Saturday, yes, another beautiful day. I went to Zurich yesterday, for a meeting at Creative Inc. After, I was due to meet up with mad Tanya of the Zurich "vibe" but unfortunately, 079 numbers for some reason didn't work in Zurich, which included mine and Tanya's. Great! How could we communicate? We hadn't managed to get anywhere. Anyway, one of the guys at the office used twixtel to find her name and address and home phone number so I called her and left a message. Then, Roberto, showed me how to get to her house. I waited there. She told me the party was from 6.30pm. I didn't think she'd be too late so I waited outside her apartment block (which looked like cell blocks on the outside, in typical Germanic Swiss style) and they smelt of incense inside.

Anyway, I waited until about 7pm and then left a note in her postbax and left. I headed to town, parked the car and thought I'd make my way all the way over there, I may as well stay for a bit. I wandered down the lake, wishing I'd taken a book and a swimming costume. Anyway, I stopped at a little bar on a side street, had a glass of rose Zinfandel wine, paid and then left. Quiet extraordinary events then unfolded.

As I reached the top of the street, I heard a voice from a balcony shouting "Tanya" I looked around. From the distance it could have been anyone and then I wondered whether I actually wanted to meet up if by the slightest chance it was indeed Tanya. Then I thought, bother it, Zoe, just find out, so I ran towards her as she was about to be let into the building. Sure enough it was Tanya, I couldn't believe it! So there we were, we'd met up anyway, you'd never do that in London (and perhaps that's what I'd miss too if I left here, the size, the scale, the scope) or perhaps I do miss the company?

We entered the building, it was her friend, Darryl's, party. So we met Darryl, "Downstairs Peter", Noelle, Gaby, and a guy who left early. They were all completely drunk and stoned on joints they were rolling. I just wasn't in the mood, besides, I was driving, in work clothes and too hot. We went to Noelle's apartment later for some home cooked spaghetti which was fab. Then I decided to leave. Tanya, of course wanted a lift home "darling". She was pretty stoned too and had a massive row on the mobile with her mate "Indie". It was all "gorgeous that""darling this".

They've asked us to join them in Locarno on Saturday 4th August, to a party. I just know how it will be though, so I'm inclined to decline. I've booked the hostel on 10th and 11th anyway (they looked at me astounded when I mentioned the word "hostel" as if it were a little spec of grub on the floor). They've also asked us to a party on 24th August in Zurich. Sounds fab – a lovely place. Noelle is organising it for the bank where he works. Noelle's apartment is fantastic. Tanya told me her parents are rolling in it but Noelle later told me she'd been married once (to a banker, half Persian, half English, didn't want her to work) for 4 weeks only before she wanted to get out. So, I can imagine all the pre-nuptual agreements and money paid out. They don't talk anymore and that was 3 years ago. She's 33. (Tanya's 31 I found out). There seem to be so many 33-year olds or thereabouts here – I've never met so many in one place.

I feel a bit sick and tired but I want to get up now. I didn't smoke anything, but I guess I probably inhaled a bit.

A strange couple were sitting outside my apartment block when I returned last night. Very odd. She was in the car. He came down the stairs (from my level). It was 1.30am! I never got to the bottom of it.

Darryl reckoned I should live by the station in Zurich and commute to Basel everyday – yeah right. Noelle's all right, she'd had her problems in the past – family, but she says "You're OK" so I like her. I think she's fought to be where she is today – nice apartment. Tanya keeps saying it's just because her parents are filthy rich but in some ways I don't believe that. I don't understand Tanya sometimes, so many chips and yet she must have led the most amazing life – she'd lived in Barbados, Hong Kong, London, Africa, India, Australia and now is back in her home town of Zurich, yet everyone else is better than her… I hope I don't sound like that. I must get rid of my debts, then there's no baggage on me.

Danny ket calling me "Box fresh" last night (clean apparently, whereas normally, all UK girls have a grubby reputation). Danny calls all UK girls,"boys with tits". How awful. Then he went to "shake hands with the unemployed" (ie. Go for a wee - apparently). He's a horrid little man.

I just had a weird phone call – similar to that one a few weeks ago. He said he was calling from the UK. Said he knew I was not going out with anyone at the moment, that he knew where I lived, that my ex boyfriend had told him that I gave good blow jobs. I just said "Gosh, is that true, I'm flattered". Git. He also said that he had some video footage that my ex boyfriend had taken whilst I had given him a blow job, that he would send to me. I said "OK, wonderful. I'd like to see what I was doing that was so good". He told me to stay on the line for 5 minutes and then he said he'd tell me who had told him. OK I said, let me know then. He said it could have been my ex boyfriend I'd left behind in the UK, before I came to Switzerland (Yeah right, I just said OK so not the guy I really miss then). Something tells me it could be one of SBP's friends, or, that lorry driver from the Gottard. Perverts – all of them. But how else could he have got my telephone number? M? No, surely not. I don't think he could lower himself to that. JB, no. Don't think it's his style. Andy, no, he was always so pissed he'd never remember anyway, I

I called Kate. She was really concerned.

Went to the Natural History Museum to meet JimBob today – from the Crans Montana team – to go around the treasures of the Munster exhibition. It was amazing. I learnt that Basel was devastated by an earthquake in 1356 – amazing, that's why most buildings date from then onwards and it's very medieval.

I was supposed to meet Sabine and her boyfriend, GuyC afterwards, to go swimming in the Rhine as it was so hot. However as I left the museum, it was raining, so I called Sabine and there was no reply, so JBob and I went for a drink at Des Artes – such a cool bar, good fun atmostphere, a little quirky but it's OK: Then I cycled to find out where we would have met, and got hopelessly lost but it was fun. Sabine telephoned me later. She then mentioned that tonight they were going to see some "enlightenment" chap and suggested that it may be good for me to go too.

Now, I like her a lot but I hope she's not hoping I'll end up joining some cult or other and worshipping some enlightened humanoid form of budda. I am worried. I went home for an evening of writing letters (to Anna, Nikki, to M...will I ever send it, well, yes, he needs to know why I sent such a rude and abrupt reply, if he doesn't have the sense right now). Having thought about having an early night, it's now quite late, but it's ok, I don't need to avoid anyone etc/or even stay out because of anyone or give anyone a lift anywhere. Consequently, I got a bit squiffy on my own (v sad) and ate lots of chocolate.

Mum called. I still sounded a bit upset to her – well, I'd just been relating my mysterious telephone call to Nikki in the letter to her and I just realised how alone and how a little bit scared I was. Why was mother calling on Saturday night though. I should be out enjoying myself! But I wasn't clearly

Sunday, a beautiful morning again. I feel a bit groggy after all that wine and chocolate last night. Damm, hungover. Still, it's probably about time, even though I drank alone. (I wonder what my writing looks like in M's letter – probably dreadful, I'll have to write it out again).

I just thought, if Marco does come over this week, it would be great on Tuesday. I could take him to the BBQ and then the fireworks – it would be lovely to have some UK company – also he could speak Italian to everyone.

Well, the 2nd night I'm eating out on my terrace and how civilised it is – why didn't I think of this before? It's worth the effort. Just me, the moon in front of me, a glass of wine, Georgey Michael in the background, Brutus by my side. I think I overdid it on the herbs. This is my bit of "enlightenment" for my soul. (I didn't call Sabine, I hope she's not offended, but I'd rather not get roped into all sorts of culty clubs. I know what's right and wrong in my life and how I must sort it out, well, I think I do.

I keep thinking about that call yesterday. I want to know which idiot it was. How did he know so much information about me? I want to meet up with Theo so much, with anyone. I keep thinking about the wonderful fresh Greek salad food and how cheap it is over there. I'd be over tomorrow if only it wasn't for the conferences I have to organise here, there and everywhere! I can't believe I'm sweating still and it's 10am and all I have on is a vest and knickers.

Chapter 27

What did I do today?

1. Think of M. Arghhhhh!!!!

2. Brush my teeth/have shower

3. Went for a hack in the forest behind my apartment. It was fab, a bit slow, but it was 30degrees, even at 10am this morning. The hack lasted approximately 2 and quarter hours, good value. I was on Grace – I think we understand each other now. I have to "work her" hard (keep pushing my knees in) but she's quite responsive eventually.

4. After riding, it was so hot, I just wanted to dive in a lake, so I drove to Luzern to Weggis, dropped off the car, got on my bike and cycled to Gersau, to visit my little spot with diving area and island etc. Unfortunately, it also came complete with hot-headed Zurich guys, so arrogant. I did not exchange numbers – one weird 'phone caller is enough. Anyway, I met "Kurt" from Gersau – he's a chef and used to work at a big restaurant in Zurich but now works 3 days a week somewhere in Gersau. The arrogant Zurich boy was Thomas or, Bondi, as he liked to be called ("like James Bond with an eeee at the end" he said). Groan. He told me he was going to be "Adonis" on a float in the love parade in 2 weeks' time which is happening in Zurich. He then took a drag on Kurt's dope he'd just rolled in front of me (his 2nd). He told me I should go. "Everyone is there, everyone from Basel".

From what I've seen of the Zurich festivities to date, I think I'll pass).

Bondi told me that Zurich was the place to be "from zee banhof to downtown, it's party party party, everyone dances in the bahnhof even".

I shared some water with them, they then went onto beers (and more dope). I read the paper I'd bought (to catch up on news back home) and my Bridget Jones. Bondi said I looked like an angel as the last rays of sunshine lay around my body on the "beach" where I sat in the corner.

Back home, it seems in the UK that the battle is on for the successor to be leader of the Tory party. In addition, they think flight delays will continue for many years. Then I read about how warm it has been over there at the moment – dam.

Back home…
I'm homesick.

I read and re-read the letter I've written for M – will I have the courage to send it? He's got to know why I replied so curtly on the email.

Night 3 on my terrace. A lilac smoke blue sky in front of me, the moon slightly to my left. All these times I could have eaten out in my back garden in Battersea, but I never made the effort, because East Enders was on or something equally as unproductive, depressive and solemn. Excuses, excuses.

I read and re-read M's letter again. Should I send it?

Tonight, I played squash by myself. Dale couldn't make it in the end, but I thought I would only go home and start to eat earlier so I made the effort.

I emailed Marco to advise him of the BBQ and fireworks party on the river and the National free day on Wednesday, but I did not hear anything. He's such a tease – I'll never believe he's coming over.

Ben Ledge sent me a response to my email Cheeslette news last week. It was nice. He says he may pop over. I've given him a few free dates and suggested he join me in Locarno in a couple of weeks' time for the film fest. It would be fab if he could make it, a laugh with no strings.

Fireworks are going off in all directions again tonight – more practice for tomorrow night.

Tuesday, wow, what a beautiful blue sky. What a day.

Tuesday 31st July. A full day at work, then left, on time. (Hans-Peter was away for the day at a meeting in London). Then I cycled to Dierk and Catherine's tonight for their BBQ to celebrate 31st July and watch the Basel fireworks – it was a fabulous evening, everyone from the "Terrific" event in Crans Montana was there (Ermen, Lorena, Peter, John, Oliver, Phil and Carla, and of course Catherine and Dierk and their lovely little daughter, Estelle with her grandmother, a typical French grandmamma, very sweet). It was a lovely evening. The fireworks were AMAZING. They must spend 1000's of CHFs on them, if not more. I've never seen such a display.

Anyway, I left there at about 12.30 to cycle back, part of the way with Ermen – we're planning to go out this weekend – apparently to the Cargo bar, it's the place to be by the river when the sun is out and the nights are long.

It's August 1st, Wednesday. It's a beautiful day and it's a Freitag, so I'm free for the day. Gosh, what should I do? Waterskiing in Zurich? Windsurfing on Lake Geneva? Rollerblading in Interlaken and swimming in the lake? Which lake? Thun? Brienz? I really fancy going rollerblading, although I may bump into SBP. There again, what the hell if I do? He's a pratt anyway, total fuckwittage if he passed my way to make those funny 'phone calls (if he's searching for a way to my heart then that's definitely not that way).

I'm eating breakfast (Frustücke) on my balcony. Just had some porridge, and croissants. After all the food last night too - such comarardaree it was fab – most people took something, like a cake or something as well as wine or beers whatever. Their generosity was quite overwhelming. I'd asked Catherine whether she wanted me to take anything, but she'd saidnot really unless there was something particular I had wanted to eat and drink, as there would be plenty of salads and meat etc (and boy, was there). So well organised. They're looking forward to their move to England – I offered to be their tour guide and recommend

269

via email where they could go at weekends.

Oh yes, yesterday, I posted letters to Anna, Nikki and…of course, to M. I don't know what he'll think of it when it arrives .

Oh well, 08.48am. I'd best make a move.

At least this anti-mossi plug in device seems to be working – no more midge bites for a while.

I have decided, roller blades and a lake, here I come. Don't know where I'll get to, what adventures I'll have, but I'll share them with you later.

I can't believe tonight, I'm sat on my balcony again, with fireworks going off in all directions around me. Even the "Greek house" on the corner of my road has a party going on – it's great here, I don't know whether to look left, right, behind me, in front of me. One of my neighbours is playing Swiss music. And, my pasta even tastes great. I wish I could share it with someone, anyone, even SBP seems appealing at this moment – NO NO NO (I must be desperate to even contemplate it).

I'm glad I didn't go riding tonight. I don't think the horses would have liked it much.

There are some fireworks where the garden centre is, some where roughly Munchenstein is (Midge's 2nd home, ie. the MG garage), where the Rhine is – all along it, where the wood is, where Valentino jogs, where the post office is, where boss Hans-Peter and Denise live. There are fireworks going off everywhere.

Looks like I just got home in time to unpack, make dinner, have a bath and appreciate them all – I think they're going to go on all night at this rate. In gardens, people have set up little displays with candles and lamps and BBQ grills. It's really lovely.

Today, I took my roller blades, bike and bathing suit to the Bernese Oberland. (I decided that if SBP saw me, he saw me, it's a free country) so I went down to the old airfield in Interlaken to practice my rollerblading, which I haven't done since I last went out with SBP, so it was a good opportunity to practise. (ooh, there are now fireworks in a garden to my right. Now in the forest again. At this rate, I think they'll set off an earthquake).

I rollerbladed for about one and a half hours, then went to find some water. I wanted to check out Thun, so I headed down there, found the lake and went for a dip. Unfortunately, you can't dive in there, but it was great – the water was about 18-20degrees, so quite warm, compared to Luzern. I swam, sunbathed, read (I've nearly finished Bridget Jones) oh, and tried to have a windsurfing lesson, but he was busy all day, so I've booked for next Sunday at 3pm.

I think I've developed a stitch from running around my balcony whilst eating trying to take in all these fireworks.

At about 6.30pm, I cycled into the town centre and found a beautiful restaurant on the edge of the lake, where it was silver service and a pianist was playing. Very civilised. I cycled to a bar on the banks of the Aare – it starts in Thun – and had a 3dl glass of Sangria – a complete rip off at 8CHF per glass but worth it for fun and the feeling of being on a boat as the bar had a bit that extended into the river.

Oh yes, I had a bit of a stupid accident. Whe finishing my rollerblading, I went hurtling towards my car, I cannot brake properly yet, so I decided to just break by crashing into my car. I misjudged my bike on the bike rack on the boot. As I swept towards it, stretching out my arms to stop myself, my right hand was sliced open by the bike cog, taking a gash of skin out of it. A bit of flesh hung off and blood spurted everywhere. It was disgusting. It's OK now, the lake water did it good, but it hurts quite a bit. It's quite a deep slice and perhaps I should have a stitch, but I wouldn't know where to start, so I kissed it better, wrapped it in a piece of tissue, washed it with my spare water bottle and moved on.

As I drive along, I notice lovely smells in the air, with the windows open and the roof down. It smells kind of farm fresh, yet not disgusting, as it sometimes does in the UK, more rich, lush, like the grass and the milk – does that sound stupid?

I wonder where M's letter is at this moment? Is it in the UK? At which depot? In which postman's sack? Has he left for Greece already? Has his sister been to stay? Has he taken a photo of little Sam, complete with Swiss bib on? Have I ruined our friendship with my snappy email? I'm partly glad I sent the letter to explain my reaction. I think he knows why though, and I think perhaps that's why he sent it, to test me. Well F*** him.

No, no hard feelings, come on Zoe, be super calm, like him. I just ate a Cross Air choccie – well, there are many of them in my fridge and I felt like it.

Thursday, a lovely day. A bit fresher than it has been of late but still beautiful. I had a dream about Ceroc last night, about M again, maybe nighmtmares now.

Tonight, I went to a Muskulatur class – it was so so hot – about 32 degrees I think today, however, tonight, it's now raining – a dramatic thunder and lightening display, follwing the man made displays of last night.

I went to meet Lorena, Rita and the girls at Munsterplatz to watch "Himalaya". It was a beautifully shot film, fab scenery, but in Tibetan, which I'm not that fluent in (contrary to popular belief) but I managed to follow the French subtitles and the yaks.

A typical boy meets girl. Girl's husband dies. Man brings husband's body back to girl. Girl thanks man. Man is wonderful, strong, caring, has beautiful eyes, beautiful hair and body. Man and girl end up sharing a Tibetan version of the duvet, a sac, and it's all beautiful, wonderful. Even son of girl loves man and all live happily ever after.

There you go, I'm fluent in Tibetan.

It started to rain as we started the movie at the outdoor cinema. Suddenly we were surrounded by assistants handing out rain macs and then we all sat there like we were some laboratory rats in our free white coats all watching the screen. It must have looked quite funny from the air to any passing planes.

It was a very hot and steamy night. A shame I am alone. I think of Bridget Jones and perhaps should use this time alone to find inner peace, harmony and spiritual epiphany as well.

Oh yes, I had an email from Theo – he sent it Saturday night – boy, does he seem to know just when my "down moods" are. Last time he rang, he more or less saved me from jumping off my balcony after M's email.

Friday. A fairly nice day. Pretty warm still even though it's a little cloudy. I had quite a good sleep last night (I must stop eating all these free ice creams at the cinema though, otherwise, all this gym effort will go to pot).

Chapter 28

Oh fuck oh fuck oh fuck. M sent me an email today (well, last night actually). He's off to Vass, Greece, on Sunday on holiday. He's dyed his hair blonde (??!!!??? I can't believe it – he says he'll send me a photo sometime! I just can't imagine it!)

I still feel mad, sick, helpless, I cannot concentrate on anything, sick again, happy, sad, confused, perplexed, butterflyish, when he writes. I replied and eluded to the fact that I'd sent him a letter I said it was really stupid and asked him to ignore it/etc/I had felt pretty low when I wrote it – oh shit oh shit, now I wish I hadn't sent it – I keep remembering the things I'd put in it – oh shit. He said he was planning to buy a boat with Dave to go up and down the river with – wow, fab. It's just typical though isn't it – when I have him, he hasn't got anything. Now he's getting everything and I'm not with him. Oh shit, what will he think of the letter. Oh shit.

Friday night. Later. Wonder if the letter is waiting for him at home when he returns, or will it arrive tomorrow.

Worse, will it arrive when he's away (actually this is probably better – at least he will know about it).

Saturday, it's a bit cooler today though still bright – it had been raining last night, but not too heavily.

I wonder if M's letter arrived this morning?

Saturday, spent too much shopping. I went to the gym for a good workout this morning. Everyone's started to recognise me now and say hello which is nice. They probably think "there's that mad English girl going on the treadmill again", but who cares. I have to work off this cheese and chocolate (I put on some Capri pants tonight that I'd worn for the Ceroc competition last year and they're tight, too tight – oh my goodness, weight, where did you come from? It cannot be. Perhaps I just used to wear figure hugging things in London – I will have to wear them before I get all lapse and start becoming a fat slob – is my fat starting to graduate down to my hips – god forbid). I bought some new gym things today (they're so expensive here) and a waterproof jacket plus some walking sandals for all terrain but comfortable and trendy too. So, a practical day, albeit expensive. And I went to the market to buy some fresh mushrooms and cheese. Simplest pleasures.

Tonight, I went with Ermen, to one of her friend's, Claire's, leaving party. She's from New Zealand and will be leaving for Hamburg soon. Her flatmate, Julie, (also from New Zealand and who I'd also met before with Rita – everyone seems to know everyone) and she's off to Madrid next Saturday for good too. Wow. She speaks fluent Spanish though.

I cycled to the party and back home, it was quite a civilised party and I met a few more English people – all the English people I meet are from London I think compered to anywhere else in England. Switzerland is definitely better" most if them say. I met, gosh, I can't remember their names, but they all go to "Paddy's" (an Irish pub which sounds awful and looks awful – it reminds me of those tacky places on Lavendar Hill that you would not dream of going to). (Ermen says it's awful too). By the look of their friend, Lou, as well (a beer swilling, plump and non so attractive "girl") I think I'll be staying well clear too.

August 3rd 2001 sees the opening of the first Starbucks in Switzerland – is this the road to ruin?

Sunday, absolutely beautiful morning. Off riding and then to try my hand at windsurfing. (I hope M waves to me as he passes on the plane – wish I'd written that on my email).

I've just been to see Stanley Kubrick's film 2001: A Space Odyssey. The only words to describe this cult 1958 (?) movie are: Astonishing, bizarre, incredible, captivating, yet disturbing – a film full of colour and inspiration. Quite extraordinary.

Today, I went horseriding – there was an event on at the stables – a national swiss competition, which was fascinating to watch. I'd love to be able to jump like that.

I went to Thun for my windsurfing lesson afterwards too. It was fab. I can do it, a bit. I managed a few times to stand up and "plane" it along the lake (well, not so fast) but even the instructor told me to stop before I reached the other side of the lake. (Yes, Tom, the instructor at the windsurf school, was a typical boarder typoe of person – he works in Wengen during the winter, teaching skiing and snowboarding "as you like" – the most annoying Swiss Man saying – SBP used to say it too – but then he teaches windsurfing and hires out all the kit in Spiez and Thun in the summer. I went out there on my maiden voyage and damm typical, he spins like a piroet on his board, flying up to me, quite literally, "handbrake turning" in front of me, whilst I clamber on my knees to my board, struggle to pull up the mast, hang onto the boom ans sail and rope and balance, feel the wind, lose balance and splash, off I fall into the water again. Tom's blonde hair breezily blowing in the wind and his lean limbs dance aroud in the mast like a lap dancer on water.

Anyway, I made it, I've done it and now M will be having the first of many drinks (probably) down on a Vass beach in the beautiful heat and sun and probably chatting up everything in a bikini this very second with Paul.

Monday, beautiful. A little fresher but beautiful blue skies with sweeps of white dusting that look like they could be clouds.

The pressure was on today to do this, do that, get it sorted, with a client asking me for more than is feasibly possible. Ridiculous. "Oh and Zoe". Sometimes, I feel like throwing my hands in the air and ringing Theo and saying "I'm comig over" (for good). Just imagine though if I went to see him and he was ugly and small and his horrible teeth (and rough hands). And, I'd decided to spend a whole valuable week putting up with it. Well, I suppose I could always sail off somewhere else. It's really easy and not too expensive.

I wonder if M did receive his letter and things on Saturday before he left? I wish I'd taken a photocopy then at least I'd remember exactly what I'd written.

I wonder what JB is doing now? Probably watching his motorsport video and shagging some tart whilst his lodger is looking on.

Well, tonight's a night in. It's raining a bit. I was going to go to the outdoor cinema to see "In the mood for love" but I think I should have a night to me, to gather my thoughts (and save some money) besdides it's raining (not that I should be worried about that with my new waterproof fab jacket thing), but then I think, I'd like to go windsurfing in Ascona, so I shouldn't spend all my money before I get there.

I sent Michele a text, but typical, no news. What's he up to I wonder? Dating some Italian girl with beautiful long dark hair and sultry skin. I feel a bit of a lost soul at the moment with no direction except trying to survive here – sometimes it feels like I'm doggy paddling just trying to keep my head above water and always someone's pulling at my legs to try to pull me under and sometimes I think it may be easier to just give up, give in, stop trying so hard and let go.

Chapter 29

7.8.01

Bit of a cloudy morning but a steady 25 degrees this afternoon, so I could have dinner on my terrace again.

Had several erotic dreams again last night, it was very strange – must have been the wind blowing through my apartment (I dreamt of M – well, obviously – and of JB, strangley, I've never dreamt of him before – quite funny really, his masterpiece was chopped off – he did it. Bizarre, quite extraordinary. But he still wanted me in the dream. (His friends were there too). Dreams. Bizarre. Anyway, I wonder what that meant.

Tonight Aston Villa are in town to play Basel in the new stadium – I wonder if anyone's watching the match back home – well, M won't be, unless it's in Greece, but I doubt it, wish I could be there, lying on a beach waiting for him as he comes off his windsurf and then make love to me in the sand dunes, then to go to a disco, to have something to eat along the way with Paul and then, snog and make love and get up the following morning with the sun on our faces and our arms wrapped around each other, laughing, joking, perhaps having a pillow fight and a shower together…I'm getting the feeling it will never be with him though.

Kate sent a mail. I sent one back. Nic phoned me, was nice to hear his voice. He sounds in great spirits and I admire him so much after all he's been through, MS and all – I so wish I had a father like him. Apart from that, nothing extraordinary happened, so why does my horoscope keep telling me that this week, "this is the week, you Sagitarians" Well come on, I'm waiting!

Oh yes, now Midge is a fully fledged Swiss citizen – well, almost. I took him to the border as I'd had a warning paper from them and had been given 10 days in which to declare him as a Swiss car – they let me go, I do not have to change the plates and I can now officially drive in der Schweiz. So, he has his own papers now. He's an official resident – of course that also meant that I was qualified for a parking ticket 2 days later. Scheissa.

Border control was interesting. They only spoke German or French. At least, that's what they told me. They said, "we learnt English at school but are not very good at it" (well, I couldn't even string that sentence together in Deutsch, so they should be proud of themselves).

At 5.58pm, all left, promptly, like clockwork oranges on the dot. At 6pm, no-one was left in the place except me and the guy filling in the forms. Eventually it was done, and he told me I could drive my car for 2 years in Switzerland as it is without changing the plates etc. I paid the princely sum of 10CHF ("Praise the Lord"). So, that's the trick, go to border control, less than 30mins before they're due to close – the Swiss will always stick to their watches (which I guess means leaving for home on time – wish our office was the same).

Wed. Well, it's raining quite badly this morning – unusual. Still, I suppose Switz would not be so green if there was no rain.

Wed. pm, it was stonkingly hot again.

I had a bit of a shock this morning. I received an email from Magda, saying how furious she was that I'd forwarded a mail onto Ermen and invited her to Gladiators on Monday night. It sounded like I'd really put my foot in it. I felt really down after reading it. Here I am, trying hard to make friends yet, suddenly, this and whoosh, wham, no friends, any more.

Suddenly I feel very alone again. It wasn't just Magda's mail, it was the fact that in the mail she mentioned that I'd done it to other people, so she'd heard, so they had told her, which also disappoints me because it means that people have been talking ill of me, behind my back, without saying

279

anything. Half of me says, oh for goodness sake, life's too short and complicated enough to worry about things like that and if that's what she's like, then it's no wonder that she has no boyfriend, which only makes me think how normal I am and how I deserve a great guy and that I am an OK catch – fun, keen, enthusiastic, always willing to please, always trying to look on the Bright side, being happy, the list goes on I think. But now, I don't know whether anyone's talking to me, just about me.

It's only suddenly, when you receive emails like this, that you start to wonder why you're here on earth? Whether you've upset everyone else in te same way, who you've ever sent an email to, or, when you've tried to demonstrate your eagerness, excitement and enthusiasm to.

It was really upsetting and makes me reanalyse the way I think things through, I guess we all occasionally need emails like this to just ensure that we don't go around upsetting people unknowingly. It really knocks your confidence though. You expect emails like that from your boss at work but not from a so-called new "friend". Finding new friends in a foreign country is hard enough, without someone writing something like this (plus insinuating that others I've met, and opened my life to, may feel the same way). It's ok for them, they can discuss things together, they are from the same place, the same country. I have no-one else here. I've not met anyone I'd particularly call a fellow friend from my country – Phil and Suze are the closest, but they've got each other.

Sometimes I feel like a new born puppy with massive oversized paws, that keeps stumbling over everything in her path and knocking things over as she wags her tail in delight, not realising that it's upsetting everyone – quite nonchalant to the idea that I'm creating havoc.

I think I'd best lie low for a while. I have to start to reevaluate who my friends are, why they are my friends and who do I trust?

I sent an SMS to Michele about me going to Locarno. No reply…why did he respond so quickly last time (he had a viable excuse. Perhaps this time he has to think of one)

There's a message on my telephone. Wonder who it is. Well, it's just to say that Michele's message has been delivered – says it was delievered at 19.04pm and yet it's now 11.30pm. He's probably only just switched his mobile on. Oh well, see if he responds.

I phoned Kate tonight to appologise for the miserable mail I sent her yesterday. She's busy at work and having fun…sometimes I get the feeling that I'm just a nuisance to her, that she doesn't really have the time, or energy, to talk with me. As time slips by, I feel I'm growing farther and farther away from the friends I've built up, the people I like and life, and I feel like they are moving away from me as I'm not there anymore – out of sight, out of mind, and I can't bear that.

Thursday. A few clouds, but a beautiful and bright morning, Meeting with Chameleon this morning (an 8am – 6pm meeting ☹)

And it's the weekend…

Andrea's parents have a house in the mountains – the valley opposite Bosco Gurin. Impressive? (Nothing impresses me after Andy. I want to be totally in love with someone for who they are, not for the houses that their parents own).

Well, a bizarre turn of events. Bizarre, bizarre, bizarre.

I left locarno at 2.30pm, met Andrea for a pizza around 7pm, then we went to the piazza. Despite my ticket, he had 2 VIP tockets – again. He bought my pizza and for a moment, I feel like I am being taken care of, then after "Moulin Rouge" (an interesting if not slightly bizarre film about the place with the same name in Paris).

After that, Andrea suggested going for a coffee, so that I

stayed awake during my drive home. We had some water and coffee (and he likes his bitter lemon). (Bitter lemon is to Andreas what Rivella was to SBP).

Anyway, then he produces a VIP invitation to the closing night ceremony. I thought, I can't miss that, and he suggested going for just 20 minutes or so – well it was more like 1 hour. It was fab though – it was held in the teaching school for primary teachers. They handed out massive pieces of Panatone and champagne, (now this is more my style I thought to myself) and we had 2 glasses each – I'd not drunk a bean all day – and an ice cream each – the Swiss are very proud of their "Movenpick" ice cream (but I still prefer Haagen Daaz).

There was beer, music, salads, etc etc, it was wonderful. I wished so much I could have danced though. No-body seems to dance in Switzerland, perhaps I should start a class here. It sometimes feels like my legs have been tied up and I am desperate to dance. I miss my Cerocing Monday nights.

This guy Andreas, seems to know everyone under the sun too. We walk into this party, seemingly full of starlets, producers, and people we don't know, and he claps this guy on the back, shakes his hand, shakes another's hands, etc etc, like tarzan swinging from rope to rope, but here it's hand to hand. We leave at 2am and we cross the road and he says Hi to someone else. Just Hi, how's it going – nothing else – quite cool, calm and collected. Just a quiet confidence. It felt nice and good to be with him. I had not felt that for so long, SBP was not like that, this felt good.

He sent me a "good morning" message via sms this morning, Monday. I sent him a reply and tonight, sent him another. He sent me one back, then called later. (oh shit, I thought, it's happening all over again – friends, I keep thinking, friends, it's important to be mates first, friends).

Tuesday, Rhine swim. It's a beautiful day (wow, blue blue skies and already pretty warm) I had another dream last night about JB – I keep dreaming about him, why? I'm not particularly fussed about him.

Andreas sent me a mail, to which I replied, naturally.

Ok so here are some of the irritating and annoyng statements by Swiss men that send me emails:

"Unbelieeeevable"

"Bye bye, Andrea" (means "bye for now, see you later, see ya" – but feels like he is talking to a 2-year old).

"Keep attention" (=take care/pay attention etc)

"As you like" (= whatever, if you can, what I'd do etc etc)

"Handy" = mobile

"Top fit" (=very sporty, as I was described by heidi at the gym – I'm flattered, but it sounds hilarious spoken with an emphasis on the feeeeet=fit)

Oh yes and "that's swiss for you" (ie. It is expensive, it's such an annoying expression, and that's the only time they have a smile on their faces, when they say that, Bea does it all the time at work – if she thinks it cannot be done)

"oops la" (= oh dear, another annoying one of SBP's)

Who teaches them these phrases? In their accents, or perhaps it's just SBP's accent, it sounds silly, damm, I wish I'd never gone out with him, it's made me so wary of all foreign men, especially Swiss ones which is a shame as any are truly nice gentlemen.

Spoke to Tanya on the mobile today. She's so full of bullshit sometimes. Sorry T but that's the way it seems sometimes, we love you to bits, and everyone needs that in their lives sometimes, to liven things up, but why full of bullshit – it's party party and then nothing happens, it's "oh no, not swiss men, not men from ticino, they're the worst because they even think they're Italian but they're not, they are swiss through and through". But her first reaction when I mentioned Andrea was "oh fab, great, wonderful darling – is he gorgeous babe?" I mean, I wouldn't exactly call Andrea gorgeous, I mean he's not bad looking (in a Hugh-ish Grant sort of way, with trendy specs – and with a bit of imagination) but not gorgeous. My first impression of him was: quite nice, trendy specs, lovely pale shirt and chinos –

nice dress sense and style. Nice wavy chestnut hair (just like Sydney the horse) and he speaks Italian (very sexy) although he speaks English with more of a Swiss-English accent (damm).

What I did like about him though, was that he seemed to care, even to guide me through the crowds on Friday night, when I didn't even know him and every 2 seconds, he looked around at me to make sure I was following him. Also, he was so "masterful" at arrangements for Sunday night. Not pushy, so not meeting on Saturday was cool. He has lots of friends, obviously (as he acknowledged just about every person walking down through Locarno on both Friday and Sunday night – nicely though, not showy, arrogantly or anything, just quietly confident. He has quite a nice smile when he uses it, too (I just wish he'd use it more often) and also has a good sense of humour – he made a few jokes at which he nudged me on the shoulder with his shoulder – this was a bit lady, and it became a bit irritating after a while – the first 2 times, were quite funny, but there is such a thing as over-egging the joke.

At least though it was not serious heavy-duty sniffing, like SBP, or, with a serious look, smile, head bowed type.

Oh yes, I forgot to say that I was bang on time to meet with Andreas tonight (remarkably) an he was not there, tut tutting at his watch (like SBP used to, sending me an sms if I was 2 seconds late. What an asshole).

I will have to stop eating this Swiss chocolate bunny – well it's been in my fridge since boss Hans-Peter gave us all one each for Easter, it was just in my fridge saying "eat me". I just read in a medical journal though, that oolder people with a penchant for choccie live to be older, have less heart attacks etc etc, so it's justified (a little) I will have to work twice as hard at the gym tomorrow.

Andreas has a day's holiday tomorrow – all Catholic religions have in the relevant parts of Switzerland. (Basel is not of course, Catholic), Well, it's half and half really,

Catholic in Basel land, Protestant in Basel Stadt.

Andrea is going to walk in the mountains – I mean, what would you do in England? Go to Brighton beach? Go horse riding? Go swimming in a swimming pool, go to Devon (more than 3 hours and a traffic jam?), watch a movie, go shopping at Do it all.

What else, argue with your partner? Hopefully not, clean the car? Clean the house? Read, go for lunch on Battersea rise, Northcote road. Go to the gym, see my friends – they feel a lot closer to me now that I've moved away, (well, the ones that stay in touch do), to be honest you have the feeling of needing them so much more when you move away. I don't think they know that. It's a shame about some girls, as long as they are ok, and have a man, all else does not matter too much, I guess they assume that everyone is as happy as they are, or are they? They will be in touch again soon, I hope.

I think about Marco. Mmm, well, he's just one of those gigalos that wants his panetone cake and eat it and have some spare panatone stored in the cake tin, just in case he ever needs it – well, nothing's going to be left of THIS panetone (ie me!) except crumbs, by the time he wants to open the lid. I'm out of there.

I think of Theo and his sexy deep greek voice.

Chapter 30

"Have courage"

"I walk in the sand and I can see the wind burying my footprints as I turn back. Sand is following me. Man, don't forget that call from the deep of sand."
  Rev DF Zudnochovivs, Lithuanian

6th June 2002

I met up with Evelina tonight after Deutsch class (why am I still bothering with class?) We had a great laugh. She's going for an interview tomorrow to be a marketing manager based back home in Lithuania (where the above quote was from). I love that quote. I'm not sure what it means, what's gone is gone, or is it? Should we keep hold of it, it's not forgotten, or, how things can follow you, you're there to make an impression that others will want to follow, or, a bit sinister, that whatever you try to cover up, it's always there, deep down. Whatever, this line of prose was to have a greater meaning in my life as time wore on in Switzerland.

And how do I feel one whole diary year later, about love, life, and men?

I'm here, I survived, I've been single since February 2002 – almost parallel to when the mighty Robert came over from the USA to dislocate our freetime, our routines, our coordination and, our happiness. That's also the time when I started German classes, started to become totally stressed out, with every job under the sun with no help to help me out.
I am buckling under the pressures and ranted at M in text messages with my words of hate, disdain and bitterness. How simply awful and no wonder he couldn't be bothered with me anymore and yet no, I don't want to be used as a

doormat, my friends are genuine friends who like me for who I am, who appreciate me. I like to believe I'm here for them when they need me and likewise, when I need them too sometimes.

I think I have a big heart, but it easily bleeds. In fact, I think it's haemophiliac – it bleeds and bruises so easily. Well, that's my heart. Perhaps it's not meant for this world, but I hope I've brought some joy to some people here in the meantime and taught others a few lessons and how to respect others, how not to hurt feelings, to respect sensitivities, to be humble, to forgive and forget, how to cry, how to ug, how to love.

Mike says that hopefully one day M will read my book and will be heartbroken. It doesn't matter. At the time, I just wanted to give him everything, anything.

But here I must start a new chapter to my life, perhaps we'll meet again one day and our moons will pass.

So, the new edition, the new book.

I've learned to scale mountains (well, the climbing wall at the local gym), to understand (or not, as the case may be), the Swiss and their taste in undergarments. How to fly (well, hang off a bungey rope down 700m of 007 heaven), to cycle like a lunatic to the top of valley versasca, to swim in the high seas (and a number of lakes), windsurf in the lake of Thun, to dive into a waterfall canyoning in the Ticino Valleys, to rollerblade around a disused airstrip in Interlaken, to stay in a mountain hut and walk across a glacier in May, to ski like a champ, to appreciate the difference between Ticino Latte Machiato and All Bar One Cappucino, to learn German (ein bischion), to live on my own, to believe in myself, to cycle everywhere, to cry alone, to cook better, to enjoy myself, to listen to others, to ask others for help, to reach out to them, to depend on them sometimes, and for them to depend upon me, to be open, to be honest, to spend money, and save money, to find things to spend my money on other than clothes, to love every chance that I can get a facial in London, to love the smell of fresh flowers and the hedgerows first thing in the morning, the smell of rain, the warmth of sunchine, the sound of snow and wind, to make the most of other cultures, and appreciate their diversity, to work hard, to play hard, to appreciate music even more, to be happy.

I listen to Moby and I think of crying but I don't want to. It plays "Speak to me baby, speak to me". I love this song.

And …

For the first time in so long, I feel stronger, happier, more beautiful(?) more positive, perhaps just more in control.

Reason: Just been on the phone with frineds - like Tanya, who despite my initial impression, and her flagrant way with darling type words, is actually great. She cheers me up no end. She's made me feel really positive about myself and we all need friends like Tanya, when we need them. I hope I am useful for her when she needs me too.

"Think of what you've done girl" "You're incredible".

"You're an incredible woman" she says. She gives me hope. We talked about when we're not happy and how sometimes, if you're in the wrong place, there's something that's missing in each of us, like she said in Hong Kong, she felt she had something "you know" I said, "That's just how I feel, something's missing in me, therefore something's not quite right, it is, it's my surroundings, it's here, it's just not making me feel the way I should." I thought about London, I felt good, generally, attractive (vaguely?) confident, happy, (or as much as I thought) and yes, yes, I'd miss weekends here, badly, now that I've tasted the mountains, the lakes, the rivers, I've made a few friends, everything (as long as you can put up with the Swiss) it is fabulous. It's here, It's Basel, Basel is just not me, it's this apartment.

Everything I bought in Spain, here today, (tops, skirts, aerobic tops, aerobic bottoms to cycle in etc) I bought them thinking either – this would be good for cycling in Ticino, or, for wandering down Northcote road, or for going dancing at Ceroc in London, I did not buy anything for here, for looking lovely here in Basel.

Tanya suggests I move to Zurich, she always has and you know, I always just assumed that was because she was there and biased etc, but I think she has a point.

She talks about "Wink advertising" a new agency that handles the Swiss account (the new airline) ie. Big bucks, but not just that, interesting, what's more, apparently, they are looking for people, people like me.

"you should send your CV" she says.

Suddenly I start thinking positive, hopeful, a way to get out of this rut. Sometimes you just need a little help to point you in the right direction.

Should I leave here, go back to London, o the new CEO at Creative Inc, or, apply for a job back here at Wink. Sounds good. Could be fun. A fun account at last. That's what it is, that's what's wrong, the miserable faces of my clients, (Carla's miserable look at me when I was dancing with Felix in Seville, Bridgitta swearing at me, all prima donnas, boring, pond life, in their grey boring office and I think of the clients I had in the UK – in their cold grey dark and boring offices too, and their miserable faces too. In fact, my happy clients I can count on one hand:

Rog, Stef. I like both of them. Wow, incredible, suddenly I realise why I am not happy, suddenly I feel like I know where I'm going, suddenly I feel the huge sense of positive self worth, this surge of happiness, warmth, I've, control, happiness, reasons.

Wow, that simple. Wow, I do need to leave Creative Inc healthcare here in Basel. I suddenlty feel great, great to be alive, great to be lying here, naked on my bed with a face mask on, and looking totally gorgeous (yeah right) and suddenly I know what I want for me, and then I'll find the right man.

M I will never ever forget him, I love him still, but he has to love me too. I cannot accept anything less. I'm starting to feel what I must do to do that and I'm starting to

289

realise what I have versus what I want and I almost feel like crying again.

And my Texas album plays "I'm so in love with you, whether it's right or wrong..I'm so in love with you…to take your fears away, give me anything to keep your feet on the ground and help you on your way…"

"..when you see your reflection, you're standing in the queue and in turn and look away and please don't fade away, you're all that I need, all that I need. I'm so in love with you..whether it's right or it's wrong…" "yes, I'm right there.."

I also bought a rucksack backpack today from the shop, Kostsport. I knw it was 499CHF that I should not have spent but hey, I've got rid of the car now. And I'm not sure whether it was my statement to Basel that I'm …out of here.

And then, I come back to bed.

And M's last words echo on my pillow "Sometimes, somethings are just not there for one, or other or maybe both" and I struggle to understand quite what he meant. Something was certainly there for me – I did not shut my eyes when I lay on top of hinm that morning and prayed to God that this would never ever end, for no reason whatsoever.

I feel so sad, so betryed almost because when we were together, there seemed to be so much there for both of us, something happened, something stopped him, and I have to know, I cannot settle until I knowit must have been something I said, something I did? Or was I just someone to "muck around with" Why did he ask "I don't want to be on the rebound" and tell me his dreams and hopes, desires and share with me his passions.

When I spoke with him in the new year, in Jan 2000, he said on the telephone "I used to really like you" What was it? What did he mean? It mut have been something to change his mind?. "Used to" why not "do" why not "I do really like you but…" and it makes me cry to start to analyse that sort phrase to myself time and time again. Perhaps that's how my father felt – he used to really like us…

I cry inside and somehow all the positiveness that I felt before has drained out of me, like a hole in a bucket, that's been slowly leaking all night since Tanya's telephone call.

And all I crave is some loving arms around me, someone who's as mad as me, and as adventurous as me, quite independent and happy with themselves, their friends, not reliant on me, but who can add something to my life, make me smile inside, make me happy, not make me squirm with embarrassmen at an SMS message, who I want to make love with whilst standing in the kitchen, in the bath, in the garage etc, not forced, not feeling like a rebound.

If I go to the UK next week, to this meeting, I know I'll want to pop in to see M but that would be such the wrong thing to do, deep down I know.

He doesn't need me anymore. He's so shallow.

I want to believe that no-one is the same as me.

And now I wish I'd not sent the SMS about my bungey jump, nor the SMS when I was in hospital after falling off my bike and being knocked unconscious in front of a tram, nor the email about the world cup, nor included him on the email thanking everyone for taking time to telephone me.

I sent an email to Fiona, Dave's wife to appologise for sharing my heart 'n soul with her. I attached a joke. She's not responded, she never responded to my last mail when I asked her advice, it was not fair on her anyway and I should not have done it. I know she will have probably forwarded it to M.

What a foolish and desperate thing to do I thought and I felt very silly – usually in hind sight, we all know best don't we.

Met up with Dave tonight – he's going to give me a thing for tickets to the Henley ball. It suddenly brought back massive memories of this time last year when M sent me a mail all about it. Gosh how this year seems to have arrived at June already. I'll never know, but I think my life's been put on hold since M sent me the mail in March about him seeing his new girlfriend. How long has he been seeing her? Not even 3 months now since his message and yet it feels like a lifetime since we last spoke/contacted/communicated – I hate him for that, I hate him so much and yet he's probabl trying to give me space, to let me carry on without him, the only problem is, 'm not sure how to.

I now understand silly love songs and people like Barry Manilow and the inspiration behind him writing a song like "I can't smile without you, I can't dance, and I can't sing, I just can't…. without you" etc. I have fallen into a Baz Manilow fan? Seriously. Now no street cred.

Now I feel happier that it's not even 3 months since I last received something from M. I want the 26th of this month to come but very slowly, unless he replies before, then it can come whenever it likes. I must promise myself NOT to send him anything, nothing.

As Evelina said, "it's no good telephoning or sending SMS messages, they're no substitute for an expression in the eyes, on the face. Only then do you know exactly what the person means and how they really feel". Even Chris's email to say "You've made the right decision. People will look different when you see them face to face – SMS's and the telephone are just not the same". Strange that 2 very different people in 2 different parts of Switzerland, say exactly the same thing on the same day.

Lisa Stansfield plays on the radio, it sounds a bit like the way I'd like to feel…"one day I'm coming back, and it won't be long, before I'm home and in your arms. Some day, some way. I never wanted anyone so bad, some way some day..why so sudden the change of heart, why do I feel that I've done wrong, when all I want is for you to ask me for more… Some day I'm coming back, and it won't be long, before you beg me to come back and ask for more. Some day I'm coing back and it won't be long before I'm home, home and in your arms…"and so it goes on.

Why can't I forget M?

Even this morning I wake to think of him. I pretend he is kissing me and rolling on top of me and running his hands up and down me and I feel so whole. And how I regret not asking him to come into bed with me when he was here. I suppose I was scared of him saying no. He was probably too scared to ask/assume.What do guys want? I feel I know what I must do, I must see him soon, face to face, no letters, no emails, no SMSs, just face to face, one on one, I miss him so.

Chapter 31

Thursday 13th June. A day of enlightenment?!

Sabine's lent me one of her enlightenment tape cassettes. A bit off the wall but some of it is interesting. A strange guru. Going into hysterics with the phrase "Would the world exist if we weren't here?" I suppose he has a point. He continues: "You believe you are the centre of the world and the whole world revolves around you and you are the centre of all creation." He makes you feel pretty stupid and insignificant really.

To continue his analogies… "When a star explodes and is dusted around the galaxy, and it starts to build a little spacesuit..(nice analogy if a little weird)…" and then the tape ran out ☹ to turn over… " and so in each little inconsequential little world, it becomes more and more complex and has lots of DNA and then lots of chemicals, then develops sacs of chemicals that can reflect on themselves. Each individual sac of chemicals has its own survival programs and so there is survival of the unit and reproduction of the unit and as long as you are identified with that group of DNA, can survive and we are seen as reproducing that and it's called 'falling in love'

That's where the beginning of life, when you can reflect on life, before that it's just seeds/harvest/seeds/harvest living in ignorant belief that it will never happen to you."

Making much sense?
He didn't ask anyone's opinion, but then why should he, he is the guru.
I'm not sure this has helped and I ceryainly haven't considered thinking of falling in love like this before. Interesting.

The passage continues: "Should I really be going. Should I stay and have family. It's choiceless. As long as there are choices, the ego then chooses, 'it's my destiny', and rationalises it. As long as you can tell you my kind of story – who's talking to who about what, but you will notice if you listen carefully, and listen to ego act it out, that really there is no story at all, just the Unverse's decision and it's really just going with the flow.

Subconscious latent identification of the ego with the Universe and when it's seen for what it is, under that is a deep unknowing. 'Unknowing' and if you feel completely in, there's a pristine clarity that knows nothing in particular but everything in potential – this is the opposite to ego, who knows everything in particular.

As long as there is someone that needs an outcome, and now, the best way to get that outcome is to 'let life do it for me, just go with the flow' but it's still the strategy of someone wanting something.

And so, in that you can uncover this attachment which turns up in love then love overwhelms that bubble, it's infused with love, then love becomes a lens through which love flows through, therefore the body becomes an instrument for this love, therefore we serve love or your idea of yourself, so whatever you do is not within your power/ You have the power to stay true to love – that's in your power, but you're willing to give that up, to go with the flow.

But it takes intelligence, willingness, all attention, therefore attention is off the flow and onto love, therefore what you have power over is about circumstance, just looking in the wrong direction. Look to where you have full power, look to where you can be still. Stillness is the strongest power. Surrender to love, it's the best place to be…"

And so it goes on.

This man gets paid for this.

It's now 01.50am and I should be fast asleep, gosh. I'll feel dreadful tomorrow. I cannot sleep though. I am too excited. I want to return to the UK, I want to go now. (I hope this feeling will last even when it snows, when it rains, when it's cold, dark and damp in the mornings as I leave for the gym and the office, as I queue for the bus for 40 minutes in the rain with no umbrella, and then 3 turn up at once, as I walk through puddles and cry alone at night in my lovely little flat on Limburg Road, as I go up the M1 to Milton Keynes in rain and traffic jams, as I pour a bath and listen to soft music in my flat, as I have fun redecorating and cutting the hedge and cleaning the garden, buying flowers from the flower stall on Northcote Road, as I have fun with friends in the bars around Battersea, as I skip to Ceroc on Monday nights, whether M's there or not – his loss and he will see that I feel sure, as I hear the voices and laughter and the shouts "Ciao Bella" from the Italian boys at Pizza Metro, as they'll be no more juggling finances across 2 continents, 2 rents to pay, 3 visa bills.

I consider what it's cost me to move here and the effort I made and the effort the company did (or didn't) make, and the tears, the pain, the suffering, the blood, the sweat, the boys – yuk, apart from Swiss Chris, he was so lovely in so many ways, so gentle and yet so scary toowith darkest of dark moods, and then I think of when I passed out on that tram line, and coming back around when I thought "No, let it be, I feel so at peace, so serene, so calm, let me stay here, away from you all, away from all the angst and problems and pain, away away, let M go, but then for some reason, God slapped my cheeks and I came around, surrounded by gasping ambulance men shoving pen torches in my eyes, to squeezing my arm to insert a needle, to having a blood pressure cuff attached to my left arm, to waking up and feeling the sting in my arm, my leg, my elbow, my head, and feeling so sick, and dizzy, yet frightened, and so wanting to 'just go home and have a nice hot bath and some tea. The usual routine, spoiled by a Doctor taking my hand and advising me that I would be staying in hospital for at least 24 hours. (It was like tying down a tiger and I just wanted to flee and yet I couldn't, totally disorientated, so I just had to go woth the flow, let it go , let it flow, and let them take care of me as I lay there shivering – for no apparent reason, it was quite humid outside – and shivering.

I wrote my letter of resignation to Robert (the new boss of Creative Inc in Basel) that night.

"I hereby give notice..blah blah blah" or words to that effect. Perhaps he will congratulate me on my copywriting skills in his sarcastic way. Well, let him, to be honest, I could't be bothered now. It's the right thing to do.

Having spoken to David (the new boss in London) tonight though (from the hospital bed), I just hope that Steve (ex-London boss) sends that official letter pretty soon...

So here I go again, A new start, new adventure, a new beginning, or is it?...

So my advise to my children, and to my childrens' children. My nephews, nieces and anyone else...Listen to the clues, listen to advice, heed everything you hear but at the end of the day it's what's in your heart. Listen to your heart calling and you'll know where to go...

Small things end. Great things endure.

Basel Art Messe, 2002

And, I awoke (because I did get a couple of hours sleep last night) and it's a beautiful beautiful day, but I have to be strong and have the courage and stick with my decision. I must leave this place and go to where they need me, warts and all.

And I look out from my bedroom window on the world and see the Bruderholtz hospital on the horizon, where I spent 24 frightened hours being sent uner an MRI machine. I look at the rolling hills in the distance where I spent many an evening running with the team form the bank with head torches through the snow or under the cherry trees in the summer heat. I see the tops of the apartment blocks beyond, feel the gentle breeze blow in through my huge French windows.

I know what I have to do, book my flight next week, call my apartment landlord, call the estate agent in London....

I don't know whether it's Sabine's tape or what but do I feel the urge to go home now, even though it's so beautiful outside.

I went to Basel Art Messe tonight after work. Met up with Evelina for a drink after too. She thinks I've made the right decision. I feel I know I have and once Robert signs my expenses and I receive the note from Steve, then I'll hand in my resignation note. Monday. It will be on Monday. I'm not waiting until 24th, it's Monday and I'm trying to heed Sabine's tape, because I feel I am that bubble on the wave, rolling with the wave, but desperately finding ways to get out of it and then giving up and going with the flow, hoping that something else will take me out of it and waiting until I disappear, to be replaced by another bubble. Amd the wave is just one of thousands of waves in an ocean of waves, amongst many oceans in the Universe. It does now seem to make sense and makes me feel very small and humble and makes my problems seem pretty insignificant after all, so here I am, about to take my next bungey jump onto dry land.

I mentioned that I was thinking of moving back, to the estate agents, to the property manager. She responded by saying "No, you don't know that you've done the right thing until you're there." I think they are wise words.

And I return from my weekend in Zurich, having had probably one of the worst nights and the best days of my life here.

The evening progressedand my story continued….

It was time to go. Or was it….

Thought for the day: All our dreams can come true- if we have the courage to pursue them. Walt Disney.